HUMAN
SACRIFICE

Dear Ardi
To New friends And
Night Readers!

Cindy Hull

The year of Covid, 2020

HUMAN
SACRIFICE

A Mystery Novel

by

Cindy L. Hull

Readers are encouraged to go to www.MissionPointPress.com to contact
the author or to find information on how to buy this book in bulk at
a discounted rate.

Published by Mission Point Press
2554 Chandler Rd.
Traverse City, MI 49696
(231) 421-9513
www.MissionPointPress.com

ISBN: 978-1-950659-27-2
Library of Congress Control Number: 201991723

Cover design: Jim DeWildt

Printed in the United States of America

To my husband and soulmate:

We have shared a life of travel and adventure that I will always cherish; to our children, who have filled our lives with joy; and to our grandchildren, whose love and ability to find humor in all things remind me of what is truly important in life.

In memory of my parents, Arthur and Lorraine Vandenbergh, whose encouragement and love guided their children to follow their own paths in the world, even the wayward path of the anthropologist.

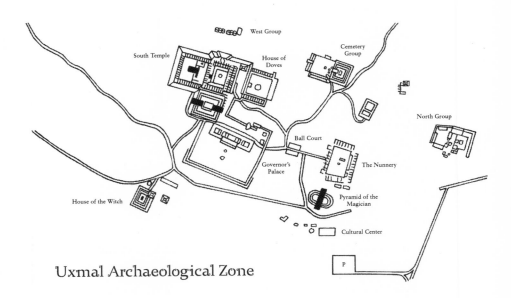

West Group

South Temple

House of Doves

Cemetery Group

North Group

Ball Court

Governor's Palace

The Nunnery

House of the Witch

Pyramid of the Magician

Cultural Center

P

Uxmal Archaeological Zone

A note on Mayan pronunciation:

1. In Mayan, the "x" is pronounced "sh", so Uxmal is pronounced "Ush-mal."

2. The Mayan word for shaman/priest is h-men, pronounced "huh-men." The plural is "h-menob."

Program for the 10th Annual Meeting of the Society for Mayanist Studies
Intercultural Hotel, Merida, Yucatán, Mexico
May 5-9

Hosted by
The University of Yucatán, Merida, Yucatán, Mexico,
and the newest academic member of the SMS,
the Keane College Interdisciplinary Mayanist Program,
Westport, Michigan, USA.

Program Chair:
Doctor Bradley James Kingsford
Director of the Keane College
Interdisciplinary Mayanist Program

Events for Sunday, May 4
- Early Registration and Preconference Field Trip to Uxmal Archaeological Site
- Reception and Special Event: Sound and Light Show

CHAPTER ONE

Sunday Evening: Uxmal Archaeological Site, Yucatán, Mexico

The young man lay at the foot of the Magician's Pyramid, his body intact, his heart lifeless but in its proper place. Dressed in blue jeans and a bloodied maroon T-shirt instead of a loincloth, he embodied the metaphor of his surroundings, a warrior sacrificed to the gods. Above him, the full moon cast ominous shadows over Uxmal, more formidable in the quiet darkness than it had been earlier that day when merely a tourist attraction, an ancient Magic Kingdom. Tonight, only the ambient floodlights leading along the pathway marred the magic of the ancient Mayan civilization—that, and the body.

Nine Hours Earlier: Sunday Afternoon, Uxmal, Yucatán, Mexico

At least I won't be sacrificed today. Claire Aguila Carson looked over her shoulder, embarrassed. Did she say that out loud? She was alone for the moment, except for an iguana perched on a low wall that had once formed one side of an ancient Mayan ball court. She focused her camera, but the reptile tired of her company and slithered off its limestone perch, its tail trailing far behind its massive, mottled, and spiny body.

"*Mierda!*" Claire took the giant lizard's place on the wall. She unclipped her dark hair, letting it fall below her shoulders before sweeping it back into place, capturing the loose strands caked in sweat against her neck. She closed her eyes and inhaled the moist air promising rain that would not be delivered until early June, when the Mayan *h-menob* performed their supplications to the rain god Chac.

Around her, temples, palaces, and stately buildings erupted from the porous Yucatecan earth, cleared of rainforest, evidence of ancient engineering genius. Built a thousand years before, without wheels or draft animals, the structures told a tale of raw political and religious

3

power, of priest-kings, scientists, farmers, and slaves existing in an environment devoid of rivers or streams. This was Uxmal.

She had visited the ancient city many times before, but today it felt different. This time, she hardly noticed the turquoise motmot birds perched on the branches of the Royal Ponciana tree, or the spectacular architecture. Today, death enveloped her: the death of the war prisoners who lost a dangerous ball game, their hearts ripped from their chests and their bodies thrown from temples, such as the one looming above her; the death of an ancient civilization whose scientific knowledge rivaled that of its conquerors; but even more painful, the death of her husband.

Yucatán, Mexico was Claire's ancestral home, though not the place of her birth. Here, she felt suspended between the Midwestern culture where she was raised and the world of her ancestors. The latter world pulled her in and held her in an embrace so powerful that she could barely breathe. It was here where, over a span of thirty years, she had explored her Hispanic roots, met her husband, and frequently lived in a nearby village, Yaxpec. The only thing that prevented her from running immediately back to "her" village was a conference of Mayan scholars beginning the next day in Merida, the capitol city of Yucatán.

"Claire! Claire! Up here!"

Jolted from her thoughts, Claire bent her head upward toward the top of the Magician's Pyramid, shading her eyes against the piercing midday sun. From the middle platform near the summit of the pyramid, her friend and colleague, Madge Carmichael, waved to her. George Banks, chair of the anthropology department, stood next to her, his hand gripping Madge's arm. Both wore straw hats that partially blocked their sun-creased faces.

Claire waved back in disbelief that her elder colleagues had climbed the pyramid, and that Madge had survived, dressed in her characteristic post-hippy garb. In contrast, George resembled an escapee from a golf course. Her department chair pointed to his watch, and Claire glanced at her own…twelve-thirty. She gave him a thumbs-up and stood, pulling her dress, damp with perspiration, from the back of her thighs. She couldn't believe George had called a meeting at an archaeological site.

CHAPTER TWO

Eighty feet above Claire, Professors George Banks and Madge Carmichael stood side by side on the massive temple. Unlike other Mayan pyramids that rise like children's building blocks, each level smaller than the one below, the Magician's Pyramid was ovaloid, its texture smooth. It rose three levels, like the layers of a cake. The ancient inhabitants built the structure in stages over three hundred years, as new priest-kings established their legitimacy in the Mayan world. George and Madge stood on a wide ledge forming the base for the second level of the pyramid.

From their perch, they gazed at the panoramic view of Uxmal, surrounded by hundreds of miles of lush rainforest nestled in the Puuc Hills, the highest point in the Yucatán Peninsula. Wisps of cloud lingered in the blue sky but did not filter the rays of the brilliant sun. In the distance, facing south, openings appeared in the forest, revealing the archaeological sites that formed the famed *Ruta Maya*.

Below them in the clearing of the rainforest, they had an eagle's view of Uxmal, spreading out for more than a half-mile. Nearly fifty multinational Mayan scholars, primarily anthropologists and archaeologists, were exploring the site as the kick-off event for a conference where they would share their research with other experts in Mayan studies.

From their lookout, they watched scholars meander in and around the Nunnery Quadrangle, four low-lying buildings surrounding a vast courtyard. To their left, others struggled up the steep stairways that led to the Governor's Palace. Beyond the Palace, the scholars spread out toward the partially excavated Great Pyramid, the Quadrangle of the Doves, and more distant structures along the boundaries of the site, leading them deeper into Mayan history.

Like all tourists, the academics posed for photographs or examined the plaster Mayan calendars and statues of Mayan gods offered by vendors along the path leading from the site to the Cultural Center and park entrance. Madge aimed her binoculars downward and saw that Claire had abandoned her position and was strolling toward the vending tables, her camera clutched in her hand.

"I worry about Claire," Madge mused.

"Why?" asked George, scanning the site through his binoculars.

"She's sad, distant," Madge said, struggling for the right word, "apathetic, since Aaron died."

"She's grieving," George said. "She'll recover."

"She needs to move on...I keep telling her."

"It's not your business, Madge. Just because you moved on multiple times..." he looked down at her and smiled. "Sorry, just joking."

George loosened his grip on his binoculars, attached by a leather strap around his neck, and they dropped to his chest. "Shall we head down?"

Madge grimaced and glanced briefly down the steep stairway. "I need to get out of the sun and rest first."

"We'll be late for the meeting," George fussed.

"They won't start without you."

Madge edged toward a chamber built into the second level of the pyramid. George took her hand and guided her into the low, narrow chamber as she fumbled with her skirt.

"Why did you wear that get-up to an archaeological site?" he grumbled.

"Shut up and help me in." Their familiarity reflected years of shared educational and professional experiences as long-time friends and colleagues, archaeologists working together in Guatemala.

Madge lowered herself slowly onto the cool stone floor and removed her hat, freeing her wild tangle of curly gray hair. She rested her head against the damp wall. George stood at the entrance, glancing at his watch. He frowned but followed her in. Mayan temples were not constructed for six-foot-tall Americans, so George had to squat to enter the small enclosure. He sat next to Madge, wiping his forehead with a handkerchief he pulled from his hip pack. They sat in silence for a few minutes, recovering from the heat.

Fanning herself with her hat, Madge asked, "What do you think of the two candidates for the teaching position?"

George scowled. "I'm not convinced either one is suitable for us. I'm curious to see how the others feel."

"Who will Brad want?" Madge asked.

"No idea, but as director of the Mayanist program, he'll want his say." George used the wall to maneuver himself back to his stooped position, his sixty-eight-year-old body resisting the effort. Once back on his feet, he reached down to assist Madge—of the same age but with less flexibility—as she struggled to stand.

Madge rearranged her skirt and placed her hat on her head. "Speaking of Brad and the program, do I have to attend Eduardo's lecture?"

George frowned at his friend. "Of course you do. We all do. After all, Eduardo is making a substantial loan to our new museum. That's thousands of dollars' worth of artifacts we would never be able to purchase on our own, and Brad made it possible." They stood for a moment in the doorway, their eyes adjusting to the brilliant sunlight outside the chamber. "And don't forget, it lured you out of retirement."

"Don't remind me, George."

They stepped back out onto the ledge. Madge, feeling mild vertigo, stayed close to the pyramid wall while George moved along the platform toward the stairs. A park employee motioned to them to descend from the pyramid. The park had allowed the scholars to climb the Magician's Pyramid as part of their excursion, but now the barriers were being placed to protect the temple from further damages incurred by thousands of tourists. George turned to Madge. She stared down from the edge of the platform, her face white, her knees shaking under her skirt.

"Oh shit," said Madge. She looked down to the ground, the steps barely visible from where she stood, and her stomach churned. She sat on the top step and inched her way down. George said a silent prayer to the Mayan Gods and descended carefully alongside her.

CHAPTER THREE

Tanya Petersen rummaged in her tiny leather purse for a tissue, gave up, wiped her nose on the back of her hand and then surreptitiously rubbed it along the edge of her pink tank top. "When you said you had something important to tell me, I thought it was good news."

Jamal Kennedy, her companion, shortened his stride to match hers but did not take her hand or attempt to appease her anger. "I talked to George, but you assumed the good news." He looked down at her. "George begged Madge to come to Keane College because she's an established archaeologist and curator. Why would he offer the position to you?" He pulled his hands through his micro-braids and continued, "Did you think Madge would leave the University of Michigan to teach introductory anthropology courses? Be real, Tanya."

"It's a gerontocracy, Jamal. They should retire and let young scholars shape the program."

"Brad would agree with you, and I don't disagree, but we have to earn our positions, like they did."

"But I have ambitions."

"We all do, but frankly, I think you have been using me to achieve yours."

"I don't know what you mean." She stumbled over a carved limestone hieroglyph, part of the rubble strewn around the archaeological site. Jamal reached out to grab her elbow, but she brushed him away.

Rebuffed, he looked at her, his dark eyes unreadable. "I think you do, Tanya. I love you, but I have doubts about your feelings."

Tanya's mouth set in a pout. "I do...love...you."

Jamal clenched his jaw. "You can't even say the words, can you?" His tone was hard and low. "Why don't you talk to Brad yourself? You don't need me."

"I already did. Last fall."

He stopped and stared at her. "And he said?"

"That the decision was already made…a done deal."

Jamal grabbed her arm, turning her toward him. "I was Plan B?" He released her, afraid of his own emotions. "It's no good, Tanya. I'm done with your manipulations."

From their position between the Nunnery and the ball court, Jamal saw Brad Kingsford, the program director, standing with a job candidate on the vast terrace of the Governor's Palace. "There's Brad now, talking to Paul Sturgess. Go work on him again."

She followed his gaze. "Shut up, Jamal."

Ahead of them, they could see Claire near the Magician's Pyramid, watching them as they approached.

"What do I do now?" Tanya whined, drying her eyes with the hem of her shirt.

"Get a grip, Tanya. You're a good actress. Act."

At the base of the pyramid, Claire watched in fear as the two sexagenarians made their way down the west stairway. When they arrived safely at the bottom, she sought out the rest of their group. Tanya and Jamal appeared from the direction of the Nunnery. They presented a study in contrasts: Tanya's sharp Scandinavian features juxtaposed sharply with Jamal's mahogany skin and Lenny Kravitz-esque hair, which sent freshman girls into ecstatic swoons and exaggerated interests in bio-cultural anthropology. They walked close together but did not touch, their faces set in angular lines—a lover's spat? Their relationship was the worst-kept secret in the program. Even George, who rarely left his office except for meetings, had figured it out.

Brad Kingsford approached from the opposite direction, the image of the hero from the cover of a romance novel—brown leather vest over a blue Keane College T-shirt, wrap-around sunglasses, and straw hat straddling his graying-blond ponytail. He strolled slowly from the direction of the Governor's Palace, his backpack hoisted over one shoulder.

A voice from behind Claire startled her. "Excuse me?"

Claire turned to see an elderly woman with short permed hair sticking out from under a straw hat. She stood next to her husband, wearing a Detroit Tigers T-shirt and holding a small digital camera.

"Yes?" Claire said.

The woman asked, "Could you take our picture?"

Claire looked around. Brad had not yet arrived. Madge sat on the bottom step of the pyramid, catching her breath; George sat next to her glancing at his watch and then up at Brad, frowning at his progress; Tanya and Jamal stood side by side, each attempting a look of nonchalance.

"Sure," Claire said, and posed them in front of the pyramid. As she handed the camera back, she asked, "Are you from Michigan?"

"Lake Odawa," the woman answered. "Lois and Dale Stuart."

Dale produced his map of Michigan by opening his right hand and pointing to a spot about an inch under his middle finger. "Would you like us to take your photograph?" he asked.

Claire smiled and roused her colleagues. "Just one photo," she promised as everyone groaned at her suggestion.

George mumbled, "We don't have time for this, Claire."

"Come on," Madge pleaded. "This will be the first official portrait of the Keane College Mayanist Program."

George rolled his eyes as Madge urged him forward; Jamal and Tanya wandered over slowly, still not speaking. As they watched Brad approach, the Stuarts chattered on about their hotel and travel itinerary. Everyone waited for Brad.

Joining the group, Brad smiled and shrugged. "Sorry, I didn't know you were all waiting."

George fussed, "It appears we're not ready yet." He scowled as Claire organized the positioning, situating George and Madge in front of the pyramid.

"Do we have to do this?" Brad grumbled, removing his sunglasses and hat.

"Humor me, Brad," Claire said, handing her camera to Mr. Stuart.

"Let's make it quick, can we?" said George.

"Just smile, George," Madge said as she smoothed out her skirt and removed her hat.

Moments later, the Stuarts wandered away, and the members of the Keane College Mayanist Program made their way through the gauntlet of vendors toward the promise of a cold drink and a dull meeting.

CHAPTER FOUR

George Banks led his entourage of exhausted and thirsty scholars into the Uxmal Cultural Center. The blast of air-conditioning offered a welcomed reprieve from the Yucatán sun. Around them, the center pulsated with activity. Multigenerational and multicultural families stood in line waiting for their tickets to be stamped while their children or grandchildren broke away, jostling small clusters of retirees huddled near a central fountain, struggling to understand the accented English of their tour guide. The arrival of a tour group led by a tiny woman waving a German flag added yet another language to the cacophony.

Claire's colleagues joined a short line at the entrance of a small restaurant, taking in the aroma of Mexican spices that enveloped them as they waited for the hostess, a young girl wearing a traditional Mayan *huipil*, impossibly white with embroidery at the neck and hem. She seated them in front of the window at two square tables that had been pulled together, each with its own distinctive wobble. George maneuvered his girth onto a padded wooden chair at one end of the table; Brad, tall and lean, situated himself at the other end. Madge and Claire sat so they had a view through the window, leaving Tanya and Jamal to sit together, facing them. Tanya shifted her chair away from Jamal, adding physical distance to the emotional chasm clearly existing between them.

A young man approached to take their order. A classic Mayan nose dominated his bronze face and his ready smile disclosed a gold front tooth. When he retreated with their order, the group turned its attention to George as he pulled a small spiral notebook and ink pen from his black hip-pack and adjusted his glasses. He scanned the faculty from under bushy gray eyebrows.

"As you know, the Dean gave us permission to interview four candidates. When I learned that two of them would be at this conference,

14

I thought we might interview them here. I appreciate your willingness to meet with them early this morning at the hotel, and I would like to discuss their qualifications while they are fresh in our minds." George looked around for the waiter. "We can interview the remaining two applicants later this summer. It is important that we have someone hired for fall semester to replace Helen."

Brad leaned forward. "Why did Helen wait to announce her retirement so late in the year?" He released his hair from its ponytail. Unleashed, it fell into a wavy mass brushing against his shoulders. "She should have announced last year. We could have hired her replacement by now."

George frowned, adjusted his glasses again, and gave Madge a slight shake of his head. In response Madge sat back, arms folded, lips pressed together. George cleared his throat as the waiter returned to their table with icy cold Coronas, limes, and four small bowls of spicy nuts, tortilla chips, and salsa. The faculty members seized their bottles greedily as they waited for him to respond.

George sipped his beer, taking his time. "Helen had personal reasons for retiring early…"

"Oh, for Heaven's sake, George," Madge blurted. "Helen has cancer…again."

George glared at Madge, Brad and Jamal looked at each other, and Tanya said, "Again?"

George shifted his gaze from Brad to Jamal, then Tanya. "It was before we hired you three. You had no reason to know."

Claire stared at George, then Madge. "I thought she was in remission."

"Unfortunately," George said, "her cancer returned, and she starts treatments this month. She and her husband decided she should retire early to concentrate on her health."

Hurt, Claire clutched her heart-shaped necklace, the last gift she'd received from her husband. "Why didn't she tell me?" She looked from George to Madge. "I should have been told."

"I'm sorry, Claire," Madge said. "You should have been told, as senior faculty. But we…I…knew how it would affect you."

"Were you protecting her or me?" Claire's eyes stung. "I could have talked to her. I know…"

George interrupted, "She insisted, Claire. She didn't want pity or the teary-eyed retirement party. She hopes…plans…to have a healthy retirement when this is over."

"I'm sorry, Claire," Madge repeated, and tapped Claire's knee under the table.

Brad said, "I'm sorry I over-reacted."

George shrugged, relieved to escape the emotional landmine. "At least the Dean permitted us to search this summer. She could have made us wait until the next hiring cycle." George took a sip of beer and everyone at the table followed his lead, except Claire. She stared out the window in front of her, willing herself not to cry.

George glanced at Claire, then continued. "So, to review, the Dean has approved the hiring of an anthropologist who is comparable to Helen in teaching and expertise, preferably with research in either Guatemala or Chiapas, Mexico. Since we couldn't conduct individual interviews with either candidate, I hope that each of you will find an opportunity to speak with them this weekend. It's important that the person we hire can fulfill our teaching and culture-area needs."

Claire's eyes stung. She focused her gaze outward through the window, toward the towering pyramid. *More sacrificial victims*. She knew what Helen and her husband were experiencing. She and Aaron had the same hope, but Aaron did not recover. There was so much she could have said to Helen and her husband. Afraid to look at her colleagues, she let her mind wander, barely listening to George's monologue.

Claire's life with Aaron Carson had started in the Yucatán. In fact, it had started here, at Uxmal. The recollection startled her. It had been on a group trip to Uxmal, during a university internship program nearly thirty-five years ago, when she first talked to the handsome student she had previously observed from a distance. She had been assigned to the university bilingual/bicultural program; he had been a pre-med student assigned to a medical clinic. The intern groups only mingled during program outings to colonial towns or archaeological sites.

She and Aaron first spoke in the Nunnery Quadrangle. She had been sitting on the steps of the west building, writing in her journal. Aaron was taking photographs of a stela that stood in the courtyard, a carved obelisk that marked the important events of one twenty-year period, or *katun*. He had asked her to stand next to the stela to demonstrate its height, and she had modeled next to it, tipping her straw hat over one eye and pursing her lips in a kiss. That had been the beginning.

CHAPTER FIVE

Claire wiped away a tear as George reviewed the hiring process with the newer faculty members. She watched with misty eyes as several men set up a reception area on the lawn outside. An older man, with graying hair combed back from his face, gestured as he directed two young waiters in situating a large sign on a home-made easel near the cloth-covered tables: *'Bienvenidos! The 10th Annual Meeting of the Society of Mayanist Studies.'* The man nodded his approval as he straightened his crisp white *guayabera* shirt, pulling it down by the hem, fingering the buttons and the vertical pleats that strained over his extended stomach.

George's "ahems" brought Claire back to the conversation. Her colleagues stared at her, their faces marked with worry. George cleared his throat again. "We have Paul Sturgess and Laura Lorenzo to consider."

Anxious to move beyond her grief, Claire asked, "May I start with Laura Lorenzo?"

"Please do." George turned his palm to her as he reached for a tortilla chip.

Tanya looked up sharply, then slapped her notes down on the table, folding her hands tightly on top of them.

Claire looked at Tanya. "I'm sorry, do you want to start?"

"No, go ahead," she said, pressing her lips tightly.

Claire pulled a small spiral notebook and reading glasses from her bag. "Laura completed her undergraduate work and master's degree in Chicago, the same university where Paul Sturgess studied. She will finish her Ph.D. in linguistic anthropology at Georgetown by September. She's currently teaching courses in Guatemalan languages and cultures." She looked at her colleagues, who studied their own notes or concentrated on the drinks in front of them. Tanya sat stone-faced, holding her beer tightly in her hand.

18

Claire continued, "Laura conducted her linguistic research in Guatemala. She would complement the cultural areas in our program. With Brad, Jamal, and me all working in the Yucatán, and Tanya's linguistic and hieroglyphic studies in Chiapas, Guatemala is a logical geographic area to pursue." She looked up to assess the reaction of the group. "Of course, George and Madge did archaeological work in Guatemala, but Laura's work is linguistic and cultural."

Tanya spoke up, "But we agreed that we were looking for a cultural anthropologist with an economic focus." She paused and looked pointedly at Claire. "Paul fits that category." She pulled at her ponytail. "Paul is *very* ambitious. He has reviewed our publications and knows about our projects and our research sites. Laura didn't seem as well-prepared."

"It seems that perhaps Tanya is feeling a little threatened by another linguist?" Brad said.

Tanya stiffened, directing her rebuttal to George. "I don't feel threatened...really."

Claire stifled a frustrated sigh. "In addition to her linguistics research, Laura has presented conference papers on cultural topics such as the Guatemalan civil war and migration of Guatemalans into Mexico and the United States. Those are economic topics."

"That's political, not economic," Tanya persisted. Claire cleared her throat to disagree, but Tanya continued, "No one asked for my report." She looked at George. "You *did* assign me to check Laura's references."

"And what did you find out?" George asked, his voice tense.

"It seems that everyone *loves* Laura." Tanya rolled her eyes, pausing to sip her beer. "Her doctoral committee chair gave her accolades about her work, but seemed reluctant to give me details on her dissertation, other than it examined linguistics *and* economics...doesn't that seem strange?"

"They don't want to pigeonhole her," Madge reasoned. "If they label her a linguist, it might jeopardize her chances for this job."

"As it should," argued Tanya. "And another thing," she said, looking at each of her colleagues in turn, "Her committee chair said I was the second person from Keane College to call her regarding Laura's credentials." She paused a few moments to make eye contact with George. "I'm wondering if anyone else checked up on her, besides me."

Claire bristled at the accusatory tone. "Why would we?"

"Maybe I'm not taken seriously?" Tanya's hand shook as she reached for her beer and took a large gulp.

"That's ridiculous," George sputtered. "Did the contact give a name?"

"No," Tanya responded shortly. "Just that *he* was a member of the search committee."

"It wasn't me," exclaimed Brad.

"Or me," Jamal said, glaring at Tanya.

An uncomfortable pause ensued as they directed their attention to their drinks and snacks.

Madge finally spoke up. "Can we move on to Paul Sturgess?"

Jamal, who had been tapping the table nervously, started, "Paul's research on tourism is important, but he worked in several communities near those where Brad and I worked. As for being prepared, usually job candidates flatter their interviewers. I felt interrogated."

Madge removed her hat and smoothed her hair, which sprang back into life, resuming its original state of disarray. "You all remember what it's like, applying for your first post-doctorate teaching job. Desperation and nervousness can cause you to say things you don't mean. Paul's strange, I agree, but I'm not concerned about his comments." She tapped George's hand as it hovered over the nuts as she moved the bowl closer to herself. "He is trying to impress."

George turned to Brad. "You researched Doctor Sturgess. What did you find out?"

Brad flipped through a small notebook he had taken from his backpack. "Paul is currently teaching part-time in Chicago, and his department chair seemed very anxious to be rid of him."

"You mean the chair gave him an excellent recommendation?" Madge asked, her hazel eyes directed at Brad.

"Yes, but too much. We've discussed his credentials. They seem valid, but I just don't like him."

George furrowed his brow. "I'm not sure either of them fits our needs. Fortunately, we don't have to decide today. We still have two candidates to interview this summer."

Madge pulled the conference program from the folds of her bag and adjusted her glasses on her nose. "Paul is giving a formal paper tomorrow. That will give us another look at him."

The heightened activity on the lawn drew Claire's attention. The Cultural Center staff had put out food trays and connected blenders to an electrical strip leading from the center to the food and bar areas. A mariachi band was setting up nearby. A small group of university-aged guests, wearing conference badges, congregated at the perimeter of the reception area, talking amongst themselves as they waited for the party to begin.

She noticed one couple already seated at one of the white cloth-covered tables. Laura Lorenzo, the linguistics candidate, and Eduardo Ramirez, the art collector who was making the donation to Keane College, sat deep in conversation, unaware of the head waiter hovering over them. Claire had only met Eduardo once before, but recognized him, primarily because of his striking good looks and the fact that he seemed out of place in his western suit and tie.

Laura appeared enchanted. She smiled as he spoke, making eye contact. She fingered the neckline of her peach-colored sundress in response to Eduardo's careful, mannered movements—lightly touching her arm and tipping his head toward her as she spoke. When he pulled out a cigarette case, the waiter reacted, pressing his hands over his *guayabera* and pulling it down again over his stomach. He approached the distinguished-looking guest, making apologetic gestures. Eduardo smiled graciously and placed the cigarette case back in his suit pocket.

Madge, following Claire's gaze, said, "Well, what is *this*?" Everyone turned to the scene outside the window.

Jamal said, "Do you think they know each other?"

Tanya said, "How would she know him?"

Brad lowered his voice. "Perhaps she has connections that could work for us in our museum collections."

Tanya turned sharply to Brad. "Look at her. She's almost in his lap."

Brad narrowed his eyes but said nothing, his attention diverted. "Well, look who's also waiting for the party to begin." He nodded toward two men in their late twenties, one with black curly hair and horn-rimmed glasses, the other with reddish blond hair, neatly trimmed. They skirted the edge of the reception area. "It's Paul Sturgess and his boyfriend."

"Boyfriend?" Jamal said. "How do you know?"

"I'm an anthropologist. I observe," Brad smiled.

The two men sat on a cement bench just outside the reception area. Paul dominated the conversation. His friend, whose pale, freckled skin was reddened from the sun, listened, his hands clasped in his lap, his lips often opening as if to speak, but closing again, silenced.

Inside, the anthropologists were enthralled by the two scenarios. Claire, however, felt like a voyeur. She turned her attention back to her notebook, flipping through the pages.

Tanya persisted, asking Brad, "Did Paul tell you it was his partner?"

"No. Why would he tell me? Besides, I didn't talk to him privately."

Tanya furrowed her brow. "You did. I saw you…Jamal and I saw you…at the Governor's Palace. I recognized Paul's university T-shirt."

Brad looked at her, his eyes narrowed. "You're right. I forgot. He came up to me, but he didn't say much—just thanked me for the interview. I think that was when I suspected he was gay. His friend stood nearby, watching him."

"We can't discuss this," Madge said.

An uncomfortable stillness settled on the group. George squirmed in his chair and cleared his throat once again. "Does anyone have anything pertinent to add to the discussion?"

Getting no response, George raised his hand to call for the check. He pushed his glasses further up the bridge of his nose. "I hope you all understand that the conversation we had today remains within this group."

The waiter brought the check to George and, at that moment, the mariachi band began to play. The lively music, performed with trumpet, guitar, and tinny drum permeated the glass, muting the conversations in the restaurant. Outside, the anthropologists and graduate students, their clothes wilted from the heat, flooded into the reception area, forming lines along the food and drink tables.

"Well," George said loudly to be heard above the din, "I guess that does it." As his colleagues rose to join the party, he added, "Don't worry, I'll get the check."

Preoccupied, the professors merely nodded and walked away. Rolling his eyes, George took the check to the cashier. Madge strolled ahead of the group, snapping her fingers above her head, twirling so that her tie-dye skirt flared out around her thick legs. Restaurant patrons smiled at the eccentric lady and clapped along with her.

"Olé!" Madge said as she danced out of the restaurant, patrons laughing and encouraging her on. The other scholars, trying to maintain a modicum of decorum, trailed behind her, like children following the pied piper. Claire, smiling at her friend's performance, waited for George. Meeting adjourned.

CHAPTER SIX

Sunday Afternoon

Outside, the heat had intensified into a seething inferno. Perspiration settled on the waiters' foreheads as they stood at the bar or buffet table unprotected from the sun while the guests filled their plates, chose their beverages, and retreated to the relative cool of the umbrella-covered tables. Claire took a margarita from the bar and stirred the golden liquid with a plastic stick depicting an unidentifiable Mayan god.

She watched as a three-generation Mexican family herded their children and grandchildren down the path toward the pyramids, the adults glancing at the foreigners, their children oblivious. The family reminded Claire of her research years in Yaxpec.

She remembered one day when an ancient widow, with a deeply creased face and sparse gray hair escaping from a loose-tied bun, invited her into her oval, stick-and-daub house. Strips of plastic sheeting covered the gaps where the cement filler had fallen away from the tree branches that formed the shape of the house. She had invited Claire to sit in a wobbly wooden chair and disappeared out the back door, returning with a large naval orange, sliced in two. She had offered both halves to Claire with hands gnarled by arthritis before balancing herself on the edge of a hammock strung from one side of the room to the other. Her smile had displayed a nearly toothless mouth, and she spoke softly in a part-Spanish, part-Mayan style characteristic of her generation, telling Claire her story, one of thousands she had heard during her stay. Now thirty years later, a full professor, Claire remembered those days as among the most fulfilling of her life.

Claire scanned the tables, locating Madge seated with Paul Sturgess and his friend. Paul studied his laptop screen while his friend sat quietly, his eyes surveying his surroundings as if seeking a familiar face.

The men held beer bottles, their hands curled around icy glass necks, while Madge, like herself, had switched to tequila.

Madge's pursed lips and squinted eyes betrayed an irritation with her companions, but her demeanor brightened as Claire joined them.

Claire pointed toward a plate of tacos. "May I?"

"Of course," Madge said. Claire reached for a taco as she placed her drink on the table. She took a bite, savoring the rich corn tortilla and spicy meat.

"I'm having a nice chat with Paul and his friend, Cody…um…" Madge paused, embarrassed.

"Detwyler," Paul said. "Cody Detwyler."

Madge shifted in her seat, reached down to the ground and fumbled with her cloth bag. "As a matter of fact," she said, "I need to find George." She turned to Paul and then Cody. "It was very nice talking to you both."

She stood, pulling her skirt away from her legs and lifting her bag to her shoulder. She gave Claire a brief glance, her hat hiding her face from the view of the two young men. She raised one eyebrow and retreated as quickly as her legs would carry her, her skirt twirling around her ample frame.

Paul leaned in toward Claire, speaking softly. "Doctor Carmichael told me about your husband. I am so sorry."

Claire sat back, stunned at his abruptness. "It's been two years," she said.

Glancing briefly at Cody, Paul continued, "How did your husband feel about following you to Yaxpec? Did he resent it?"

"He completed a medical fellowship in Merida while he was here," Claire said. "Why do you ask?"

"Anthropological research is difficult for spouses, especially if they each have a career."

"That's true. I have friends whose marriages suffered or failed. But many became stronger, like ours."

"Did your husband follow you to Keane College too?"

It seemed an odd line of questioning, and she noticed that Cody stiffened and gave his friend a pleading look. Claire suspected that he asked these questions for his friend's benefit more than for his own edification.

Claire replied, "Aaron was a doctor. He started a private practice."

Cody suddenly stood. "Can I get anyone a drink?"

Paul nodded, but Claire shook her head. After Cody left, Paul turned to Claire. "He's a little bored, I think. This is my gig, and he feels a bit out of place."

"Is he concerned about moving to Michigan if you get this job?"

"Maybe, a little." Paul fiddled with his laptop for a few seconds, then said, "I really liked your book."

"Which one?" Claire responded quickly, without thinking.

He clicked a few keys on his computer. "*Yaxpec: A Village in Search of an Identity*. I respect your honesty about your research."

"What do you mean?" Claire wasn't sure she'd heard him correctly over the music. She peered at Paul over her glass. Perspiration appeared suddenly on his forehead.

He stammered. "In the introduction, you admit to your discomfort about your own Mexican heritage and how it might affect your work in Mexico…and about your Catholic upbringing, how you have come to question Catholicism…."

"We all take our experiences and beliefs into the field," Claire said, interrupting him. "We are challenged to examine not only the culture we are studying, but our own beliefs as well. You know this, I'm sure." She remembered Jamal's comment about Paul's interrogation technique, and she thought of the strange look on Madge's face as she left the table.

Paul didn't make eye contact but took refuge in whatever was on his computer screen. He self-consciously wiped the sweat off his forehead. "What's important is that we respect the indigenous history."

"That's correct, but what are you saying?"

He shrugged. "Nothing, nothing…I meant no criticism. I have always admired your work, and that of the other faculty members. I would love to work with you." Flustered, Paul snapped his computer shut and looked at Claire, his blue eyes pleading. "Please forgive me if I said anything wrong. I wasn't speaking about you."

Before Claire could respond, Cody returned with two beers. He sat down, pushing one beer toward his friend. She placed her empty margarita glass on the table and said, "My second book, *Yaxpec Then and Now,* considers the economic and social changes in the village over thirty years. I discuss the evolution of my thinking as well." Claire regretted her comment when Paul's face reddened. "It just came out recently," she added

Paul's face brightened. "Oh, yes. I can't wait to read it."

Claire stood to leave, but as she did so Laura Lorenzo approached their table, a large colorful Mexican woven bag hanging from her shoulder. The linguist adjusted the folds of her sundress over her muscular legs.

"Doctor Aguila," she said, thrusting her hand out to shake.

"Call me Claire, please," she said, taking her hand. "I hope you are enjoying the reception."

"Very much," Laura responded, briefly glancing at Paul and Cody. Claire introduced her to the young men, wondering if she and Paul knew they had interviewed for the same job.

Paul held his hand out to shake Laura's, answering Claire's silent question. "Can I assume we are competitors?"

"I guess so, yes," Laura responded. She smiled uncertainly, and Claire noticed that she might be older than she first appeared. Her dark hair framed a face marked by gentle lines and creases, not the look of a fresh-faced graduate student.

Claire said to Laura, "I was about to socialize. Do you want to join me?" Laura nodded, and Claire noticed a look of disappointment cross Paul's face.

He quickly recovered and smiled. "Time to circulate," he said, stuffing his laptop into his backpack. Cody reached behind him to grab his pack off the back of his chair. They picked up their beers and stood, awkwardly.

"I look forward to hearing your paper tomorrow," Claire said as she turned away from Paul.

Paul smiled. "I hope you like it."

Laura and Claire strolled to a small clearing near the reception area where a poinciana tree stood majestically, its red flowers in deep bloom. The band still played, but they had lowered the volume, and the distance made it easier to converse. "I'm sorry I haven't had a chance to talk to you privately since your presentation this morning," Claire said.

"It has been a busy day," Laura responded. "It must be exciting to have a new program and be able to hire faculty members...I understand you'll be receiving a collection of artifacts from Doctor Ramirez. A program *and* a museum!"

"We are fortunate," Claire said. "Do you know Eduardo Ramirez?"

"Not really," Laura said. She pushed her hair behind her ears and Claire noticed her earrings, small Mayan jade posts. "He invited me to sit with him while we waited for the reception to begin." She smiled uneasily. "He explained why he was here. I knew he must be important by the way he felt comfortable moving into the reception area...and then there's his clothes." She raised her eyebrows.

Claire laughed, and Laura added, "Is he associated with Keane College?"

"Just through Dr. Kingsford, and now the collection."

Laura's gaze wandered away from Claire. "There's Tanya...Doctor Petersen. I would love to talk to her. Do you mind?"

Claire watched Laura stroll to Tanya's side. *Paul talks too much; Laura is cautious. What a contrast,* she thought as she pulled her camera from her bag. Through her camera lens she watched Laura approach Tanya. They spoke for a few minutes, then Paul joined them. Tanya moved away slightly, staggering a bit and nearly spilling her margarita. Paul ignored Tanya and continued speaking to Laura, saying something that caused Laura to frown slightly. Tanya laughed too loudly, drawing the attention of those around her. *Something is wrong with Tanya,* Claire thought, as she absently clicked the photograph and tucked her camera back in her bag.

She watched as Paul took Laura by the arm and drew her away from Tanya. He smiled as he imparted some information to her, but Laura's eyebrows furrowed. She recovered and smiled briefly, turning away from him and walking toward Madge and George, who sat together near the bar. Claire saw that Tanya also watched the scene. Catching Claire's eye, Tanya winked at her, and moved in her direction.

The music stopped, much to Claire's relief. She saw Brad and Eduardo make their way to the buffet table. Claire turned to follow them, but Tanya appeared at her side.

"Well, that was interesting," Tanya said, holding her now-empty glass. She smiled at Claire and winked again.

"Damn!" Tanya said, looking over Claire's shoulder. Claire turned to see Jamal speaking with a middle-aged man with short gray hair and a square jaw.

"Who's that?" Claire asked.

Tanya turned quickly back to Claire. "Someone..." Her response was interrupted when Brad spoke loudly, to get everyone's attention.

"On behalf of the Society of Mayanist Studies, I would like to welcome you all to Mexico, and to one of Yucatán's premier Mayan sites. Isn't this spectacular?" He motioned to the pyramids looming in the distance, and the participants applauded.

"As director for the newest program in the Society, I am proud that the Keane College Mayanist Program of Westport, Michigan, has been asked to sponsor this year's event. I would like to thank my colleagues for their tireless work in planning and bringing the conference to Merida this year."

Brad paused and motioned to Eduardo. "I am especially proud to present my friend, Doctor Eduardo Ramirez." Eduardo bowed to the participants. "Eduardo and I earned our doctorates from the same great university..." Brad paused for laughter, "and he is an expert in Mexican artifacts and art. His family is renowned in Mexico and Texas for their galleries and museums, *Galerías Indígenas.*" Mild applause followed as Brad motioned Eduardo to speak.

"I am very pleased to be with you this week," Eduardo said, his English mildly accented and velvet-smooth. "It has been an honor to have Doctor Kingsford as a friend, and I look forward to meeting you all during the conference. I am hosting a reception on Tuesday evening at the Casa Montejo. I hope to see you there."

More applause as Brad put his arm awkwardly around his friend's shoulder. He said, "I encourage you to hear Eduardo's lecture tomorrow evening. He has a fascinating topic for us, 'The Mayan Art of Murder.'"

CHAPTER SEVEN

Sunday evening

After the reception, the anthropologists dispersed on their own until the Sound and Light Show that evening. Shuttle buses transported conferees and tourists back and forth between the Cultural Center and the exclusive on-site hotels and restaurants. Students attending the conference took local buses into the small town of Uxmal where more reasonably priced food could be found.

Later, Claire, George, and Madge stood in front of the Hotel Uxmal Restaurant, waiting for the next shuttle back to the archaeological site. Laura, Paul, and Cody had caught an earlier shuttle, and the rest of the Keane College group waited behind them.

They boarded the shuttle and rejoiced in the blast of cold air. Madge and George took one of the long seats along the aisle behind the driver. Claire sat across the aisle, facing them. The bus followed a route between the on-site hotels, dropping off tourists and picking up others who wanted to attend the evening event. George tipped his hat over his face, and within moments, Claire could hear him snoring from under the hat. *How do people do that?* she thought. Madge leaned against the barrier separating her from the driver and closed her eyes. Claire relaxed her head against the window. Her mind wandered over the events of the day, and how nice it would feel to be in her hotel bed, this day behind her.

At the Cultural Center, Madge opened her eyes and prodded George in the side. He snorted to attention as the children and others paraded past him and exited the bus. Inside the building, Madge and Claire visited the restroom, and rejoined George at the fountain where Madge sat on a bench and refused to move.

"I'll meet you at the Nunnery Quadrangle for the show," she said.

"Are you okay?" Claire asked, worried.

"I'm fine. I need to rest a few minutes."

George stayed with Madge, and Claire set off by herself.

The archaeological park had closed, admitting only those with tickets to the program. Claire followed the tourists who had shared her bus past the abandoned vendor tables. The park guards attempted to keep the tourists on a marked path around the Magician's Pyramid toward a back stairway to the Nunnery Complex, but Claire and others circled away from the security guards to take photographs of the setting sun displaying a brilliant orange aurora around the pyramid. As she did so, a flash of maroon drew her attention.

She recognized Paul and Cody just beyond her, at the foot of the pyramid. She lifted her hand to wave but hesitated and stepped back into the shadows. They were arguing. She could hear Paul's tone rising and falling in the evening air, but she could not discern his words. He glared at his friend, his hands punching the air for emphasis. Cody started to speak, but Paul, making a horizontal swipe with his hands, silenced his companion. Cody slouched, his hands in his pockets, and looked toward the Cultural Center.

Claire stepped back and retreated toward the Nunnery Quadrangle. She passed Brad and Laura, who stood near the pyramid, and joined the tourists climbing an ancient stone stairway leading to the first tier of the north palace. There, metal scaffolding and bleachers had been erected over the ancient steps to protect the deteriorating stairways.

Seated in a middle row of bleachers, Claire spread her purse and camera along the bench to save seats for her colleagues. The sun had set, and the pyramid was cloaked in shadow. It had been a long day: several hours of interviews with the two candidates, an hour bus ride from Merida to Uxmal, traipsing around the site in the blazing heat, a meeting, reception, more traipsing, eating, drinking, the Sound and Light Show, and, after the show, another hour bus ride back to their Merida hotel. She once again thought longingly of her hotel room, or more ardently, for a hammock at the home of her *compadres* in Yaxpec, her goddaughter's parents.

Claire stood and waved when she saw George and Madge at the top of the stairs. They moved across the long row, sitting heavily onto the bleachers.

"Damn it, Claire," Madge said. "Couldn't you find a more inconvenient place to sit?"

"Well, you left me to choose." Claire smiled as she moved down the row to save the place for others.

The pyramid stood in deep shadow now, backlit by the floodlights that led to the Cultural Center. The evening air vibrated with energy as tourists settled into their rows. Cameras at the ready, they chatted among themselves as they waited for the show to begin.

"Where is everyone?" Madge asked. She pulled her binoculars from her bag and stood to scan the audience.

Claire was beginning to wonder if her colleagues had found seating elsewhere when she heard her name called. She turned and saw Tanya skipping down the bleacher steps toward them. She slid into their row and sat next to Claire with a heavy sigh.

"Where's Jamal?" Tanya asked. "He said he was on his way. Can I see?" She held her hand out for Madge's binoculars, and Madge handed them over. Tanya's gaze moved along the bench rows and toward the stairway leading up to them.

"Probably too embarrassed to attend these hokey shows," George said.

"Aren't we all," Tanya said, distracted as she scanned the area surrounding the pyramid and the walkway by the metal stairs. "Whose idea was this anyway?"

Claire, whose idea it had been, said nothing. Perhaps a day at an archaeological site had been a little optimistic for this group.

"Looking for us?" Brad's baritone, coming from behind, startled them.

Tanya jumped, nearly losing her balance as she turned to see Brad and Eduardo sit just above them in the bleacher seats.

"Sorry we're late," Eduardo said. "I had to rescue Brad from Laura." He laughed, and Brad followed suit.

"And I thought she was the quiet one," Brad said as he stuffed his hat into his backpack and pulled out a light jacket. He crammed his pack between his feet.

As the floodlights dimmed, Jamal pushed past a large family that had settled in their row.

"Sorry," he said as he sat down. "I ran into Laura Lorenzo in line, and she wanted to summarize her academic credentials." He reached into his backpack, pulled out a Bob Marley sweatshirt and pulled it over his head.

"You don't have to explain," Tanya pouted, indicating that perhaps he did.

"You too?" said Eduardo. "She's a politician…and beautiful too." Eduardo raised his eyebrows at Brad. Tanya turned back to Eduardo and scowled at Brad.

"I didn't say anything," Brad said, blushing. "Eduardo's the Latin lover."

Warning noises from their neighbors directed their attention to the program just beginning. The show depicted a complicated story describing the mythological origins of Uxmal. It involved a sorceress who managed to hatch a child from an egg. She sent the child, who in one year had grown to be an adult dwarf, to challenge the King of Uxmal to a series of tests that culminated in the king's defeat. The king, in retaliation, demanded that the dwarf build a palace overnight, which he did, the result being the Magician's Pyramid.

A choreography of greens, reds, and golds accompanied the drama, highlighting carvings on the stone façades: warriors, the mythical feathered serpent, and the rain god Chac. Exclamations from the audience competed with the exhausted cries of numerous babies in the audience. When the narrator described how the dwarf was then proclaimed Magician and supreme leader, the pyramid lit up in a spectacular blaze of purple.

Above them an endless expanse of stars filled the darkness. The air had cooled, and spectators who had shown foresight donned sweaters or light jackets. Claire pulled a nylon jacket from her shoulder bag and followed her group. The clanking of heavy feet on the metal stairs reverberated in the night air. Park officials holding large flashlights directed the traffic behind the north building of the Nunnery Quadrangle, away from the pyramid. Footlights followed the path toward the Cultural Center.

Despite the size of the exodus, visitors departed as if from a church, conversing in subdued tones, except those of fussing, overly tired children, herded along by similarly exhausted parents. Madge and Claire joined a small group of tourists who wandered away from the path to take night photos. While the others rejoined their groups, Madge and Claire meandered farther afield, maneuvering carefully along the limestone outcroppings. The illumination cast ominous shadows in the crevices of the structure, and Claire paused to adjust the settings on her camera.

A piercing scream shattered the darkness, followed by cries of alarm emanating from the far side of the Magician's Pyramid. Claire and Madge stumbled toward the sound, Claire in the lead, dodging ankle-breaking clumps of limestone while Madge struggled behind. Just past the west stairway a crowd was coalescing, like flocking birds waiting for the signal to journey south. Indistinguishable noises, like the shrill cries of blackbirds, collided in a Babel of questions and gasps as tourists jostled to fill in the gaps of the growing semi-circle that formed around the body lying at the foot of the pyramid.

A young, female security guard stood among the growing crowd. The guard held her flashlight on a middle-aged woman trying to make herself understood as she explained how she came upon the horrific scene. The guard punched numbers into her field phone as the witness turned her back and addressed the crowd, providing her narrative to those around her.

"Someone's dead!" she said.

The guard fought back tears as she continued to push numbers, listen, then disconnect. Several people pulled out cellphones and began taking photographs, to the protest of more sensitive tourists around them.

The guard clipped her phone to her belt and shined her flashlight around the group. "*Se mueven, por favor, y no tocan fotos!*" she begged, but the tourists largely ignored her.

Claire elbowed her way to the young guard. As she approached, she could see a figure lying in the shadow of the pyramid balustrade, but she forced her attention toward the crowd. "She wants you all to move away and not take photographs."

An elderly man spoke from the midst of the crowd. "Why doesn't she do something? My God!"

Claire turned to the guard, who once again attempted a call. In frustration, the young woman held up her radio with one hand and held the flashlight on Claire's face with the other.

"No answer," she said in accented English.

In Spanish, Claire said, "Get help! I'll watch the crowd."

The young woman turned and ran toward the Cultural Center, and Claire looked closely at the body for the first time. Blocking out the voices bouncing around her, Claire's eyes locked on the unnatural position of the neck and the huge gash at the back of the head, a man's head, matted with blood that had flowed freely over his gray nylon jacket. She couldn't see his face, yet there was something familiar about him. Claire scanned the crowd and saw her colleagues huddled together at the edge of the circle that had formed around her and the body. She sighed with relief when Brad joined her in the circle. He looked down at the body and frowned at Claire.

"I told the guard I'd keep everyone away," Claire said as Brad threw off his backpack and knelt next to the body. He used his fingers to test for a pulse behind the man's ear, then leaned down to look closer.

Gently, he turned the body over. Claire reached out to stop him, but she was too late. When the face was visible, a new rush of gasps erupted from the anthropologists in the crowd.

CHAPTER EIGHT

Claire looked into the staring eyes of Paul Sturgess. His face was bruised; his wire-rim glasses, broken in the fall, hung from one ear. Instinctively, she reached out to touch him, but Brad pulled her hand back. He looked up at the crowd bearing down on them, a mixture of tourists and anthropologists with facial expressions ranging from horror to poorly disguised voyeurism.

"Can someone find that security guard? Call someone?" Brad demanded in English and Spanish. Bystanders looked helplessly at their cellphones or surreptitiously took photographs of the gruesome scene. "*Por favor!*" he shouted.

A student wearing a University of Yucatán sweatshirt took off in a sprint. "*Me voy!*"

Claire's colleagues inched closer to the inner circle as they realized who had died. Tanya stared at Paul, biting her lower lip, her eyes wide. Madge, unsteady, leaned into George, and George, deathly pale, put his arm around her. Laura Lorenzo stood off to the side. Only Jamal was missing.

Tanya forced her eyes away from the body. "Did he fall? What happened? I don't understand!"

Madge wiped her eyes with her fingers. "He must have fallen from the ledge," she said. "George and I stood in that same spot this afternoon." She choked back tears, "Why was he up there?"

Claire stiffened as Brad struggled to remove Paul's jacket, displaying the maroon shirt that would have identified him sooner.

"What are you doing?" she asked, watching his ashen face as he fumbled with the jacket sleeves.

"Help me, Claire," he said. "It's only proper to cover him."

Claire helped him remove the jacket, and Brad placed it over Paul's face, carefully smoothing the jacket with his hands.

"Um, Miss?" Claire looked up to see the elderly couple from Michigan standing at the edge of the circle. She struggled to remember their names as the woman tried to recall hers.

"Lois?" Somehow, it came to her. "You need to stay back." Claire approached them so they could speak quietly.

Lois's husband, Dale, said, "We saw him on the temple. We wondered why he was up there when the show was about to start."

Claire stared at them. "Did you see him fall?"

"Oh, my, no!" cried Lois. She placed her hand on her heart, as if it might give out at any moment.

"He was walking along the platform," Dale said, pointing to the ledge that separated the first and second levels of the pyramid, "like he was looking for someone."

Claire asked, "Did you see anything else?"

Lois answered, "No, we had to get to our seats." Tears came to her eyes, and she pressed closer to her husband, whose gaze moved up and down the pyramid and settled on the balustrade at the base of the stairway. They now stood directly below where Madge had stood earlier, calling down to Claire to remind her of the meeting. It seemed like days ago, not hours.

Claire looked at her watch…nine-thirty. *How long had they been here? Why hadn't anyone come to help?* Tourists also looked at their watches or phones, deciding whether to stay for the drama or leave. Families opted to leave, pulling their children along the path.

Fearful that important witnesses might disappear, Claire pleaded with the crowd. "If any of you saw something, you should stay. Someone will be here soon."

"Do you think Dale and I should stay?" Lois asked. "We would be witnesses. Oh, dear," she lamented as she grasped her chest again. "We'll miss our bus. So will you."

Claire hadn't considered this. "We should all stay."

A middle-aged balding man wearing a golf jacket and a beret that looked out of place in Mexico, scoffed loudly. "It was an accident, lady. The kid fell." He and his wife, a stick-thin, platinum blonde wearing skintight jeans and leather jacket, turned to go. "Besides," he added, "if anyone shoved him, do you think he'd be hanging around waiting for the *policia* to come?" He stressed the Spanish pronunciation in derision, *po-lee-see'a*. They joined the sprinkling of tourists forming a slow procession toward the exit.

Claire suspected he was right. Yet there was something odd about where Paul had landed. With her eyes, she followed a line from the body up the wall of the pyramid, a narrow area between the stairway towering eighty feet to the first landing, and the balustrade. It *could* have happened that way, she thought.

She remembered her reason for straying from the designated exit route. Although, she had been repulsed by the tourists snapping photographs, she knew she should record Paul's location before security arrived, if indeed they arrived at all, just in case there were questions later. She took her camera from her bag, where she had stashed it unconsciously when they came upon the body. She moved toward a footlight to adjust her settings.

The crowd shifted suddenly as the university student pushed through, followed by Cody and, a few steps behind, the security guard. The student rejoined his group, and the guard stopped to catch her breath. "*La ambulancia y policía*—it come. Please wait."

But Cody didn't wait. He pushed into the circle and collapsed on the body of his friend. Brad reacted quickly and pulled him away.

"No!" Cody's scream split the air as Brad lead him to Madge and Tanya at the edge of the circle.

Amidst murmurings around the circle and the anguished choking cries of Cody nearby, some of the remaining crowd obeyed the guard's request. Others proceeded slowly toward the exit, finally exhausted and bored with the slow-moving drama.

Claire addressed the guard in Spanish. "Can you help me take photographs?"

At first the young woman pulled back. "*No quiero*," she protested. "I don't want to." She refused to look at the body. "I'm not really a security guard," she admitted, "just a night employee…they let me wear the uniform."

"You're in charge until the police come," Claire continued softly, to put her at ease. "It would be a great help to the police if someone took photographs of the scene." Claire hoped this was true, and that the woman wouldn't get into trouble for interfering.

The young woman nodded slowly, her eyes flitting from Claire to the body. Claire introduced herself and the woman responded, "I am Maria Socorro May Uc," drawing courage from somewhere within. "People call me Socorro."

Easing Socorro slowly to the pyramid, Claire asked her to aim her flashlight at the point where the balustrade protruded from the base of the temple. She thought that if Paul had hit the balustrade when he fell, he should have landed away from the temple. Instead, he lay in the shadow of the balustrade, along the wall of the pyramid.

Brad, who now stood at the perimeter of the group, turned as he saw the camera flash. "What's that for?" he asked.

"You aren't thinking…?" Tanya said, edging into the circle.

"I don't think anything," Claire said, aware that her hands shook as she held the camera.

"You're right, Claire," said George.

Brad looked from George to Claire, deep in thought. He nodded solemnly and began to walk the perimeter of the circle, urging the remaining onlookers to move away.

Laura took her cellphone from her bag and used the flashlight function as she walked away from the circle. Claire watched her as she climbed the pyramid, scanning the side of the balustrade and the steps.

The presence of the cameras and flashlights drew the attention of the remaining bystanders, who pulled out their phone flashlights and began to scan the area around the pyramid. Claire groaned as she watched tourists kicking up loose limestone chunks as they walked around the temple.

George stepped into the circle and projected his professorial voice to move the crowd back. Giving George a grateful nod, Claire brought her camera back into position. She photographed segments of ground where she and Socorro had not yet walked, capturing several sets of footprints.

They moved slowly toward the body, Claire taking photos as she walked. "You didn't move him?" she asked Socorro.

"Oh, no! I wouldn't touch him…" She stared at the covered body, stammering, "B-but somebody did…while I was gone."

Claire didn't respond. Instead, she knelt next to the body and asked Socorro to hold the flashlight up over her shoulder. She forced herself to remove the jacket from Paul's face and take several photographs. His eyes were open, and dried blood had settled below his broken nose and around his mouth. Deep bruising was evident on his forehead. The frames of his glasses were bent and still hanging over one ear, the lenses shattered. None of these injuries seemed consistent with landing face-first on the balustrade. The massive gash on the back of his skull seemed the most likely area of contact.

She lifted Paul's shoulder and asked Socorro to shine the flashlight toward the back of his head. The flashlight wavered as Socorro huddled behind her to avoid looking at the body. Claire photographed blood-like splotches on the ground beneath the body, then lowered the shoulder to the ground. She closed Paul's eyes.

Replacing the jacket over Paul's face, Claire asked a relieved Socorro to shine her flashlight along a line of disturbed limestone rubble and dirt that stretched between the body and the place where Claire suspected the body should have landed. There, the ground was relatively clear of rubble and the flashlight picked up discolored dirt. Unfortunately, this area had been trampled by the first onlookers at the scene. She took photographs anyway, hoping that the area had not been destroyed. She was quite sure these drag marks indicated the body had been moved. But by whom? As she stood to stretch, she saw headlights bobbing up and down as a vehicle moved slowly up the walkway, approaching them. An ambulance had arrived.

Claire heard Brad say, "Well, finally!"

CHAPTER NINE

Lights flashed, but the siren did not sound. The circle—which had thinned to twenty die-hard voyeurs or potential witnesses—opened to allow two paramedics into the space. The older man maneuvered a stretcher over the uneven ground and limestone rubble. The younger man carried a medical bag. They ordered Claire and the others aside, and the younger man squatted down to examine the body. Claire joined Laura, who had returned to the group, her lips pursed together in concentration. Jamal had joined the group and taken Madge's place next to Cody, who whimpered at the outer edge of the shrunken circle.

"Did you see anything up there?" Claire asked Laura.

"I'm not sure," Laura admitted. "I wondered if there might be something on the ledge that indicated how he fell, but I didn't see anything." Her intonation didn't reveal any suspicions on her part, so Claire kept private her own concern over how the body had ended up next to the balustrade instead of in front of it.

A few moments later, the police arrived in a battered white pickup truck with *Policía de Uxmal* stenciled on the side and a portable red flashing light affixed to the roof. The vehicle needed no siren. The noise and smoke from its missing muffler provided all the warning any criminal might need.

The officers conversed briefly with the medics, then identified themselves as Constable Luis Pech and Deputy Reymundo Tun. The younger man, Deputy Tun, sought out Socorro and they walked together past Claire, who suspected they knew each other. Socorro addressed him as "Mundo" as she led him away from the crowd to give her report.

In hesitant English, Constable Pech asked witnesses to identify themselves. The woman who had discovered the body raised her hand, and the constable joined her at the edge of the circle, where she clung tightly to her husband's arm. Trembling in fear, the chilled air, or both, she struggled to understand the constable's questions. George came to their rescue, offering himself as translator.

The witness explained that she and her husband had wandered away from the crowd to photograph the Magician's Pyramid. The flash of her camera caught the clump of clothing at the base of the temple. When she realized what she had seen, she screamed, and the security guard came. No, she didn't move the body. No, no one moved the body until that man—she pointed to Brad—turned the body over and then covered it with the dead man's jacket. Then she pointed to Claire. "And that one there, she took pictures."

The constable frowned in Brad's direction, then at Claire. After dismissing the jittery woman and her husband, he directed Brad and Claire away from the tourists. He motioned to Deputy Tun who abandoned Socorro and joined the constable who had already begun to question them.

"You moved the body?" Constable Pech asked Brad, his pencil pausing over his notebook.

In Spanish, Brad defended his actions. "No one was in charge."

The constable lowered his eyes and answered in an apologetic and uncertain tone. "*Pues, Señor,* we came as soon as we heard." He looked at the body, and added, "It was probably an accident, but still…"

Brad interrupted. "I turned the body over to check for a pulse. He was dead, so I covered his face. People were taking photos."

Pivoting from Brad to Claire, Pech demanded, "*Señora,* you took photographs?"

Without Brad's self-confidence, Claire stammered, "I thought it might be helpful, in case they are needed."

"Do you think you are—what is it called—CSI?"

His sarcasm irritated her, but she sensed that his bravado was due more to his insecurity than rudeness. From her field experience, Claire knew how village deputies differed from their city counterparts. These men were hand-picked by the village president, often nephews, brothers, or *compadres*. They weren't trained in police procedures, and they earned little for whatever authority they possessed.

"I am very sorry if I have made a mistake."

Constable Pech said, "I will need your camera."

Claire flinched. "No, I won't give it to you, but I'll take it to the authorities if required." She would not relinquish her camera, or even her memory card, unless she was attached to it.

The two officers turned away and discussed the stubbornness of the anthropologist in their indigenous language. The ancient Mayan language didn't have the vocabulary to discuss such modern concepts as camera, memory card, or uppity anthropologists, so their conversation consisted of both Mayan and Spanish.

Claire listened carefully to their exchange. She mustered her Mayan language skills and broke into their huddle, saying, "I did what I thought was right."

The officers stared at her and then smiled. Their mood altered, as suddenly there existed kinship, of a sort, between them.

Constable Pech said, "*Señora*, you can take your camera. But the Merida police may request it and you will have to obey."

"*Entiendo*, I understand," Claire said, and gave him her name, hotel, and phone number. "Perhaps you need the information for other witnesses?"

Pech nodded, "*Ni'bo'olal.*" Thank you.

Claire explained the request to the tourists who remained, and Deputy Tun made his way around the circle to collect contact information. The tourists had wandered off by the time Tun approached the Keane College group. After Cody provided his contact information, Claire asked him if he knew how to contact Paul's family.

"What?" Cody asked, confused, as Claire explained her question to the deputy.

"Paul's parents. Do you have their phone numbers?"

"I'm not sure." Cody reached into his pocket, retrieved his phone and scrolled through his contacts. He sniffled and nodded. Tun handed him his notebook and pencil.

The chore of writing the parents' names and checking his own phone for phone numbers calmed him, but he raised his head in a jerk when he saw the medics carry the body away.

"Wait! Wait for me!" He stood, dropping the pad and paper, and ran after the medics.

"*No, Señor*," said Constable Pech, reaching for Cody's sleeve. "*No puede ir!*"

Jamal ran to Cody's side and urged him back to the officer. "Cody, you can't go with them."

"He can't go alone!"

"They'll take care of him," Claire said, handing him the pad and pencil. Cody watched as the ambulance started up and crept down the walkway toward the parking lot. He took a deep breath and concentrated on his chore. When he finished, he passed the notebook to the constable.

Jamal announced that they should hurry for the buses, but this news didn't increase the sense of urgency for the Keane College entourage. They proceeded toward the Cultural Center like refugees, exhausted and dragging their feet along the path, the tragedy of the event weighing on them.

Program for the 10th Annual Meeting of the Society for Mayanist Studies
Intercultural Hotel, Merida, Yucatán, Mexico

Events for Monday, May 5
The Mayan World in a Global Context

Morning Sessions:

- Paul Sturgess, *Micro-tourism: The Role of Small Tourist Vendors in Rural Yucatecan Economic Development* CANCELED
- Miguel Muñoz, *The Role of Maquiladoras in the Proletarization of the Yucatecan Worker*
- Ana Alvarez, *Si, Podemos Mandar: Women as Leaders in the Cooperative Movement in Yucatán*

Afternoon Sessions:

- Wendy Wallers, *The Landscapes of the Maya: Applications of Appadurai to Global Issues in Mexico and Guatemala*
- David DeHaan, *Do you Facebook? The Use of Social Media in Maintaining Family and Social Networks in Mexico and Abroad*

4:00 Distinguished Lecture
Doctor Eduardo Ramirez
"The Mayan Art of Murder"

CHAPTER TEN

Monday Morning

Claire glanced at her watch as she waited for the elevator. She was late for breakfast with her colleagues, and the elevators were unusually slow as the conferees descended to the lobby for morning sessions. Claire squeezed in among the scholars who, credential badges dangling around their necks, shifted their positions to allow her in. As she settled into her allotted twelve inches of space, conversations that had paused as she entered resumed. It didn't surprise her that they were discussing the poor man who fell from the pyramid. Claire listened, but did not join the muted conversation.

A short, round man, who took up more than his share of the elevator, added, "I heard the guy was giving his paper today."

The elevator stopped on the next floor, the door opened, and three anthropologists groaned as they realized they wouldn't fit. The door closed, and the elevator jerked into action.

A young man, whose badge identified him as a graduate student from Florida, picked up the conversation. "Today? Really?"

Those who could access their programs in the cramped space opened them up to the morning sessions and someone read off the male presenters: Sturgess, Muñoz, DeHaan.

Another woman said, "Do you think it's the distinguished lecturer, Eduardo Ramirez?"

"It's Paul Sturgess," Claire said quietly.

The door opened on the lobby, and Claire plunged into the chaos of anthropologists reacquainting themselves with fellow scholars they saw only at conferences. Claire paused at a tall easel that held a poster with the daily presentations. The first presentation, by Paul Sturgess, was marked: "Canceled."

Claire quickened her pace, her leather sandals squeaking on the polished tile floors. She had tried for years to overcome the "Mexican Time" gene that she blamed for her predisposition of rushing into department meetings and classrooms at the last moment. She tried to be prompt, but something always delayed her—that last-minute student demanding a grade change or an email requiring a quick response. She strode past a spacious meeting room set aside for exhibits and the conference book sale. She would have to explore it later.

She paused for breath at the entrance to the hotel restaurant that spilled out onto a large outdoor terrace. As she suspected, she was the last to arrive at the table where Tanya's shrill voice dominated. Claire's colleagues turned toward her with wistful gazes, as if they wished they too had just arrived. When Tanya stood on her soapbox, even George couldn't quell her hyperactive monologues.

"You're late," Tanya said, with barely a pause in her narrative. "We need your input."

"Coffee first, then input," Claire pleaded as she lowered herself into a chair between George and Madge. The group heaved a collective sigh of relief. Their waiter approached immediately, left a menu, took Claire's coffee order and departed. The men had already delved into huge portions of *huevos rancheros*. Madge moved her fork around a mound of scrambled eggs, and Tanya nibbled pineapple from her tropical fruit plate as she waited for Claire to settle in.

When Claire's coffee arrived, and she had ordered her breakfast, Tanya spoke, as if there had been no gap in the conversation. "I'm trying to find out who talked to Paul and what they learned about him." She pointed her fork at Madge. "It's your turn."

Madge sipped her coffee. "We all talked to him, Tanya. He was applying for a job." She finished her coffee and looked around for the waiter. "I talked to Laura too. They both thanked me for the interview, gushed about my archaeological excavations in Guatemala...yada yada...they're hungry for a job."

Tanya ignored Madge and turned to Claire. "What did you think of Paul?"

"Socially awkward…naive," Claire responded. She remembered their conversation and regretted her subtle reprimand. "Cody seemed bored…the political spouse at a cocktail party."

Tanya's fork went to Jamal. "Jamal saw Paul and Cody arguing after the reception yesterday."

"I'm not sure they argued," Jamal protested. "They both looked unhappy and Cody walked away from him. They seemed fine at dinner."

The waiter returned with Claire's breakfast and a carafe of hot coffee for the table. Coffee cups replenished, Claire buttered toast and shook pepper on her scrambled eggs as she considered how much to contribute. "I saw Cody and Paul just before the show, near the vendor tables," she said at last.

"And I saw Cody hurrying back from the archaeological site toward the Cultural Center as I returned to the site for the program," Jamal said, "And…"

George sighed heavily. "Can we eat in peace?"

Jamal peered at George. "But there's more."

George glared at Jamal over his coffee cup.

Jamal continued, "After the program, when I heard the screaming, I ran to the Cultural Center…"

Tanya interrupted, "I wondered about that, Jamal. Why did you run away?"

"Can I finish, Tanya?" Jamal squinted his eyes. "I looked for security, but I think they were all out in the parking lot, directing traffic. Cody was in the Cultural Center, writing in his tablet and sniffling. I ignored him because I was looking for someone in authority. Then that female security guard arrived, yelling into her radio. She disappeared into an office, and a few minutes later a student rushed in and said that someone had fallen off the pyramid. The guard and the student ran from the building. Cody's face turned white, he picked up his backpack and ran for the door." Jamal paused for effect. "Like he knew what had happened."

"What did you do?" Madge asked.

"People were coming in from the archaeological site, chattering over each other about someone falling off the Magician's Pyramid, and I realized that we might not be leaving anytime soon. I checked with our bus driver, but the drivers already knew about it."

"It's possible that Claire was the last one of our group to see Paul last night," Madge said, pensively.

The group sat silently, concentrating on their food and coffee. Tanya's eyes narrowed as she surveyed the table. Her fork returned to Jamal, the last chunk of papaya dripping onto the table. "I thought I saw you talking to Paul near the pyramid."

"When?" Jamal asked.

"Before the show," Tanya said. She wiped papaya juice from her chin with her free hand, but her eyes stayed focused on Jamal.

"No," Jamal said. He glared at Tanya across the table. "I talked to Laura before the show, but you know that."

"Ah," Tanya shrugged. "It must have been someone else."

Jamal sat back in his chair and picked up his coffee cup with shaking fingers. His eyes moved from face to face around the table.

Brad shoved his coffee cup aside. "What the hell does it matter who talked to whom? The poor pathetic creature fell to his death."

"But aren't you curious about him?" Tanya asked.

Brad looked at George as if to challenge the department chair to speak. George pursed his lips as if in deep thought, so Brad turned his attention to Tanya. "None of us knows anything about him or his death. Besides, if anyone is responsible it would be his boyfriend. He could have killed him and returned to the Cultural Center as if nothing happened."

Madge raised her eyebrows. "He could kill him in Chicago anytime he wanted to, theoretically."

"This is silly," Jamal said. "He fell. Listen to us trying to accuse a stranger of murder."

Brad turned his attention back to Tanya. "You never told us what *you* know about Paul."

Tanya pushed her empty fruit bowl away. "I talked to him at the reception, just for a few minutes. He asked about my work in linguistics and my research," she said, her posture defiant. "I assume we all had similar conversations."

"Then, why are you asking all these questions?" Claire asked.

Tanya sat back, her body folding in on itself. "Because he seemed so odd. And everyone is acting strangely since we met him."

"You mean, since he died," Madge said.

"Perhaps," Tanya conceded. "George, what do you think?"

George leaned back, closed his eyes and pursed his lips, gestures Claire knew signified that either he was trying to remember something or control his temper. When his eyes opened, they locked onto each faculty member, one by one, and finally fell onto Tanya. He moved his plate away and pushed himself up from the table. "This isn't a parlor game." He turned away from the table and strode back into the hotel, out of sight.

CHAPTER ELEVEN

The group sat in silence, staring at Madge as if she could explain George's behavior. Madge leaned back in her chair, the creases in her face deepening in concern.

"I don't think you appreciate the seriousness of this," Madge said, her eyes darting from one colleague to another.

Tanya blushed, Brad and Jamal looked at each other, and Claire sat back, feeling the reprimand. She resented the inclusive "you," but she understood Madge's meaning.

Before anyone spoke, the waiter brought checks to the table and retreated. Madge picked up George's check, and the others signed for their meals. It was into this vacuum that Cody Detwyler arrived. He approached their table in a crab-like pattern, as if he might turn and run at any moment.

As Claire watched him approach, she thought about Paul. How would his family cope with this tragedy? Could she have done something to avert this disaster? *You can't fix this.* Aaron's words came back at her. Her husband had often reproached her for internalizing everyone else's problems and trying to solve them. She always denied it, but now she admitted to herself he had been correct in his assessment.

Everyone had been preparing to leave, but the appearance of the grieving lover changed their minds, and they resettled themselves. Claire invited Cody to sit with them. Anthropologists are, after all, avid gossips.

"I wanted to talk to Doctor Banks," Cody said, "but he just rushed past me." He collapsed into George's abandoned chair.

A waiter came for the signed checks and to take an order from the newcomer. Cody shook his head, so the waiter took the checks and cleared the table, leaving the coffee carafe and cups.

"We are very sorry about Paul," Claire said. A chorus of agreement circulated the table.

"I don't know what to do," Cody said. "The police have contacted Paul's family. I don't know how he…his body…will be sent home." He ran his fingers through his hair. "I wish we hadn't come. I don't know why he wanted to leave Chicago."

"Why *did* Paul apply to Keane College?" Jamal asked.

"He was born in Western Michigan. I think he wanted to be closer to his family. When he heard of your new program, he became very excited. He seemed confident he could get a teaching job at Keane."

"You didn't want to move?" Madge asked.

"I love Chicago. I'm a writer…an aspiring writer."

"A writer can write anywhere, so they say," Claire said, trying to be helpful.

Cody smiled for the first time. "Yeah, that's what Paul says…said. He tried to interest me in his work. We've been together a year, and this was my first trip to Mexico with him. He took me to the town where he worked and introduced me to some of the people he interviewed for his research." Cody paused, collecting his thoughts.

"We talked a lot yesterday, but then…last night…he said he wanted some time alone and told me he would meet me back at the Cultural Center before the show. But he never came. When that guy ran in and said someone fell…I had a terrible feeling, you know how you just know something? Anyway, I knew that it had to be him."

Cody's eyes filled with tears, and his shoulders slouched forward. Madge, closest to him, reached over and touched his hand. Claire, who thought he had given more of an explanation than he needed, heard Brad say, "Oh Lord," under his breath as he rose from the table. Jamal, taking the opportunity to do the same, excused himself, giving condolences to Cody, who turned his attention to the women who remained.

Claire opened her mouth to speak when suddenly the room grew quiet. She and her companions followed the gaze of patrons to the restaurant's street entrance. Two policemen entered, scanned the room, and moved resolutely toward their table. Cody gasped and shrank into his chair as the officers approached, their eyes hidden in wrap-around sunglasses, their hands resting ominously on their belts, near their revolvers.

"Oh, my God," Cody said. His eyes widened in fear. "What's happening?"

Madge leaned forward. "It's okay," she said quietly.

"Señor Detwyler?" The older man, identified as Sergeant Juarez by his badge, addressed Cody. He was large in height and width, his ample girth spilling over his gunbelt. He dwarfed his younger counterpart.

Cody nodded, sweat dripping from his hairline. He pressed his lips together to control their quivering.

Sergeant Juarez removed his hat and sunglasses and introduced Deputy Chan. Chan stood ramrod straight, his facial features unreadable, hat and sunglasses intact, and his hand near his gun.

Madge spoke for Cody, in Spanish. "What is this about, *Señores*?"

The sergeant stepped aside, allowing Deputy Chan to speak. The latter stood even straighter and adjusted his sunglasses. "We have orders to take *Señor* Detwyler to the police station to answer questions."

When Cody looked at him blankly, he added, in accented English, "Do you speak Spanish?"

Cody shook his head and looked to Claire, who switched to English for Cody's benefit. "Is this about Paul Sturgess?" she asked.

"Who are you?" Chan turned his dark glasses toward Claire.

"We are here for a conference. We met Paul and Cody yesterday." Claire looked from Chan to his superior officer.

Sergeant Juarez ran his hand through his graying hair and stroked his matching gray mustache. Unlike his deputy, Sergeant Juarez stood casually, holding his hat and sunglasses in both hands. He spoke softly, in a conversational style. "Our business is with *Señor* Detwyler," he said.

Tanya directed her attention to Chan. "Can't you ask your questions here? We could help you."

"No," Chan said, his voice cracking a little under Tanya's gaze. "Detective Salinas may ask to see you and your friends later."

"Salinas?" Claire asked.

"A detective?" Cody said.

Tanya's blue eyes focused on Deputy Chan. She softened her tone and brought her hands to her chest in a gesture of surprise. "Really?"

Chan raised his hat momentarily to rub his hand over his hair, and Claire thought he might remove his glasses, but he regained his self-control, returned his hat to his head and said, "We're following orders." For a moment, Claire thought she saw the sergeant roll his eyes.

Madge stood to her complete five-foot-three inches and stared up at the sergeant. "Surely you don't suspect him of hurting his friend?"

"*Sin embargo...*" the deputy answered, shrugging his shoulders. Nevertheless.

Claire looked at Cody's face, frozen in fear, then studied her companions. Madge's belligerence hadn't worked. Tanya's flirtatious manipulations nearly succeeded, but not quite. Claire decided to take George's path—skeptical and practical. She said, "Then you need to inform the consulate."

Chan stepped closer to Cody. "He doesn't need the consulate."

Sergeant Juarez softened the message. "There is no reason to fear. The detective needs information about *Señor* Detwyler's friend."

Claire picked up her purse from the floor and stood defiantly. "I'll go with him to translate."

Deputy Chan's authoritative façade wavered in the presence of the persistent women. "That's not necessary. The detective speaks English."

Sergeant Juarez handed a card to Claire, and she stared at the name. "If you wish, you can come to the police station on your own, to pick him up," he said. "Ask for Detective Salinas."

"I'll go too," declared Madge. She picked up her purse, pushed her straw hat down on her head, and rearranged her pink hibiscus blouse.

Claire turned to Cody, who stood, barely able to hold himself upright. "You should go with the officers. We'll be right behind you."

"A-Are you sure? You'll come right away?"

"We're on our way," Claire said.

Once Cody and the policemen had left, conversations surrounding them resumed, quietly at first, then returning to normal volume. People continued to glance toward their table; as newcomers joined them, they were filled in on the excitement.

"Let's go," said Tanya, her face flushed and eager.

Claire gave a sideways glance to Madge, which Madge missed, but Tanya saw.

"What?" she said. "You don't want me to go?"

Madge said, "We don't all need to go. You can return to the conference. You'll benefit from that more than a trip to the police station."

"Don't patronize me. I want to know what's going on with the case, too."

"There's no case, Tanya," said Claire. "It's just questions."

"Why you two and not me?" Tanya complained.

"Cody seems to trust Claire," Madge said. "She should go, but not alone."

"Well, I want to go. Besides, I'm the one who thinks something is suspicious about this case."

"No case," Claire repeated, but she too thought something was amiss.

"I'm going." Tanya said, and pulled her small purse over her shoulder.

Outside the hotel, three taxis in varying states of disrepair lined up along the circle drive of the hotel, awaiting fares. Claire bypassed the first taxi, its passenger side doors dangerously askew, and approached the next cab in line. The driver, surprised at his fortune, jumped from the driver's seat to negotiate a fare.

Madge and Tanya followed Claire, as Madge fumbled in her bag and pulled out her phone. "I'm calling George. He'll wonder where we are." She tapped a number, and after a few seconds clicked off. "He didn't answer," she said. "I'll call him later."

Claire helped Madge into the front seat, and she and Tanya settled into the back. As the driver edged his way between the other waiting cabs, Madge pointed toward a black Ford Escape pulling into the driveway that led to the parking lot behind the hotel.

"There's Eduardo Ramirez," Madge said. "Maybe he wants to come too."

Claire recognized the sarcasm, but Tanya responded in her own sharp tone, "I'm sure he has more important things to do."

Madge snorted. "Like finishing up his lecture on the murderous Maya."

Their taxi pulled away from the curb as the driver, who had been ignored, lay on his horn in anger and frustration. Claire was certain that, while many cars ran without mufflers, tailpipes, turn signals, or operating windows, they all had working horns.

The city traffic, horrendous at any time of the day or year, hindered their progress. The three women held a collective breath as the taxi wove around multiple obstacles, braking for light changes or to avoid a collision with something or someone.

Once they passed the plaza and turned away from the central district, the traffic lightened. They passed through neighborhoods where stucco houses shared narrow streets with house-front businesses, mechanic shops, and grocery stores. Through their open windows, the aroma of freshly baked pastries and tortillas competed with car exhaust. Finally, the taxi screeched to a halt in front of the police station, jolting the women in the back seat, unencumbered by seat belts, up against the front seat.

The station, constructed from huge limestone slabs, stood high above the street, accessible by a vast cement stairway and guarded by men in military uniforms wielding rifles. Claire could imagine the awe inspired by such colossal buildings, likely built by the Maya themselves for their new masters. It seemed to Claire that whoever the masters happened to be, the Mayan peasants had built temples and monuments for them.

"*Estamos*," the taxi driver said. We're here.

CHAPTER TWELVE

Tanya led the way up the wide, stone staircase, Claire following as quickly as her middle-aged knees would carry her. Madge hobbled behind, moving with determination if not ease. At the front desk, Claire and Tanya asked the desk sergeant where the young man had been taken.

The sergeant lay her romance novel, open and faced down, on her desk. "Which young man?"

Claire gave his name. "I think he is with Detective Salinas."

"Ah, the American," she replied. "Your names?"

Claire handed over her university business card as Madge caught up with them at the desk. The sergeant punched buttons on her phone and spoke briefly to someone at the other end, reading Claire's name off the card.

Hanging up, the sergeant pointed to a tall, colonial wooden door. *"Por ay, y entences directo…directo…"*

"Thank you, Sergeant Gutierrez," Claire said, reading her badge.

The sergeant nodded and picked up her book, *Amor Prohibido*, the cover of which featured a scantily attired, light-skinned blonde in an erotic pose.

The trio started off in the direction the sergeant had pointed, but immediately became lost in the confusion of hallways and rooms. They passed through several corridors lined with offices whose massive doors were open to allow for air flow. Large standing fans stood in doorways, moving the hot air around and causing a white noise that followed them down the hallway. Finally, after several wrong turns, they entered another reception area.

Claire explained their mission to another female sergeant, whose name tag identified her as Detective Sergeant Rosa Garza.

"Profesora Aguila?" she asked, reading off her notepad.

Claire nodded. Sergeant Garza made a phone call and, within moments, a tall man wearing black slacks and a white *guayabera* shirt came to greet them. He appeared to be in his mid-fifties, with a mass of thick, black hair, turning gray at the temples. Unlike the stoic policemen who took Cody away, this officer smiled slightly as he assessed the women through horn-rimmed glasses. He introduced himself as Detective Roberto Salinas, and, when he turned his attention to Claire, her heart stopped.

He directed them to an office, larger than the others they had hurried past. A computer sat on a large wooden desk, surrounded by stacks of file folders. A bookshelf held replicas of Mayan pots next to a ceramic Virgin of Guadelupe. Claire stared at a photograph of the detective with his family, his wife and two children, situated next to a photo of an elderly couple, presumably his parents. The Mexican flag stood in the corner of the room, and a photograph of the Mexican President adorned the wall behind Salinas's desk, just above his head.

Claire's gaze went back to the family photograph and to the man looking at her with interest. *Oh, no,* she thought. *Now what?*

Detective Salinas motioned Madge to a worn, leather chair with a slight rip along one seam. Claire and Tanya sat in wooden chairs, all facing his desk.

Claire spoke first, in Spanish. "We came to pick up Cody Detwyler."

"Of course," Salinas responded in English, his hands opening as in praise, palms up. "Don't worry, he is fine. We had a brief chat, and now he is writing his statement."

"Can we take him to the hotel?" Claire asked.

"*Ahorita,*" he responded. *Ahorita*—a word Claire knew could mean 'right this minute' or 'sometime next week.'

Madge asked, "The fall was an accident, correct?"

"We have no reason to believe otherwise. But I do need to close the file."

"Do you need to talk to us too?" Tanya asked, fingering her hair, worn long today, blonde waves brushing her shoulders. "We were all there."

"Since you are here and willing, I may have a few questions," he mused, "but, I don't want to make trouble where there is none." Salinas straightened a few files on his desk. "However, now that there is a video of a death at one of our most famous archaeological sites..." he sighed heavily, returning his hands to his desk. "It won't be long before media spin—is that what you say?—makes it into something sinister." He sighed again.

"Video?" said Claire.

Salinas pushed a button on his desk intercom. "Rosita, please bring in your computer." He smiled apologetically at the women, adjusting his glasses. "Sergeant Garza will show you."

Garza entered the room with a small electronic notebook, clearly her personal computer. Photographs of children and family members had been taped to the lid, and an enlarged photograph of two beautiful children graced her wallpaper screen.

In stilted English, Garza explained, "My son, he saw this on YouTube. He doesn't read English well, but he saw 'Uxmal' in the title." She clicked on the media player. "He made a copy and sent it to me."

Within moments, they were looking at the Magician's Pyramid. The anonymous photographer scanned the crowd before aiming his camera at Paul Sturgess, lying on the ground in deep shadow after being turned over. Luckily, his face had been covered. Yet, the idea that someone would record and share this appalled Claire. As the video played, she watched the crowd scenes. She saw Madge, hugging her huge bag, George pursing his lips, Brad pacing back and forth, and Tanya peering, her eyes wide with fascination. Claire stared, dismayed, as the camera caught her squatting near the body and taking photographs.

"Oh, my God," Claire exclaimed, watching herself contaminate the scene.

No one else spoke as the video camera returned to the crowd, panning over a study of faces from the horrified to the curious. The title of the video was "Tourist Falls to his Death at Uxmal, Mexico."

Salinas turned to Claire. "So, you see, I could have a few questions for you, Doctor Aguila."

Claire nodded, her hands clammy with perspiration.

After Sergeant Garza left the room, Salinas continued, "There weren't any close-ups of the body, *Gracias a Diós,* and the video has been taken down." He folded his hands on the desk, lost in thought. "But, because it exists, my captain has assigned me to investigate further, so we can assure tourists that it *was* an accident and nothing else."

Claire hadn't thought of this but knew it would be true. The presence of the drug cartels in Mexico had done enough damage to the tourist industry. A suspicious death of a tourist would be a further disaster.

The detective turned to Claire. "Why did you take photographs?"

Embarrassed, Claire folded her hands in her lap to hide their shaking. "I had planned to take night photos of the pyramid, so my camera was on my mind. When I noticed the footprints and…a few other things…I thought I should take the photographs in case the police got involved." Claire paused for breath, breaking eye contact with the detective. She looked at Madge for encouragement, and then forced herself to return Salinas's unflinching gaze.

"The two Uxmal deputies asked for my camera or memory card," Claire added, "but I refused. I hope I've not made a mistake."

Salinas said, "No, you did right, but I would like to see the photos." He paused and tented his fingers. "You can call Sergeant Garza, and someone will pick them up."

A long silence ensued, during which everyone looked at their watches.

Madge finally said, "Will Cody be here soon?"

"*Ahorita,*" the detective repeated. He gave Claire a look again, and she lowered her eyes to avoid his gaze.

Claire sighed gratefully when Garza knocked on the open door and entered with Deputy Chan and Cody. Cody's hair was disheveled, and dark stains under his arms suggested either a warm interview room or tense interrogation, or both. His eyes, puffy and red, had sunk into his face. He looked warily at the detective but brightened when he noticed his rescuers.

"Thanks for coming," he said nervously, his lip twitching.

"We said we would," said Madge.

Salinas took a folder from Deputy Chan, who glanced quickly at Tanya before leaving the room. Salinas directed Cody to sit next to Claire. Garza sat next to the detective and took a small notepad and pen from her pocket.

After skimming Cody's statement, Salinas asked the women for a summary of what they knew about the incident. Since Claire had been designated the official spokesperson, she recounted the scene at the pyramid as she remembered it.

She spoke in English for Cody's benefit, but Salinas held his hand up and turned to Garza. "*¿Entiendes?*" She nodded.

During this narration, Cody sat quietly. He started to sob again as Claire described the scene at the foot of the pyramid. Madge handed Cody a tissue packet that she pulled from the depths of her purse, and Cody took it in a pathetic gesture of thankfulness and grief.

Salinas asked, "Did anyone touch the body?" He glanced quickly toward Cody, who reacted with a sharp gasp at the reference to his friend as 'a body.'

"I touched him to take the photographs." Claire shuddered as she remembered the revulsion she felt as she removed the jacket from Paul's face and moved his head to take the photo.

Tanya said, "Brad Kingsford checked Paul for breathing." She paused, looking toward her companions. "And he turned the body over."

Cody pulled another tissue from the packet and blew his nose.

"Did anyone else come close?" Salinas asked.

"An elderly couple from Michigan hovered along the inner edge of the circle, Dale and Lois Stuart. We had met them earlier," Claire explained. "They saw Paul on the pyramid before the program but didn't see anyone with him." She paused. "I think they stayed at the Hotel Chac." She looked to her colleagues for confirmation but received only shrugs in return. Claire added, "They took a photo of our group earlier in the day. The Uxmal officers have their contact information."

Salinas nodded. "Yes, Sergeant Garza has it."

Madge cast a sideway glance at Cody. "Could it have been suicide?"

Cody's head jerked up. "No! He wouldn't kill himself! He had his whole career ahead of him! He had me…" This last statement became lost in another burst of sobs and sniffles, the tissues now just shredded wads in his clenched fist. He pulled out another tissue, the last one in the small packet.

Claire glanced at Salinas before asking Cody a question. Receiving an intense gaze in return, she asked, "Cody, why would Paul climb the pyramid in the evening, just before the show started?" Salinas gave her an appraising look but said nothing.

"He liked to be alone, to write notes or to think," Cody said. "We are alike that way. It would be like him to do that. He had no fear of heights and would have ignored the barricades." He sniffled and rubbed his nose with the wad of tissues.

Detective Salinas tented his fingers and turned to Madge. "Perhaps the elderly couple and the photographs may help me clear up—how do you say—the loose ends, but I hope to conclude my investigation within a few days." He brought his hands back down to the desk. "The Uxmal police gave me your contact information. I may call on you again."

"Are we done?" asked Tanya.

"Yes, for now. But, please, if you think of anything else, or if your friends know something, they should call me." He handed a card directly to Claire, the recipient of privileged information. "You can take your friend back to the hotel."

Outside, Cody clung close to the women, as if afraid he might be snatched up and sent back to the interrogation room.

"Now what?" said Madge. She looked at Claire. "What's wrong?"

"Nothing," Claire said, trying to control her breathing.

Tanya looked at her watch. "The morning sessions will be ending soon, but I'm in no mood for meetings."

"That's why we're here," Madge reprimanded, but she too had lost all interest in the conference.

CHAPTER THIRTEEN

When George left the breakfast table, he had no other thought but to escape Tanya's incessant chatter. He returned to his room, changed from his flip-flops to walking shoes and exchanged his tweed jacket for a short-sleeve shirt more agreeable to the weather. He took the conference program from the dresser and skimmed the sessions for the day. Seeing nothing archaeological until Eduardo Ramirez's lecture, he decided to take a walk and clear his head.

Brad joined him as he waited for the elevator. In shorts, a university T-shirt, tennis shoes, and straw hat, Brad resembled a graduate student more than a faculty member, especially with his hair tied back in a ponytail. His sunglasses hung from a strap around his neck, and he carried his backpack over his shoulder.

In the elevator, Brad pushed the button for the first floor. "Sorry, George, but I'm playing hooky this morning. I'm going to Progresso Beach to rework my speech and get away for a while...you know...I can only take so much departmental drama."

George grabbed the handrail as the elevator stopped at a lower floor. Two women anthropologists he recognized but did not know entered, speaking Quiché Maya. Both wore the brightly colored shirts and blouses characteristic of their region of Guatemala. George greeted them in their language, but they switched to Spanish to grill George on the death of the young anthropologist. Brad stood quietly, perched at the elevator door, as if hoping for a quick get-away.

George disappointed him. Exiting the elevator, he motioned to Brad, "Can we talk?"

Brad looked at his watch. "I have to hurry to return in time for Eduardo's lecture. My rental car is ready."

"I'll walk with you," George said.

"What's on your mind, George?"

"Tanya."

Brad frowned at George. "We have to do something about her."

"What do you mean?" George asked.

"She has no sense of decorum. She talks to us like we're students, not senior colleagues. It would be a mistake to give her tenure. She'll be nagging us to death for the rest of our careers."

They stopped at an intersection where a beleaguered police officer maintained order with frantic hand gestures and a whistle.

"You know that's not our decision," George said. "Linguistics hired her and grants her tenure."

"But we'll have input," Brad insisted.

The crowd forming behind them pushed them into the road as the whistle blew for them to cross. "She is a little…informal," George conceded.

"You know that she's a problem for Jamal. Her behavior borders on harassment."

"It seems the relationship has been mutual. I can't imagine Jamal being forced to date a young pretty faculty member."

"You'd be surprised," Brad said as they approached the rental office. He grimaced as he noted the tourists crowded around the counter or sitting in metal chairs, flipping through vacation magazines. "I gotta go."

George opened the door for Brad and followed him in. The blast of air-conditioning brought goosebumps to George's arms. "You're not getting to that counter any time soon."

Brad reached over the heads of an elderly couple to pull a paper tab from a machine—Number 35. He moaned as he saw number 28 on the screen above the heads of the two employees patiently explaining to their customers how to navigate Merida's one-way streets. He returned to George's side, lowering his backpack to the floor.

"I actually wanted to talk about something else," George said. "Jamal asked if I would support Tanya for the position of museum curator."

Brad smiled. "He did, did he?"

"Did he talk to you about it?"

"No. What did you tell him?" George asked.

"That Madge had the position until she retires." George pursed his lips, thinking. "Why do you think he went over your head to come to me?"

"Because he knows I would laugh at him. Tanya? Curator? She has no experience." He smiled again. "But this proves my point. She's manipulating him." He looked up at the numbers on the board.

"One more thing," George said as Brad glanced at his watch. "Madge could be a strong ally in getting funds and contributors if you gave her the chance. I understand that she has not been included in your communications with Eduardo."

Brad's face hardened, and his jaw tightened. "Do you know what she's doing?"

George adjusted his glasses and looked at Brad. "What?"

"She's researching the provenance of the artifacts the college already holds, and the artifacts designated by Eduardo's family to be loaned to us."

George furrowed his brow. "That's her job. We can't take the chance of holding undocumented artifacts. You know that."

"She doesn't trust me?"

"It's not a matter of trust, Brad. It's protocol."

Brad sighed and pointed to the number board. "I gotta go."

George relented. "Well, have a great day."

He waved to Brad, who waved back, squeezing his tall frame past an elderly couple who sat along one wall and a probable newlywed couple nuzzling on a small bench. George left the building, feeling the warmth of the morning sun on his face. Now, where could he find a computer with a good browser?

CHAPTER FOURTEEN

Cody and his rescuers settled into a cab for their return to the city center. Tanya had jumped into the front seat, leaving Cody pinched between the two older, less sleek women. The odor of perspiring bodies wafted through the cab, despite the open windows. Cody rested his head against the seat, eyes closed. The three women sat silently, watching the sights from their respective windows: streets now filled with locals and tourists, stores with merchandise overflowing onto the sidewalks. The taxi jolted them out of their musings as it skidded to a stop at a red light. The driver uttered an expletive in Spanish.

Recovering her composure, Tanya peered back over her shoulder at Cody and said, "So, what did the detective ask you?"

Cody, now wide awake, shifted in his seat. "He wanted to know if I had any reason to kill my lover," he responded bluntly. "I told him we had argued that evening, but that I didn't push him off a pyramid."

His hostile tone surprised Claire. "I guess he had to ask," she said. "I doubt he really thinks you would come all the way to Mexico to kill him."

"That's what I told him." Cody stared ahead, eyes widening as the taxi veered strongly to the left to avoid a woman stepping out into the street. "He took my passport."

"What?" Madge asked. "Why?"

"Standard procedure," Cody said, slumping back into the narrow wedge of seat between Claire and Madge.

"What else did he ask?" Tanya said.

"He asked if Paul was upset or depressed about anything." Cody paused here and looked at Claire. "Paul would not kill himself."

The taxi lurched to a halt in front of the hotel, and the foursome stepped out into the steamy heat. Cody reached in his pocket, but

Madge had somehow found her wallet in the folds of her bag first and paid the driver.

Tanya took a quick glance at Cody, then turned away from him. "I need to walk."

Madge looked at her watch. "It's lunch break. Shall we find a café?"

Tanya agreed, but Cody turned toward the hotel. Claire declined, remembering the photographs she had promised Detective Salinas. She waved to her colleagues and joined Cody at the hotel entrance.

"Would you like coffee?" Claire asked Cody, more as an offer to talk than a desire for anything to drink.

"No, thank you. I have a lot to do." He counted on his fingers. "I have to call the airport to ask about flying his...Paul's...body home, call my parents and tell them I no longer have a passport, pack up Paul's belongings, and call his parents again to calm them. They are frantic."

He seemed calmer since they left the police station, not exactly optimistic, but purposeful. His shoulders were straight and his mouth firm. "And I seriously need a shower," he added. "I have never been so scared in all my life." He attempted a smile.

Claire touched his arm. "Be sure to tell Paul's parents we are very sorry about their son's death. We'll call them soon to talk with them."

In the lobby, they met a crush of conference participants, filing out of the meeting rooms for the lunch break. They milled into colorful polyglot groups. She and Cody followed the flow of traffic that led to the elevators. They stood aside until the area emptied out, the din of overlapping conversations decreasing as the elevators swallowed the hotel guests and delivered them upward.

Claire peered at the young man as they waited. Despite his disheveled appearance, there *was* something different in his demeanor. Was it possible that Paul's death had released him from something?

"Can you tell me about Paul?" Claire asked.

Cody's eyes moved around the crowd before he spoke. "You have to understand that I loved him, but he was a hard person to decipher."

"In what way?"

"It took me awhile to put it all together, but when I met his parents it clicked, and I began to understand him." They moved a few inches closer to the elevator and Cody whispered, "His parents own a car dealership. His father, Paul Senior, is a strong believer in the axiom, 'Knowledge is Power.' He said it several times over the weekend we visited them. He knows everyone in the small town, and he is a master salesman. He can push buttons like you wouldn't believe. It's how you get ahead, that's what he thinks. When Paul was growing up, his dad always told him to know his enemies, so they couldn't hurt him."

He looked behind him before continuing, "Paul upset his parents when he announced he was gay. He was in high school. His mom came around, as moms do, but his dad worried more about how it would affect his business than his sexual orientation itself. His father urged him to stay in the closet, like most parents do, mine included. He wanted Paul to go into the family business."

"But Paul wasn't interested in the car business?"

"No, he loved anthropology. When I asked him why, he said that anthropology teaches that cultures have diverse values. He said that in many cultures, homosexuality is accepted, and homosexuals can be spiritual leaders. Is that true?"

Claire nodded. "Some Native Americans use the term "two-spirit" to describe men and women who feel that they have dual genders. Some cultures and religions accept the idea of third genders."

"Paul said that the men sometimes take on women's occupations."

"And women two-spirits can become warriors," Claire said.

Cody's eyes brightened just a little as he heard this. "I think this understanding gave him some hope."

"What was he like as a person, Paul Junior, I mean? Obviously, he won your heart."

"Paul is...was...very complex. He was very smart and engaging. I loved that about him, but he could put people off. I think you saw it. He wanted...needed...to know about others' work and personal lives, almost like a defense mechanism. If he knew a secret about someone, they would have a connection.... He asked questions that made people uncomfortable. But I don't think he did it with bad intentions… at least…" His words trailed off as they neared the elevator doors and people pressed around them.

"At least?"

"Nothing." An edge came into his voice. A touch of anger, or frustration.

"Did he use knowledge against you?" Claire whispered.

"Sometimes," he admitted as he glanced at the numbers flashing above the elevator doors. "He never threatened me," he said cautiously and softly. "And it never meant anything."

CHAPTER FIFTEEN

With the camera memory card tucked away in her purse, Claire left the hotel and was again assaulted by a wall of heat and the incessant blare of vehicle horns and police whistles. She turned toward the central plaza where she remembered seeing a Kodak store, the name reminiscent of the golden age of film cameras. She found the shop at the edge of the plaza, tucked between a tourist boutique and a small café.

Downloading her photographs into the kiosk, she obtained a receipt from the clerk who indicated a twenty-minute wait. Reluctantly, she exited back into the stifling heat and walked toward the central plaza.

Merida, like most colonial Latin American cities, comprised multiple plazas, each dominated by a parish church and lined with the colonial homes of the Spanish landlords. In Merida, the central plaza was a city-block garden with trees shaped by topiary and brilliant flower gardens crisscrossed by sidewalks.

Congested one-way avenues flanked all four sides of the plaza. Along these avenues, the conquerors built spectacular stone structures documenting their political and religious power: The Catholic Cathedral, Governor's Palace, Colonial administration, and the Casa Montejo, the residence of the family that conquered the Yucatec Maya. In modern days, interspersed between these structures, and indeed still part of them, stood small tourist shops, ice-cream parlors, a lottery and newspaper kiosk, and a video arcade, all defying any logical city planning.

Claire collapsed onto a cast-iron bench facing the cathedral, basking in the shade of a small tree. It took a mere two minutes for the first hammock salesman to approach her, a stick of a man, with a creased face, bent forward under the weight of the bulky load strapped to his back. He held a colorful hammock, unfolded and slung over his arm, to demonstrate its size. Claire wondered how he had identified her as a tourist, rather than a native. Perhaps, she chided herself, the conference identity badge she'd forgotten to remove when she left the hotel had tipped him off.

Offering the hammock to Claire to touch, she replied as she always did in Spanish, "No, thank you. I have one at home."

To which the salesman replied, as they always did, "*Oh, pero siempre se puede utilizar otro.*" She could always use another.

Claire loved this plaza, suffused with memories of her internship year in Merida, her first adventure away from her family—but in search of her heritage. Here, she had met Roberto Salinas. *And what was she going to do about that?*

She stared at the massive cathedral, looming over her from across the avenue. She thought about her conversation with Paul—just yesterday—that all humans are shaped by their culture and beliefs. Unfortunately, she had lost her faith: in herself, her chosen career, and in the possibility of finding love again.

Claire's recent conversation with her daughter had shaken her confidence further. She closed her eyes and remembered Cristina, arms crossed, seated on Claire's sofa, watching as her mother finished packing her suitcase for her flight to Merida.

"Why Africa, Cris, not Paris or London?" Claire had pleaded.

"That's where the sick children are, Mom. They're not in line at the Louvre."

Claire couldn't dispute Cristina's logic. Her own mother had lost the same argument before Claire had left for Mexico the first time. She had been younger than Cristina was now.

"It's only for six months," Cristina reasoned, "and I'll be working in a hospital…with doctors and nurses. What can happen?"

"Malaria, Ebola, AIDS," Claire had responded, deflated.

Claire had tried to hold back tears, the grief from Aaron's death resurfacing, the memories of his horrible struggle and her emotional turmoil as she had watched him fade away. "I don't want to lose you."

"You're not losing me, Mom." Cristina had slumped from the sofa onto the floor, the luggage sitting between them. "Dad's death taught me to live life now. We never know what's in the future." She too had blinked back tears, and mother and daughter sat misty-eyed, facing each other across the suitcase.

"We'll talk when you get back from your conference," Cristina had promised. "You can help me plan the trip and make sure I take every inoculation imaginable."

Remembering this conversation, Claire knew that her daughter was right. Hadn't her own goal as a mother been to raise an independent daughter?

Hunger finally gripped Claire, and she decided to eat lunch before picking up the photos and returning to the hotel. Crossing the plaza, she saw George seated at a small sidewalk café with Laura Lorenzo. Neither of them noticed her approach; they were deep in a conversation that she couldn't hear over the street noises.

"Can I join you?" Claire pulled out a chair and sat, without waiting for an answer. She sensed that she had interrupted something important. The awkward silence broke when a waiter approached with a menu. Glancing at it briefly, she ordered bottled water and *sopa de lima*, the famous Yucatecan chicken soup.

"Hello Claire," George said, when the waiter had left. "Laura and I have been discussing the Mayanist program."

Laura nodded. "I would love to visit Keane College." She paused, blushed, then said, "But I have to go now. I have some errands to run before Doctor Ramirez's lecture."

She started to reach for her wallet, but George stopped her. "It's my treat. I invited you to join me."

Laura thanked him, waved goodbye, and left in the direction of the market.

Claire raised an eyebrow at George. He ignored her and pulled a small notebook out of his shirt pocket. He flipped the pages and finally looked at his colleague. "So, it seems that you skipped the morning program, too."

Claire grimaced. "Guilty." The waiter returned, and she paused to taste the delicious soup. "After our excursion to the police station, we were exhausted."

"Police station?"

"Madge called you."

George pulled out his phone and pursed his lips. "I missed her call. What happened?"

Claire summarized their morning with Cody and Detective Salinas, and the now-deleted YouTube video.

"YouTube?" George harrumphed and pursed his lips again. "It seems we all skipped out," he said.

"Who else?" Claire asked.

"Brad went to the beach to work on his keynote address."

"I didn't think he was the beach type."

"I didn't either."

"What did you do this morning?" Claire asked, straining to look at George's notebook open on the table next to him.

"Tanya, damn her, got me thinking about Paul. I wanted to learn more about his research. He showed us that slideshow on his computer, and it intrigued me."

"How?" she asked.

"His research centered in Motul as a center of regional tourism, separate from the larger urban areas and archaeological sites. During his presentation, Paul implied that he knew these villages where Jamal and Brad worked. Normally we would call that good interviewing, but why was Jamal so upset at breakfast?"

"It *was* different," Claire admitted.

"Did Paul say anything to you?"

Claire hesitated. "He indicated that he read my first book. He made a reference to my section on shedding religious biases, and something about anthropological ethics. What do you think he was up to?"

George's eyebrows furrowed in their characteristic way, and he pushed his eyeglasses further up the bridge of his nose. "I'm not sure.

It doesn't make much sense to critique the research of your future colleagues."

Claire told him about her conversation with Cody about Paul's father. "Paul seemed flustered when he realized I had written two books and he hadn't known it," she said. "Do you suppose this is what Cody meant by 'knowledge is power?'"

George's brow creased into deeper crevices. "Very curious."

Claire raised her eyebrow again. "Talking about curious, Laura left quickly. What were you two talking about?"

"I told you. The Mayanist program." He sighed and scowled. "She wanted to explain that, while she and Paul both attended the same graduate program in Chicago, she hadn't known him personally."

"Is Laura a suspect?" Claire smiled at him.

George blushed, "So, Tanya's conspiracy theories have gotten to you too?"

"I really don't know," Claire admitted. She told him about Detective Salinas' interest in her photographs. "I have to pick them up now. I hope the police settle this soon, so we can get this conference back on track for all of us."

"That might be easier said than done."

CHAPTER SIXTEEN

Claire entered the hotel through the restaurant patio entrance to avoid the commotion at the auditorium, where scholars would be congregating for the lecture. She decided that the Exhibit Room would be a quiet place to examine the photographs before turning them over to the officers. In the excitement of the past days, she had not yet seen the exhibits or the book-sale tables set up for the conference. The Exhibit Room door was unlocked and the room unoccupied. The exhibit cases, as well as the book tables, had been left unattended.

She studied the two exhibit cases, positioned on one side of the room. The first case held a Keane College collection, including replicas of Mayan tools, pots, grinding tools, jewelry, pottery, and a sacrificial dagger. The second cabinet held replicas of the artifacts Eduardo had designated for loan to the college. The most intriguing were the replicas of stone carvings portraying religious specialists using the large flint knives to open the chests of sacrificial victims—usually prisoners of war—the bloody dagger in one hand, the beating heart in the other. The original carvings were too heavy and valuable to put on public display.

On the other side of the room, Claire scanned the tables set up to display books available for purchase. She paused at each table, viewing the books published in Mayan studies: anthropology, archaeology, religion and myth, history, and linguistics. She paused to rearrange the copies of her two ethnographies on Yaxpec. Thirty years of research condensed into two books.

Claire sat on a metal chair behind the bookseller's table and pulled the photographs and her reading glasses from her purse. The gruesome scene of Paul's death had not affected her as she had taken the photos, the camera acting as an emotional barrier between her and the awful sight. But now, her stomach wrenched as she stared at the vision of

Paul, his blood soaking into the hard earth. Studying the area around Paul's body, she remembered her concern. The body seemed too close to the pyramid. But she was not a forensics expert, and her working knowledge of physics was negligible. Marks on the hard earth might indicate that the body had been moved, but by whom and why?

Shuffling through the other photographs, she didn't notice anything that might be of interest to the detective. She paused at the photograph Lois and Dale Stuart had taken of her group, she and her colleagues standing together physically and symbolically in a complex web of personal and professional relationships.

Claire looked at her watch. She couldn't avoid her obligation any longer. Brad would certainly notice her absence and reprimand her if she missed his friend's speech. She rummaged in her purse for the card the officer had given her and called Sergeant Garza.

As she ended the call, the Exhibit Room door opened, and a young woman wearing jeans and platform sandals entered, balancing a jelly roll on top of a take-out coffee cup. She looked at Claire, then at the books on the table in front of her.

"I had to go to the bathroom," she said, embarrassed, "and I needed some food. No one was around to watch the table."

"Your books are valuable," Claire said. "The display articles are replicas, but still expensive to replace."

"I don't have a key," she said. "I didn't think I'd be gone long." She rearranged the books at the table, waiting for Claire to relinquish her seat.

"I'm sure it was okay," Claire consoled. Stuffing the photographs and her glasses into her purse, she left the embarrassed exhibit monitor and hurried to the auditorium. She paused at the entrance as her eyes adjusted to the dim lighting, then edged her way along the last row to join Madge and Tanya.

Eduardo was discussing the Mayan society, not as agriculturalists who eked their existence from the thin Yucatecan soils, but as warlike imperialist city-states in constant conflict for power and territory, the

"Apocalypso" version. He stood at a podium in front of a large screen displaying archaeological evidence of the warring Maya.

Claire's mind wandered as Eduardo droned on. She didn't want to hear about human sacrifice, especially one that involved bodies thrown from pyramids. She leaned back with her head against the wall. She wondered if there could be something else for her. She loved teaching, thrived on her own research and the relationships she formed with her students and the people in Yaxpec, but the politics and the academic dramas tired her. Brad's arrogance, Jamal's puppet-like dedication to his mentor, George's surliness, and Tanya's incessant chatter wore on her. Only Madge invigorated her and reminded her why she chose this profession: the seeking of knowledge about other ways of life, and the wonder of all things cultural.

The house lights went up, and Claire's attention returned to Eduardo, who was now explaining his family's place in both American and Mexican history.

"So, here I am, descended from a Mexican mother whose ancestors found themselves in the state of Texas after the Mexican-American War, and a middle-class Mexican businessman living temporarily in the United States. My parents ultimately settled in Mexico City and made a commitment to preserve ancient Mexican cultures…"

Claire heard a snort and turned to see Madge roll her eyes in the dim light. "Preserving culture, my butt," she whispered.

"Shh," Claire said, and stifled a smile.

Eduardo then turned to the story, familiar to Claire's colleagues, of how he and Brad met. "Brad was my first friend in graduate school. I am honored to thank him by loaning artifacts from my family's collection to Keane College." He motioned to Brad, coaxing him to the front of the room. Brad stood awkwardly as Eduardo reached under the podium and pulled out a box about six inches long. He opened the box and extracted a translucent green statue of a Mayan deity, a corncob erupting from its head.

"I would like to present this statue to Brad, and to the Keane College Mayanist Program, as a representation of the first item I will be loaning to their new museum," Eduardo announced. "Of course, this is a replica of an important piece in our family collection at *Galerías Indígenas*. The original is jadeite, a symbol of Mayan royalty." Eduardo paused, expecting sighs of appreciation, but instead the audience became restive. People turned to each other, and whispered comments floated through the room.

"Where do you suppose the original came from?" Claire whispered to Madge, who was rummaging in her bag for her notepad.

Eduardo held his hand up to still the undercurrent. "I see you are interested in this beautiful piece." He smiled and looked out at the audience. "The original of this deity, the Corn God, Ixim, dates to the mid-800s AD." Eduardo cradled it in his hands like a tiny chick.

"As you all know, the Mexican Antiquities Act prohibits any exporting of artifacts for sale after 1972. My grandfather acquired this piece in the 1940s near an unexcavated Yucatecan site. He received it from an old friend who obtained it from a relative who had found it while planting henequen in his fields. The actual provenance is unknown. My grandfather did not sell the original but kept it safe in his collection. The original, and all other loaned pieces, will be accompanied by documentation of legitimacy. I am very proud to be able to loan these beautiful items to my old friend and his wonderful colleagues."

Polite applause spread through the lecture hall, but a whispered undercurrent continued. Madge jabbed Claire in the ribs. "Look at Brad. He looks ill." Brad stood stiffly at his friend's side, staring at the statue.

"He's embarrassed," said Claire.

Madge guffawed, and wrote notes in her notepad.

Eduardo broke into the restless atmosphere. "I have another small announcement."

The audience began to look at their watches and shift in their seats. "In the spirit of the Mexican concerns for the repatriation of exported items, and for the return of items now housed in private collections, I am offering scholarships and internships to students at Keane College and our Texas alma mater to research artifacts from my family's private collections. I am calling this enterprise 'The Provenance Project.' Any artifacts whose origins can be determined will be returned to their home villages or closest museums."

Eduardo's eyes scanned the audience, his charisma finally winning over the skeptics. He continued, "This is a long-term project, but one that allows me to undo some of the damage done by those who knowingly stole items from excavated sites, or innocently acquired them. I hope to make amends to the communities that have lost their heritage to foreign or national museums and to private collections. I think my family would approve of my actions."

A more enthusiastic round of applause spread through the room. Eduardo turned to his friend and asked him to step forward. Brad stood stiffly and hesitated for a moment before stepping forward. He stared at the statue as if it held the powers of Mayan sorcery. Eduardo offered the statue to him, and slowly Brad raised his hands to accept it. Eduardo placed it gently into Brad's hands as if it were the real thing.

Brad moved back to the podium. "I don't know what to say. This is an amazing piece…I have admired the original in your collection. I don't know how to thank you. We will treasure it." He held it up for the audience to see. "All of us at Keane College will treasure it."

CHAPTER SEVENTEEN

Claire rushed from the lecture hall, squinting at her watch. She had told Sergeant Garza she would turn the photographs over to one of her officers at 5:30, but Eduardo's lecture had started late and had just ended. She recognized Sergeant Juarez at the front desk, wisely dressed in slacks and a *guayabera* instead of his uniform. He was scanning the crowd leaving the auditorium as the receptionist made a call, presumably to Claire's room. When Juarez saw her rushing toward him, he motioned to the receptionist, who hung up and turned to another guest.

"*Buenas tardes,*" Claire said. "I'm sorry I am late."

"*No problema, Señora.*" He led her away from the commotion, and Claire extracted the photo envelope and memory card from her purse. She handed them to the officer, looking over her shoulder as she did so. She felt like a spy delivering government secrets to the enemy.

"Please tell Detective Salinas that I need my memory card back. I have an extra one for now, but I still need it."

"*Cierto,*" he replied. "Oh, and Detective Salinas sends his greetings." Before she could respond, he turned and walked away.

Claire observed Laura seated in the lounge, reading. Claire approached her.

"Are you busy?"

Laura placed the typed sheets she had been reading on a small table. "Please, join me."

"What are you reading?" Claire asked.

"It's a copy of Evelyn Nielander's paper on the Zapatistas. Her research has a connection with my interest in Guatemalan refugees and the loss of indigenous languages."

"Can I ask you a few questions about your academic background?" Claire asked.

Laura nodded, but looked uncomfortable. She clasped her hands in her lap.

"You applied for a position in economic anthropology, but your credentials seem to indicate more interest in linguistics and Guatemalan political movements."

Laura grimaced. "My grandparents came to the United States during the Guatemalan civil war, with my parents and my brother. I was born in the United States, but many in my family were killed or disappeared in the 1980s. I studied linguistics because I wanted to carry on my family's cultural heritage, but my interest has turned more to human rights."

"Thus, your interest in Evelyn's work with the Mexican Zapatistas?"

Laura nodded. "Many Guatemalans, those lucky enough to have survived the genocide, made their way to the United States, but others settled in Chiapas and integrated with the Maya living there. Some became involved with the Zapatista movement." She picked up the papers from the table. "It was a bit of a deception, I admit. You advertised for an economic anthropologist. But to me, language, economics, and politics are linked to power."

"It might have strengthened your application to address that interest. Small departments are always looking for broadly trained faculty."

"I'm really sorry," Laura said.

Two candidates, both deceptive, Claire thought. "Madge, Tanya, and I are going to dinner. Would you like to join us?"

Laura smiled, biting her bottom lip between her teeth. "Thank you, but I made plans with friends." She stood. "This had been a terrible day. I can't get past the idea that Paul Sturgess and I both interviewed for the position yesterday, and today, he is gone."

Claire had been thinking the same thing. She said goodbye and watched Laura move toward the elevator.

"Professor Claire!"

Now what? Claire thought as she turned and saw Cody rushing toward her.

"I've been looking for you," he said, as he collapsed on the chair abandoned by Laura.

"What is it, Cody?"

He gulped. His hands and voice both shook uncontrollably. "I'm packing Paul's things..." he paused and looked around the room. "I can't find his computer."

"His computer?" Claire remembered the small laptop Paul had used during his interview to illustrate his presentation. "He had it at the reception. I remember he put it in his backpack."

Cody's eyes widened. "His backpack is missing too."

Claire tried to visualize the scene at the pyramid. She didn't remember seeing Paul's backpack there. She had covered the ground carefully as she took photographs. She certainly would have seen it. "Could he have put it on the bus so he wouldn't have to carry it around that evening?"

Cody shook his head. "Never. It was too valuable."

Claire said, "Call Detective Salinas. This might be important."

"Will they understand me if I call?"

Claire considered this and pulled her cellphone from her purse. The station's number was the last one she had called. She touched the number on her screen, spoke to Sergeant Garza, and ended the call. "Go now. Detective Salinas will wait for you, but, listen to me carefully." She whispered, "Don't tell anyone else about this. No one, except Detective Salinas."

Cody nodded.

"You promise?" She spoke as a mother might speak to a child, and immediately regretted her tone, but he didn't seem to notice.

"I promise."

CHAPTER EIGHTEEN

Monday Evening

Claire suggested a small restaurant near the Plaza Santa Lucia. The three women walked slowly for Madge's sake, Tanya dominating the conversation with her own interpretation of Eduardo's talk on the warrior Maya. Claire tried to concentrate on Tanya's monologue, but her own thoughts were several miles away in another direction. She wondered what Roberto Salinas's reaction would be to Cody's discovery—or rather, his lack of discovery. She also wondered if he had examined her photographs. Most of all, she wondered what he thought about seeing her again.

At the Plaza, they turned up a narrow one-way street, passed the Santa Lucia Cathedral, and stopped in front of a small restaurant named "La Paloma." Inside, a young woman wearing a dress-length white *huipil* asked if they wanted to sit inside or in the courtyard. Deciding to take advantage of the cool evening breezes, they chose the courtyard. Following the hostess through the restaurant, they passed a long table where a lively multigenerational family celebrated what looked like a birthday for an elderly great-grandmother.

They greeted other like-minded anthropologists as they passed into the open courtyard of what once had been a Spanish aristocrat's home. Claire looked up at the darkening sky. She breathed in the clear air, knowing she would be returning to a Michigan spring that might greet her with beautiful lilacs—or a snowstorm. She heard a shriek of recognition and looked to see Madge, waddling as quickly as her legs would take her, to a table on the far side of the courtyard beyond a small fountain. Claire smiled as she recognized her friend, Evelyn Nielander, a cultural anthropologist at Central Wisconsin University. It was her paper Laura had been perusing in the hotel earlier.

Evelyn was famous, or infamous, for her ability to disappear into the Chiapas rainforest every summer. Evelyn conducted her research on the Zapatista Movement, initiated by the Maya of Chiapas, but which had expanded into a major Mexican indigenous movement. Evelyn's ability to enter the world of a Mayan social and political movement both awed and terrified her department chair. That same department chair, Steven Sorenson, sat with Evelyn at a square table located ominously under a mural of The Magician's Pyramid.

Some commotion erupted as a second small square table materialized to accommodate the newcomers. Claire studied the two elder female anthropologists, opposites in appearance but so much alike in their personalities: Madge, gray hair as rumpled as her mismatched clothing, exemplified the 1960s love-child; Evelyn, hair lightly tinted and neatly styled around wireless eyeglasses, was Gloria Steinem, long skirts, boots and flowered scarf, even in the Yucatecan heat. But both represented women of their generation—dedicated feminists raised in a time when women had to fight for their place in academia.

A waitress came to the table and took their drink and dinner orders. Steven asked that his and Evelyn's dinners be held until the newcomers received theirs.

"So, Evelyn," Madge said when the waitress left, "when do you leave for the Lacandón Jungle?" She knew this question would irritate Evelyn's department chair, and that was exactly why she asked it.

Indeed, Steven blushed as Evelyn responded, "I leave from here on Saturday. I'm just getting my marching orders and my curfew from my boss." She smiled as Steven's blush deepened, reaching to his receding hairline.

Accepting the good humor in which Madge had asked the question, he responded, "Like I could ever give Evelyn an order." Evelyn, at least ten years senior in age to the department chair, was known for her independent streak. "I keep trying to get her to take my job as department chair, but she refuses."

"And sit in a chair all day sending emails and writing reports to the dean? Never!" Evelyn laughed.

"My sentiments exactly," Madge said. "Every department chair I have known has retired in complete exhaustion after resigning from their position." She paused. "And George will probably be next."

When their drinks arrived, Tanya, who had been quiet during this exchange, said, "I'm Tanya Petersen."

"Oh, I'm sorry," Claire said. "I didn't realize you didn't know each other." She introduced them. "Tanya is a linguist who has also worked in Chiapas."

"She also studied the Palenque hieroglyphs," Madge added. "Sorry, Tanya."

Tanya shrugged and pressed her lips together. "It's okay," she said in a petulant tone. "Chiapas is a big state. There's no reason why we should know each other."

"Where did you do your linguistic work?" Evelyn asked.

Tanya sipped her beer and bit her lip again. "I lived in the city of Palenque," she said. "I studied Tzotzil, Tzeltal, but especially Ch'ol, the language spoken by the original inhabitants of Palenque."

"And studied the hieroglyphs, also," Evelyn said. "I'm impressed. That's like two careers."

"The hieroglyph research arose because of my knowledge of Ch'ol," Tanya said. "Local archaeologists asked for translations of Mayan texts held at the university library. I enjoyed that work, and if I had the chance would love to pursue curation."

Tanya gave a sideways glance at Madge before turning her attention to Evelyn and Steven. "But everyone is distracted by Paul Sturgess's death." She paused, her eyes brightening. "We knew him."

Evelyn leaned forward. "We heard he interviewed with you yesterday."

"Yes, can you believe it?" Tanya said.

Evelyn straightened in her chair and looked briefly at Steven, then turned back to Claire. "How did the interview go?"

This seemed an odd question, given the fact Paul would never become a member of their faculty, but before Claire could respond Tanya blurted, "He knew a lot about our research...perhaps too much?"

Claire caught a quick glance flit between Evelyn and Steven. Madge caught it too.

"What?" Madge asked. "Did you know him?"

"He interviewed with us last year," Steven responded. He gave a glance at Evelyn, as if in warning, but his colleague sat forward, eager to speak.

"In our one-on-one meeting, he hinted that I might be a secret Zapatista, one of the *Sub-Comandante* Marcos's female comrades, *Sub-Comandante* Evelyn." She laughed at the idea. "Later, I found out he did similar things to others, like he was trying to get a job through extortion."

"We thought the same thing!" Tanya exclaimed. "But he had things wrong," she added. "He insinuated that I had an affair with my faculty advisor." She blushed at this unintended admission. "Which wasn't true…well, we dated, but he was separated at the time." She blushed again but blundered on. "He also knew things about Brad and Jamal, but they aren't talking." She turned to Madge and Claire, anxious to move the conversation away from herself. "What about you two?"

Madge took a gulp of her margarita. "Nothing other than remarking that I conducted my archaeological research during colonial times—little twerp, but I considered it youthful arrogance."

Tanya turned to Claire. "What about you, Claire? 'Fess up. Did he know any of your deep, dark secrets?"

Claire thought that Tanya acted agitated, too talkative. She pondered her response. "He made some strange comments about my faith, but interview-by-extortion doesn't seem to be a viable strategy." She turned to Evelyn and Steven. "Why do you think he did this?"

"We decided he was just immature," Evelyn said. "He thought if he demonstrated that he knew our work and could critique it, or, us…" she nodded to Tanya, "then we would see him as an equal. It certainly doesn't make sense, but I don't think he meant to blackmail anyone. It seems he didn't learn his lesson if he used the same technique with you."

"He seemed very enthusiastic about working with us and joining our department," Steven added. "I didn't think he was threatening."

They were saved from further deliberation on the topic by the arrival of their dinners. Gratefully, conversation moved to other topics such as the sessions, most of which the Keane College contingent had missed.

During dessert, discussion turned to Eduardo's gift to Keane College. Steven congratulated them. "Must be nice to have friends in high places," he said.

"A mixed blessing, I think," said Madge. "It would have been better to wait a few years until we had a more developed program and museum protocol."

"Oh, Madge," said Tanya, "don't be so negative. I think it's great!" She pushed her custard around with her spoon. "I think Brad is a genius, setting this up for us. We'll be the envy of all the big universities."

When the busboy appeared to clear the table, conversation returned to Evelyn's work with the Zapatista movement, and her promise to Steven that she would return to campus at least one week before classes started.

As the group rose to leave, Madge and Tanya retreated to the restroom. Claire, Evelyn, and Steven exited into the cool night air. When Steven walked down the street to smoke a cigarette, Evelyn pulled Claire aside, speaking softly.

"I might be wrong, but I think I know something about Tanya."

Claire moved closer to Evelyn. "What do you mean?"

"Where did she earn her Ph.D.?"

Claire told her. "Why?"

"When she foolishly disclosed her relationship with her advisor, I remembered something." She looked back toward the restaurant entrance. "A colleague of mine told a story about an archaeologist who had worked with a graduate student at Palenque and had an affair with her. I never learned her name, but the assignment and Tanya's admission of their affair are similar. He later agreed to be on her dissertation committee. I think he eventually divorced, but he shouldn't have been on her committee."

Evelyn looked back over her shoulder again. "There's something else that I don't remember clearly. It has something to do with some of the stone fragments they had worked on together. They disappeared, and the translations couldn't be corroborated. The archaeologist claimed he didn't know what happened to the segments—I guess they were relatively small chunks of hieroglyphs. I think one of the graduate students working on the site dropped out of the program."

Claire felt her heart pound; she looked back before speaking. "That couldn't have been Tanya. There are teams of graduate students at many sites. It might not even be the same team," Claire protested. "Besides, she successfully defended her dissertation." Evelyn straightened quickly as Madge and Tanya came out of the restaurant. She whispered, "I think you should watch Tanya."

CHAPTER NINETEEN

The two groups separated at the plaza where the street traffic had lessened to taxis and a small number of vehicles. Claire took in deep breaths. Competing aromas from open-air restaurants replaced the fumes from car exhaust. A blanket of stars shone high above the muted street lights. No one spoke, and Claire let her mind wander in the quiet. She thought about what Evelyn had disclosed and what it might mean.

As if reading her thoughts, Tanya said, "I guess I made a fool of myself."

"What do you mean," Claire asked, unnecessarily.

"About having a relationship with that professor," she said, biting her lip. "I just wanted to make a point about Paul…that he was investigating us…it really wasn't a big deal, and the professor was separated from his wife anyway." She was agitated, and her sharp tone disturbed the serenity of the night.

"I'm sure it happens all the time," Madge said. "I don't recommend it as a career move, though, Tanya."

"It wasn't," Tanya protested, "but you all probably think so because of me and Jamal."

"What about you and Jamal?" Madge said.

"We've been dating, that's all," Tanya insisted. "Jamal wanted to keep it quiet. He said George wouldn't approve, but I think it was more that Brad wouldn't like it." She bit her lip again. "Like either of them is my father."

Madge said, "It causes complications sometimes, especially if the relationship sours and warfare ensues." Madge tipped her head up to look at Tanya. "Believe me, I've been around long enough to know."

"We're not even in the same department," Tanya complained. "We wouldn't be voting for each other's tenure or anything." Tanya paused for Madge to catch up with them. "Jamal has been moody and distracted. He says he needs space." She made quotation marks with her fingers. "That's so male. Personally, I think it's Brad. He hates me, and Jamal is his little puppy dog."

Claire wondered about her shifts between adulation and rebuke regarding Brad.

"I don't think either of those things is true," Madge said, "but that proves my point."

The trio walked in silence until they approached the hotel. As the automatic hotel doors opened, Tanya exclaimed, "Oh, I almost forgot!" She pulled her companions away from the door as it closed behind them. "I have something to tell you."

Claire and Madge exchanged glances of disbelief. Tanya had more to reveal?

Tanya herded her companions to the lobby lounge, where they huddled together on a brightly upholstered sofa. Tanya paused for dramatic effect, looking around the room. "I think that the great Brad and powerful Eduardo had a falling out." Her eyes widened in excitement, her words a forced whisper.

"What do you mean?" Madge asked.

Tanya scanned the room again. "I overheard them in the Exhibit Room after Eduardo's lecture." She looked at the scowl on Madge's face and the questioning look on Claire's. "I was passing by and couldn't help hearing. I...stood just outside the door." She paused again, reconsidering her statement. "Actually, I could see them too," she confessed. "They stood behind the display case looking away from the door."

She paused and looked at her colleagues, expecting further comment. Receiving none, she continued. "Eduardo opened the display case to put the statue inside. They turned toward me, so I stepped back and didn't see anything else."

"They didn't see you?" Claire asked, in a whisper.

"I'm sure they didn't."

"Well?" Madge prodded. "What did you hear?"

"Eduardo said something to the effect that Brad should appreciate the gesture...and Brad said he, Eduardo, shouldn't have done it. But he didn't say it in a positive way, like it was too generous, but angry, like a growl." Tanya paused again, pressing her lips together. "Eduardo swore, and then I heard a sound, like the case being closed and locked. I had the sense that Eduardo thought he had done Brad a favor, and Brad didn't appreciate it. Eduardo sounded miffed…like it had been a big favor."

"Like loaning a small museum collection to an unappreciative recipient?" Madge said.

"I don't know," Tanya said. "It sounded more personal."

The conversation halted when Madge's eyes widened, and she tapped her mouth with her index finger. Tanya and Claire followed her gaze to see Brad and Jamal approaching from the front desk. Tanya blanched and fumbled with her purse.

Claire wondered if the two men had overheard their conversation, but they seemed preoccupied with folded notes, reading them as they walked.

"Did you get one of these?" Jamal asked the women, waving his paper in the air. "They're notices from the Merida Police Department. They must have been hand-delivered."

"We just got here." Tanya held her hand out to take the note, but Jamal handed it to Madge who read it aloud: "'Detective Roberto Salinas requests that you meet with him tomorrow, Tuesday morning at eight o'clock in the Exhibit Room.' What does this mean?"

"It must be about Paul," Tanya said. "I knew it…there is more going on here."

Claire, who suspected it concerned the computer, suggested they all check their boxes. They followed Brad to the front desk phone. "I'll call George," he said.

Claire stopped at the session board located near the desk, where an announcement had been posted next to the daily program schedule. It requested, in English and Spanish, that anyone with information about Paul's death meet with the Merida police the following morning.

Claire joined her colleagues at the desk. Madge and Tanya had received the same message as Jamal; Claire claimed the note from her box and saw similar folded notes sticking out from other mail cubicles, including George's. When Madge asked Claire if she got the note, Claire said she had, but she lied. Her message asked her to call Detective Salinas at his personal cellphone number.

CHAPTER TWENTY

Claire called Detective Salinas from her room. She grabbed her hand-woven shawl, a gift from her *comadre*, the mother of her goddaughter. She headed back out to the cool Merida evening. She knew El Caracol because it had been Aaron's favorite bar, located away from the hotel and the central plaza, near the section of the city called San Francisco. It was owned by a gay Canadian couple and was popular with the American and Canadian ex-patriot community.

Detective Salinas stood at the entrance, dressed informally in blue jeans, a light-weight jacket over a button-down shirt, and sandals. Claire could visualize a younger version of the face, now a bit thickened with age, but with the same dark eyes and expressive eyebrows.

"Good evening, Detective."

He smiled, but his eyes were wary. "I'm glad you came. I thought you might stand me up…again." Salinas led Claire up a narrow staircase leading to the second floor of the building. "And don't call me 'Detective' unless you want me to call you 'Professor.'"

It had been four years since she had been here with Aaron, but she remembered the walls, multicolored in bright oranges and greens and vibrant Mexican murals. In a far corner, a small group of twenty-something locals watched a soccer match between the Yucatán *Venados* and the Hidalgo *Cruz Azul* on a large flat-screen television. A cheer arose, followed by a chorus of "Gooooal!" as the *Venados* scored. Beer bottles tapped together in congratulatory toasts.

The owner, a young man in his mid-thirties, waved at the detective from the bar. "¡Hola, Berto! ¿Cómo está?" The bartender winked at him, a gesture that Claire did not miss. Detective Salinas was clearly a regular here.

"*Feliz*, Todd," the detective answered, to which the bartender winked again.

The waiter led them to a small table away from the television, in a corner where bright orange and red paint met. Along one of these walls, an artist had painted a mural depicting a rural village with thatch homes under a bright Yucatecan sun, women in traditional dress, and children playing in the park. Claire had already imbibed a margarita at dinner and hesitated to order another drink, but the waiter encouraged her to try a white wine that Todd had brought from Canada. Claire agreed, and the detective ordered beer for himself and an appetizer platter.

Claire clasped her necklace, then folded her hands in her lap, conscious of the wedding ring she still wore. "I was surprised to see you at the station, and under these circumstances. You have done well—a detective."

"You have done well also," Roberto said, his eyes studying her with an intensity that made her look away. "An anthropologist, no less." He tented his hands in front of his face. "But what I really want to know is why you left Mexico without telling me."

Claire's hands went to her necklace again. "I am so sorry. You knew I was leaving."

"But I thought we had things to talk about...to say." He paused as the waiter brought their drinks and retreated. "I thought there would be more. And you never wrote. I never had your address."

Claire sipped her wine, stalling. "I was wrong, and I am sorry." She sipped again, holding the wine glass to control her hand shaking. "I didn't really think that you were serious...that you meant it to be more than a fling with an American student...I thought you wouldn't care."

"Fling?" he asked.

"Temporary, fun, but not serious."

"You based this on...what?"

"We were young and didn't know each other well. It would have been a long-distance relationship with no future."

"That's what you thought?"

"That's what I thought you thought too," Claire said, miserable. "And I had met someone else during the trip...and I married him."

"So perhaps you had the fling, not me."

"Please, don't torture me. I am sorry. It wouldn't have worked. I know it, and I think you know it also."

The appetizers arrived. Roberto took a wedge of quesadilla and Claire twisted her wedding ring, staring at the man whom she had hurt. "I saw the photograph in your office. Is that your family?"

Roberto nodded. "Was. My wife and son were killed in a car accident five years ago. I live with my daughter and my widowed mother."

"I am so sorry," Claire said again. "I can't imagine losing a child and spouse at the same time."

"If it hadn't been for my daughter and mother, I wouldn't have survived the grief." He paused, looking at Claire's wedding ring. "Did your husband come with you to the conference?"

"My husband died of cancer two years ago. I too have a daughter."

They both drank silently, aware of the emotional charge between them. Aware of the circumstances that brought them together.

Claire said, "Why did you invite me here?"

"I wanted to see you again. Was it a mistake?"

"No, not at all. It's this death. I can't think of anything else."

"Or anyone?"

Claire smiled. "I remember you now. You were the romantic...and you became a cop."

"And you were the beautiful American woman, so near, but so mysterious."

"Beautiful? Mysterious?" Claire said. "Hardly either, I'm sure."

"You conquered me...then left me in despair."

"And now, I'm a suspect?" Claire smiled, trying to change the conversation.

"Not yet," he said, and finally smiled. "But I need your help."

Claire felt her heart settle and head clear. "Is it about the computer? Is that why you called a meeting tomorrow?"

"Yes. Thank you for sending Cody to me."

"Do you think it's a coincidence that Paul's computer disappeared when he died?"

"I don't like coincidences," Roberto said, and continued as if Claire were a colleague, not a potential suspect or former love interest. "Let's assume that his death was not an accident, and that the missing computer is important. What could be the motive to kill Paul?"

"You're assuming murder, not accident or suicide?"

"I'm assuming the worst and hoping for the best."

"It seems to me the person most likely to have a motive would be Cody," Claire said. "Who else?"

Salinas tipped his hand in a now-familiar gesture. "But why did he tell me about the missing computer? I didn't suspect a crime. We didn't even search his hotel room."

"Do you think he tried to misdirect you? He could have taken it himself, thrown it away."

"Misdirect?" he asked, struggling with the word.

"Deceive you, send you in the wrong direction, to make you think it was someone else who took the computer. Why mention it otherwise?"

Salinas frowned. "Why would Cody kill his lover here, when he could have done it anywhere, or just left him?"

"Perhaps it was something that happened here…an argument, and the opportunity available…or perhaps it was an accident and he was scared." She realized she had been clenching her fists in her lap and released them, reaching for her wine glass. "Several of us witnessed tension between them."

"Yes, he admitted that much to me."

"Who else could it be?" Claire asked.

Salinas looked at her in a thoughtful manner, his fingers drumming softly on the table. "Can you think of other possible motives for harming him?"

Claire wondered how many enemies Paul might have made as he meandered from college to university applying for positions. It could have been someone else entirely, someone they had no reason to suspect, another man with whom he had a relationship, a woman even.

Roberto watched her closely, as if trying to read her thoughts. "Claire?" he asked.

"There is something." She paused as Roberto pulled a small spiral notebook and pen from one of his jacket pockets. With a sigh of resignation, she summarized the faculty discussion at Uxmal concerning Paul's candidacy. She also reported on what she and her colleagues had learned from Evelyn Nielander about Paul's interview tactics, and what Cody had told her about Paul's family. "Perhaps, Paul's personality contributed to his death," she said.

"Do you mean he was blackmailing people?" Salinas asked, his hand poised over his notebook.

Claire shook her head. "I don't think so, but his comments could be construed as threatening." She told him about Tanya's confession. "I'm not saying that Tanya would kill Paul for hinting at this indiscretion, but someone else, threatened by a disclosure, might feel the need to quiet the source, not hire him, which is what he obviously wanted."

"It doesn't make sense."

"That's what we thought."

"But it does increase the number of possible suspects and motives," he said, looking at her with raised eyebrows.

"Including me," Claire said.

"Including anyone at the conference whom Mr. Sturgess had threatened." He picked up a chicken wing and examined it. "Technically, everyone at Uxmal that night is a suspect, but you are not on my A list...is that what you call it?" Claire nodded. "You could have discouraged Mr. Detwyler from coming to me, but you placed the call." He attacked the chicken wing and deposited the bone on the platter. "Besides, despite how you treated me, I can't see you pushing someone off a pyramid."

Claire, frustrated, protested, "Are you sure it couldn't have been an accident? Perhaps he climbed up and just fell." She paused to gauge his response, a slight shrug. "Perhaps he committed suicide."

He sat back, studying her face. "There's no evidence of it, such as a note, and neither his family nor Cody told me anything to make me suspect he was depressed."

"Perhaps the note was in his backpack."

"But then, where is the backpack?" He studied his beer, not looking at Claire. Finally, he said, "I need you to consider the possibility that one of the Keane College faculty or another anthropologist might be involved with Paul's death in some way."

Claire opened her mouth to protest, but Roberto did not give her a chance to speak. "I know that you don't want to think about this, but I need your help. You know your faculty members, and you know where they were during that evening. It will help me if you can describe their movements, so I can compare your observations with the statements they will give me tomorrow."

Claire felt exasperation rise from within her. She tried to control her hands as she struggled with her conscience. What would happen if, because of her observations, one of her colleagues was wrongfully accused of a horrible crime? What would happen if she did not cooperate and someone she knew, and probably respected, avoided responsibility?

Roberto moved his chair so that he sat to her side rather than across from her. Speaking more softly, he said, "Anything you observed will stay between us. I am not anxious to accuse anyone of a crime." His eyes narrowed, and his eyebrows furrowed in a manner reminiscent of George when he was deep in thought. He was a cop now, not Roberto. "Believe me," he said, "my captain wants this conclusion. It's not good for the tourist business for people to fall off pyramids, but it is far worse to have them pushed."

Claire leaned toward him, remembering the charge she had felt years ago when he had touched her hand. He did this now, and the same feeling came over her. "Okay. I will tell you what I know about last night."

CHAPTER TWENTY-ONE

When Claire finished her narrative, she sat back as Salinas continued to write in his notebook. When he had laid his pen down and took a sip of beer, Claire asked, "Have you contacted the elderly couple who saw Paul on the pyramid—the Stuarts?"

Salinas flipped through his notebook. "My sergeant tried to contact them at the hotel, but they had already left." He paused. "Can I ask a favor of you?"

"Certainly."

"Sergeant Garza got their home phone number from the hotel, but they haven't returned her calls. It's possible they don't have international service." He spread his hands on the table in front of him. "Could you try to contact them through the internet? Perhaps you can get their email and ask them if they have any photographs of that night."

"Yes, I'll try."

Roberto flipped a few pages back in his notebook, wrote the phone number on a blank page and ripped it out for her. He then pulled a packet of photographs from his other jacket pocket, the photos from Claire's camera. He organized the photos into two stacks, pushing one toward her and turning the second stack upside down on the table.

Roberto pointed at the top photograph. "Can you identify your colleagues? I assume this is the Keane College group?"

Claire identified the faculty members, providing a short summary of their areas of expertise. They flipped through the photographs together. Claire touched Salinas' hand as one photo appeared. It depicted Eduardo and Brad standing together on the Governor's Palace platform.

"This is Eduardo Ramirez." She turned the photo slightly, so she could see it more closely. "My God," she said. "That's Paul." Paul was on the far edge of the photograph. His body faced the pyramid, but he was looking toward Brad and Eduardo. His face was blurred as the camera was not focused on him, but it was clearly Paul, his shirt, glasses, and curly dark hair unmistakable. She could discern the straps of a backpack.

Salinas looked carefully at this photo, tapping his finger on Eduardo's image as if thinking of something. He turned the second stack of photos over and placed them in front of Claire. "Can you look at these?" he asked.

Claire knew which photos they would be and preferred not to look at them again. "I'm sorry they aren't very clear," she said. "That's why I gave the officer the memory card."

"Ahh," he said, and reached into his pocket again. "I almost forgot." He handed the memory card back to Claire and she put it in her purse. "Thank you for including it. We enlarged them for detail."

"As I looked through them," Claire confessed, "I realized that I hadn't taken photos of the crowd." She could tell by the wrinkle in his brow that he too had hoped for more, but had refrained from mentioning it.

"Perhaps you could help me with that."

Claire named those at the site that she could remember, including those from her group, and he wrote them down. "Oh, and Laura Lorenzo, the other candidate for the job, and the Stuarts, of course." She paused to think. "The YouTube video should help with that also."

He nodded. "So, everyone from your group was there?"

She thought a moment. "Not at first. Jamal arrived later. He told us that when he heard the scream and saw people running, he ran to the Cultural Center for help."

"But you didn't believe him?"

"Why wouldn't I?"

"The way you answered, like you weren't sure you believed what he said."

"It just seemed strange for someone to run away from something like that. Most people run toward an accident, but I was relieved that he had thought about getting help. And, he did give Cody an alibi."

Salinas shrugged. "Perhaps, but Cody could have returned to the site before the show."

He turned his attention back to the photographs, arranging them on the table. He moved the appetizer platter away from them. When a waiter came to take it, Salinas quickly laid his napkin over the photographs and ordered two more drinks.

Another chorus of "Gooooal!" erupted from the fans. Claire strained to hear what Salinas was saying. He raised his eyebrows and waited for the din to lessen.

"These photos are very helpful," he said. "I want to draw your attention to a few things."

Claire nodded and forced herself to look at the photos she had taken of Paul, lying on the ground, face up.

"First," Salinas asked, "did you find the body in this position?"

"No. Brad turned him over to check his pulse. That was when we realized who it was." Her hand shook as she touched the photo. "He was on his stomach, his legs crumpled underneath him. I saw the gash on his head and I wondered—after I saw the blood on the ground—if he had landed there…"

"Go on," Salinas urged.

"He seemed too close to the balustrade, and his face…" She touched the photo again. "His face was bruised, and his nose broken, but it didn't look like his face had hit the lower platform. His glasses were broken, but still hooked around his ear."

The waiter returned with drinks, peering at the photos as Salinas covered them again. When the waiter had left, he continued, "You were correct in questioning the position of the body and the blood on the ground and around the pyramid platform. The body had been moved, at least once, perhaps twice." He paused as they sipped their fresh drinks. "Brad turned the body over, but someone dragged the body, which had been face-up, from near the pathway to the base of the pyramid, and then turned it over."

"So, it wasn't suicide or accident," Claire acknowledged, sitting back in her chair.

"Think it through," Salinas said. "Let's say, you see someone fall or lying on the ground. What do you do?"

"I'd call for help."

"Most people would, yes." He raised his eyebrows. "Would you move the body?"

"Of course not. Everyone knows that from television."

"Yes, but what if the person isn't the honest, good citizen that you are? Why might you move the body?"

Claire thought about this. "The backpack? Someone moved him to a dark location and turned him over to get the backpack?" She was incredulous. "That's so risky! They could have been seen."

"Very risky indeed, but with everyone's attention on the program, it would be possible."

"Could it have been opportunistic?" As much as Claire preferred that interpretation, she knew it was unlikely. Someone had pushed him to get to the backpack.

"Do you think that's what happened?" Salinas asked.

"Not really," she admitted. "Not unless the person knew it had valuable contents...but I doubt it happened that way."

Salinas nodded. He pointed to a photograph of Brad kneeling next to a backpack. "Is this Brad's backpack?"

"Yes," Claire answered. "He took it off to work on Paul."

"The enlargements will give us a better look at the footprints around the body and the steps. Unfortunately, people moved around, so this will be a difficult chore. We may have to request witnesses' shoes at some point. I'll know when I get more lab results. Is there anything else you remember about the scene?"

"There is one thing, but I don't think it's important."

Salinas looked up. "Tell me."

Claire told him about seeing Laura climbing partway up the pyramid while Claire took photographs. "I just thought it was odd."

"Laura Lorenzo—the job candidate?"

Claire nodded.

"Interesting," Salinas said thoughtfully.

He continued to thumb through the photographs. Claire wondered if she should mention the breakfast conversation, or Tanya's disclosure about Brad and Eduardo's argument in the Exhibit Room. She didn't think it related to the death, but it puzzled her.

Roberto interrupted her thoughts. "You have changed."

"How?"

Roberto tipped his head to the side. "I remember you as a bit of a—how do you say—rebel? Spirited, bending the rules, dating me even though it was against the rules of your program."

She smiled. "And now it seems I am doing the same thing."

"Yes," he responded. "But you are cautious now, *melancolía*. Is it your husband's death?"

Claire realized she was twisting her wedding ring. "Yes, but not only that." She sipped her wine. How much to disclose? "I am suffering a sort of mid-life crisis," she admitted. "I've lost my passion for academia. I hoped that the Mayanist program would rejuvenate me, and to some extent it has, but there are still the internal dramas, interpersonal squabbles, and turf-building that I don't have the patience for anymore."

"Anything that might cause someone to push a job candidate off a pyramid?"

Claire looked up at him sharply. "Of course not!"

Salinas laughed. "There's the spirit I remember."

Embarrassed that he had been able to provoke her, she sat back and sipped her wine. "Tell me about your daughter."

"She is a student at the University of Yucatán…and yes, I live with my mother, or I should say she lives with us."

"I like the idea of the traditional Mexican family. I have missed that in my life."

"And how are you not traditional?" he asked.

She pushed her glass away. "My father is of Mayan heritage. His grandparents followed the migrant stream from Yucatán and settled in Michigan, where my father was born. He married my mother, a red-haired Irish girl, and here I am, browned skinned with brownish-red hair, a Spanglish speaker with a Latin/Irish temper that you call spirit…a hybrid."

"A beautiful hybrid, still. If I may say so."

Program for the 10th Annual Meeting of the Society for Mayanist Studies

Events for Tuesday, May 6
The Future of Mayan Archaeology and Ethno-Botany

Morning Sessions:
- Samantha Sanchez, *Field Report on the Excavation of La Pacificacion, Guatemala*
- Keith Kramer, *The Economic and Cultural Costs of Looting at Mayan Archaeological Sites: Who owns Mayan History?*

Afternoon Sessions:
- Wayne Williamson, *The Last Shaman: Loss of Indigenous Healing in Mayan Communities*
- Jacob Jamieson, *The Commodification of Mayan Pharmacopeia*

4:30 George Banks
"Who Owns Mexican Culture? The Future of Museum Curation in the Age of Privatization"

Evening:
7–9 pm Reception Hosted by Doctor Eduardo Ramirez
and the Museos Indígenas,
at The Casa Montejo, Central Plaza

CHAPTER TWENTY-TWO

Tuesday Morning

Sergeant Rosa Garza and Detective Salinas arrived at the hotel early to prepare for the meeting. Garza aligned several rows of metal chairs at the center of the Exhibit Room. Nearby, Detective Salinas examined a large poster Garza had prepared, featuring an enlarged photograph of Paul Sturgess.

Garza paused in her chore, located Officer Chan near the door, and asked Salinas in a whisper, "So you're telling me you had a *cita romántica*, a date, with a suspect last night?"

Detective Salinas had never attested to having insight into the mind of women, especially women like Rosa Garza who were difficult to read, serious in nature, and professional to a fault. That she had made this comment indicated either criticism of his behavior or a softening in her touch. Unfortunately, he had no idea which possibility was correct.

"It wasn't a date, Sergeant," he said. "It was an informal interview."

"And it involved food and drink?" she pressed.

"Perhaps."

"That's a date. I know. I used to have dates...then I got married, had children, got a divorce, earned my sergeant stripes...now I have no time for dates."

Salinas' hand paused as he wrote on the poster board, the Sharpie pen soaking into the paper. Was this a quip, sarcasm, or an attempt at collegial conversation? *Mierda*.

"It was an informal interview with a social element." He explained how he and Claire had met, omitting the details. "It was a long time ago."

"Hmph," Garza said, and unfolded a few more metal chairs. "Are we ready, sir?" she asked.

"Yes." Salinas turned the easel so that the photograph was clearly visible to those entering the room.

Garza motioned to Officer Chan, who had sidled over to the exhibit cases, feigning interest in the artifacts so he could overhear their conversation. On her command, he returned to the Exhibit Room door, and opened it.

Salinas watched the faces of the scholars as they entered and saw the photograph. Some approached the easel; others, engrossed in private conversations, ignored the image of Paul Sturgess altogether. They slipped into chairs and continued their conversations quietly; others paused, looked at the photo, and moved along.

Professor Madge Carmichael entered with a colleague whom he recognized from Claire's photograph as Professor George Banks. Madge nodded to Salinas as she and George approached the poster. Salinas identified the other Keane College faculty members as they arrived together: the tall and striking blonde Tanya, whom he had met at the police station; the two men he recognized from Claire's photograph, Jamal Kennedy and Brad Kingsford. They joined Professors Carmichael and Banks at the easel, spoke together for a moment and then found seats near the center of the room. There was no sign of Claire, Cody Detwyler, or the mysterious Eduardo Ramirez. At that moment, a tall Mexican man entered, distinguishable by his black suit, pink shirt, and leather shoes. So, this was the great Doctor Ramirez.

Claire had told Madge she overslept and would meet the group at the Exhibit Room, but the truth was more complicated. She feared how she might react when she saw Roberto after their meeting the night before. She felt embarrassed: by how she had treated him years ago, by her conflicted feelings for him now, and by the ease with which he had persuaded her to discuss her colleagues.

Claire was surprised to see Cody Detwyler just outside the Exhibit Room, peeking around the corner, his face blotched, his eyes red.

"What is it?" Claire asked when she reached his side.

He pointed into the room and Claire saw the large photograph of Paul.

"I can't go in," Cody whispered. "Those cops are here too." He pointed his finger at Sergeant Juarez and Officer Chan, who stood nearby.

"I'll go in with you," she said.

The atmosphere was funereal. It wasn't just the image of Paul pinned to the easel, but the pockets of people either standing at the photograph or sitting uncomfortably facing it. Cody did not approach the photograph, but dipped into the back row, near Laura. Eduardo Ramirez also sat in the back row, one ankle crossed over his knee, casually watching the detective at the front of the room. Claire joined her colleagues, taking a seat next to Brad and Tanya.

Detective Salinas stood before his audience, wearing an American-style suit and tie. Sergeant Garza stood next to him. Claire found it difficult to look at him and not remember his words of the night before. She had deflected them successfully, she thought, but they hung there in the air, nonetheless. Roberto's gaze skimmed over the audience and his eyes fell on Claire, but only momentarily. It seemed to Claire that Sergeant Garza stared at her for a long time.

When the room quieted, Salinas motioned Chan to close the door. He thanked the group for their attendance and introduced himself and the other officers.

"As you all know, Doctor Paul Sturgess died at Uxmal Sunday evening. Mr. Sturgess's parents and his friend, Mr. Detwyler, are understandably concerned about his death, and certain facts have come to our attention that suggest further investigation might help us understand what happened that night."

As Garza and Chan handed out clipboards and pens, Salinas continued, "Rather than interview you individually, I am asking that each of you write a statement, in your own words, focusing on what you know about the events of that day and evening."

Salinas held up a copy of the questionnaire he had attached to the clipboards. "I ask that you use the questions to organize your thoughts.

Please print your name, hotel, and phone number clearly on the top of the sheet in case we need to talk to you in person.

"I assume you have come today because either you received an invitation, or you attended the excursion and might have some information about Mr. Sturgess or events surrounding his death. If you weren't at Uxmal but know something about Mr. Sturgess that might be important, please fill in the comment section at the end of the questionnaire."

Salinas continued, "I have also asked you to outline when and where you saw Mr. Sturgess on that day or evening, whom he was with, or a description, what he wore, including if he had a backpack, jacket, or other identifiable clothing, so we know you saw Mr. Sturgess, not someone who looked like him.

"If you spoke with Doctor Sturgess, please summarize your conversation. Don't speculate on what you have seen or heard. Finally, fill in the comment section with any additional information you might have and indicate if you have any photographs that might be helpful."

Salinas paused and looked around the room. "I know this is difficult, but I know you are all trained observers, and I have no doubt some of you saw something that might help us understand how Doctor Sturgess came to be on the pyramid, and how he fell."

Salinas scanned the audience again. "You might know that someone posted a video of the accident scene…" Voices erupted around the room at this information. "Quiet, please," Salinas said. "It is no longer online. But if you saw the video or posted it yourself, we would like to know."

Claire looked back at Cody and saw a look of horror on his face as he heard about the video. Salinas continued, "When you are finished, please sign and date your statement and give it to Sergeant Garza before you leave, with your clipboard and pen. Does anyone have any questions?"

An elderly man in the back row broke the tension when he asked, "Do you prefer the answers in English or Spanish?" Several people laughed, but Salinas held his hand up. "As you teachers always say, there is no such thing as a stupid question." He smiled at the man. "Either language is fine…but we prefer you not answer in Maya." The audience laughed again.

Claire could feel the mood of the room lighten as the group settled into their task. She understood Salinas's attempt to put people at ease, but she worried about how the levity would affect Cody. She turned around to look at him again. His head was bowed over the questionnaire. He chewed on the end of his pen, like a student concentrating on a difficult exam.

Within fifteen minutes, the potential witnesses lined up at the door where Garza stood with a large cardboard box at her feet. The Keane College faculty joined the end of the line that wound alongside the exhibit case where the corn-god seemed to stare at them in judgment.

Behind her, Claire heard Tanya ask her companions what they had written.

"It's none of your business," Brad said.

"I'm just curious," she said, and turned to Jamal. "Can I see your statement?"

"No, Tanya. It's my statement, not yours."

The men held their clipboards to their chests as Tanya walked between them, her mouth set in a pout.

The witnesses approached Sergeant Garza with trepidation. A small group of anthropologists huddled near the sergeant, correcting errors or filling in information. The mood of the group was generally jocular, as those who had successfully passed her station teased their colleagues and friends for their predicament.

"I haven't been that scared since Catholic school," said Brad as the group walked together to the lobby. They joined the remaining conference participants, who maneuvered through the crowd toward the meeting rooms.

"What now?" Tanya asked.

She sighed. "I have to find two elderly needles in a haystack. I hope you all can enjoy a few sessions." She turned and headed toward the elevators.

In her room, she called the Stuarts in Michigan using the number that Roberto had given her but was unable to make the connection. She opened her computer, searched for Lake Odawa, and sent an email message to the township supervisor. She could only hope that the township officials read their email. On impulse, she Googled Eduardo Ramirez and *Galerías Indígenas* and found several links to his family museums and art galleries. One of the sites provided a virtual tour of the Ramirez collections.

She skimmed the photographs of statuettes, pottery, and other artifacts his family had accumulated over the years for their various museums. The massiveness of the collections both impressed and worried her. How does one family gain access to such treasure? As she considered this, her finger froze on the computer mouse. She clicked on an image and an enlarged photograph appeared. It was the original of the statue that Eduardo had presented to Brad yesterday. Its provenance was listed as: anonymous donor, from Dzibichaltún, circa 800 A.D. Dzibichaltún was the archaeological site closest to the locations where she, Brad, Jamal, and Paul had done their research.

CHAPTER TWENTY-THREE

"What's with her?" Tanya asked, as she watched Claire join the throng of anthropologists congregating at the elevators.

"She's lovesick," said Madge. She had observed the amount of time Claire and Salinas had spent trying not to look at each other, both at the police station and the meeting they had just left.

"Lovesick?" said Tanya. "How old-fashioned." She raised her eyebrows at Jamal, who clenched his jaw and flashed his dark eyes in her direction.

"What?" Brad said. He had been studying his own program. "Who's lovesick?"

"Keep up, Brad," Tanya said. "Where's everyone going now?" She turned, seeking out Jamal, who had disappeared from her sight.

Brad said, "To eat. I missed breakfast this morning." He looked at his watch. "If I hurry, I can hear the end of Keith Kramer's talk on looting Mayan sites."

George said, "Madge and I are going to Samantha Sanchez's field report on Guatemala archaeology. Do you want to come?"

Tanya caught a glimpse of Jamal heading toward the hotel entrance. "No thanks. I'm going shopping." She gave a backward wave as she sprinted toward Jamal.

"Wait for me." Tanya caught up with Jamal at the entrance. He stood back so others could pass through ahead of him. "Where are you going?" she asked.

"Taking a walk before the afternoon sessions on ethno-botany."

"Come with me to the market." She reached for his arm. He started to pull away but relented and allowed her hand to rest in the crook of his elbow.

They pushed past a cluster of University of Yucatán students who stood just outside the hotel entrance, engaged in excited discussion about the police meeting.

Disentangling from the crowd, Tanya said, "I need to talk to you." She moved closer to him. "I have a theory about Paul's death. I didn't tell the detective everything in my statement. I want to know what you think."

Jamal looked at her, confused. "What do you mean, a theory you didn't tell the police? Why hold back?"

"He said not to speculate, remember?" She pulled on his arm again, smiling up at him in the way that used to warm his heart, but now chilled him to the bone.

"What's your theory?" Jamal asked.

"Later," Tanya teased, a sly smile returning to her face. She quickened her step as they wove their way past vendors selling palm-leaf crosses in front of the cathedral. "Why did the detective call us all together?" she asked. "Don't you think that was strange?"

Jamal sighed. "He explained it to us. If it were my son, I'd want to have answers, especially if it happened in a foreign country, wouldn't you?" He looked at Tanya with questioning eyes. "Besides, it's likely the YouTube video got them moving on it. I'm sure they don't want negative publicity."

"I saw the video," Tanya said. "Didn't I tell you?"

"When?"

"At the police station. It was a copy." Tanya opened her eyes wide. "Ah, now you're interested." She pulled him closer.

"Did the video show the body?" he asked.

"It was dark," she admitted. "You could see him, but he was covered with a jacket by then, thanks to Brad."

"I'm glad it was taken down from the site," Jamal said thoughtfully. "I can't imagine seeing my dead child on an online video."

Pedestrian traffic increased as they approached the market. They turned onto a brick street that was closed to traffic. Tanya peered into shops and, at her insistence, they entered a leather shop at the end of the street. Inside, the powerful odor of leather accosted them, as did the relative cool of the shop's interior. Once they assured at least three aggressive salesmen that they were just looking, they moved toward the back of the shop.

Tanya, examining a variety of leather belts, whispered to Jamal, "I'm thinking about opportunity and motive." She pulled Jamal to a display of leather purses along a side wall. "I think opportunity is more important, don't you? It had to be someone who could have climbed the pyramid during a short period of time."

"There were hundreds of people there," Jamal protested.

"But how many knew him? How many could have lured him to the top of the pyramid?"

"Only Cody, I think," Jamal said.

"Perhaps, but it's something that someone said that night, at the show. I don't think it happened that way." She picked up a leather belt with a jaguar buckle and took a place in the check-out line.

"What do you mean?" Jamal asked, looming over her as she counted her pesos.

"Someone wasn't where he said he was."

"Who?"

"I can't remember, but the backpack is the key."

CHAPTER TWENTY-FOUR

"The backpack?" Jamal asked. "What backpack?" They had crossed a small plaza lined with horse-drawn carriages.

Tanya sighed, impatient. "Detective Salinas mentioned it," she said. "It must mean something. If you had been there, you would have seen that Paul's backpack wasn't there...on the ground."

Jamal's hand shook as he took Tanya's arm and led her across the busy street and into the market, where the bright colors and blended aromas of fresh vegetables and fruits greeted them. Mayan women stood at tables, carefully stacking their produce into neat, impossible pyramids of oranges, grapefruits, mangoes, and papayas.

"I was there. I saw a backpack."

"That was Brad's."

"Why is that important?"

"His computer, Jamal."

Jamal pulled Tanya to him. "Are you saying that someone took the backpack with Paul's computer? Do you know for sure he had it with him?"

"He had it at the reception." She snorted, "And you call yourself a trained observer."

Jamal frowned. "That means someone killed him for the backpack?"

Tanya shrugged. "Maybe." She smiled at Jamal. "And that brings me to motive."

"Cody is the only one who could have motive," Jamal protested. "We didn't even know Paul before this week."

"Perhaps, but I have a theory...two theories actually." Jamal followed Tanya past the produce into a section dominated by household goods, plastic buckets, hardware, and kitchen utensils. "At the Uxmal department meeting, you said that you felt interrogated by Paul. What did that mean?"

"It wasn't what he said, but how he said it. I assumed he did the same to others."

"Yes, that's it. Paul seemed to know things, or hint that he knew things, about our work. And it's not just us."

"Who else?"

"There's this anthropologist at Central Wisconsin, Evelyn Nielander. Have you heard of her?"

"Sure. She works in Chiapas, with the Zapatistas. I read her book."

"I guess Paul implied that Evelyn had joined the Zapatistas." She laughed, her eyes wide. "Can you imagine? Evelyn looks like one of those beautiful senior women I've seen on television advertising osteoporosis medication." She pulled on Jamal's arm again. "Maybe that was his *modus operandi.*"

They skirted the fresh-meat section of the market where the mingled odors of beef, pork, fish, and fowl collided in a putrid stench that permeated the air. Averting her eyes from the long wooden tables laden with animal heads and piles of offal coated with flies, Tanya turned to Jamal, meeting his eyes. "What do you think of Laura Lorenzo?"

"What do you mean? As a job candidate? As a murder suspect?"

"Laura has been everywhere, talking to everyone."

Jamal followed closely on Tanya's heels as she hurried though the meat section, catching up with her at the jewelry kiosks near the edge of the market. "That's what people do at conferences," he said, huffing to a halt.

"She talked to Paul several times at the archaeological site, and she sat with him and Cody at dinner that evening."

Jamal shrugged. "So?"

"We know that she and Paul both attended the same university in Chicago. They might have a history."

"Laura might have a motive to push Paul off a pyramid? Really? That's your theory?"

Tanya turned her attention to the jewelry displays, ignoring Jamal. She took her time examining several silver bracelets. Jamal's frustration surfaced as she patiently purchased two bracelets and a necklace.

When she had placed her wallet and purchases in her purse, Jamal demanded, "What's her motive?"

"Why do you care?"

"I just can't see it. Besides, how could she steal a backpack? She had one of those Mexican woven purses."

"So, you paid attention to her," Tanya said, raising her eyebrows again. "But there's something else. Before the cops came, and while Claire was doing her CSI routine, Laura climbed up the pyramid. Her purse looked heavy, and she also used the flashlight function on her phone, like she was looking for something."

"Like what?"

"Something she might have dropped? Or Paul dropped? She came down and acted casual, like no one would notice."

"This is crazy."

Tanya smiled, showing her small white teeth and a tip of tongue. "Perhaps she just went up to talk to him…and he fell. That could happen, right?" She took his arm again in a flirting motion. Jamal tilted his head toward her, lifting her sunglasses so he could look into her eyes.

"Are you okay?" he asked. "Are you on the pills again?"

She pushed her sunglasses back down over her eyes. "Don't change the subject."

"There is no subject. This is ridiculous. No one killed that guy!" Jamal stepped out from the covered market into the sunlight. He turned toward the central plaza as Tanya struggled to keep up with him.

"I've only taken a few oxys this week," she said as she reached him at the corner. "It's your fault, you know."

"Just a few? That's impossible."

"I thought we would discuss things this week…about us. We've become so obsessed with the death, we haven't talked at all."

"We? You're the only one obsessed. Everyone else thinks it was an accident…which it was." Jamal looked over at her, their eyes level. "Besides, I thought we had talked Sunday. You were more concerned with getting Madge's job than with our relationship, as I recall."

They retraced their route to the hotel, Tanya one step behind Jamal. "So, it's over?"

"You don't think so?" Jamal asked, harshly.

"No," Tanya pleaded. "I thought everything was fine, really. You're the one acting differently, and I don't know why. What has changed?"

"I think we made a mistake."

"We or you?"

"Me. You don't love me. You never did."

"That's not true!" Tanya protested. "I…I really do love you."

"Too late, Tanya."

Tanya sniffed. "Will this affect your recommendation for my application to be curator of the museum?"

Jamal stopped and pulled her down onto a bench at the edge of the central plaza. "Listen to what you're saying." Jamal clenched his jaw, then sighed and softened his tone. "This is exactly why intra-department relationships are dangerous. We need to do this like adults, and without drama. It can only hurt both of us professionally."

"You promised."

"I kept my promise. I talked to George, as you asked—demanded." He took her hands in his and looked closely at her eyes through her tinted glasses. "The chances have always been slim for you," he said. "I told you that on Sunday. George hired Madge as curator, and you know that Claire will support her. Brad doesn't like the idea that Madge was crowned curator before his arrival, but he's stuck with her. Frankly, I don't think Brad would support you anyway. Who would he choose—you, a linguist, or Madge, an archaeologist with eons of experience?"

"You would have a vote," Tanya pressed. "But it appears that you have already made up your mind." She stood and crossed her arms. "Does this have anything to do with Paul? You seemed flustered by him."

Jamal glared at Tanya but stood to walk with her. "I am not flustered by Paul, or his death. But I'm fucking pissed that you won't let this go. The police are in charge. We are here for a conference, in case you've forgotten."

Tears sprang to Tanya's eyes. She pushed her glasses up onto the top of her head to wipe her eyes.

"Tanya, we've been having these circular arguments for months. We just met Paul two days ago. He has nothing to do with me, or you."

She reached into her purse and pulled out a prescription bottle. "I don't want to lose my chance for the curatorship." She looked at Jamal, shook a pill from the bottle and swallowed it without water.

"What the hell?"

Tanya became still, replacing the bottle in her purse. "I saw you talking to Paul. Did he tell you about Tom Freeman?"

"I met Tom Sunday afternoon, at the Uxmal reception. We had a chat. He told me a few things about you, not knowing about our relationship. He said you broke up his marriage, but I don't believe that. It was probably already broken, but it told me something about you." Jamal studied Tanya closely, watching her eyes dilate and her mouth relax. "Is that what Paul knew about you?"

Tanya's eyes misted over momentarily. Then, they hardened. "I never told you about my second theory."

"You mean in case the Laura Lorenzo theory doesn't pan out?" Jamal glared at Tanya. "You have got to get off the pills. You're not making sense."

Tanya smiled a crooked smile. "Perhaps you're worried about something else."

"What?"

"Something Paul might have known about you."

Jamal's jaw tightened, and his hand went to his earring. "What?"

"You know," she turned toward him. "You have secrets, too." She put her index finger and thumb close together at her lips and inhaled.

"I've made mistakes, but I no longer have a problem. But it's clear that you do." He leaned toward her and whispered, "My only problem seems to be you."

Tanya clenched her hands together. "Don't you think it's interesting that all of us…all Keane College faculty…were there at the scene of the fall, except you?"

Jamal stared at her. "You're crazy."

"I'm worried about you, Jamal. I didn't write anything about you in my statement. I don't want you to get into trouble."

"No, Tanya. It's all about you. You're wondering how it will affect your career if I killed someone." Jamal stood. "Be careful about making accusations. You can get yourself and others in a lot of trouble. Paul's death is none of our business."

Tanya faced him. She replaced her glasses over her eyes and clenched her fists. "Is that a threat?" Tanya weaved slightly, then caught herself. "Don't worry. I won't be climbing pyramids with you anytime soon." She turned on her heel and strode away, stumbling as she made her way through the crowd.

CHAPTER TWENTY-FIVE

Tuesday Afternoon/Evening

George stood in the semi-dark, the large screen behind him. He clicked the remote, and an image of a large archaeological site, deep trenches crisscrossing the landscape, filled the screen.

"This is Río Azul, Guatemala," George said. "The American archaeologist, Richard Adams, visited the site in 1962. At that time, they found several looters' trenches. The site was so remote that archaeological excavations had not been feasible, yet by the time Adams raised the funds to excavate the site in 1983, a very wealthy Guatemalan collector had moved onto the site and employed workers to open the tombs and scavenge them. They found 125 open looted trenches and twenty-eight looted tombs. This represents not only the loss of artifacts, but the loss of historical context, as sites are destroyed."

George clicked off the slideshow and motioned for the lights to come on. He squinted at the audience. "But, of course, this is not a problem only in the New World. If you visit any museum, you can be assured that many of the items, the beautiful antiquities that we enjoy, have been stolen or, more delicately, transported from the ancient world to the coffers of the conquerors." George picked up his notes, straightened them, and tapped them on the podium. "Until we address the ownership of ancient history and culture, we will continue to allow the rich and powerful the ability to buy and sell that history."

George looked out at the audience. "Thank you. Are there any questions?"

Eduardo Ramirez stood, his voice resonating through the auditorium, startling George. "Surely, Doctor Banks," Ramirez said, "you're not saying all private collectors hold stolen property. That would be an egregious misstatement."

George cleared his throat. "I would not presume to claim that. But the truth is that until developing and undeveloped nations had recognized the theft of their history, thousands of valuable items had already left their countries to fill a growing international demand for ancient art and artifacts."

"But most of those items ended up in museums," Eduardo argued. "What is the difference?"

"There may be little difference historically, except that museums display artifacts so that history can be shared. Private collectors and auction houses profit from the sale of antiquities. Sometimes, demand increases value, and increased value creates incentive to steal. Profit is the difference."

Brad raised his hand and stood. "We can't forget that without museums, most people would know nothing about ancient history and indigenous cultures."

"You are correct, I am sure," George replied. He looked at his watch. "I would like to remind everyone that Doctor Eduardo Ramirez is sponsoring a reception tonight at the Casa Montejo. All members of the Society of Mayanist Studies are invited to attend. Thank you."

As the audience filed out of the auditorium, Claire and Madge stayed behind to discuss their dinner plans. Claire watched as Tanya left the room with Brad; she was speaking to him, but he looked distracted, placing a folded manila envelope into his blazer pocket. Claire looked toward the stage where Jamal was assisting George in dismantling his computer and digital projector. But Jamal was also watching Brad and Tanya.

"La Paloma, again?" suggested Madge. "Or La Chaya?"

"La Chaya," Claire said, looking at her watch. "Do you mind checking the Exhibit Room first?" Claire explained how she had found the room unattended the previous afternoon.

Madge stood, straightened her skirt, and hoisted her bag over her shoulder. "I wish you had told me."

"I'm sorry, Madge. I did remind the bookseller and I told the manager. He promised the room would be locked at four o'clock."

"Well, let's hope it is," she said, looking at her watch. "It's five-thirty now."

The Exhibit Room was dark, but when Madge turned the knob, it opened. She flipped on the light and cursed as she examined the two cases.

"Something's gone," Madge said, her eyes wide.

Claire followed her gaze, expecting to find that Eduardo's statue had been taken. But it wasn't the statue that had disappeared. It was Keane College's sacrificial dagger.

"Shit!" exclaimed Madge as she reached out to touch the glass door that had been left ajar.

Claire pulled Madge's hand back. "Don't touch anything."

"Why?" asked Madge, though she pulled her hand back to her side. "How many people have touched that door, do you think?"

"What should we do?" Claire asked.

"Yell at the hotel manager for one thing." Madge stomped her foot and crossed her arms. She looked behind the cabinet. "Where's the key?"

"There, on the floor." Claire looked in the second case again, assuring herself that nothing had been taken from it. She said, "Call Brad and tell him what happened. I'll hurry back and see if Jamal and George are still in the auditorium."

Madge pulled her phone from her purse and Claire returned to the auditorium. Jamal had left, but George remained, speaking to several anthropologists whom Claire recognized but did not know. George introduced them as Carlos Gonzalez and Pablo Perez, retired archaeologists who had worked with George in Guatemala many years before. Claire hesitated, not wanting to make her report in front of the two men.

"I'm sorry to interrupt," Claire said, "but we have a problem in the Exhibit Room." The archaeologists moved back a few steps but didn't leave. "The room was unlocked, and the sacrificial dagger is missing." She explained how she and Madge had decided to check on the room.

Carlos Gonzalez, a portly man with a white beard and tufts of white hair erupting Einstein-like from his round head, pulled his unseasonable tweed jacket over his ample belly. "Was the dagger valuable?" he asked.

Claire shook her head. "It's only a classroom teaching item, and nothing else appears to be stolen."

Pablo Perez adjusted thick glasses over his wide nose. Unlike Carlos and George, Pablo was tall and lean, with neatly trimmed hair and narrow brown eyes. Pablo said nothing but looked intently at his colleague, Gonzalez.

Claire continued, "Madge is calling Brad. Should we call the police?"

George looked at his colleagues. "It's likely a hotel staff person or graduate student wanted a souvenir." He smiled weakly at his friends. "In any case," he added, "Brad can decide what to do."

Madge and Claire stepped out of the restaurant and into the cool evening breeze. It was after six-thirty when they entered the central plaza, humming with activity: families with children running and laughing, young couples sitting closely together on park benches, and tourists perusing the indigenous and not-so-indigenous handicrafts, spread out on plastic sheets along the ground.

Hammock and toy vendors competed for the attention of tourists, and in the center of the park a mariachi band played tinny music, heavy on the trumpet and accordion. Along the edges, vendors sold fruit drinks and *panuchos*, luscious deep-fried puffed tortillas stacked with black beans, turkey, lettuce, avocado, and onions. The rich aroma of grilling meat and onions followed them as they passed.

Their destination was the Casa Montejo, located across the plaza, where Eduardo Ramirez would be hosting the reception sponsored by his family business, *Misterios Indígenas* and its galleries, *Gallerías Indígenous*.

As they dodged families and tourists, Madge quipped, "It's a mystery where they found the indigenous artifacts."

Claire laughed and returned to the topic that had dominated their dinner, what to do about the missing dagger. "You haven't heard from Brad?" Claire asked.

Madge stopped, rummaged in her bag and pulled out her phone. She checked her messages and missed calls. "Not yet." She dropped her phone into her bag. "I'll tell him at the reception."

"We should tell Detective Salinas," Claire urged.

"Why? It's a minor theft."

Claire struggled with her conscience. She had promised Roberto she would keep their conversation private, but she sighed and pulled her friend close. "There's more going on," she said. "And you have to promise not to tell anyone."

Madge's face dropped. "Not even George? I have to tell George."

"Why?" Claire asked, puzzled.

"Because he'll know I am keeping something from him. It's a skill he has."

"Oh, Madge," Claire said. "I suppose, but no one else."

Claire told her about Paul's missing computer and backpack.

"What does it mean?"

"Maybe nothing. Maybe someone saw it lying on the ground and took it—an opportunistic theft. Or it could mean something important."

"A motive?" Madge said.

"This can't all be coincidence," Claire insisted. "Paul's death, a missing computer, and a disappearing artifact…"

Madge interrupted, "Don't let Tanya's dramatics influence you. Someone wanted that dagger. It's as simple as that."

They passed the crowd listening and dancing to the mariachi band. Claire saw Jamal ahead of them. She pointed him out to Madge.

"I wonder what's going on with Jamal and Tanya," Claire asked.

"Feels like high school to me," Madge responded, pulling her shawl over her shoulders. "Forget them. I want to know about you and that handsome detective."

"What do you mean?"

"Don't give me that innocent look. You were my student. We've known each other for years. I saw how you two looked at each other at the police station when he introduced himself. And I saw you look at his photographs. It's a good thing you're not a criminal, but I expected more reserve from a detective."

Claire looked at her friend, miserable. "Oh, Madge."

"So, tell me, Claire," Madge persisted.

"We met here during my internship year. Because I was bilingual, I was assigned to the university as an English teacher for professionals. Roberto—Detective Salinas—was a recruit attending one of my classes. The university strongly discouraged dating locals...too many potential complications, you know." Claire held her hair up as she walked, letting the evening air tickle her neck. "However, I broke the rules and we dated from time to time."

"You dated? Did you...?"

"Absolutely not...but it was wrong. When I met Aaron toward the end of the internship, I knew he was special. Then, I understood why the university rules existed. I eased away from Roberto. We both knew I'd be leaving soon. I thought he understood, but his feelings were stronger than mine. I left Merida without saying goodbye. I didn't write him, and he didn't have my address—this was long before email. I never thought I'd see him again."

Madge said, "There's a song about this...the Doobie Brothers, I think. The guy goes through life with a crush on a girl and when they meet later, she doesn't even remember him...!" She stumbled through the lyrics, ending with, "...what a fool believes."

"The Doobie Brothers?"

"Hey, look at me.... Do I look like the Lawrence Welk type?"

"But I did remember him," Claire admitted.

"Have you talked to him?"

"Can I plead the fifth on this?"

"I expect a full accounting later."

"I promise." Claire looked at her watch. "It's seven o'clock. We're late."

"Party won't start until at least eight o'clock, Mexican time."

"But we're Americans," Claire said. "And Brad will notice."

"Why is everyone afraid of Brad?" Madge said, taking Claire's arm as they crossed the boulevard toward the Casa Montejo.

CHAPTER TWENTY-SIX

Madge and Claire studied the façade of the Casa Montejo before entering. Built by the Montejo family as a tribute to their success in conquering the Maya in the 1500s, the architecture represented an odd blending of medieval gargoyles and Renaissance statues.

"This building is spectacular and creepy at the same time," Madge said as they entered through immense wooden doors into a large courtyard. Twenty-foot-high walls separated the conquerors from the conquered. Surrounding the courtyard, grand rooms opened onto a hallway of black and white marble floors.

Tonight, descendants of conquered Maya mingled with the descendants of European conquerors. Indigenous scholars formed vibrant clusters of traditional clothing representing diverse Mayan cultures: brightly woven skirts and colorful blouses depicting important symbols and designs that identified the wearer's region of origin, from Mexico to Guatemala. The American scholars, dressed in pastel dresses or casual slacks, paled in comparison.

A bar had been set up at the far end of the courtyard. To the left of the bar, double doors opened into the dining room. Behind the bar, staff entered the courtyard from a rear door, carrying trays of food and setting up an elegant buffet table.

A door along the walkway to the right of the bar opened into a parlor. A sitting room and museum took up the hallway to Claire's right. She knew from an earlier tour of the building that the parlor and the sitting room both opened into a large bedchamber located in the corner connecting the two perpendicular wings.

The fourth wing of the building, where they stood, was now taken up by the bank that owned and managed the mansion, and a souvenir store. A staircase led to the upper level, where former bedchambers had been converted to meeting rooms, a small museum, and restrooms.

Above them tiny lightbulbs had been strung from wires draped across the courtyard, casting the trees and the garden area in shadows that flickered with the slight evening breeze.

"Well, look who snuck in," Madge said, pointing to Cody, who had already snagged a beer from the bar and was heading in their direction.

"Professor Claire! Professor Madge," Cody said in a soft-but-urgent tone. He approached them warily. "I've been looking for you. I need to show you something." He pulled a black-and-white composition notebook from his backpack.

"What is it?" Madge asked, her curiosity piqued.

"It's Paul's journal. It has notes in it, and information about professors."

"It sounds like he was preparing for the interview," Madge stated, holding her hand out for the book.

Cody pressed it into Claire's hand instead. "But it's more...you know, with the other...?" He looked askance at Madge. "Please, read it and give it to the detective."

"You should take it to him," Claire said. "If you think it is important, he should see it first."

Cody's tone was conspiratorial. "You should read it first. You'll know what to do."

"This is a police matter," Claire said. "I don't want to be a go-between."

Claire tried to give the book back to him. He pulled his hands away, refusing to take it.

Resigned, Claire placed the notebook in her purse. "I'm not sure you should be here," she said.

"I'm leaving," he said, then turned away from the entrance and into the party.

Madge wandered off to visit friends, and Claire made her way toward the bar. To her right, Brad had just joined George and Eduardo who stood near the parlor, a huge mural of the three Montejo conquistadores looming behind them. George and Eduardo moved apart to allow Brad into their space. The tone of the conversation changed as Eduardo patted Brad on the back, and the three men held up their glasses in a toast. It seemed whatever conflict Tanya had observed between Brad and Eduardo had been resolved.

She watched Jamal approach Tanya, who stood awkwardly near the bar, her eyes darting around the room to settle on the group of men toasting each other. Jamal said something, and she turned toward him, accepting a margarita he offered her. Her hand shook as she reached for the glass, but she took a large gulp, licking salt from the rim. She looked unsteady, and, as Claire watched, Tanya became animated, her eyes widening. She started to speak, but Jamal silenced her by touching her mouth with his finger. She brushed his hand away and spoke, her words drowned out by the cacophony of conversations in the open space.

There is something wrong with Tanya, Claire thought again. Her eyes seemed unfocused and her hands shook, nearly tipping her glass. Claire took a glass of white wine from the bar and moved in their direction.

"Ah, Claire," Jamal said, "Tanya and I are discussing George's lecture." Tanya, who normally expounded at length on any academic topic, stared blankly at Claire. Jamal, noticing Claire's look of concern, asked her, "What did you think of Eduardo's defense of private collections?"

"I think it was very brave of George to give that lecture knowing Eduardo would be here, offering us part of his private collection."

"Brave?" Jamal asked. "Brad said it was inappropriate at best, perhaps even foolish."

Claire shrugged. "I'm sure Eduardo is aware of the academic perspective on private collecting. He's not stupid. In fact, his gift to Keane College is a stroke of brilliance—he can show appreciation to a friend, demonstrate philanthropy, and stifle criticism about the business side of collecting all at the same time."

"Claire, always the cynic." Jamal laughed uneasily, but they both focused on Tanya, who had staggered away from them. Claire followed Tanya to an iron bench near the center of the garden. A small *Flamboyan* tree provided a brilliant umbrella over her.

"Are you okay?" Claire asked.

"I have a headache."

Claire steadied her as they sat together on the bench. Tanya smoothed her sundress over her thin legs and took a sip of her drink. Her eyes met Claire's, and then flitted away, back to the trio of men still standing near the parlor.

"Actually, I'm fine," Tanya said, turning back toward Claire. She gave a wry smile and took a sip of her margarita. Her demeanor suddenly changed, and she looked directly at Claire, who saw that her eyes were dilated. "I think things are looking up for me." She took a gulp of her margarita, spilling some on her dress. She wiped it with her hand. "I've been thinking. I've been wrong about Paul's death."

"What do you mean?"

Tanya spoke softly, glancing over her shoulder. "I think it was an accident...what I said before...you know...I didn't mean to accuse anyone from our group." She wiped perspiration from her hairline with the fingers of one well-manicured hand. She paused, as if remembering something. "There's really nothing suspicious about the backpacks."

"Backpacks?" Claire wondered if Tanya knew about the missing backpack and computer.

"Oh, nothing." Tanya looked over at Jamal, who, Claire noticed, was staring in their direction.

Claire put her hand on Tanya's forehead. "Let me take you back to the hotel."

Tanya shook her head. "It might be over for us," she said.

"What?"

"Me and Jamal," she said impatiently. She looked over her shoulder again. "What is *he* doing here?" Claire turned to see Cody hovering in the corner of the courtyard.

Tanya wiped her brow again, as if trying to remember something. "There's something amiss with that guy." She looked at Claire, as if trying to focus. "Oh, never mind."

Claire stood. "Let's talk later, when you feel better."

"Yes, please go ahead...I'm fine."

Claire wandered toward the group of faculty and students from the University of Yucatán. She had seen these students from time to time in the hotel lobby as they attended the various meetings and lectures. One of them, a young woman with large dark eyes and shoulder-length hair, addressed her.

"Doctor Aguila," she said, reaching into her shoulder bag. She pulled out a copy of Claire's most recent book. "Would you sign your book for me?" she asked.

"I would be honored," Claire said. "What is your name?"

"Marta."

"What do you hope to study?"

"I want to study Mayan women, like you." She paused. "I'm studying Yucatec Maya to prepare."

Claire opened the book and wrote: "*Estimada Marta, Jach ki'imak in wóol in wilikech y Ka xi'ik teech utsil,*" and signed her name.

Marta beamed as she read it aloud: *Dear Marta, I am pleased to meet you and good luck.* "Thank you," she said.

"*Mixba'al,*" Claire said. "You're welcome."

Claire returned to the bar for another glass of wine and visited with colleagues she had not seen for several years. Surprised, she saw that Cody had not left the party. He sat on the bench with Tanya, who held her margarita glass in one hand while her other hand fluttered around her head, like she was trying to catch an idea escaping her mind. She spoke in short muddled bursts. Cody was trying to explain something to her, and then her voice rose in anger.

"I don't believe you!"

Cody jumped up from the bench, and Jamal looked over from his place at the bar. He put his drink down and pushed past the guests toward Tanya.

He took Tanya's arm and lifted her from the bench, taking the empty glass from her hand. He turned to Cody. "What are you doing here?"

CHAPTER TWENTY-SEVEN

The room grew silent as the anthropologists stared at the intruder. Cody blinked and moved away without answering.

Jamal spoke softly to Tanya, but the guests were alert and listening. "Let me take you to the hotel."

"This is *my* night. Leave me alone."

Jamal looked at her closely. "You shouldn't be here."

Tanya smiled and walked away. Jamal placed the margarita glass on a serving tray, filled with empty glasses and plates, and retreated toward the buffet table, pulling his hands through his braids. The onlookers exchanged glances with each other but resumed their conversations as the room took on a less vibrant, more subdued tone.

Claire watched Tanya sway as she made her way to the bar. A tall middle-aged man with a chiseled face and gray hair approached Tanya from behind. He caught her by her bare arm as she nearly lost her balance. She turned to thank him, but her smile disappeared as she pulled her arm away. She said something to him, and he turned away from her, his jaw set, his eyes angry.

Tanya continued to the bar, but Laura intercepted her before she could take another drink from the counter. Laura spoke to the waiter, who handed her a glass of water. She took Tanya's arm with her other hand. Tanya resisted at first, squirming from Laura's light touch, but finally she allowed Laura to lead her out of the courtyard, to the parlor.

Thank you, Laura, thought Claire.

Claire joined Evelyn Nielander at the buffet table and succumbed to a small plate of cheese and tropical fruits.

"What happened?" Evelyn asked.

"I'm not sure," Claire admitted. "I think Tanya has had too much to drink, sorry to say."

Evelyn leaned over the table, placing several wedges of quesadilla on her plate, speaking softly. "My sister has a dependency on prescription drugs. I know what that looks like."

Claire looked at Evelyn. "Are you thinking...?"

"I don't want to disparage Tanya any further than I already have. I feel badly enough telling you about her research in Palenque." She paused again. "I just think you should watch her closely...perhaps talk to her when you get back to Michigan."

Claire looked back toward the parlor. "I'd better check on her now." She put her plate and wine glass down at the end of the buffet table. "Thank you for the warning, Evelyn."

Claire entered the parlor as Madge and George were leaving the room with a group of students, whispering among themselves. Madge paused as Claire stood at the door.

"It's not good, Claire," Madge whispered. She tilted her head back toward the parlor.

Inside, Laura was pacing. "Where's Tanya?" Claire asked.

"In the bedchamber. Jamal went in to check on her."

"Why is she there?" Claire asked.

"I asked the docent...a very nervous man...he allowed her to lie down on the bed." She pressed her lips together. "He wasn't happy, but I think he saw how sick she was. He put a blanket down to protect the bed."

Jamal came out from the bedchamber, his eyes dark. "Brad was in there with her," he said, and slumped into a chair. "He left so we could talk."

"How is she?" Claire asked.

"Determined to stay. I don't know why," Jamal said, shaking his head.

Claire walked past him and into the bedchamber. Heavy velvet curtains blocked the windows, and muted wall tapestries further darkened the room. A narrow band of light from the open door behind her highlighted a set of red velvet chairs positioned at either side of a gold gilt dressing table, and beyond that a tall four-poster bed. Tanya lay on the bed, her eyes closed. She opened them when she heard Claire enter.

"I'm very tired," Tanya said.

"Let me take you to the hotel."

"Why does everyone want me to leave? I just need a short nap."

Claire looked at the water glass. "Have you taken any pills?"

"Pills?"

"Anything?" Claire said.

"No...well, just something for migraine at the hotel. Please let me sleep."

Claire frowned at her. "I'll check on you later."

"It's cold in here," Tanya said, and Claire could see that she was shivering.

Claire saw a large wooden quilt display stand next to the massive dresser. She removed a Mexican blanket from the rack and placed it over Tanya.

"Thanks," Tanya murmured, nearly asleep already. She turned away from Claire and pulled the blanket up to her face.

CHAPTER TWENTY-EIGHT

Exhausted and worried, Claire returned to the atrium. She rested on the bench where Tanya had sat earlier. In a shadowed corner of the courtyard, she saw Brad and Eduardo conversing. They separated; Brad walked past her toward the stairs to the bathrooms and Eduardo turned toward the kitchen behind the bar. Neither acknowledged her. She watched as George and his archaeology friends exited the mansion, engaged in conversation.

"Professor Claire?"

Claire turned to see Cody, staggering slightly behind her.

"I'm sorry I crashed the party," he said, slurring his words.

"But since you did, you should take this with you." Claire motioned to her purse.

He swayed slightly, and Claire thought she might have to catch him. "No. You need to read it." He looked around the courtyard. "Have you seen Doctor Kingsford?"

"Upstairs. Are you sure you want to talk to him? Perhaps tomorrow would be better." She doubted this, but she knew that Brad would not look kindly on an intoxicated party crasher. Cody gave her a wave and staggered toward the stairs. She looked at her watch. Ten minutes had passed. She stood and returned to the parlor where Jamal still sat, his eyes wary, a half-empty beer glass at his feet.

"How's Tanya?" she asked.

"Still sleeping," he said. "I'm trying to stay away until she wakes up so I can take her to the hotel."

Claire opened the bedchamber door to peek in on her colleague. She heard a click and thought she saw the sitting room door close on the other side of the room. Tanya lay still on her back.

"Where was George going with his friends?" she asked Jamal when she returned to the parlor.

"Don't know. They came in to check on Tanya. One of them got a phone call, and they all left the room…The Three Musketeers. I haven't seen Madge."

Claire left Jamal at his vigil and returned to the atrium where she met Madge, who also had come to check on their colleague.

"Have you seen Tanya?" Madge asked.

"She's sleeping."

Madge looked toward the parlor door. "I'm looking for Brad. I need to tell him about that dagger."

"I saw him go upstairs. You'll have to get in line behind Cody."

"He's still here?" Madge said. "Brad won't be happy. I have to use the little girls' room, so I'll be the referee."

As Claire watched her friend trudge up the stairs, she felt a hand on her elbow. She turned to find Eduardo Ramirez standing behind her.

"Good evening, Doctor Aguila."

It seemed odd that she had not yet spoken to him, but so much had happened in the past few days, the ordinary activity of meet-and-greet had fallen to the wayside.

Claire smiled at her host. "The reception is lovely, Eduardo. Given the tragic circumstances, we all need a reprieve, to be sure." She thought briefly of mentioning her intoxicated friend asleep on sixteenth-century furniture but decided against it.

Eduardo bowed and focused his dark eyes on her. "I am so sorry to hear about Mr. Sturgess." He motioned to the entrance of the Casa Montejo. "I desperately need a cigarette. Will you join me for some air?"

He took her elbow and led her outside, directing her to sit with him on a wrought-iron bench tucked up against the stone wall of the mansion. He drew a cigarette from a small container and offered her one. Claire declined, but stared at the gold cigarette case. She had no idea that people still used them. He lit his cigarette with a gold lighter, engraved with his initials, and slipped both items into his jacket pocket. In the distance, across the road and in the plaza, she saw George standing with the Professors Perez and Gonzalez, cigarette smoke encircling their heads.

Claire said, "I haven't had the chance to thank you for your generosity."

"It's the least I can do for my friend and his friends." He paused and smiled. "I understand we are similar...you and I...both bicultural...and a little lost in two cultures."

"Perhaps we are 'found' in two cultures?" she said.

"Ah, that's what I hoped you would say." He paused, "I want to talk to you about something." He inhaled deeply. "I would like to offer you a job."

Claire suddenly felt uncomfortable. "I have a job."

He laughed and small creases appeared along the edges of his eyes. He was very handsome when he smiled. "Yes, but I think you might be interested in this one." She shifted slightly on the bench to avoid the cigarette smoke that blew toward her in the evening breeze. "I am looking for a bilingual researcher, someone who knows Mexicans and Mexican culture and can maneuver between the United States and Mexico flawlessly. I think you are that person." He paused to inhale. "You would be the perfect director for the Provenance Project I mentioned in my lecture, overseeing the research on my family's collections."

"I plan to retire in a few years, not start a new career," Claire said. "Besides, I'm not an archaeologist or curator. I am an ethnographer—I study living people, not artifacts." She continued to think of objections. "My parents and daughter are in the United States. I have no desire to leave my country."

"But, consider, Claire. The northern winters are brutal. You could work in Texas and Mexico City, or even Merida. You could do your field research here in the winter and computer research in Michigan during the warm months. You could write your ticket."

"Why me?" she asked. "There are hundreds of students graduating from museum programs every year, dying for a position like this."

"Not with your experience and background." He dropped his cigarette on the ground and crushed it with a shiny black wingtip shoe. "I have been learning about you from others. You are a person with integrity."

Claire shook her head. "I'm sorry, but I don't think I would be interested in changing careers at this stage of my life."

Eduardo tipped his hand in a gesture that reminded her of Roberto Salinas. *I could live in Merida,* she thought.

He continued, "Just think, no more teaching introductory anthropology classes to undergraduates who took your class to fulfill core requirements, no more department meetings, living on the academic calendar, and," he stressed, "you would have a significant increase in salary."

"I'm very flattered at your offer, Eduardo. I'll think about it, but I seriously doubt that I'll accept it."

"That's all I expect from you now. You have a lot to think about." He reached into an inside pocket and pulled out a business card, handing it to her. "I would love to work with you."

He stood and took her elbow to help her up. She accepted the card and stuffed it into her purse. He extracted another cigarette from his case, ending the interview.

She thanked him, though she didn't know why, and watched Eduardo walk along the street away from the central plaza. As she pulled on the massive door leading back into the mansion, a large group of students pushed the door from the other side. She noticed that Cody was part of this mass exodus. *Finally,* she thought.

Inside, Claire looked upward toward the balcony, and saw Madge making her way slowly down the stairs. Laura was making long strides toward Claire.

"I've been looking for you!" She whispered to Claire. "You have to come! I've called the ambulance."

Claire turned to Madge, who had finished her descent and sensed the emergency. She followed Claire and Laura as they hurried toward the parlor. Inside, Jamal stood at the bedchamber door, his hands gripping the ancient knob, his eyes wide.

Laura took Jamal's arm and led him to a chair, directing him to sit. She and Claire entered through the mahogany door, their eyes adjusting slowly to the darkened room. Tanya Petersen lay peacefully on her back, like a queen in her bedchamber, eyes closed, blonde hair falling around her head like a halo. She was still covered by the beautifully woven Mexican blanket. But she lay too still. She was too pale.

Madge entered the room, panting. She looked at Tanya. "Someone covered her up."

"I did," Claire admitted.

Claire looked closely at Tanya, then to Laura. She didn't have the strength to look at Madge. Laura touched Tanya's forehead, her neck. There was a bulge under the blanket, and Laura folded it down, over her chest. Madge looked at Claire, her eyes wide, her face drained of color. Laura covered her again, quickly. Before they could react, an ambulance siren shattered the air.

CHAPTER TWENTY-NINE

The bedchamber door opened, and two paramedics rushed into the small room, followed by the docent, his eyes wide, his mouth opening and closing like a puppet's. The docent closed the door behind him and gaped at the woman on the bed.

Claire, Madge, and Laura turned and stared at the medics, unable to speak. The older man moved Claire aside and uncovered Tanya's body. The medics looked at each other, then at the women who had found her body.

The dagger was lodged deep into Tanya's chest, at an odd angle. Her hands cupped the handle. Blood had seeped from the wound and settled into a puddle under her hands. Not much blood, but enough for Claire and Madge to gasp as the medic stood aside for the photographer. Tanya's purse lay open next to her body.

The younger man, his assistant, addressed the women in Spanish. "Who called us?" he asked.

"I did," Laura responded, studying the wound while Claire and Madge turned their heads.

"Why didn't you call the police?" he asked.

"I didn't know about this…" Laura said, indicating the replica ceremonial dagger buried in Tanya's chest.

The assistant turned to the docent. "*Señor*, did you know she was here?"

The small man leaned against the door. "She was just sleeping," he whimpered.

The medic pulled a phone from his pocket and called the police. When he rang off, he noticed the second entrance to the bedchamber.

"What's this door?"

"It goes to the sitting room," the docent stammered. "I brought you through the parlor because there are fewer people there."

144

The assistant pointed toward the sitting room door. "*Señor*, guard that door. Don't let anyone enter." The docent nodded and left, closing the sitting room door behind him. The assistant then directed the women to leave by the parlor door. "And stay until the police come."

They nodded and left the bedchamber, finding that George had joined Jamal in the parlor.

Jamal, his eyes wide, spoke first. "Is she okay? They wouldn't let us in."

Madge went to Jamal and took his hands in hers. "She's dead, Jamal."

"No! That can't be!" Jamal moaned. "Dead?"

Claire collapsed into a chair, her hands clasped in her lap. "We have to stay here until the police come." She looked to Madge as tears began to flow freely, and she could no longer speak.

Madge said, "She was stabbed with…" She couldn't say the word. The guilt was hers to bear.

"Stabbed?" said Jamal, standing and taking two long strides toward the bedchamber door.

Laura intercepted Jamal and guided him back to the chair. Jamal sat obediently, in shock.

"Stabbed?" repeated George. He stared at Claire and Madge, both wiping their eyes with their hands. But before they could respond, Brad stormed into the parlor from the atrium.

"What happened?" Brad looked at the stunned faces. "Why is the ambulance here?" He stood, eyes wide, then looked toward the closed bedchamber door. "Tanya?"

Madge spoke. "She's dead, Brad."

"But she was just sick," he pleaded.

"She may have been sick, but someone stabbed her," George said, leaning back in the chair, his hands shaking.

"Jesus," Brad leaned heavily against the wall. "Murdered?"

Claire sighed heavily to regain control and repeated their discovery. "She was stabbed with the sacrificial dagger." Claire placed her fingers on the soft area between her ribs. She began to sob again.

George looked at Claire. "The stolen dagger?" Brad and George stared at Claire, who nodded.

"It can't be," Brad said, incredulous. "Madge just told me about it." He collapsed against the wall. "I don't believe it."

CHAPTER THIRTY

The group waited in the parlor, Madge, Claire, and Jamal weeping and the others sitting in stunned silence. Moments later, they heard commotion in the courtyard as an accented voice requested that everyone stay within the walls of the mansion. Exclamations arose as the news of a death floated around the courtyard.

When Sergeant Juarez entered the parlor, Claire felt a sense of relief. Visions of Juarez and Chan leading Cody away to the police station seemed distant now. She no longer feared them.

Juarez scanned the room, taking in the grief-stricken and shocked faces surrounding him. He reintroduced himself and gave Claire a slight nod. "Can someone tell me what happened?"

Brad and George started talking at the same time. George gave Brad his department chair stare, and Brad stood back.

George pointed to the closed door. "Professor Tanya Petersen is dead. She is in the bedchamber with the medics."

Juarez opened the bedchamber door and turned to the group. "Please, stay here."

When the door closed, Jamal paced the room, wiping his eyes with the hem of his shirt. "I thought she was drunk…but the dagger? I don't understand." He choked, "While I sat here, in this room…she was dying in there." He pointed to the door. "Six feet away, we let her die."

George said, "But she was stabbed, Jamal. We don't know when that happened."

The bedchamber door opened, and Eduardo Ramirez stormed into the parlor, his eyes hard and his jaw tight. The docent followed in his wake, his hands tightly clutched as if in prayer. Eduardo stopped abruptly when he realized he had an audience. The anthropologists turned toward the two men expectantly.

"Did you talk to the sergeant?" George asked Eduardo.

"He demanded that we leave," Eduardo said, his anger palpable.

Beside him, the docent rubbed his hands together and spoke to Eduardo in Spanish. "I'm sorry, *Señor.* She seemed so sick. I thought it was okay." He looked to the anthropologists, as if for sympathy.

Eduardo looked down at him. "You had orders not to allow anyone to touch the antiques, and you let someone sleep on the bed?"

He pointed at Laura. "She asked so nicely, and the young lady…she looked so sick."

Eduardo raised his hand to dismiss the docent, who moved back a few steps as if expecting to be slapped.

George stood quickly. "He had no choice," he said. "We thought you knew she was there."

"We all thought she had too much to drink," Madge said. "Please don't blame Mr…"

"Freddie," said the docent, giving her a grateful smile.

"Please don't blame Freddie," Madge continued.

Eduardo's demeanor softened. He glanced briefly at Claire. "I'm sorry about your friend. I knew she was ill, but I didn't know she was in the bedchamber." He straightened his tie. "However, I understand that she was stabbed? I don't understand how that happened."

Sergeant Juarez re-entered the parlor, followed by the medics, who silently exited into the courtyard. Juarez stood in front of the fireplace.

"I am very sorry for the loss of your colleague," the sergeant said. "I know you have questions, but I'm afraid I can't answer them. Detective Salinas and his team will be here directly. In the meantime, he has asked that I identify those in the room when Miss Petersen was found." He turned a page in his small notebook. "Please introduce yourselves."

George listed himself and his colleagues. Laura introduced herself and explained how she had called the ambulance because she was worried about Tanya. "Professors Carmichael and Aguila entered the bedchamber with me and we found her," Laura said.

"Were you all here when she was found?"

"All but Professor Kingsford," George said.

Juarez addressed Brad. "I am sorry, but I must ask you to leave for now," Juarez said. "And please, don't talk to anyone about this."

"But..." Brad began.

"If you don't mind," Juarez said, "could you stand outside the door until the detective arrives? That would be very helpful."

Brad squared his shoulders, nodded briefly and left the room.

Juarez turned to Eduardo, who stood quietly against the wall, his jaw tense. "*Señor* Ramirez, were you in the room when the body was found?"

"No, but I am the host of the event."

Juarez looked at the docent, who hovered in the corner. In Spanish he asked, "What is your name, *Señor*?"

"Frederico Flores," he said. He came out from the corner and began to pace nervously, explaining in rapid-fire Spanish, "I was in the sitting room...keeping people from putting their glasses on the tables...I just let the lady lay on the bed to rest...I put a blanket down first..." He looked toward Eduardo, whose face contorted.

"Who brought Miss Petersen into the room?" Juarez asked.

"I did," said Laura. "It was about seven forty-five, I think."

Something bothered Claire, but she couldn't put her finger on it. She stared at Laura, trying to remember.

Juarez turned to Freddy. "You can leave now. Can you arrange for the staff to make coffee? Also, no more alcohol, and please, say nothing." Freddy left, but Eduardo remained, leaning against the wall.

Juarez said, "*Señor* Ramirez, you may leave and tend to your guests. Thank you for your time." Eduardo frowned and narrowed his eyes, but he followed the docent from the room.

When Ramirez and Freddy had left, Sergeant Juarez studied the five remaining guests. Claire and Madge sat, holding hands, their eyes red and swollen; Laura stood at the fireplace, deep in thought. George leaned forward in the largest chair in the room, staring at the floor, and Jamal paced like a zoo animal, his eyes reddened.

Juarez addressed the women. "Please describe what you saw when you went into the bedchamber. Be specific."

Claire explained how she had covered Tanya with the blanket earlier. "She was still covered when we found her. We folded the blanket down and saw…" Claire choked. She closed her eyes and clenched her fists in her lap.

Laura continued for her. "The dagger was stuck into her chest like this." She clenched her fist under her chest to show the angle of the dagger, not perpendicular, but upward, under the ribcage.

"Anything else?"

Claire's head came up suddenly. "The water glass."

"Water glass?" Juarez asked.

Claire turned to Laura. "You took a water glass in with her," she said. "Is it there?"

Juarez nodded to Laura who crossed to the bedchamber, entered and returned, shaking her head. "It's not there."

"Did she take any pills with it?" Claire asked.

"Not when I was with her," Laura answered.

"What do we do now?" George asked.

Juarez checked his watch. "We wait for the detectives. Please remain here. If you need to move around or use the restrooms, you may do so, but please don't talk to others."

Juarez left the room, and the group sat quietly, listening as the sergeant spoke to the guests in the courtyard. Exhausted, the imprisoned KC faculty were left with their grief. Claire sat with her elbows on her knees, her fingers clasping her necklace. Madge and George stared at each other from across the room. Laura wrote in a small notebook she had taken from her purse. Jamal paced back and forth between the bedchamber and the fireplace.

The silence was broken when Brad entered the room. "I convinced the sergeant that I should be with the faculty," he said, leaning against the wall. "Will someone tell me what happened? Am I the only person who didn't know about the dagger until tonight?" He moved away from the wall and sat on a folding chair. His gaze moved from person to person, his eyes piercing.

George turned to Brad. "Claire told me it was missing. It's my fault the police didn't get called."

"I didn't know about it either," Jamal protested. He sat in one of the chairs and clenched his hands in his lap. "Are you sure it's the same dagger?" he asked.

Madge nodded. "I used it in a class demonstration last week…I'll never use it again." She sniffled into a soggy tissue.

Jamal, tears coming to him again, said, "She was sick."

George turned to Jamal. "It's time you told us about Tanya."

Jamal lowered his voice, "I think she was taking oxycodone. She injured her back in a car accident in graduate school, and it was prescribed to her. She had been dependent on it for a while but told me she was through with it…but I guess…I think…she might have started up again." Jamal looked at his colleagues, who wore a variety of expressions: disbelief in Madge, scorn in George, pensiveness in Brad, and concern in Claire.

"And then she was drinking," Jamal continued. "I should have helped her instead of badgering her about it. I…how could this happen?" He rubbed his nose on his sleeve. "I should have taken her back to the hotel."

"*I* should have," insisted Claire. "I knew she was sick, but she was determined to be here. I don't know why."

Brad said, "She was talking nonsense tonight."

"Well, if there is blame, I share some." George aimed dark eyes at Brad. "She seemed agitated at the hotel. I should have insisted that she rest there, but, as Claire said, she wanted to come."

"Don't look at me, George," Brad said in a harsh whisper. "I almost had her convinced, but then you came, and suddenly she changed her mind."

Jamal looked up in surprise and glared at Brad. "You were in her room? When?"

"I checked on her to see if she was okay," Brad explained. "You saw that she acted odd at dinner." He paused and looked at George, then brought his hand to his mouth. "In fact, she took a pain pill, for migraine she said. Right, George?"

Jamal glared at Brad, then George, who nodded. Jamal opened his mouth to say more, but instead he looked away, tightened his jaw and clenched his fists.

George pushed his glasses up his nose. "But the fact remains that she was stabbed. If she didn't do it herself, someone wanted her dead."

CHAPTER THIRTY-ONE

Sergeant Juarez peeked into the parlor and directed the Keane College faculty to the atrium. Detective Salinas and Sergeant Garza were speaking with two uniformed officers and the crime scene technicians, two men with black satchels and a woman with a camera slung over her shoulder. George's group found chairs and huddled toward the edge of the courtyard near the stairway as the technicians disappeared into the parlor, led by Garza.

To Claire, Salinas looked as if he might have been called from a date. He wore khaki slacks, loafers, and a lime green *guayabera* embroidered with colorful tropical birds. She envisioned a woman sitting in a restaurant wondering what happened to her romantic evening.

In contrast, Garza wore the same clothing she had worn on earlier occasions, black slacks and a white blouse, but tonight she had not bothered to wrap her hair up in a bun. Instead she had pulled it into a long thick black ponytail, tied at the nape of her neck.

Salinas surveyed the crowd, his eyes pausing momentarily when they met Claire's.

"Good evening," he said. "I'm very sorry to report that there has been a death here tonight...Professor Tanya Petersen. I cannot give you any further information at this time, but because of the nature of her death, we will need to interview you all. I'm afraid we have a long night ahead of us. Unfortunately, the sitting room and the parlor are no longer available to you. Please leave your name with Officer Morales before you wander to other areas of the mansion, so that we don't forget any of you."

He pointed to a hefty policeman with dark curly hair and thick mustache, and continued, "Once I learn the details of Doctor Petersen's death, I will begin my interviews." Amid groans and whispers, Salinas and Juarez retreated through the door to the parlor, leaving Chan and the other officers behind with the guests.

"Are you ready?" Salinas looked at Garza.

She nodded slowly and followed Salinas and Juarez into the bedchamber where the crime team had changed into white scrubs, shoes, head covers, and gloves. The medical examiner stood at the bed, the technician looking over his shoulder. The photographer was documenting the area around the bed.

Garza opened her notepad as Salinas spoke to the medical examiner, Dr. Hernandez, a tall man with gray hair and narrow brown eyes.

Doctor Hernandez introduced his team and then asked, "Can you identify the victim?"

Salinas nodded. "It's Professor Tanya Petersen. Can you tell me anything?"

"Her purse contained an empty prescription bottle, unlabeled, but with tablet residue. I suspect drugs were involved, and probably alcohol."

Salinas looked on as the doctor examined the dagger wound.

"I think this is very strange," Doctor Hernandez said. He moved so Salinas could look at Tanya's hands curled around the dagger.

"Is this how the body was found?" Salinas asked Sergeant Juarez.

"Yes, except that blanket there…" Juarez pointed to the blanket that was now folded down over Tanya's feet, "was on top of the dagger and covering her to the neck."

"Do you have a time of death?" Salinas asked Doctor Hernandez.

"With the information I have now, less than an hour, but there is something else interesting." The doctor indicated the area around the wound.

"Yes," said Salinas. "I see."

Rosa Garza looked at the body, then up at her boss, waiting for him to expand. Instead he said, "Let's go back to the parlor." To the doctor he said, "Thank you. We can talk later."

Garza, Juarez, and Salinas returned to the parlor, and pulled chairs together so they could talk quietly. Garza recorded Juarez's report. When he had finished, Salinas sat back in his chair.

"Professors Aguila and Carmichael found the body?" he asked, giving a quick glance toward his sergeant.

"And Ms. Lorenzo," Juarez said. "She called the ambulance and brought the two professors into the room to check on her."

Juarez removed his hat and scratched his head. "Do you think it was a suicide?"

"I doubt it very much," Salinas said, "but someone wanted us to think it might be."

"Do you think it's related to Paul Sturgess?" Garza asked.

"Time will tell, Rosa," Salinas said. "Let's keep the two deaths separate for now."

"There are two problems that I see, Detective," Juarez said.

"Go on."

"First is the second blanket. Professor Aguila admitted she covered Miss Petersen with the second blanket just after she had lain down on the bed. That means that she might have been stabbed at any time during the evening, and no one who looked in to see her would know."

Salinas nodded. "Second?"

"Second, Professor Aguila said that Miss Lorenzo had taken a glass of water into the room and she said it was still there when she checked on her later, yet it is not there now." He sat back, satisfied with his report.

Salinas interrupted him, "And third...?"

"Third?" Juarez said.

"Yes, the doctor referred to it just now." Salinas joined the fingertips of both hands forming a tent in front of his face, the index fingers touching his mouth. "Third, there is very little blood around the wound." Salinas turned to his detective sergeant. "What does it mean, Sergeant Garza?"

Garza threw her boss a quick look of appreciation for the opportunity to share her knowledge. "It means she was dead, or very nearly so, when she was stabbed."

CHAPTER THIRTY-TWO

George, Madge, Jamal, and Brad collected folding chairs and placed them in a small circle at the corner of the courtyard. They sat quietly, too exhausted to speak. Guests, including Laura and Evelyn Nielander, visited their circle to offer condolences, but wandered off, not knowing what else to say. When Claire saw Eduardo come their way, she stood.

"I can't take this," she said, tense with fatigue and nerves. "I'm going upstairs."

"Do you want me to come with you?" Madge asked.

"No, please. I need to be alone for a few minutes."

Claire left her name with Officer Morales and climbed the stairs to the restroom. Afterwards, she drifted through small groups of guests. Those who knew her approached with condolences. She could do no more than nod in return. She peeked into a small museum of colonial artifacts where several students had congregated. She backed out quickly before they noticed her.

Finally, Claire discovered a tiny room, empty except for scattered metal tables and chairs. She moved a chair to the window, opened the tall wooden shutters, and looked out over the plaza. The street was strangely quiet, a string of police cars and the crime-scene SUV lined up along the curb. She removed her purse from her shoulder and placed it on her lap. She closed her eyes, trying to take her mind off the contraband she possessed, but a desire to think of anything other than Tanya's death took over. She extracted Paul's notebook and her reading glasses from her purse and began to flip through the pages. She knew Salinas should be reading it, not her, but her curiosity overcame her conscience, and she started to skim.

The format resembled a field notebook that all anthropologists carry with them to take notes and record ethnographic details. But this notebook focused on other anthropologists, not ethnographic data. As

Madge suggested, most of the entries entailed questions or comments consistent with notes a job applicant might want to pursue. She did not see a page dedicated to her own research, but he had scratched a short notation to the top of a new page: LL—credentials. But there was also more.

Claire heard heavy footsteps in the hallway. She closed the book quickly but recognized the hesitant clomp-clomp of Madge's Birkenstocks. Claire crossed the room and opened the door a crack.

"Madge," Claire said softly. "I'm here."

Madge hurried along the hall and entered, closing the door behind her. Claire took another chair to the balcony window. They both breathed in the night air: cool, fresh, and free of the exhaust fumes that lay so heavy over the city during the day.

"How are you holding up?" Madge said, settling into the chair and dropping her bag at her feet.

"Terrible," Claire said. "Poor Tanya."

"Yes, indeed," Madge said. She pointed to the notebook. "I see you're examining the evidence. What's in it?"

"Random notes on our faculty and research sites."

"Really?" Madge said, grabbing at the book. "What's in it about me?"

Claire, torn between grief and curiosity, handed her the notebook. Madge flipped through to her page.

"My research sites," she said, then her eyes fell on a comment: "'The Margaret Mead of Archaeology.' That little shit," Madge said. "Sorry to say that about the dead…" she added quickly. "Just because Mead and I both had three husbands…lots of people have a few missteps along the way."

Claire smiled. "You've never told me your story. I'm sure it would cheer me up."

"I'm sure it would, my dear." She turned pages, pausing to glance at entries. "He wanted to know about Brad's research site, Tixbe, and he wrote the initials BS and ER…Eduardo?"

"Perhaps," agreed Claire. "Nothing really earth-shattering."

Madge turned a page and read, "'Jamal, research site Dzib.' Paul wanted to talk to a shaman, and wondered if Jamal knew someone with the initials BS." She paused. "Who's BS?"

"No idea," said Claire, staring down at the central plaza where the streetlights cast shadows on the sidewalk. A group of young Mexican adults, dressed in nightclub clothes—low-cut dresses and spike heels, men in western slacks, sharply creased, and button-down shirts, with the top three buttons undone—passed by the cathedral. Claire could hear them commenting on the police vehicles along the street.

"Watch out, Jorge," one of the young men teased the other. "Hide your drugs."

"*Cállate*, shut up," the other young man said, laughing.

Their youthful exuberance reminded her of her first visit to Merida when she was their age: strolling the dark streets, laughing in the night air, and being in love.

"Did you see this?" Madge was saying.

"What?" Claire said, bringing her attention back to her friend.

"He listed Tanya's research at Palenque, and someone with the initials TF. Who's that?"

Claire remembered the conversation she had with Evelyn Nielander. She looked at Madge, frowned and pressed her lips together.

"I know that look, Claire," Madge said. "It's the 'I want to tell you but shouldn't' look."

"I don't know TF," Claire said, "but Evelyn told me something last night after dinner, when you and Tanya went to the restroom."

"You two got suddenly quiet when we joined you," Madge remembered.

"She told me a rumor about Tanya…she wasn't sure it was Tanya… but the facts were consistent with the story Tanya told us about her research with the hieroglyphs and the affair with a professor she so foolishly admitted to. Evelyn heard that the professor in question turned up on her dissertation committee."

"Was that professor TF?"

"Maybe."

Madge shook her head. "Dear me," Madge said, returning to the notebook. She turned to George's page. "Just a list of his research sites," she said, turning the page.

Claire said, "I notice that you and George worked on several sites together—Uaxactún and Yaxhá."

"We met at Uaxactún."

Madge leafed through a few more pages. "Interesting. There's no page for you, but there's a cryptic note about Laura…he didn't waste any time before researching her."

"But Madge, he didn't have this with him at Uxmal," Claire said. "It would have been stolen with his computer. That means he made this entry before he met her on Sunday."

"He knew she was applying for the job and researched her?"

Claire remembered Tanya's accusation that someone, also claiming to be from KC, had called Laura's university for her credentials.

"Look," Madge said. "There are a few pages torn out, very close to the binding."

Claire looked over at the notebook on Madge's lap. "Hmm," she said. "I hadn't noticed."

A square, blue sticky note stuck up from a page near the back of the notebook. Madge turned to the marker and found several pages of drawings, crude sketches of Mayan artifacts—bowls, statues, and weapons.

Claire tipped the notebook so she could look. "Are those drawings of originals or replicas?"

"Originals, I think," said Madge. "See, the drawings include chips and cracks. Tourist replicas are perfect molds."

One piece drew Claire's attention. She turned the page back toward Madge. Madge looked at it carefully, adjusting her bifocals to get the details.

"This is it, isn't it?" Claire asked.

The drawing, though rough, was a fair representation of the jade corn god statue Eduardo had presented to Brad. Claire had seen the original in Eduardo's catalogue.

"Did he know Eduardo planned to present this to Brad?" Claire asked.

"How could he? He died before Eduardo presented it."

An officer called the guests back to the atrium. Slowly, people returned to the open area, weary and rumpled. The evening breeze brought a chill into the courtyard. The lighting along the edge of the courtyard dimmed but did not obliterate the stars above the guests.

When Madge and Claire returned downstairs, the atmosphere of the mansion had quieted markedly as the effects of alcohol wore off and fatigue grew. Most people spoke in quiet tones as they sat in small groups or lined up for coffee. Madge and Claire joined the coffee line, then returned to their group.

"I can't get past the idea of the dagger," Madge said to the group as she sat heavily on a chair, interrupting their conversation.

Brad sighed as he removed the rubber band from his ponytail and let his hair fall to his shoulders. "You said that she had her hand around the dagger...I thought..."

"Suicide?" Jamal said. "Impossible."

"But if she hadn't been drinking...or overdosed...or whatever, she could have fought back, or screamed. We heard nothing."

Claire's cup clanked on her saucer as she nearly dropped it. "Someone knew she was sick and couldn't fight back...someone who happened to have a reason to kill her...and who happened to have *the* dagger handy...that's impossible!"

"But who would do such a horrific thing?" Madge protested.

"It couldn't have been any of us," Brad said.

CHAPTER THIRTY-THREE

After a few minutes, Detective Salinas and Sergeant Garza emerged from the parlor. The guests became suddenly alert as Salinas addressed them. "Because of the time, and the number of people here," Salinas said, "I have requested that Sergeant Juarez and Deputy Chan assist me. They will conduct interviews in the sitting room. With your help, we can finish these interviews efficiently." He paused to survey his captive audience, ignoring the deep sighs and mumblings around him.

"Unfortunately, I have to request your passports. If you have them with you, we will collect them before you leave. Otherwise, please give them to the hotel clerk tonight at the hotel after the interviews. With everyone's cooperation, you should have them back before the end of the conference."

The guests became more restive, some women rustling in their bags, others shrugging their shoulders or whispering to their neighbors.

Salinas turned to Claire's group. "I would like to talk to Doctor Aguila."

Claire stood, self-conscious at being chosen first. As she moved toward the parlor, she heard Sergeant Juarez call the name of an anthropologist she knew from Michigan State University. She felt sure that Detective Salinas would be keeping the Keane College faculty for himself.

Claire followed Salinas and Sergeant Garza into the parlor. Folding chairs and a small serving table had been moved into the room for his use. The detective sat at the table and Garza sat off to the side, her notebook in her lap.

Salinas directed Claire to sit across from him. "Good evening, Doctor Aguila." He smiled, and then turned to his sergeant. "Do you remember Sergeant Garza?"

"Yes, of course," Claire said, forcing a smile at the sergeant. Claire wondered if Salinas had told her about their history, but the sergeant's face remained unreadable.

Salinas said, "We will conduct the interview in English, but please speak clearly so Sergeant Garza can get it all down." Garza threw her boss a sharp glance but covered it quickly when he looked at her. Salinas added in appeasement, "Her English is excellent, but note-taking is difficult."

Claire nodded and smiled at Garza, whose approval, for some reason, she desired. Claire sat back in her chair, placed her purse on the floor, and folded her shaking hands in her lap.

Salinas asked Claire to describe the evening and events leading up to the reception. When Claire told him about her dinner with Madge, he asked, "Why didn't Doctor Petersen go to dinner with you and Doctor Carmichael?"

"She said she had a headache and wanted to rest before the reception."

"When you saw Tanya at the reception, how did she seem?"

"She looked pale and unsteady. When we talked, she was incoherent, saying things were looking up for her, something about Paul's death being an accident, and something about how the backpacks didn't mean anything."

Claire realized that her knuckles had turned white from the pressure of her clasped hands. She tried to relax them in her lap. "I offered to take her back to the hotel, but she said she wanted to rest. I thought she might be intoxicated."

"Was she drinking?"

"Jamal gave her a margarita. Other than that, I don't know." Claire paused to think. "She also admitted she had been silly to question us about Paul."

The detective immediately straightened in his chair. "When did she do this?"

Claire remembered she hadn't told him this. "At breakfast after Paul died, Tanya asked us when we had talked to Paul and what we talked about. It was a stupid game of 'Who saw him last?'"

Sergeant Garza cleared her throat, and Salinas paused to give her time to catch up. After a moment, he continued. "Was your entire group there?"

"Yes, but nobody took her seriously."

"Did you?" His countenance turned serious. His eyebrows furrowed, and his eyes narrowed.

"Not at that time. Later…" She paused, not knowing if Salinas had shared their private conversation at El Caracol with his sergeant.

"Sergeant Garza knows that you have shared the photographs and other pertinent facts with me. You can go on." He paused, his eyes burrowing into hers. "Later…" he prompted.

"When I heard about the computer and looked at the photographs," Claire said, "I began to think that Tanya might have been right. Maybe there was something unusual about Paul's death."

"Yet, you didn't mention this breakfast interrogation to me earlier?"

Claire clenched her fists. "I forgot. I'm sorry." She silently chastised herself for allowing Salinas to flatter and manipulate her with wine and quesadillas. He was clearly only interested in what she could tell him.

Salinas frowned. "Can you tell me now, please? How did the others react to her so-called game?"

"Madge played along, Jamal and Brad downplayed their interactions with him and criticized her for insensitivity, and George refused to say. He left in disgust at the whole conversation."

"This was before Cody joined you and my officers came to pick him up?"

"Yes. Jamal and Brad left after hearing Cody's story of what happened that night. Is this important?"

"We know that someone from your group went into Cody's room yesterday morning, looking for something."

"That's impossible," Claire said. "Everyone was at breakfast." She clutched her necklace as she thought. "Besides, the computer was stolen Sunday night at Uxmal."

"But nobody knew that except Cody and you."

"Who was it?" Claire asked.

"You know I can't tell you that." He paused. "I understand that Ms. Lorenzo took Tanya to the bedchamber around seven forty-five. When did you see her?"

Claire sat back in her chair, concentrating. "I went in just after Laura came out of the bedchamber. Madge and George had left with a group of students. Jamal had gone in to see her and I went in after Jamal." She paused to remember. "Jamal said Brad had also been there. He must have entered from the sitting room."

"Was Brad still there when you entered?"

"No. I offered to take Tanya to the hotel, but she refused. She said she needed a nap. I covered her up with a blanket—probably worth thousands of pesos—then left her alone."

"Tell me about the water glass."

"Laura took a water glass into the room. I asked Tanya if she had taken any pills and she said she had taken something for a migraine earlier that evening. Later...after we found her...I realized the glass was gone."

"Why did you ask about pills?"

"It was something someone said to me tonight...that Tanya had acted like she was on drugs. I wondered if that might explain her behavior."

"Did you check on Tanya after that?"

"I peeked in around eight-fifteen. I didn't want to wake her, so I left, but when I entered, I had a sense that someone had just left through the sitting room door."

"But you saw no one?"

"No, just a sound of the door closing. It might have been my imagination."

Salinas jotted in his notebook. "What time did you realize she had died?"

"About eight-thirty. Laura found me in the atrium. She had called an ambulance and asked me to go with her to the bedchamber. Madge followed us. Jamal had just come out of the bedchamber, so we knew it was bad news."

"Can you tell me anything about the dagger? It is not the kind of item that people might carry with them to a reception."

Claire explained how she and Madge discovered the dagger missing, and their negligence in reporting to the police.

Salinas said, "I assume you know the significance of the dagger?"

"Do you mean that her death was somehow symbolic?" Claire sat back, thinking. "How could someone steal the dagger with the intention of using it tonight, without knowing if there would be an opportunity?"

Salinas shrugged. "It does seem unlikely, yet…"

Claire interrupted him, "Both Paul and Tanya's deaths replicated Mayan sacrifices."

Salinas raised his eyebrows and referred to his notes. "Let's go back to the reception. After you spoke with Tanya, did you see anyone else approach her?"

"I was socializing, so not paying much attention."

"Do the best you can."

"Jamal offered her the margarita and I joined them, as I already said. She acted strangely but wanted to stay. I think Laura talked to her. It seems she stood near Tanya at one point and then…¡Mierda!"

Sergeant Garza looked up quickly, then put her head down to write. Salinas raised his eyebrows and gave her a half-smile.

"Yes?"

"Cody talked to her."

Salinas's brow furrowed, and he exchanged a confused expression with his sergeant. "Mr. Detwyler was here?"

Claire sighed deeply and recounted how he had attended the party uninvited and had spoken with Tanya. "I could hear Tanya's voice above the surrounding conversations. She yelled that she didn't believe him, or something like that, then turned pale and swayed like she might fall. Cody just stood there, dazed, then Jamal rushed over to her."

Garza raised her hand, and Claire stopped so she could catch up. This gave Claire a few moments to remember the scene.

Claire continued, "Cody walked away, and then Jamal had a few words with Tanya. She waved Jamal away, then walked toward the bar. Then someone came up to her...a tall man, fifty-ish, with gray hair. They spoke, and then she sent him away too. She said something to him that I didn't hear."

"It seems she was having a terrible time," Salinas suggested. "I wonder why she stayed."

Claire shrugged, her body relaxing as the details came back to her. "After that, Laura approached Tanya as she reached for another margarita from the bar. Laura took the drink from her, asked the bartender for a glass of water, and coaxed Tanya toward the parlor."

"Is this man—the one who spoke with her at the bar—still here?"

"I haven't seen him since that happened."

Salinas looked at his scribbled notes and reviewed them aloud, while Sergeant Garza caught up with her more detailed transcription. "So, between seven-forty-five when you first checked on her and eight-thirty, someone entered the room, stabbed her and re-covered her body."

Claire stared at Salinas. "I can't imagine who would have the dagger and even think of such a thing, let alone be able to take advantage of the opportunity in such a short period of time."

"Exactly," Salinas agreed, sitting back in his chair. "What did you do during the evening?"

He spoke so softly that it took a few moments to register that he was asking for her alibi.

"I...I talked to students and friends." She paused, trying to remember what she did do during this time. "I talked to Cody. He was looking for Brad, so I sent him upstairs. I had seen Brad speaking to Eduardo Ramirez, then go upstairs." She paused and felt herself blush. "Then I spoke briefly to Eduardo."

"What time was this?"

"About eight-twenty." Claire's guilty conscience niggled at her. She wasn't sure why she shouldn't tell Roberto about their conversation, but she couldn't bring herself to do so. "We went outside for some fresh air."

Salinas waited for an explanation. Getting none, he asked Claire, "Did you see Mr. Detwyler leave the party?"

Claire thought, "Yes, he left with a group of students as I returned indoors, just before Laura sounded the alarm about Tanya."

"One more question—why did Cody enter the party uninvited?"

Claire looked up at Salinas as she remembered what she had in her possession...like the Ring of Mordor in her purse. "Because of the notebook."

CHAPTER THIRTY-FOUR

Claire left the parlor feeling like she had undergone a waterboarding ordeal. She feared that any amorous emotions Salinas might have felt toward her had surely been dispelled by her dreadful performance. She rejoined her colleagues in the courtyard. Brad and Jamal spoke quietly together. George had found a glossy hardcover guidebook for the Casa Montejo to read, and Eduardo sat on a metal folding chair, perusing the Merida newspaper. To her relief, no one spoke as she returned to their cluster. She sent Madge into the parlor per the detective's request and joined George on his bench. The remaining faculty members and Eduardo paused briefly in their activities to watch Madge trudge off toward the parlor.

"Tough?" George asked, looking up from the book.

"It's a good thing I'm innocent because I would make a terrible villain. He made me feel guilty—and I thought he liked me," she added in a whisper.

"That's his job, Claire."

"I hope Madge does better than I did."

When Detective Salinas looked at Madge Carmichael, he remembered vaguely the youthful American tourists who crowded the Merida streets when he was young—tall, blonde girls wearing mini-or-maxi-skirts and tie-dye shirts, and lanky men with long hair, grotesque beards, and frayed blue jeans, all laden with beads, floating through the market in a marijuana haze. This woman resembled an older, hopefully wiser, version of this image.

After reintroducing Madge to Sergeant Garza and repeating his request to speak slowly for her benefit, Salinas began. "Doctor

Carmichael, can you tell me about the events of the evening, what you saw and heard during the reception?"

Madge recounted the evening as she remembered it. Her version and timeline of Tanya's behavior and the events surrounding the discovery of her body agreed with Claire's.

"When did you become aware that Tanya was in the bedchamber?"

"Maybe seven forty-five. I was in the sitting room and Laura—Lorenzo—came in from the bedchamber and spoke to the docent. He followed her back into the bedchamber, then came out and talked to Brad.

"I went into the courtyard, thinking I'd get a fresh drink. I saw Jamal standing in the middle of the courtyard like a zombie, staring toward the parlor. He told me what had happened, and we entered the parlor together. George was there with his students. Laura had settled Tanya in the bedchamber and asked us to let her sleep. Jamal paced for a few minutes but went in to see her." She paused, thinking. "George and I led the students out of the parlor and as we left, Claire arrived."

"Did you check on Tanya?"

"George and I went to see her a little after eight. Jamal said he and Claire had checked on her and she was sleeping, so we left."

"What did you do then?"

"George went outside for fresh air with his friends. I went upstairs to tell Brad about the missing dagger…I didn't know it was being used to murder our friend." Madge blinked back tears.

"How did he react?"

"He apologized that he didn't get my message about the theft but agreed with me that it probably wasn't important." Madge sniffled, "How could we be so wrong?"

"And then you met Claire and Laura in the atrium?"

"I used the restroom first, then went down."

"Was Brad still upstairs when you returned to the atrium?"

"I don't remember seeing him."

Salinas looked at his notebook again. "Why didn't you want to report the missing dagger to the police?"

Madge fingered her wedding ring, the one she received from her third and last husband, the only one who had died before she divorced him. "That was my fault," she pleaded. "Claire wanted to report it to you, but I couldn't imagine the police bothering about a missing teaching aid." Tears welled in her eyes. She rummaged in her bag for her pack of tissues, remembered she had given them to Cody, and sniffled. "Claire was right, of course. I feared she was getting caught up in the drama of the death—Paul's death—and I didn't see how it could be important."

Madge wriggled to the front of her chair, thinking Salinas was finished with her, but he said, "And the notebook? Did you and Doctor Aguila decide not to tell me about that as well?"

"Oh, no." Madge fumbled anew with her ring. "I'm sure she would have given it to you tomorrow. She didn't want to take it from him."

"Do you have any idea why he might have insisted she take it instead of bringing it to me himself?"

Madge shook her head, the chaos of her gray natural curls falling out of her leather hair clip. "I think he wanted her to see something...I don't know what...and decide what to do with it." She puffed her hair with both hands and pulled it back up, securing it with the clip. "In fact, he seemed conspiratorial."

Salinas raised an eyebrow but did not comment. "What did you think about Mr. Detwyler's journal?" he asked.

Madge sniffled again. "Not much, really, just random comments about our research sites. I'm not sure why Cody thought they were important."

Salinas shifted his position, checked his notes, and said, "Tell me about the drawings."

Madge straightened in her chair, regaining composure as the topic shifted away from Tanya. "I saw eight or ten drawings. One was of a replica statue that Eduardo...Doctor Ramirez...had presented to Brad. Do you have the notebook?"

"Yes, I do, and I may ask you to look at it more carefully later."

Madge nodded. "Do you think it's important?" she asked.

Salinas gave the senior professor a sympathetic smile. "That is all, Doctor Carmichael. Can you please send in Doctor Banks?"

CHAPTER THIRTY-FIVE

Salinas invited George to sit as he assessed the senior member of the anthropology department, his staid dark slacks and Mexican *guayabera* in stark contrast to his colorful colleague, Madge. Salinas re-introduced George to Sergeant Garza.

"Doctor Banks, I understand you dined with the victim before the reception. Can you tell me who dined with you and describe what happened there?"

George straightened his black-framed bifocals and directed his full attention to the detective. "I dined at the hotel restaurant with Tanya, Brad Kingsford, and Jamal Kennedy." He pushed his glasses up his nose. "We had decided to eat early, at five o'clock, and rest up before the reception. Our conversation centered on the upcoming reception."

"How did Tanya seem at dinner?"

"She seemed quiet, but she kept looking at her watch."

"Do you know why she chose to eat with the men instead of dining with Claire and Madge?"

"No. I hadn't thought about it."

"So, everyone ate and left the table together? And went where?"

George rearranged his glasses again and thought. "Tanya left first. She said she had a headache and wanted to return to her room. We all signed for our meals and I signed for Tanya's. Jamal left next, then Brad. I had ordered coffee, so I stayed for a few minutes longer and then went up to my room."

"Does everyone in the Keane College group have rooms on the same floor?"

"Yes. We're all on the third floor."

"Are your rooms along the same hallway? I'm just trying to understand the room placement."

173

"They are all along the same corridor. Madge, Claire, and my rooms are to the right of the elevator as you exit. Jamal, Brad, and Tanya's are to the left."

"Did you see anyone in the hallway?"

"I don't know why this is important," George protested. "She didn't die in the hotel."

"No, but she got sick in the hotel, at some point. I am just trying to—how do you say—set the scene."

George sighed. "I saw Jamal in the hallway, walking from his room toward Tanya's or Brad's. He had a bottle of wine."

"Do you think he was taking a bottle of wine to Brad's room?"

"Well, they are friends, but probably not."

"Were Jamal and Tanya involved romantically?"

"I think so. I'm the department chair and not likely to be informed on these types of matters."

"Were they having difficulties or worse? Arguments?"

"I've heard they had problems, but I can't put Jamal in the role of murderer."

"Nevertheless…"

George reasoned, "If he were thinking of murdering her, why would he be taking wine to her room?" As he said this, he considered the possibilities of such a gift, and looked away from the detective.

"Did you call out to Jamal? Talk to him?"

"No. I went to my room and rested. I watched a few minutes of a news program and decided to check on Tanya before heading to the Casa Montejo."

"You went to her room?"

"Yes, but Brad was there already."

"Brad? Not Jamal?"

"Yes, I wondered about that." George shrugged, "Brad was pacing the room. Tanya was dressed to go out. I asked her how she felt, and she said she felt much better now."

"Now?" Salinas asked.

"She held up a prescription bottle and shook it. She said something like, 'This will get me through.'"

"How did Brad react when he saw you?" Salinas asked. "It must have appeared strange for him to be there. Did he act embarrassed? Nervous?"

"No," George responded, "he said he stopped by to see how Tanya was feeling. He didn't think she should go to the reception. I thought she looked pale, but she seemed excited. She said she wanted to celebrate."

"Celebrate what?"

"She said she had received good news."

"Did she explain the good news?"

"No, and Brad didn't offer any elaboration. He kept looking at his watch like he wanted to leave. Tanya put the pill bottle on the dresser next to her purse, went into the bathroom, then we all left together."

"Did you see the wine that Jamal brought?"

George thought. "Yes. It was on a table in the corner of the room. It was about three- fourths full and had been recorked. I noticed two glasses placed upside down on a towel next to the bottle, as if they had been used and rinsed out."

"Did anything else in the room look unusual?"

"There were two small liquor bottles, like you get on airplanes, on the dresser near the pill bottle."

"It seems like a lot of alcohol and pills in her room," Salinas mused.

Salinas paused to let Garza catch up, and George used these minutes to think about the scene in the room. He readjusted his glasses and confessed. "I'm a fool," he said. "There were *two* pill bottles—the one she placed on the dresser didn't have a label. I wondered what kind of pill she had taken. But there was another bottle with a prescription label next to the bed."

Salinas sat straight in his chair. "Was the unlabeled bottle still on the dresser when you left? Could she have put it in her purse?"

George furrowed his brow in thought. "She might have, but I don't remember seeing her do it."

"Did you see if the small bottles were still there when you left?"

"I don't remember," George said, pursing his lips. "Won't her room be searched?" he asked.

"It is being searched as we speak," Salinas said. "Did you all leave her room together?"

"Yes. We arrived at the Casa Montejo around seven o'clock. Brad was in a hurry to meet with Eduardo. He went directly to the kitchen when we arrived."

"And what did you and Tanya do?"

"Tanya saw someone she knew and wandered off to talk to him."

"Do you know who it was?"

"I'm not sure. It might have been the archaeologist she worked with in Chiapas…at Palenque." George paused. "I don't remember his name, but it seemed that he had been waiting for her or looking for her."

"What did you do?"

"I went to the bar. The bartender had lined up red and white wines alongside the margaritas, so I took a glass of wine and stood aside for others." George cleared his throat, thinking. "Eduardo and Brad came out of the kitchen. Eduardo had a glass of wine and walked toward the parlor, greeting guests. I hadn't had a chance to thank him for his gift, so I followed him there." He furrowed his brow. "Brad approached the bar as I walked away."

"Had anyone else from your group arrived?"

"Brad joined Jamal at the bar." George's brow furrowed again. "This might not be important, but I think Jamal saw Tanya talking to that other man. He was talking to Brad, but he was watching Tanya."

"Did you see Jamal give the margarita to Tanya?"

"No, but I did hear her speak from time to time."

"Did you hear what she said to Cody?"

"Jamal told me later. I was in the parlor by that time."

"You were in the parlor when Ms. Lorenzo brought Tanya through to the bedchamber."

"Yes, around quarter-to-eight. Tanya looked pale. She mumbled about something…it didn't make sense."

"Can you be more specific?"

"She said that Madge would be upset, but she didn't care." George resettled his glasses. "When she saw me, she put her hand to her mouth as if to stop herself talking."

"Because?" Salinas prompted.

"Presumably, she didn't want to discuss Madge in front of me."

Sergeant Garza put her hand up and asked Salinas to translate 'presumably,' and to give her a minute to catch up. The two men sat quietly while she made rapid notes.

When Garza nodded, Salinas asked, "Did Laura take Tanya directly into the bedchamber?"

"No. We watched Tanya while she found the docent."

"We?"

"A small group of local students had wandered in. I admit I was embarrassed when Laura brought Tanya in. She could barely stand, and students had to help Laura steady her. I thought she was drunk."

"Did Tanya say anything more while Laura was gone?"

"No. I offered to take her back to the hotel, but she said something about a special day."

"Then Laura returned?" Salinas prompted.

"Yes. She said that the docent was setting up the bed for her, and she led Tanya into the bedchamber."

Salinas paused, folding his hands again. "Do you remember a glass of water?"

George thought. "I think Laura was holding a glass of water when she brought Tanya into the parlor. She must have put it down somewhere when she went to find the docent because she didn't have it when she returned to the parlor to get Tanya."

"Where was Jamal when this was happening?"

"He came in with Madge just after Laura put Tanya to bed. When Laura came back into the parlor, she asked that no one bother Tanya, but Jamal paced a bit then went in anyway. When he came out, he said that Brad was with her."

"Did you see Tanya's archaeologist friend go into the bedchamber?"

"No, but he could have gone in through the sitting room."

"Did you remain in the parlor most of the evening?"

George said, "Yes, but I went out for air with my colleagues, Perez and Gonzalez. When I came back inside, I heard the ambulance."

Salinas turned a page in his notebook as if to change the subject. He looked at Sergeant Garza, then settled his gaze on George. "Doctor Banks,' he said, "Doctor Aguila has observed your conversations with your archaeology colleagues. Do you have any updates for me?"

George looked at Garza, then at the detective. Salinas turned to Garza. "Why don't you take a break? We will be ready for Dr. Kennedy when you return."

Garza frowned, narrowed her eyes and placed her notebook on the chair. After she left, George took his small spiral notebook from his pants pocket. He said, "I have found out a few things that I think will be very interesting to you."

CHAPTER THIRTY-SIX

Jamal Kennedy entered the parlor hesitantly and looked toward the closed door to the bedchamber. He sat in the metal chair and avoided eye contact with the detective. Salinas thought he was a striking young man, with delicate facial features and deep piercing brown eyes.

Salinas cleared his throat to bring Jamal's attention back to him. "Thank you for your patience, Doctor Kennedy. I know this is very difficult for you." He reintroduced himself and Sergeant Garza.

"Is she…still in there?" Jamal asked the detective, nodding his head toward the door to his back.

"Yes, I suspect they will take her away after we all leave." Salinas watched Jamal carefully, noting how he ran his fingers through his micro-braids and fiddled with his tiny earring. He took Jamal through the dinner that he had shared with Brad, Tanya, and George.

"After dinner, when did you see Tanya again?"

"At the reception."

"I see." Salinas folded his hands on the table. "What did you do during the time between dinner and the reception?"

"I went for a walk and arrived at the Casa Montejo a few minutes after seven."

"Were you the first from your group to arrive?"

He fingered his earring. "George, Brad, and Tanya arrived before me. I just learned that they came together."

"Did you talk to Tanya when she arrived?"

"Not right away. I joined Brad at the bar, then Tanya came over."

"So, you didn't see Tanya until she came up to the bar?"

Jamal pressed his lips together. Salinas waited patiently for his response. "I saw her," he said simply.

"But you didn't speak to her?"

"She was talking to someone…an archaeologist."

"Someone you knew?"

Jamal sat back in the chair. "I just met him at the conference. His name is Tom Freeman. Tanya worked with him at Palenque."

"Ah," Salinas said, and Jamal turned dark wary eyes toward the detective.

"They knew each other a long time ago," Jamal said, his voice rising.

"Do you have a temper, Doctor Kennedy?"

"No."

Salinas frowned. "What happened when Tanya came to the bar?"

"Nothing. She said she wanted a margarita, then wandered away."

"How did she seem?" Jamal looked confused. Salinas added, "Happy? Depressed?"

"She looked ill," Jamal said.

"But you took a drink to her?"

"Yes. We talked about the lecture. Claire came up to us, and she and Tanya went off together. Later, I heard Tanya say something loud, like 'I don't believe you' or 'I don't believe what you did' or something like that. I saw Cody with her, and I went to see if he was bothering her. Tanya seemed agitated again, and Cody just walked away."

"Did you ask her why she said those words?"

"She insisted Cody was talking nonsense about Paul's death. I tried to calm her—she said, 'it has to be him,' and then she started to mumble. I offered to take her to the hotel, but she refused."

"What did you do then?"

"I was frustrated with her behavior, so I left her there and went back to the bar."

Salinas put his pen down. "Weren't you concerned about your friend? She was agitated, perhaps ill, and you left her alone?"

"You didn't know her. I thought she wanted attention."

"Oh?" Salinas said and tipped his hand. "Can you explain?"

"It's not important."

"Are you sure? She is dead."

"It had nothing to do with me."

"Then who?"

Tears came to Jamal's eyes. "I wouldn't hurt her."

"Did you argue?"

"Earlier, but we had settled it."

"We'll come back to that later, then. Did you happen to see what happened to the margarita glass?"

Jamal clenched his fist on the table. "That was hardly on my mind, Detective."

"Did you follow Ms. Lorenzo and Tanya into the parlor?"

"Yes, with Madge. Tanya was in the bedchamber. I went into see her…" Jamal put his hands over his face. When he pulled them away, tears had formed in his eyes. "Brad was with her."

"Who told him about Tanya?"

"I have no idea." He wiped his eyes on his shirt.

"Did you hear their conversation?"

"They were whispering, but Brad left so Tanya and I could talk." Jamal wiped tears from his eyes. "She refused to return to the hotel."

"Did you notice a glass of water on the table, or anyplace in the room?"

"No."

"When did you check on her again?"

"Several times, but the last time, she looked different. She lay on her back and she looked…terrible. I grabbed Laura in the atrium. She checked on Tanya and called the ambulance."

Salinas turned toward Garza, who was writing rapidly in her notepad. She looked up and nodded at Jamal. Salinas asked, "Doctor Kennedy, are you sure you didn't see Tanya between dinner and the reception?"

CHAPTER THIRTY-SEVEN

The detective's question startled Jamal. He sat up straight and his head turned quickly toward the sergeant, then back to Salinas.

"What?"

"You said you went for a walk. Are you sure you didn't visit Tanya's room first?" Jamal looked at the sergeant again, at his own shaking hands, and then at the detective. Salinas continued, "You were seen in the hallway after dinner, walking toward her room with a bottle of wine."

He slumped in his chair. "I wanted to talk to her."

"About what?"

Jamal shrugged. "It's personal and has nothing to do with her death."

"You broke off your relationship, and now she's dead. I have the authority to ask."

Salinas put his hands on the small serving table and drummed his fingers. "Perhaps she broke up with you, and you were not happy about it?" Salinas shrugged casually. "Is that possible?"

"No!" he said aloud, then lowered his voice. "That's not how it was." He wiped his brow with the back of his hand. "I thought she had been using me to advance her career."

"Was she?"

Jamal sighed, "I recently learned that she had an affair with a married professor in graduate school, and that she used him to get her Ph.D."

"And was this faculty member the man you saw her with tonight? Doctor Freeman?"

"Yes."

"When did you learn this about Tanya?"

182

"I had heard rumors before, but Freeman confirmed it Sunday, at the Uxmal reception."

Salinas started. "Really? He told you he had an affair with your girlfriend?"

"He didn't know that." Jamal insisted. "We met at the reception and started talking. When he learned I taught at Keane College, he said he knew someone there—Tanya Petersen—and that she had destroyed his marriage."

"Did you tell him about you and Tanya?"

Jamal's head shot up. "Of course not. I was too stunned."

"What else did he say?"

"He said to be careful of Tanya. That she had a history."

Salinas cocked his head and looked at Jamal. "And you had heard of this before? From whom?"

"No one in particular."

"This could be construed as a motive," Salinas said, tipping his hand upward.

"I didn't kill her!"

"Did you see Doctor Freeman anytime later this evening, or see him leave?"

Jamal thought. "I don't remember seeing him again."

Salinas tented his fingers. "You said you thought she used you. What could you offer her?"

"She wanted me to influence George to change his mind and sup-port her as curator of the museum…except that couldn't happen. Madge would be formally appointed once the museum was established."

"So, after breaking off your relationship, you took a bottle of wine to her room to—how do you say—smooth her over? Or did you change your mind and want her back?"

"We say, 'soften the blow,' and I guess that was my idea. I felt badly for how it turned out. She was hurt and angry."

"Did you share the wine with her?"

Jamal shook his head. "She didn't want me to stay, but I insisted. I had a corkscrew and opened the bottle, but she wouldn't drink anything. In fact, she seemed anxious for me to leave. She said she wanted to rest, but I had a feeling she might be meeting someone because she wasn't dressed for bed."

"Did you see any alcohol bottles or prescription drug containers in the room?"

"I wasn't there long enough to notice anything. I recorked the bottle and put it on the table. She nearly pushed me out of the room."

Salinas raised his eyebrows. "There were two rinsed glasses next to the wine bottle, and some of the wine had evidently been consumed."

Jamal looked up sharply. "It wasn't me." His eyes shifted back to the bedchamber, as if he hoped Tanya could confirm his statement.

Salinas sat quietly, thinking of prescription bottles. "Did Tanya have a problem with alcohol or drugs?"

Jamal considered his words. "She had a problem with prescription drugs, once, but she told me she had conquered the addiction. But this week, I learned she was using again…and drinking." His eyes widened, and he rose quickly from his chair, his hands clenched. "Are you accusing me of drugging the wine?"

Sergeant Garza stiffened and rose from her chair, her notebook falling from her lap.

Salinas put his hand up to Garza and turned to Jamal. "So, you do have a temper. Sit down, Doctor Kennedy." Salinas turned dark angry eyes on Jamal. "It could have been in the margarita that you gave her."

"Absolutely not!" Jamal sat down, but his voice wavered.

"Did she threaten you? Accuse you of something?"

He hesitated slightly, remembering their conversation in the market. "No."

Salinas looked to his notes and asked, "Did you know that Brad was in Tanya's hotel room when George went to check up on her?"

"I just found out tonight."

"What did you think when you saw Tanya here?"

"I thought she'd changed her mind." He sat up straight as a thought came to him. "She might have been waiting for Brad," he admitted.

Salinas remained quiet for a few moments, waiting for this idea to sink in. "If you had known this, would you have been angry?"

"How could I be? I had broken up with her. But…Brad? He didn't like her—at least I didn't think so."

"Perhaps she was trying to make you jealous? Or maybe he had more to offer her than you did? That curatorship perhaps?"

Jamal's shoulders sagged. "I saw them leave the auditorium together this afternoon after George's presentation. I didn't think much of it—we are all colleagues…"

"But you noticed it, and you're thinking about it now. Did you think anything of it then?"

"Maybe a little."

"Thus, the wine?"

"No…at least I don't think so. You're confusing me."

Salinas looked at his notes and shuffled pages in front of him. "Speaking of confusion, I would like to settle another matter, while we are talking."

Jamal looked up at him, his eyes wide with anticipation. Salinas reached his hand out to the sergeant and she handed him a pile of papers that Jamal recognized as the written statements from that morning. Salinas pulled a statement from the pile and studied it. Jamal braced himself for bad news.

Salinas handed the statement to Jamal. "I want to review the statement you submitted this morning." He paused. "You wrote that after breakfast Monday morning, you went to your room to prepare your academic lecture."

"Yes. I give a paper on Thursday."

"Did you do anything else before or after you worked on your paper?"

"I don't think so."

"Well, let me refresh your memory. After collecting the statements, I talked with various staff members at the hotel. It seems that the fifth-floor maid saw you—in fact she spoke with you."

"With me?" Jamal's gaze flitted from sergeant to detective.

"It may be true that all gringos look alike to Mexicans, but unfortunately for you, you do not look like the others. The maid reported that a black man came to her cart that morning. He wore a backpack and held a book; he asked if he could put the book in room 505 because it didn't fit the mail slot at the front desk."

Jamal's mouth went slack. "I had borrowed it…"

"From Paul? Certainly not Cody." Salinas saw the distress in Jamal's face. His mouth contorted.

Salinas shrugged as if this explanation were perfectly reasonable. He said, "Never mind. The point is that this young black man convinced her to open the room for him. She didn't stay to watch, a misstep that could cause her to lose her job, but she saw him leave without the book."

Jamal pleaded, "I don't see how this is related to anything, Paul or Tanya."

Salinas spoke slowly, as if to a child. "Merida is a large city, but despite American stereotypes of Mexico, it is a safe city. There is little crime, and very few murders. *Entonces*, when two tourists—both anthropologists attending the same conference—turn up dead, I must consider that these deaths might be related. Either anthropologists are very unlucky in Merida, or they are very unpopular."

Jamal slumped once again, his knee wobbled, and his hand went up to his ear. "When Paul talked to us individually, he seemed to know a lot about our research, which is normally a positive characteristic. But in his case, it seemed malicious." He looked at Garza, who had raised her hand, "a feeling of bad will. He made innuendos—hints—about my research, and I guess about others' also."

"Do you think he was blackmailing you all?"

"It didn't feel like blackmail, but he made us uncomfortable."

"And your mistake?"

"N...nothing really...really," he stammered. "I wanted to check it out. I thought if I could get a quick look at his computer, I could see what he had written about us...especially me."

"Did you find it?"

"I didn't see it, but I had to hurry because I didn't know when Cody would be back."

"How did you know he wouldn't be in the room?"

Jamal swallowed. "He came into the restaurant that morning—yesterday—after we had finished eating. He sat at our table and started rambling on about Paul. I really wanted to leave, so I did. Brad and I both left. I'm not sure how I thought of it, but it occurred to me that I might take advantage of the situation. I knew I had a few minutes, at least."

Salinas leaned forward, his hands folded. "You seem to have some trouble with the truth, Doctor Kennedy. Did you also lie about the wine? Did you coax Tanya to drink it? Perhaps put something in it?"

Jamal jumped from his seat again. "No!"

"Sit down, Doctor Kennedy," Salinas said, his voice rising again.

Jamal sat down. "I didn't lie about the wine. I wouldn't give her drugs." He pressed his lips together. "And I didn't take the computer. Why do you insist that I did?"

"Because it is missing."

CHAPTER THIRTY-EIGHT

Salinas watched as Brad Kingsford entered the room, taking his time. He looked toward the bedchamber briefly before sitting across from Salinas. His appearance of professorial chic, his Dockers, polo shirt, and sandals, belied a less confident demeanor. He ran his hands through his graying blond hair, hanging in waves nearly to his shoulder. His eyes darted back and forth between his two inquisitors. As he positioned himself in the chair, Salinas watched his transformation from unease to confidence. He sat straight in the chair, his jaw hardened, and his eyes met those of the detective. He wondered which was the real Brad Kingsford.

Again, Salinas made introductions. "I am sorry that you have had to wait so long this evening, Doctor Kingsford," Salinas said.

"It can't be helped," Brad said, shrugging. "We are all stunned."

Salinas folded his hands in front of him. "Tell me about the dinner tonight. I understand you ate with Tanya, George, and Jamal."

"Yes," Brad said, and described the meal as did the other men.

"Do you know why Tanya ate with the men instead of the women?"

Brad ran his hand through his hair, thinking. "She said she didn't feel like going out for dinner. Actually, I'm not sure that she feels comfortable around Madge and Claire."

"Why not?"

Brad shrugged again. "They've been friends for a long time. Claire was Madge's student in graduate school. I think Tanya felt like an outsider."

"Does she feel more comfortable with men in general?" Salinas asked.

"Perhaps."

"How did Tanya seem at dinner?"

"A bit tired. She left the table early with a headache."

Salinas paused momentarily. "I understand that you, Doctor Banks, and Doctor Petersen arrived at the reception together." Salinas observed that Brad relaxed as the questions shifted to the reception. He crossed one ankle over the other knee and sat back in his chair. His description of their arrival matched those of his dinner-mates.

"We arrived at seven. I met briefly with Doctor Ramirez, then went to the bar for a drink."

"Who was at the bar?"

"People came and went. I sat with Jamal."

"Did you see Tanya?"

"Tanya?" He rubbed his hands on his knee. "She was talking to someone near the stairs, an archaeologist, I believe. She talked to him for a few minutes, then joined us at the bar."

"Did she take a drink? I understand wine and margaritas were already prepared."

"Jamal asked her if she wanted a margarita, but she shrugged and wandered off. Jamal took a glass from the bar and followed her."

"Was there anything unusual about the drink?"

Brad thought a moment. "Not unusual, but it was near him, and he seemed intent on giving it to her. I took wine and joined George and Eduardo."

Salinas asked, "How well did you know Tanya?"

"Not very well. She wasn't technically in our department, but she attended meetings of the Mayanist Program."

The detective looked at his notes and rubbed his chin. "If you didn't know her well, why visit her room?"

Brad's eyes flashed, and he looked again toward the bedchamber. His hands went to his hair. "She looked ill when she left the dinner table. I thought I would check on her."

"Very considerate," the detective mused, and shifted his focus again. "You were seen walking with Tanya after Doctor Banks' presentation. You seemed to be friendly, according to at least one witness."

"That's absurd!" Brad protested and brought his index finger up to point at the detective, but changed his mind, letting his hand drop back into his lap. "We happened to leave the auditorium together, as I remember. I don't even know what we talked about."

"Were you setting up a meeting for tonight, in her room?"

"No, absolutely not." Brad folded his hands on his knees.

"So, you went to her room to check on her," Salinas said.

"And offer to walk with her to the reception," Brad said. He switched his posture, placing his ankle over his knee again. "She said she didn't feel well, so I suggested that she stay in her room."

"What did she say to that?"

"Frankly, she acted confused, like she couldn't decide, but when George…Doctor Banks arrived, she decided to go, and we all left together."

"Did you notice anything unusual in her room?"

"Well, I had not been in her room before, so I would hardly know what might be unusual."

"Alcohol, prescription drugs…?" Salinas prompted.

"She took a pill from a prescription bottle just as George arrived."

"Anything else? Small liquor bottles, like airline or hotel single-serve size bottles?"

Brad thought. "No, I don't remember seeing any."

"Did you notice a bottle of wine?"

"Yes, I think I did."

"Did you share wine with her, or see her drink from the bottle?"

"No." He sat upright. "Why?"

Salinas ignored his question and took him back to the reception. "Did you see Mr. Detwyler at the reception?"

"Cody? Yes, and I wondered why he was there. He was not part of the conference and certainly not invited."

"Did you talk to him?"

"No."

"Are you sure? Someone said he went upstairs to talk with you."

Brad frowned. "That's right. He apologized for crashing the party. I guess he thought it would be okay to come."

"Did you see him talk to Tanya?"

"No."

Salinas looked at his notes. "Did you see Miss Lorenzo take Tanya into the bedchamber?"

"No, but I saw Laura with the docent in the sitting room and wondered why he followed her into the bedchamber. When Freddy returned to the sitting room, he told me that "*la profesora rubia*" was in the bed, resting."

"Is that when you went in?"

"Yes. Her eyes were closed, but she opened them when she heard me come in."

"Did she say anything to you?"

"I offered to take her to the hotel, but she declined. When Jamal entered, I left so they could talk privately."

"Did you go back into the chamber at any time this evening?"

Brad's eyes flickered toward the room again and he rubbed his hands together nervously. "Yes, I did. I looked in there once more, around eight o'clock. She was sleeping, or I thought she was sleeping."

"Did you see a water glass on the table or floor?"

"No."

"Which door did you enter from, the second time?"

"The sitting room door, both times."

"Can you account for your actions during the evening?"

"Every minute? I moved around...it's a reception...that's what people do."

"Did you spend time in the parlor with George, for example?"

"No, not really. I guess I spent more time in the sitting room and courtyard."

"Did Doctor Ramirez know she was sleeping in the bedchamber?"

"I don't know. I didn't talk to him during the evening."

Salinas folded his hands on the table. "Did you know that the dagger had been taken from the Exhibit Room?"

He sighed in frustration. "Not until tonight. Madge told me. We were horrified when we learned it had been used to kill Tanya."

"That has not been determined yet," Salinas said carefully.

"What do you mean?" Brad shifted positions, his knee bouncing again.

"Just that. She may have had drugs in her system," Salinas said. "Did you see Cody Detwyler leave the reception?"

"No."

"Did you see him go into either of the rooms that connect with the bedchamber?"

Brad relaxed his shoulders and took a deep breath. "No, but he could have."

Salinas sat back, watching Brad. "You can leave, Doctor Kingsford. I will be requiring Doctor Ramirez next."

After Brad left, Garza shook her head. "They are a nervous bunch."

Salinas stood. "They should be."

"Coffee, sir?"

"Please. And bring Doctor Ramirez back with you." He stretched his back and rolled his shoulders. "Be alert with him, Rosa. We'll speak in Spanish."

CHAPTER THIRTY-NINE

Unlike Bradley Kingsford's professorial persona, his friend, Doctor Eduardo Ramirez, cultivated the aura of the executive entering his personal conference room. The host of the evening's event, Ramirez wore a navy-blue suit with pale-pink shirt, striped tie, and black wingtips.

Sergeant Garza sighed gratefully as the conversation proceeded in Spanish. After introductions and a request for his background, Salinas asked Ramirez to describe his relationship with Keane College.

"I understand that you have contributed items from your collection to the Keane College program and museum. I imagine that Doctor Kingsford and his colleagues in the Mayanist Program appreciate this very much," Salinas posed, as much a question as a statement.

"I'm sure they do."

"Have you become acquainted with the Keane College faculty during this conference?"

"To some extent, yes."

"Can you expand?"

Ramirez examined his hands and folded them in his lap. "I've gotten to know Jamal best, I think, because he works closely with Brad. I don't know the others very well."

"You haven't met with Doctor Carmichael, the curator of the museum?"

"Not formally, not yet."

"It seems to me that you would be working closely with her."

Eduardo picked a piece of invisible lint off his pant leg. "I'm sure that once I start sending our artifacts, she will be directly involved."

"Can you describe your movements during the evening?"

"Are you kidding? I am the host. I circulated."

"Yet you didn't know someone was sleeping, possibly dying in the bedchamber?"

"Guests weren't allowed there. Now I learn there was a veritable parade of anthropologists in and out."

"When did you realize that something serious had happened?"

"When I heard the ambulance." Eduardo sat back in the chair and crossed his legs.

"Where were you when you heard the ambulance?"

"It was just after Doctor Aguila and I went outside to talk." Eduardo raised his eyebrows.

Salinas tipped his head slightly and asked, "How did this conversation with Doctor Aguila come about?"

"I wanted a cigarette and asked her to join me. I didn't know her well and wanted to chat with her."

"And what did you talk about?"

Eduardo smiled again. "Is that important to your investigation?"

"I honestly don't know what might be important at this point in my investigation." Salinas looked briefly at Sergeant Garza.

"Well, actually, I offered her a job with my businesses."

Salinas sat forward. "You don't know her well, but offered her a job?"

"I knew her reputation and her work in the field."

"And did she accept?"

"Not yet."

"What time did you return inside?"

"Claire went back inside first, about eight-twenty. I finished my cigarette then returned about eight-thirty. I was on my way to the kitchen when I heard the ambulance sirens. I returned to the courtyard as the paramedics arrived."

"Were you aware that the dagger used to stab Professor Petersen had been taken from the exhibit case?"

"Not until tonight."

"I understand that the dagger and the statue you presented to Professor Kingsford were both on display."

"Yes, but the dagger was not part of my collection."

Salinas turned a page in his notebook. "Tell me about the statue."

"The corn god statue is a replica of one of the artifacts we are loaning to Keane College."

"Does it have a special significance?"

Eduardo repositioned himself in his chair. "No, not really. Brad had admired it when he visited my Texas museum. He said that if he ever had the opportunity to curate a museum, he would love to raid our collection, especially that piece. When he told me later that he had been hired director of this new program and that they were seeking funds to start a collection, I remembered our conversation. He probably forgot all about it."

"When will he get the real thing?"

"Once their museum is available and secure, the documentation and certification will be provided to him along with the original artifact."

Claire watched carefully as each member of her group returned to their exotic garden prison. Madge returned looking tired and more disheveled than usual. George returned to his chair quietly, in a contemplative state. Jamal paced back and forth from the courtyard to the corner of the square near the bedchamber. Brad stomped immediately toward the kitchen, his jaw tight, his chin raised in defiance. Eduardo entered the courtyard, scanned the room, and joined Brad as the latter emerged from the kitchen, a half-bottle of prohibited red wine in his hand. They each poured wine into a coffee cup and sat at the bar.

Moments later, Sergeant Garza and Detective Salinas entered the courtyard. The sergeant hurried toward the stairs to the restroom. It had been a long sit for her. Salinas surveyed the room. The guests who had been interviewed by the second team of police had all been dismissed. Only the Keane College group and a few others remained, including Eduardo, Laura, the two archaeologists Gonzalez and Perez, and Freddy Flores, the docent, sweating profusely.

Salinas addressed those remaining in the room. "The Keane College faculty and Doctor Ramirez may go. I would like to speak to Miss Lorenzo."

Eduardo spoke up from his position at the bar. "I need to supervise the clean-up." He glared first at the docent, then at Salinas. The reprimand was clear, but Salinas did not flinch.

The detective countered, "My officers, Mr. Flores, and I will make sure that the building is clean and secure before we leave. You are excused."

He turned to the rest of the Keane College group. "I may want to speak to some of you again tomorrow, but please remember to surrender your passports to the officer at the door or to the hotel manager."

Salinas turned to the two archaeologists. "I would like to speak to Doctors Gonzalez and Perez after Miss Lorenzo. I apologize that you have had to wait so long."

The two archaeologists nodded. Sergeant Garza returned, allowing the detective to take his turn at the restroom.

Brad and Eduardo turned in their passports and left the mansion together.

Madge delved into her bag looking for hers. "Well, let's go," she said. Claire had her passport in her hand. Jamal shrugged and said his was in his hotel room. George remained seated.

"Come on, George," Madge said.

George looked toward the parlor where Laura and Sergeant Garza had just entered. "I'm going to stay to walk Laura back to the hotel," he said.

As Claire left with her colleagues, she looked back at George and the three archaeologists. Near them, the docent sat slumped in a metal folding chair, his eyes gazing longingly at the bottle of wine on the bar.

Program for the 10th Annual Meeting of the Society for Mayanist Studies

Wednesday, May 7
Free Day

Contact Doctor Emilio Hernandez, Local Events Chair,
for special excursions to
Valladolid, Chichén Itzá, or Dzibichaltún.

CHAPTER FORTY

Wednesday Morning

Claire arose early, ate breakfast, and returned to her room. Her trip to Yaxpec had been delayed because Detective Salinas had requested a morning meeting with her, George, and Madge. Claire packed for her trip and settled on the bed with her laptop. She had a few minutes to spare.

Hoping for a response from either the Stuarts or Odawa Township, she opened her email. The first message was from her daughter, Cristina, who had written to allay her mother's fear about her African internship and to invite her to Madison, Wisconsin, for Mother's Day. Claire responded with a quick note telling Cristina that she supported her decision and accepted the invitation.

The next message was from Emily Duncan, the supervisor for Odawa Township. The subject line said "Hooray!" Emily had contacted the Stuarts, who promised to send Claire the digital photos by Thursday, the next day. Claire doubted their photographs would be useful, but Salinas must have been hopeful, or he would not have given her the assignment.

Claire browsed through other emails and jumped when her cellphone rang.

It was Madge. "Claire, where are you?"

Claire looked at her watch. *Damn.* "I'll be right down."

"Are you sure you don't want to get a taxi?" George asked as Claire led them to her car, carrying a large tote bag and her overnight bag slung over her shoulder.

Claire shook her head. "You two can take a taxi back to the hotel. I'm anxious to get to Yaxpec today." Claire wedged her two colleagues and her bags into the Volkswagen, and they pulled out onto the busy street.

When they had cleared the traffic around the plaza, Claire could not contain her curiosity any longer. She turned to George who sat next to her, his knees cramped in the small leg space. "You have to tell us what happened after we left last night. Did you talk to Laura?"

Madge responded from the back seat, "He's being secretive, Claire. Believe me, I've been trying to get the scoop."

George's eyes were glued on the traffic, not trusting his colleague's driving. "Why should I share information with you two? You weren't exactly forthcoming about your findings."

Claire stopped at a red light and looked at George. "I did tell you about the notebook, didn't I?"

"Ah, no," George said. "But Madge did."

Claire looked at the department chair in disbelief. The light turned green and a taxi honked behind her. Claire proceeded slowly through the residential area. "I'm an idiot."

She turned into a large parking lot adjacent to the police station. The same desk sergeant greeted them, placing a different romance book, *El Beso Prohibido*, on the table in front of her. This time, the sergeant smiled and assigned an officer to take them through the maze of hallways to a small conference room. The detective would be there *ahorita*.

Again, Salinas did not make them wait. They were no sooner seated when he entered the room and dropped a large accordion file on the table. He looked at all three anthropologists, one at a time.

"Thank you for coming," Salinas said. He turned to Claire. "I'm sorry that your visit to Yaxpec is delayed." To the group, he added, "I have eliminated you as suspects for various reasons, and I hope that your knowledge of academics will help me understand these crimes."

"Can you tell us what you have found out about Tanya's death?" George asked.

Salinas opened the file and extracted several stapled sheets. "Because tourists are involved, the coroner rushed the autopsy and submitted a preliminary toxin report. There is evidence of a strong drug in her system. We suspect oxycodone, simply because she had a bottle of it in her room. We also know she had been drinking. The dagger may have inflicted the fatal wound, or she may have been stabbed after death."

George asked, "Did you find the unlabeled pill bottle?"

"It was in her purse, empty except for remnants of powder. The assumption so far is that she had taken several oxycodone, but the last dose, perhaps the fatal one, had been taken or given to her in crushed form. It acted very quickly and with great intensity."

"She could have taken the crushed pill herself," Madge said.

Salinas thought a moment. "It's possible, but it's more likely that someone else crushed it and diluted it in a liquid, perhaps unaware that this method is potentially fatal. Because the glassware at the Casa Montejo had all been washed, we don't have evidence of how it might have been administered there. George saw two rinsed glasses next to the wine bottle in Tanya's room, and enough wine poured to account for two drinks. The bottle and the glasses are being tested."

"If the fatal dose was crushed into a drink, it had to be at the reception," George said. "She took a pill at the hotel, and I heard at least one pill in the bottle when she shook it."

"Who at the reception would have known she had pills with her? Or have access to oxycodone?" Claire asked.

Salinas shrugged. "Jamal knew this, and he did give her the margarita."

"It's possible someone else at the reception knew she took oxycodone," Claire protested, "perhaps this mysterious Doctor Freeman."

"But is it likely he had the information he needed to commit such a crime?" Salinas asked.

"What about the dagger?" Madge asked.

"Ah, yes," Salinas said. "Was the dagger stolen to commit murder? Or did the murderer happen to have it with him?"

"And if she was already dead, why stab her?" Claire asked.

"He...or she...might not have known she had been drugged," suggested George. "Perhaps he thought she was just intoxicated."

"I'm confused," Claire confessed. "No one knew that Tanya would be sick or asleep on the bed. Yet, someone had access to pills to poison her and a dagger to stab her? Did the same person who had the dagger also have the poison? How could such a murder be planned? And, even more horribly, if it wasn't the same person, who else at the reception wanted to kill her? How could there be more than one person with motive, opportunity, and means?"

Salinas looked at her with appraising eyes. "Welcome to my world."

George asked, "Did they find fingerprints on the dagger or pill bottle?"

"The pill bottle had been wiped clean, but the dagger had only Tanya's prints, which gives us contradictory evidence. If she took the pills and stabbed herself, her fingerprints should be on both." Salinas shuffled his notes. "Tell me again about the theft of the dagger. How many people could have known how to open the display case?"

Madge explained how she and Brad had set up the displays and had taped the key behind one of them. "I don't know if anyone else knew."

"Tanya knew," Claire said. "Remember, Madge? She told us after dinner Monday night."

Madge nodded. "But what reason would she have to steal it? I won't accept the idea that she stole the dagger to kill herself."

"How did Tanya know about the key?" Salinas asked.

Claire thought she had related this story to Salinas already, but remembered this was another on a growing list of omissions. She explained how Tanya had overheard Brad and Eduardo argue outside the Exhibit Room. "She watched them open the case and put the statue inside."

"So, Doctor Ramirez also knew," Salinas said. "Did she say what they argued about?"

"No," Madge answered, "and we had learned to distrust Tanya's gossip. She liked drama." Madge put her hands to her mouth. "That was awful. I'm sorry."

Salinas lay the coroner's report face-down on the table. "I would like to talk about motives—who might have a reason to harm Tanya?"

George said, "None of us would have a motive. We have disagreements. It is a fact of life in academics. Yet we don't go around killing each other."

"Yet, she is dead," Salinas said.

Madge said, "It could be someone whom she knows from her past, or a colleague at another university, like Tom Freeman."

"It's possible," Salinas said. "Sergeant Garza is reviewing all of the interviews from last night as we speak."

"It seems to me that Cody is the common denominator," Claire reasoned. "He and Paul were observed arguing several times at Uxmal, and Jamal saw Cody hurrying back to the Cultural Center before the show."

George added, "And both Cody and Doctor Freeman left the reception before Tanya's body was discovered."

"I hadn't thought of that," Madge said.

"They have both been interviewed," Salinas offered.

Claire, aware that she was twisting her wedding ring, placed her hands in her lap. "What if Tanya saw something on her way to the Sound and Light Show?"

Madge looked at Claire thoughtfully. "What if she had accused Cody of killing Paul," Madge added. "He might have come to the party to confront her or deny her accusations. He could have stolen the dagger and carried it with him, not meaning to use it." Madge sat forward, warming to her theory. "If he saw that Tanya was incoherent and knew she was in the bedchamber, he could easily have killed her while she was incapacitated." She looked up at Salinas for support for her theory.

Claire leaned forward. "He could have murdered them both."

"I saw him go in and out of the sitting room several times," added George.

Madge's gaze flitted from Claire, to George, and then to Salinas. She said, "Do the two deaths have to be related?"

Salinas shrugged. "Paul's dead. Tanya's dead. How many anthropologists normally die at your conferences?"

CHAPTER FORTY-ONE

The anthropologists sat in stunned silence. "I know you would like to place the blame for Tanya's death with someone outside of your program," Salinas said, "yet I can see only two reasons for Cody to kill Tanya. One, that she observed him killing Paul, as you suggest, or two, that she murdered Paul, and Cody killed her for revenge. Do you agree?"

The shocked look on their faces told Salinas that the second reason had not occurred to them.

Claire said, "It has to be the first explanation. I can't see how she could have killed Paul and calmly taken her seat next to us at the Sound and Light Show."

George nodded his assent. "Impossible!" He pursed his lips. "What evidence do you have that she might have killed Paul?"

Salinas opened his folder and retrieved the notebook. He turned to Claire and then to Madge. "I understand that you both read the journal?"

Madge turned her deep blue eyes to Claire, who sat upright in a defensive mode. "I skimmed the pages and showed it to Madge." Claire clenched her fists on the table. "I didn't mean to read it, but..." Claire's jaw tightened, and her eyes narrowed. "I know it was wrong."

"Cody meant for you to read it," Salinas said. "He wanted you to know that Paul had notes."

George, who had not seen the notebook, asked, "What did Paul write about Tanya?"

"A list of names, perhaps anthropologists?" Salinas said. He looked from George to Madge and settled his gaze on Claire. "Is it possible Paul found out something about Tanya that could have threatened her career and caused her to murder him?"

"Impossible!" George repeated.

"Improbable perhaps, but not impossible," Salinas said.

Claire sat stiffly, her hands tightly folded. Salinas recognized the look of anguish on her face. "Doctor Aguila," he said, "I have a sense that you are the person the others confide in." He tented his fingers. "If you have information that can help me solve two deaths, I would like to hear it."

"So would I," mumbled George.

"Remember that I have read the notebook and have conducted interviews," Salinas warned. "I have some clues as to the information Paul had been collecting."

Claire sat back, resigned. She looked at George and Madge again before directing her gaze at the detective. "You need to understand that this is hearsay—comments from her graduate advisors during the hiring process. I was on the search committee. I have since learned additional information, as you suggest, from others." Claire folded her hands in her lap. "And I don't believe for a minute that Tanya would have killed to keep this information hidden."

"Is this about Tanya and the professor?" Madge asked.

Claire nodded. "Paul made a few notes about Tanya's research in Palenque and a set of initials—TF. I think TF is Tom Freeman. Tanya's academic credentials were impressive, but she had a reputation for having romantic relationships with fellow students and even faculty members at graduate school. She seemed to gravitate toward people who could help her, though her research seemed solid."

Salinas asked, "Did your colleagues know about these relationships?" Salinas looked at George, then at Madge.

Claire responded, "I reported to the search committee, of course, but neither Madge nor George had been on the committee. I was the anthropology representative. The linguistics department voted to hire her, and the chair assigned me to mentor her as a member of the Mayanist Program. When we met, I advised her about small university culture and the importance of maintaining proper faculty-student interactions, posing this as general orientation, not as individual counseling, and I thought she understood. She seemed enthusiastic about our college and settling in for her career."

Madge looked at Claire, her steely eyes steady on her friend. "You knew about this...problem...before Tanya blurted out her affair at dinner?"

Claire turned to Madge. "I didn't feel it would be fair to Tanya if I told others, but I told George as department chair."

"You knew?" Madge sat back, arms folded, and glared at George.

Salinas said, "How desperate would she be to keep this knowledge quiet?"

"Tanya might have confronted Paul, but if she had been responsible for his death, she wouldn't have pursued her interrogations at breakfast the next day," Claire argued. "Why not be quiet and let the accident theory stand?"

Madge frowned and disagreed. "I think Tanya could have pulled that off if she had wanted to."

Salinas nodded. "So, it seems the evidence is stronger for the first scenario—that she saw something."

George asked, "But why not tell the police? Why play this parlor game and alienate her colleagues instead?"

Claire sighed. "She was sending a message to someone at the table."

"Exactly," said Salinas. "But who?" Salinas looked at the three anthropologists, then back at Claire, who looked away. "Well?"

"That would mean Brad or Jamal," Claire reasoned, "and neither of them had a motive to kill either Tanya or Paul."

George nudged his glasses up his nose and cleared his throat. "I know that Tanya wanted to be named curator." Everyone stared at George.

Madge's face displayed intrigue and curiosity. "How do you know this?"

"Jamal told me."

Madge's eyes glistened, and small smile lines appeared at the corner of her mouth. "Tell us about it."

"Jamal came to me on her behalf," George said. "Tanya wanted the curatorship and she expected Jamal to support her in her request. He knew that I had no intention of hiring her but felt obligated to approach me. I informed him that when you decided to step down, there would be a search for your replacement, and that Tanya could apply at that time."

Madge asked, "What did Jamal say?"

"Nothing. He wanted to be able to tell Tanya that he had talked to me, and that I had held firm in my support for you."

"Did Tanya ever approach you on the subject?" Claire asked George.

"No, so I gave it no further thought."

Salinas asked, "Did Doctor Kingsford know?"

George fiddled with his glasses again. "I told him on Monday. I don't think he knew."

"How did he respond?" asked Salinas.

"He laughed. It confirmed his theory that Tanya had been manipulating Jamal," George said. "I can't imagine why Jamal would kill Tanya, and I can't believe that anyone in the program would kill her because she wanted to be curator…"

"Except me, perhaps," laughed Madge.

Salinas shrugged his shoulders. "I think these were crimes of opportunity, not passion." He folded his hands. "Tanya heard Brad argue with Eduardo. Could she have been blackmailing either of them?"

"She didn't know Eduardo," George said, "but I thought it strange that Brad went to her hotel room. He's not the sympathetic type, and he seemed to be anxious to get to the reception."

"He had opportunity," Salinas said. "Perhaps she approached him about the curatorship after all?"

"She said she wanted to celebrate," George said. "What did that mean?"

"It doesn't make sense," Madge said. "Brad had no reason to hurt Tanya. There's no way he could appoint her on his own."

"So, we're talking blackmail?" George suggested.

"I have found that the personality of the victim often provides possible motives," Salinas said. "I see two similarities between Tanya and Paul. They were both manipulative and they both collected informa-

tion. Like Paul, Tanya kept a journal on her computer. It's being ana-
lyzed as we speak. They both seemed capable of blackmail."

Madge mused, "Why did Cody insist Claire read the notebook?"

"I've been thinking about that," Claire answered. "I think Cody
wanted to divert Detective Salinas' attention away from himself and
place it elsewhere. Cody told me Paul collected information for a reason. For him, knowledge was power."

"I think Claire is correct," Salinas agreed. "He knew or suspected
that someone at that reception had killed Paul." Salinas looked around
the table. "I think he wanted to do his own investigation, and he is
lucky to be alive."

George pursed his lips in thought. "Was there anything in the
notebook that might be evidence for blackmail?"

Salinas folded his hands on the journal. "Nothing specific, just lists
of places and initials. He may have had more detailed notes on his
computer." He thumbed through the notebook. "Do the initials BS
mean anything to you?"

George shook his head. Claire said, "Madge and I wondered about
that. We don't know anyone with those initials."

Salinas opened the notebook to the photographs. "What do you
think of the drawings?" George stretched over the table to look at the
page in question.

Claire pointed to the drawing of the corn god. "This is the statue
Eduardo is donating." Claire thought about how awkward Brad seemed
when Eduardo presented the statue. "But Paul was already dead when
Eduardo presented it to us. Why did he have a drawing of that specific
statue?"

"Indeed," Salinas said again. "Did you recognize any of the other
drawings?"

Madge said, "We were called downstairs, and didn't see the others."

Salinas asked, "If I make copies of some of the pages in the notebook, would it be possible to research these drawings and perhaps find
information on their origins?"

"Provenience," George offered, "and provenance. These are two different but vital elements in archaeology. Archaeologists need to be precise about provenience, the detailed three-dimensional location where an artifact is found. Without proper recording of provenience, it is impossible to determine whether two tools were made or used at the same time, or hundreds of years later. Curators and collectors are concerned about provenance, the geographic location or site where the artifact was found and documentation that the artifact is genuine and has not been stolen or looted."

"I am not going anywhere today," Madge offered. "I could do this." George added, "I'll work with Madge."

Salinas opened the folder to replace the notebook. As he did this, Claire glimpsed the packet of photographs she had given him Monday evening. It jogged two memories. She was about to speak when Salinas addressed the group.

"I want to thank you all for coming today. You have been very helpful. I wish Madge and George good luck on your research projects, and Claire, please enjoy the trip to your village."

As they left the room, Claire asked Salinas to stay back, and they waited for George and Madge to leave.

"I remembered two things…again," she said, embarrassed.

"Yes?" Salinas said. His cool response supported her belief that his interest in her was calculated at best, waning at worst.

"After George's talk, I saw Brad and Tanya together. Brad was carrying an envelope. I had the idea at the time that Tanya had given it to him, but I'm not sure about that. He put it in his jacket pocket."

Salinas asked, "What size?"

"It was an 8 ½ x 11, but it was folded over. It fit into his sports coat pocket. It bulged, but I couldn't tell what was in it. It's probably not important at all."

Salinas shrugged, but his eyebrows furrowed. "How did they seem—angry, friendly?"

"They were walking close, but I didn't sense anything unusual about it."

"But it was unusual enough for you to mention it."

"The envelope caught my attention, and the unlikely scenario of him visiting her room. It just seemed odd. I think my imagination is getting the better of me."

Salinas said, "It might be nothing, but thank you for telling me." He paused and touched her elbow lightly. "What else? You mentioned two things?"

She told him that she hoped to get the Stuart's photographs in the next day or so.

"*Bueno*," Salinas said. He hesitated and looked down at Claire. "I will be in Motul today with my team. It seems there was a suspicious death there yesterday and the local police are asking for our assistance. What are your plans for Yaxpec?"

"I'm spending the night at my *comadre's* house and then returning sometime tomorrow afternoon for Jamal's presentation. It seems we have all but forgotten our reason for being here. I don't want to let Jamal down."

"Could you meet me in Motul tonight for dinner? We could talk."

"I have already cut my time with my friends in Yaxpec short for this meeting, but I would like to talk to you too."

CHAPTER FORTY-TWO

Claire's car bumped along the road, optimistically called a highway, linking Merida to the village of Yaxpec. The scenery had altered drastically since her first stay in Yaxpec, when fields of henequen cactus, the green gold of Yucatán, connected villages and towns. Now, miles of scrub brush, interspersed with small towns and abandoned haciendas, lined the road. The highway improved marginally when she neared Motul, a growing city with a thriving central plaza. Beyond Motul, the road deteriorated again as she turned off the highway toward "her" village.

As Claire approached Yaxpec she slowed, not only to avoid the perilous speed bumps, but to take in the village itself: how the houses had morphed from thatch to cement, how the main road had exploded with a proliferation of small storefront houses. Pedestrians stopped to peer into her car and wave as she passed. Children ran after her until their parents or older siblings called them back. She wished she remembered all their names. After all, they all knew hers.

She paused at the village's only stop sign, a mere suggestion, as the major traffic consisted of twice-daily, inter-village buses and a few private vehicles. She waved at *Don* Felix, his distinctive mustache now gray, who stood in the doorway of his store, *Dos Hermanos Super-Tienda*. Ahead, the town plaza took up a small block, a microcosm of the central plaza in Merida. After an elderly man on a rickety bicycle wobbled through the intersection, Claire turned left toward the house of her *compadres*.

Maria and Arturo were close in age to Claire and Aaron; they had become friends during her research years. When their first child, Erica, had been born, they had asked Claire and Aaron to be baptism *padrinos*, or godparents. This meant that they would become *compadres*, or co-parents, to Maria and Arturo. Now, more than twenty years later, Erica was a teacher, married with a child of her own.

Claire turned onto a narrow street lined with limestone fences. Memories of her fieldwork years with Aaron haunted her as she bumped down the same streets they had strolled together. Her *compadres* lived in a large, cement block house, their relative affluence marked by an indoor kitchen and bathroom. Arturo's parents had shared the house with them until their deaths several years earlier.

Claire pulled her two bags from the car and waited outside the limestone fence for an invitation, per Mayan custom. She did not wait long—word of her arrival in the village, if not the sound of the car engine, had already announced her.

Jose, Maria and Arturo's nineteen-year-old son, Jose, opened the door and invited her through the gate. "¡*Doña Clara, Pase usted!*" Come in.

Claire opened the gate and entered the *solar*, the Yucatecan homestead. Papaya and fragrant orange trees provided shade for several chickens that pecked for bits of corn. Along the side of the house, pots of herbs and flowering plants lined the limestone walkway.

"Jose," Claire said in awe, "you are grown up...and so handsome!"

Jose blushed and held the door open for Claire as she entered the airy living room furnished with a sofa and several chairs. A family altar filled a short wall, adorned with a framed print depicting the Virgin of Guadelupe and a collection of votive candles and photographs of deceased family members. The newest addition to the room, since Claire's last visit, was a flat-screen television perched on a wooden cabinet.

Jose led them into the kitchen where Maria and her younger daughter, Carmen, were preparing lunch, their major meal. Maria turned from the stove, smiled widely and wrapped her arms around Claire, enveloping her within the folds of her warm and ample body. Carmen, in her early twenties, hugged Claire after Maria had released her from her grasp. Carmen looked like a younger version of her mother and older sister, with high cheekbones and dark, expressive eyes.

Jose took the bags from Claire. "Your clothes, *Doña* Clarita?"

Claire laughed. "And gifts for later. No peeking!"

A thick soup of black beans, squash, tomatoes, and noodles simmered on the stove, and a plate piled high with shredded chicken indicated that tacos were on the menu.

"You are in time for *almuerzo*," said Maria.

"It smells wonderful." Claire breathed in the aromas and fell naturally back into the Spanish language.

Maria and Carmen continued their food preparation. Maria stirred the soup while Carmen diced onions and then chopped several jalapeño peppers, carefully scraping away the seeds. A wooden bowl of cornmeal beckoned Claire. She washed her hands and began to form the small balls that would be transformed into hot tortillas.

Maria smiled as she watched Claire rolling the tiny balls. "Aye, you are a true Yucateca," she said, pushing wisps of hair from her face with the back of her hand. She joined Claire at the wooden table and flattened the balls into tortillas of identical shape. Instead of a griddle perched precariously over the open fire, Maria tossed the tortillas onto a stove-top griddle. As they worked together, Maria bragged about Carmen's new teaching job and Jose's acceptance into an engineering program.

Maria flipped the tortillas over with her fingers and watched them puff up into beautiful domes. She placed them into a tortilla warmer and covered them with a cloth, then started patting another batch for the griddle.

She turned to Claire, whose mouth watered as she took in the rich aroma of the soup and home-made tortillas, "We have you to thank for our blessings. We could not have afforded to send all three children to college without your help."

"It was a small thing compared to our friendship," Claire said, "but where is Erica, my *ahijada*?"

As she said this, the front door opened. "*Bueno!*"

Claire recognized the voice, quickly washed her hands, and hurried into the living room to greet her goddaughter, Erica, who entered holding a six-month-old baby. They were followed by Erica's husband, Tomás, whom Claire had met during her last visit, just after Aaron's death. Looking at Erica, now a lovely mother, Claire could not have been prouder had it been her own child and grandchild, yet she felt a pang of jealousy that Maria had a grandchild and she did not.

"This is Clara," Erica said, handing the child to Claire.

"Clara?" Claire said, taking the child into her arms. "You called her Cee Cee on Facebook."

"We call her Cee Cee, but we named her after you." Cee Cee smiled as if she knew the strange lady who held her, tears running down her cheeks.

Tomás left to find his father-in-law while the women returned to the kitchen where they gossiped about the events—deaths, marriages, and local scandals—since Claire's last visit. They placed the food and plates on the table as Tomás and Arturo entered through the back door. Her *compadre* hung his Detroit Tigers baseball cap, a gift from Claire, on a nail just inside the kitchen door. His clothes and body were covered with white limestone powder, evidence of his construction job. He smiled at Claire when he saw her. "Ah, *mija*, you have finally returned to see us. We thought you forgot about us."

"Of course not, *compadre*. It is wonderful to be here again."

The social gender norms prohibited Arturo from hugging Claire, even in a familial way, so verbal banter comprised their social interaction. While Arturo washed up, the women filled the soup bowls, and Maria called Jose in from the backyard where he had been sent to scatter the scraps from dinner preparation to the chickens, pigs, and turkeys in the *solár*. A highchair materialized from a back room.

Dinner discussion focused on Claire's visit, her hosts mesmerized by her descriptions of the conference—especially the two deaths. Her commentary reminded Arturo that he had news of his own.

"There was a murder in Motul Monday, but I just heard about it today." Arturo stuffed a taco into his mouth, awaiting the response of his family.

"Who?" María asked.

"Benito Suarez. He had a souvenir store."

Claire paused, her soup spoon frozen in place. Roberto was in Motul, investigating a murder. And the victim's name sounded familiar. She had heard it before. But where?

"A souvenir vendor?" Claire asked.

Tomás nodded. "He sold statues and other tourist items, but people say that he had a shady business, *mal negocios*, and that he might have been selling drugs. But who knows?"

"That's him," Arturo agreed. "Do you remember him, Claire? He visited you and Aaron and tried to sell you artifacts."

Claire stared at her *compadre*, stunned. Suddenly a vision came back to her of a young man coming to their house, claiming friendship with Arturo. The man had explained how he came to have some small items that he could sell...no problem. He had taken several small shards of hieroglyphs and a broken statuette from his pocket.

"But we never bought anything!" Claire protested.

Arturo laughed. "No, and that was a good thing, I think. He was just starting his business, collecting small pieces, but he turned his attentions to souvenir artifacts. I heard he had a relative who made them."

"That was Benito Suarez?" Claire asked.

In that instant it all came back to Claire, and in the same moment she remembered Paul's slide presentation to the faculty. He had included a photograph of a vendor called *Don* Benito. She remembered the initials 'BS' in the notebook and the drawings. But drugs? Maybe her colleagues weren't involved after all. This thought gave her some hope. But it also caused a pang of fear...she had met this man before... thirty years ago.

CHAPTER FORTY-THREE

Wednesday Afternoon

After a short *siesta*, Claire struggled from the deep folds of a hammock that the family had provided for her stay. Once wrapped in the soft mesh, extricating herself was both a physical and emotional hardship—physical because it required dexterity innate to Mexicans but hard-learned by others; emotional because the coolness of the mesh and gentle rocking of the hammock enveloped one into a lush protective womb. She had one more visit to make before she met Roberto in Motul.

Even in late afternoon, the sun's rays radiated off the limestone path. Her sleeveless dress was already damp with perspiration. As she walked, she took photographs of the village, the houses, the stores, and the people as they emerged from the relative cool of their homes to resume their daily life.

She hoped she would find *Don* Santiago at home. He was one of the last shamans, or *h-menob*, who still practiced the annual rain ceremony in the area. His sons, who would normally learn the ancient rain and curing rituals, had no interest in learning the Mayan traditions and had moved away.

Santiago and his wife, Sofia, lived at the far eastern edge of the village in a traditional oval-shaped house made of crushed limestone. It stood along a narrow two-track road that led to the cemetery. For many years, the house consisted of one room with a dirt floor and thatch roof. That had changed several years before when one son, who had recently returned from work in the United States, had made major renovations: a bathroom, cement floor, and corrugated roof. This had happened during Claire's last visit, and she was anxious to see if they were happy with the upgrade.

Claire stood outside the dilapidated stone fence, readjusting her straw hat. The family dog, of indistinguishable breed, came out from behind the house and barked half-heartedly, alerting the owners. *Doña* Sofia came to the gate, opened it and, smiling, waved her in.

"*Doña* Clara! ¡*Kosh!* ¡*Pase usted!*" She invited Claire in, using two languages.

Claire entered the sparsely furnished house, with wooden chairs and an armoire along one wall that served as a closet. Their family altar held faded photographs, worn candles, and a faded print of the Virgin of Guadelupe that had been torn from a magazine. One frayed hammock hung from a hook on the wall. The second hammock was stretched across the room, the one from which Claire had awoken the elderly woman.

Sofia resembled most clearly the figures carved in stone at the ancient sites, solidly built with a round dark face and Mayan hooked nose. Her dark eyes reflected ancient knowledge as she vacillated between Mayan and Spanish in her conversations. Now she re-coiled her waist-long gray hair and secured it to the back of her head with a large plastic comb.

"I am so sorry I woke you," Claire said.

Sofia brushed her hand over her soiled *huipil* and said, "Oh, no, Clarita. I was awake." To cover her small deception, she detached the hammock from the hook on one end of the house, wound it around her arm just as she had coiled her own hair and attached it to the hook on the other wall.

"Is *Don* Santiago here?" Claire asked.

"*Sí, cierto,*" she replied. She pointed to the back door of the house.

Claire followed Sofia outside, through the lean-to kitchen comprised of a stone firepit and wooden shelf suspended from the lean-to by a strong rope made with henequen fibers. Along the kitchen area, pots of herbs grew in a hodge-podge: cilantro, several varieties of peppers, and others unrecognizable, grown specifically for *Doña* Sofia's herbal medicines. They maneuvered around aloe and pineapple plants. *Don* Santiago rested in a hammock strung between two large trees.

"Why doesn't he nap in the house out of the sun?" Claire asked.

She smiled and whispered, "He doesn't like the tin roof. It is too hot. But don't tell our son. He spent so much money to build it."

Their conversation woke the elderly shaman, who jumped from his hammock as a child would, his tiny, lithe body exploding from the folds of the mesh.

"Clarita, come, sit." He dragged a metal chair from underneath a nearby mango tree and motioned her to sit among a tropical orchard that surrounded her with the colors and scents of banana, mango, orange, lime, and papaya trees.

Don Santiago returned to his hammock using it as a swing, pushing back and forth with his misshaped calloused bare feet. *Doña* Sofia left them alone to speak.

"You will never guess," he smiled widely. "We get electricity soon. The new president has promised to bring it up our road."

"And then what will you buy?" Claire asked curiously.

"Why, a television of course...and then, some fans. That roof is too hot!"

Claire laughed and shared news of her daughter's interest in medicine and healing. She described the conference that brought her to Yucatán and eventually eased the conversation toward his memory of other anthropologists he might have heard of through conversations with family and friends in neighboring villages.

"Ah, so you are here to test my memory," Santiago teased. "I thought you came to visit two *viejitos*, old people."

Claire felt herself blush. She had indeed pushed the conversation too quickly, and he was justified to call her on it. "I came to visit you," she insisted, "but, I'm also interested to learn about other anthropologists who have worked near here after me."

Doña Sofia brought a plate of fruit and placed it on a wooden chair between Claire and her husband. The plate held sweet orange wedges and sliced papaya, freshly picked from her trees. Claire chose a wedge of naval orange. "Something has happened at the conference—and in Motul too—and it might involve Americans who have worked here."

Santiago paused in his swinging and reached for a slice of papaya. "*Don* Benito," he said thoughtfully, as he popped it into his mouth and resumed his motion.

"You knew?" Claire asked.

"*Cierto.*" He stopped swinging, intrigued now. "You want to know about anthropologists around here?" His dark intelligent eyes bored into her from his heavily creased face, testament to a long life in the tropical sun.

"I'm sure you remember them." Claire popped another orange wedge into her mouth, savoring the crisp flavor while *Don* Santiago thought about her request.

"There were several anthropologists around here after you," the shaman said.

"Do you remember a Brad or Jamal, Paul or Pablo?"

"Where did they live?" Santiago asked.

"Pablo might have lived in Motul. He studied *turismo.*"

"Ah, that was not long ago. I remember Pablo. He always bothered the storekeepers about their businesses. People got tired of him."

"And Brad and Jamal?"

Santiago thought awhile. "Jamal lived in Dzab, but I don't remember a Brad." The shaman struggled with the "Br" sound. It came out as "Bl" instead.

Claire prompted, "Brad would have been in Tixbe."

The shaman tilted his head. "That was Jaime. That was a while ago."

"Jaime?" Claire asked. "Do you know what he studied in the village?"

"My friend, the *h-men* in Tixbe, told me Jaime was interested in the rituals and the sacred items we used in the ceremonies."

Claire frowned. "And Jamal?" she asked. "What did he study?"

Don Santiago smiled. "Jamal worked with my friend, *Don* Cristo. He was studying *h-menob*, but he was more interested in the drugs. He was a black man, *un negro*."

CHAPTER FORTY-FOUR

Wednesday Evening

Claire waved farewell to her friends, avoiding their questions about her evening plans, but promising to return to the village at a respectable hour. She felt like a teenager sneaking out for a clandestine date.

She retraced her route to the plaza. It was early evening, and the village had emerged from its afternoon slumber. The sweet aroma of freshly baked pastries and bread from *Doña* Isabela's bakery wafted through her open car window. She paused for the inter-village bus as it stopped at the main plaza, discharging villagers returning from city jobs—nurses, teachers, factory workers, and maids. As she left the village behind, she sped through the countryside, slowing for speed bumps as she passed through small villages.

While Merida drew tourists seeking Mayan history from the protection of the international hotels, Motul's appeal lay in its quaint colonial feel: small hotels, produce markets, tourist shops, and restaurants offering Yucatecan cuisine. Claire parked in front of Café Flor, a small café that spilled out onto the sidewalk, facing the main plaza. She settled at a table to wait for the detective.

"Good evening."

Claire turned to see Roberto Salinas at her side. He sat across from her, and Claire felt uncomfortable as he looked at her.

"I like your hair when you wear it down, like this. It's much less... how do you say...professorial?"

Claire self-consciously fingered her hair that came down below her shoulders in natural waves. "My mother says I'm too old to wear my hair long, but I'm too Mexican to cut it. Maybe when I'm sixty, I'll chop it off."

He laughed. "No, don't do that." He waved to a waiter and they ordered drinks. "I thought we might start here, but I found a wonderful little restaurant nearby. I'm glad you came. It has been a rough day."

"You mentioned a suspicious death. I have heard about it, I think."

"Oh?" He raised his eyebrows.

"Yaxpec is a small village, but a little thing like a lack of telephones doesn't stop gossip." She paused as the waiter brought two beers to the table. Pushing her lime into her bottle, Claire continued, "My *compadre*, Arturo, heard about the death of a souvenir vendor named Benito Suarez. Arturo said he might have been involved in *mal negocios*, perhaps drugs."

"Yes, that's the man," Salinas said. "It seems he had a side business of selling marijuana to tourists and local ex-patriots, but the antiquities angle is more interesting to me, given the drawings in Paul's notebook."

"You asked us this morning about the initials BS, and I had no idea who that might be, but now that I know his name, I have to confess that I met him, many years ago."

Roberto raised his eyebrows again. "Tell me."

"Arturo reminded me that *Don* Benito had visited Aaron and me selling artifacts." The mischievous smile on Salinas's face gave him away. "But, of course, you knew this already," Claire said.

"You were in the notebook."

"I didn't see a page with my name," Claire protested.

"Paul had a page for Benito Suarez at the back of the notebook. He had listed names of people he might have suspected of purchasing items from him, and there you were...CAC."

"Claire Aguila Carson." She set her bottle on the table. "Are you investigating me?"

"Poor Sergeant Garza and our team have spent the day matching initials with conference attendees and comparing them to the list of clients that we found at *Señor* Suarez's store."

"We didn't buy anything," Claire said defensively. "Perhaps I should go." She stood to leave.

"Please, stay." He reached out and touched her arm. "There is no evidence that you ever purchased anything. You weren't listed in his customer book."

"But others were?"

"Perhaps." He sipped his beer. "Would you recognize *Señor* Suarez if you saw him?"

"I think I have seen him—in Paul's slide presentation."

"Slide presentation?"

"At his interview. It was on his computer."

Roberto sighed. "Can you describe it?"

"The presentation included photographs of vendors Paul had interviewed for his research. In one of them, an old man stood at a store counter. Several statues stood on the counter in front of him. I think Paul called him *Don* Benito. I didn't recognize him at the time, but now I think it could have been the same man. It was a long time ago," Claire repeated.

Salinas sipped his beer. "He sold replicas that his relative produced. But he also had access, through family and friends, to some—let's say 'discovered'—artifacts, and he sold them for extra cash. We are trying to find out if he had a partner or someone who may have purchased these special artifacts from him. Perhaps he was, how do you say, a middleman?"

Claire settled back into her chair. "Do you think his death is related to Paul? Or Tanya?"

"It seems likely." He looked at Claire, his face stern and unreadable. "Tell me, Claire, did anyone react when Paul showed that slide?"

"Paul asked Brad if he had met this man, since his store was on the road to Tixbe where Brad worked. Brad said he remembered the store and the storekeeper, but he didn't know him."

"Was he convincing?"

"I had no reason to doubt him." She paused as something occurred to her. "But Jamal reacted."

"How?"

"I heard him take a deep breath, like a gasp...*Dios mio!*" Claire sat back in her chair and looked wide-eyed at Roberto as if just receiving an electric shock. "*Don* Santiago!"

"Who?"

"*Don* Santiago is the *h-men* of Yaxpec. I visited him today and asked him if he remembered any of the anthropologists who worked in this area. He remembered Jamal because he studied ritual with one of *Don* Santiago's friends, the *shaman* in Dzab. It seems that Jamal might have been interested in drugs, perhaps for personal use. What if Jamal bought marijuana from Benito?"

"Paul wrote 'BS' on Jamal's page also." Roberto tipped his hand upward in a 'there you go' gesture.

Claire regretted her indiscretion and felt compelled to defend her colleague. "Jamal couldn't have killed anyone."

"It's amazing how many times I hear that." Roberto studied Claire as he sipped his beer. "What made you think to ask the *h-men* about your colleagues?"

"It interested me that Paul, Brad, and Jamal all worked in this area. Even though shamans are elders, they have keen memories and they know each other. I knew that Jamal studied the botanical aspects of shamanism and Brad studied ritual objects. I thought perhaps *Don* Santiago might have heard of them. Besides, anthropologists are a novelty. People remember us."

"I applaud your initiative." Salinas said.

Claire frowned. "I feel like a traitor."

"Did *Don* Santiago remember Doctor Kingsford?"

"There's something odd about that," Claire said. "Brad worked in Tixbe, but *Don* Santiago remembered him as Jaime. If Jaime is Brad, then he used a different name."

"Could Brad have had a motive to hurt Paul, Tanya, or Benito?"

"I can't think of a motive for any of us. None of us knew Paul before this weekend. It could have been someone local, someone he knew. He was involved in illegal activities. It could have been anyone." She cupped her bottle with both hands. "After all, Jamal lived in Dzab five…six years ago? He had no recent connection to Benito…unless he went to purchase some marijuana during the conference, but would he be that stupid?"

When Roberto made no comment, Claire continued, "It has been even longer since Brad lived in Tixbe." She paused, aware of Roberto's intent gaze. "Paul knew Benito, but, if he was killed Monday morning, Paul was already dead."

Roberto nodded. "We are questioning everyone who knew him, but it seems that Benito had several visitors Monday morning."

"Visitors?"

"Non-locals. At least three vehicles were seen at Benito's store and attached house. A large black car was seen leaving the area very early in the morning; then, a light-colored car, and finally, around noon, a white Ford Fiesta. An elderly woman remembered the Fiesta because it had a Spanish name. Witnesses all agreed that the cars looked too nice to be local."

"Could the witnesses identify the drivers?" Claire asked.

"It was still dark when the black car drove by, and the witness couldn't see his face. The second man had light skin and wore a straw hat. He knocked at the storefront, then went behind to the house. He left a few minutes later. The third man went directly to the back door, but he stood out to the witness. He was black."

Salinas watched Claire over the bottle as he drank. He put the empty bottle on the table. "Strangely, no one went to check up on poor *Señor* Suarez until later when his store didn't open. A neighbor found him dead in his house and reported to the police."

"He lived alone?"

"His wife died many years ago."

"We all ate breakfast together Monday morning," Claire insisted. "What time did he die?"

"Late Sunday evening or early Monday morning."

"It couldn't have been my colleagues," Claire said, pushing her bottle aside.

Roberto motioned for the check. "Let's walk."

The air had cooled, and Claire detoured to her car to get her shawl. They strolled quietly along the central plaza. Men in white *guayaberas* sat in their horse-drawn carriages along the plaza, awaiting customers. A driver offered them a good price for a ride, but they shook their heads and walked on.

Claire pulled her shawl tighter around her shoulders, and Roberto took her arm as they continued down the narrow sidewalk as the street-lights illuminated. "You need to think of the deaths of Paul, Tanya, and *Senior* Suarez as related. Someone is nervous, perhaps desperate, and people are dying. I think you can help me find out who that is."

"I can't imagine anyone I know having a reason to harm these people. These are my friends and colleagues."

"One of whom is dead."

They crossed the main avenue and turned down a quiet side street past a series of tourist shops. Tonight, she barely noticed her surroundings.

"Can you tell me about Brad?" Roberto prodded.

She sighed in resignation and explained how Brad came to be the director of the new Mayanist Program.

"Is he a good director?"

Claire paused just long enough to pique Roberto's interest. "But…?" he coaxed.

"Brad doesn't like dissent. Academics are notorious for talking an idea to death. Brad just decides, and then pushes his plans on the faculty. It doesn't go over well with everyone."

"Like Doctor Ramirez's loan to your museum?"

"Yes, he was quite insistent that we accept the offer."

"Do Brad and Jamal get along?"

"Yes, mainly because Jamal is a willing protégé."

"You told me earlier that Brad and Jamal left the breakfast table Monday morning after Cody arrived." When Claire nodded, he asked, "Do you remember what time this was?"

"It must have been shortly after nine o'clock. Sessions usually start at eight-thirty, but none of us seemed to be in the mood to attend, after what happened to Paul."

"Do you know where Brad and Jamal went after they left the table?"

Claire thought a moment. "George said Brad went to the beach to work on his speech. I have no idea where Jamal went." She stopped walking. "That means neither of them could have killed Benito."

"But Brad could have gone to Motul," Salinas said. They paused at an intersection, waiting to cross. "Can you think of any reason Brad might have to hurt Tanya, besides the fact that she wanted to be curator?"

Claire felt her temper rise under his interrogation. She turned to look at him. "I already told you I have no reason to suspect him." Her words came out more sharply than she had intended. "I'm sorry," she said quickly. "This is hard for me."

They approached a small, brightly lit plaza lined with boutiques.

"Do you suspect Brad?" Claire asked.

"I am starting with him. Don't worry. I have questions about others, including you." He smiled down at her. Claire wished she could turn and run. He seemed to sense this and took her arm, maneuvering her through the growing flow of evening walkers and into an intimate café, *La Vainilla*.

The waiter seated them by a window where they could watch people strolling by. He brought them water and menus and left them to make their decision.

Roberto picked up his menu but looked at Claire instead. "What do you know about Doctor Ramirez?"

"Very little," Claire said. "I've researched his businesses, and it seems he and his family have become very wealthy buying and selling antiquities." She opened her menu but returned her gaze to the detective. "But you know all this," she added impatiently.

Roberto put his menu down and tapped his fingers on the table. "Do you know him personally? Have you had any interactions with him?"

Claire crossed her arms and leaned back in her chair. "What do you mean?"

Roberto shrugged and opened his menu. "Did you speak with him at the reception?"

"We spoke briefly. The reason is personal."

Roberto raised his eyebrows slightly and took a sip of water.

"He offered me a job," she confessed. His silence indicated he already knew this also. She pretended to read her menu. "I think he was flattering me, but I don't know why."

"Did Eduardo know Tanya?"

"I don't think he knew her at all."

Roberto shrugged. "Can you tell me anything about the sale of artifacts?"

Claire reached for her water glass. "It's not my area of expertise. I am a cultural anthropologist. But I have learned that Mexican laws and American Customs laws are very strict."

Roberto asked, "Do you think any of your colleagues would be interested in antiquities?"

Claire considered. "I don't think Brad is interested in artifacts, except in the ritual sense—the religious items used in ceremonies. Jamal is interested in medicinal herbs and healing, not artifacts. Paul, however, was interested in artifacts, and he knew local vendors. Eduardo is interested in artifacts...they're his life...but I know nothing about his connections with local vendors."

"Paul wrote the initials "ER" in his notebook," Roberto reasoned.

Claire was silent a moment, then said, "Eduardo drives a black rental car. I saw him return to the hotel early Monday morning."

"Ah," responded Roberto.

CHAPTER FORTY-FIVE

They ordered wine and dinner, though Claire had lost her appetite. Claire looked through the window at the diners seated outdoors. Streetlights threw a shadow on a small diner across the plaza. She watched as an elderly tourist couple, packages in hand, stopped to look at the Spanish-language menu posted on the door, but moved on. They reminded her of the Stuarts.

"What are you thinking?"

Claire turned to Salinas, who held his wineglass up to her. She hadn't been aware of its arrival at the table.

"I'm sorry," she said. "*Salud.*"

They sipped their wine before Roberto continued his interrogation. "Can you tell me about Jamal?"

"I like Jamal," she said. "I can't imagine him harming anyone, and I can't believe either he or Brad could have gone to Motul before breakfast…and they *were* at breakfast."

"Yet a black man and a man in a straw hat were seen in Motul, and we don't yet know when Benito was killed," Roberto countered. "However, your friend Jamal may have an alibi for Monday morning after all."

Claire looked up quickly. "What?"

"I don't know what he did before breakfast, but after breakfast he tried to steal a computer from Paul and Cody's room."

Claire's dark eyes widened. "Paul's computer?" She frowned in thought. "It was already stolen."

"But, as you said before, he did run away after the program instead of following the crowd. Perhaps he wanted to hide something on the bus, quickly. He had a backpack, correct?"

Claire thought. "Yes, but if he had the computer, why go into the hotel room?"

"He may have been looking for something else."

"Like what?"

"Perhaps a notebook or some other electronic device—a tablet perhaps? I am not convinced by Jamal's statement."

The waiter arrived with the food and warmed tortillas, and conversation paused as they took in the spicy aroma of the *pollo pibil* that enveloped them. They unwrapped the meat from the banana leaves and savored the first bites of moist roasted chicken, black beans, and wild rice.

"I've been thinking about the timeline," Roberto said after a few minutes. "The times are critical." He reached in his pocket and pulled out his notebook. "According to the written statements, you saw Paul and Cody at the pyramid around six-thirty, then went to the bleachers where George and Madge joined you around six-forty-five. Jamal entered the site around six-fifty-five and reported seeing Cody run back to the Cultural Center just after seven, but he didn't report seeing Paul at the pyramid."

Roberto read on. "It seems that Brad and Laura walked to the site together between six-fifteen and six-thirty. They separated at the ball court. Neither mentioned seeing Paul or Cody."

"But they must have," Claire said. "I saw them at six-thirty and Jamal saw Cody at seven…unless they had climbed the pyramid."

"Or were on the opposite side. It is a massive structure, and neither Brad nor Laura indicated which path they took around the pyramid, right or left."

Claire asked, "What about Eduardo?"

"Eduardo took a later shuttle, arrived around six-thirty and went directly into the site. He said he didn't see anyone but joined up with Brad near the Nunnery around seven o'clock or a little later."

He looked at his notes again. "According to Tanya, she left Jamal behind at the Cultural Center. She didn't mention seeing Paul and Cody, but said she saw Brad and Eduardo near the Nunnery. She arrived in the seats before them. Brad and Eduardo joined you just before the show started at seven-fifteen, Mexican time."

"Yes," Claire responded. "So, no one claims to have seen Paul after six-forty-five?"

"I meant to talk to Tanya again," Roberto said. "Her timing seemed critical to understanding when he might have died...but...I didn't talk to her in time."

"And what she saw might be the cause of her death."

"Unless she killed Paul herself," Roberto reminded her.

"But she told Cody she didn't believe him," Claire countered.

"That could mean anything...or nothing."

"It's hard to believe that no one else saw them at the pyramid."

Roberto shrugged. "It was dusk, and people are looking ahead or at their feet, not up at the pyramid. Actually," he said, "we did a little experiment."

"We?"

"Sergeant Garza and I...actually Sergeant Garza conducted the experiment. I held the stopwatch."

"Why make her do it?"

"We needed to know if a woman could climb the back stairs of the pyramid and how long it would take." He shrugged. "She climbed to the second level, walked around it, and descended in about ten minutes. Assuming a short discussion or argument, the entire encounter could have been accomplished in fifteen minutes."

"Sergeant Garza is in good shape," Claire said.

"And a saint, she tells me."

"That means it's possible that no one would notice them up there, but who could have done it?"

Roberto considered. "Tanya, Brad, or Eduardo if their stated times are off, or Jamal if he lied about the time he entered and his claim that he saw Cody run from the site."

"Or Laura, or Cody," Claire said, then stopped. "When Tanya joined us, she borrowed Madge's binoculars. She might have seen who killed Paul."

"But in her statement, she didn't report seeing Paul." Salinas shuffled through his notebook. "But she may have told someone else."

CHAPTER FORTY-SIX

Roberto pushed his empty plate away and finished his wine. "I'd like to go back to the notebook."

Claire fumbled with her empty wine glass. "I'm sorry I didn't call you immediately. I intended to take it to you the next day." She smiled. "You are quite intimidating, you know…in two languages."

He laughed. "That's my job."

"What else have you learned from Paul's notes?"

"There was something strange." Roberto tented his fingers and looked intently at Claire. "Paul wrote notes on everyone, including Eduardo, but nothing on you, except your initials on a list of possible buyers. *You* must be a saint too, like Sergeant Garza."

"Hardly," Claire said.

He watched her closely. "It seems that several pages had been carefully ripped out. It was a composition notebook, not a spiral, you recall." Claire did not respond, so he continued, "*Entonces,* my question is, who did that and why?"

"And your answer?"

"The obvious answer is that you might have done it. You might not have wanted me to see what devious act you had committed…stealing, flirting with police officers…"

He paused, raising his eyebrows. "In fact," he said, "the seriousness of the offense might not matter. The question is, what would one do to keep information about oneself from becoming public? It could be as simple as a drunk-driving charge for a politician, or sex with a prostitute for a priest." Roberto blushed as he said this. "I am sorry—I am being too familiar with you."

Claire bit her lip to still her rising frustration. "Do you think I sat upstairs slicing pages from his notebook with a razor blade?"

Roberto sat back, silent, then smiled. "Did you?"

Claire suddenly laughed at the thought, "I understand what you're saying, but I didn't do it."

To his credit, Salinas looked apologetic. "I didn't mean to accuse you. I was merely providing insight into the mind of a detective."

Outside, the air had cooled, but the stars shone brightly above them. As they walked toward the main plaza, Roberto asked, "If there had been a page for you in the notebook, what might be on it?"

Claire looked up at him sharply. "I really don't know, other than his suspicion that I might have been involved with *Don* Benito." She paused. "But Paul did ask me about my book. He gave me a backward compliment..."

"Meaning?"

"How refreshing that I was honest about personal conflicts in my research, like rejecting my faith and how that might have affected my objectivity."

"Do you have a problem with the Church? Are you still Catholic?"

Claire knew that the questions had layered meanings. "I am nominally Catholic, but my feelings about the church are complicated." She could feel his eyes on her as they walked, but she looked ahead, avoiding his eyes. "I am also an anthropologist, and our views on religion are based on a relativistic perspective, not one that privileges one religion over another."

"Yes, I know." He paused, and Claire turned to look at him. "Did I tell you my daughter is studying anthropology, and that you have met her?"

Claire tried to imagine the many university students she had talked to over the past days. "Why didn't you tell me?"

He shrugged and pulled her arm into the crook of his elbow. "She didn't want me to. And frankly, I didn't want her to get involved with your group." Claire looked up at him to see if he was joking. His wry sense of humor unsettled her.

"Did you set her out to spy on us?" She tried to match his tone.

"Not really, but Marta found out who you were." He smiled again. "You signed her book."

Claire laughed. "I remember her. She seemed familiar. Now, I know why." She breathed in the cool night air. "I would love to meet Marta."

"Perhaps when this is over?"

"I would like that. Has she helped you in the investigation?"

"In some ways. No one notices the students who are hanging around, but the students are aware of the professionals."

They reached the plaza and sat on a metal bench near a group of jewelry vendors who had lain their handicrafts on a large blanket on the walkway.

Salinas looked to Claire. "We found Paul's computer, by the way. Several young boys found it in a roadside dump and tried to sell it at a pawn shop in Merida."

"Do people go through dumps like that?"

"Are you kidding? It's amazing what wealthy people, especially Americans, throw away. Anyway, we had an alert out to pawn and resale shops for computers, and we got a call."

"Did you find anything on it?"

"The files had been deleted. We have computer forensics working on it, but it will take time. We can't find a computer genius in every eighth-grade classroom like you can in the United States." He smiled at her.

Claire asked, "What have you found on Tanya's computer? I assume her files are being examined."

"We'll know more tomorrow. I hope to have this solved very soon."

Claire frowned. "It looks a long way from being solved from my end."

Roberto did not respond to her comment but turned toward her. "I would like to visit Dzab and Tixbe tomorrow. Will you come with me?"

Claire tried to hide her shock. "If it's appropriate, I would like that."

"Can I pick you up in Yaxpec tomorrow at eight o'clock?"

Claire did not want her friends to see a man pull up to her *compadres'* house early in the morning. It would cause all kinds of speculation.

"No. I'll meet you at Café Flor. I need to return to Merida by four o'clock tomorrow for Jamal's presentation, and the drive will be shorter from here. I keep forgetting that there is a conference going on."

Program for the 10th Annual Meeting of the Society for Mayanist Studies

Events for Thursday, May 8
Mayan Identities—The Intersection of Indigenous Knowledge and Western Cultural and Religious Hegemony

Morning Sessions:

- Sarah Sanchez, *The Interface between Indigenous Medicine and Western Health Care Delivery Systems in Rural Mexico*
- Heather Hartley, *The Last H-men: The Demise of Mayan Ritual in Indigenous Communities*

Afternoon Sessions:

- Nathaniel Newman, *The New Mayan Cosmology: The Reintegration of Indigenous Mayan Worldview into Modern Catholic Liturgy in Guatemala*
- Teresa Tellejon, *Face to Face with the Pope: How Mexican Catholic Women Redefine Women's Rights in the Context of Canonical Teachings—The Case for Birth Control*

4:00 Jamal Kennedy
"The Use of Indigenous Pharmacopeia in Modern Shamanic Practices"

CHAPTER FORTY-SEVEN

Thursday Morning

Claire sat in a booth at Café Flor, staring at her coffee, her breakfast barely touched.

"Where are you?" asked Roberto, his plate scraped clean, his coffee cup empty.

"In Yaxpec," Claire admitted. "It's hard to leave."

"Have you considered moving to Merida? You could teach at the university. It might be a good change for you."

"I have thought about it actually." She sipped her cold coffee. "Now that Cristina is on her own, I could. But I need to think of my parents. They're getting older."

"It is a difficult decision," he agreed, "and my reasons are selfish."

Claire fingered her necklace. Salinas sighed heavily and motioned to the waitress. "Are you ready to visit Jamal's village?"

An abandoned hacienda stood at the outskirts of Dzab, a tiny village, seemingly lost in time. Several cement S-shaped lovers' seats and a dangerous-looking play set dominated the small plaza where vigorous weeds grew between the cracks in the pavement. Wood and thatch houses branched out from the plaza in a series of two-track roads, and the electrical wires started at the plaza and ended not too far away.

What Dzab lacked in amenities, it gained in authenticity. Women wearing *huipiles* and colorful shawls, children or grandchildren in tow, converged on an open market near the plaza. They carried henequen-fiber tote bags that would soon be filled with the fresh foods they needed to prepare the daily meals. The men had disappeared to their jobs, and the plaza belonged to the women and children.

Roberto and Claire walked along a tiled veranda to a small government office, a miniature of those in Motul and Merida. Finding no one there, they joined a line at a market refreshment kiosk and listened to the distinctive mono-syllabic tone of the Mayan language. A multitude of deep brown eyes turned toward them, assessing the appearance of strangers in their midst.

Claire purchased a soft drink from the owner, a man wearing traditional Mayan clothing, and asked where they might find the village president.

"His name is *Don* Pedro Cuca," the storekeeper said, but before he gave directions, Roberto felt a tug on his shirt.

"*Señor?*" Roberto looked around and down. He smiled at an ancient woman wearing a stained *huipil,* her colorful shawl thrown over her shoulder. She smiled, displaying a toothless grin and deep facial crevices. Her long gray hair was knotted at the nape of her neck and the top of her head barely reached Roberto's chest.

"*Señor*, my granddaughter, Maria, can show you."

A young girl, taller than her grandmother, came forward and nodded. "He lives near my house," she said.

Claire thanked them all in Mayan, which caused a twitter among them. She gave the soft drink to the young girl who walked slightly ahead of them, her spindly legs protruding from a skirt that hung to her calves, a hand-me-down she hadn't grown into yet.

The sun radiated down on them as they made their way across the plaza. Maria led them through the rocky soccer field adjacent to the church and toward a cluster of cement-block houses. Their short journey followed the electrical power line.

Maria stopped at a house where a scrawny dog lazed in the meager shade of a papaya tree. She called out a greeting from behind the stone wall, and a girl about Maria's age came to the door.

Before Roberto could speak, Maria shouted out, "Berta, these people are here to see your papa."

Berta, short and stocky with a round face and long black braid, stared at her guests. "Mama is at grandma's house. Papa's in the back."

Maria pushed open the gate and motioned the visitors in, but Roberto turned to the young girl before she could follow them.

"Thank you very much, Maria. You have been very helpful."

Maria frowned, her attempt at obtaining valuable gossip thwarted. She thanked them for the soft drink and hurried back to the village to give her assessment of the strangers.

Berta led them through the house, past an indoor kitchen, past several tiny bedrooms and a bathroom, then back outdoors to the rear of the house where *Don* Pedro reclined in a hammock strung between two *mamote* trees. A small boy nestled with him in the hammock, and together they read a shiny new picture book.

"Papa, some people are here."

The president looked up from the book, startled at the guests.

Roberto said, "I am sorry to bother you, *Don* Pedro. I am Detective Salinas, and this is *Profesora* Claire Aguila. I am investigating the death of Benito Suarez in Motul."

"I didn't know him," *Don* Pedro said, his eyes wary.

"Could we go inside and talk? I can explain."

The president lifted the child out of the hammock. "Berta, take your brother to Grandma's house."

"Okay, Papa." She took her little brother's hand. "*Vamos.*"

Pedro extricated himself from his hammock and led them back into the house. He took time rearranging wooden chairs in the living room, and directed Claire to the only cushioned chair, situated in front of the television.

"What can I help you with?" Pedro asked, situating himself in a chair and clasping his hands between his knees.

"It's complicated to explain," Roberto said, "and I'm not here to accuse anyone of a crime."

Don Pedro's shoulders relaxed a little, and he sat back in his chair, but his hands remained tightly clasped.

"Have you heard about Benito Suarez?" Roberto asked. "He owned a souvenir store near Motul."

"I heard that a vendor named Benito was killed in Motul. *Es todo.*"

"Do you know anything about his business?" Roberto asked.

"He sold souvenirs." Pedro gave a sideways glance at Claire.

Roberto looked at Claire, then at *Don* Pedro. "Professor Aguila is in Merida for an anthropology meeting and several people from her group have also died this week. We are looking for a connection between these deaths."

"One of the anthropologists is Jamal Kennedy," Claire said. "He lived here several years ago, no?"

"Jamal died?" *Don* Pedro asked, his eyes wide.

"He is fine," Claire said. "But Detective Salinas thinks he knew *Don* Benito."

Don Pedro shook his head. "No…no…Jamal wouldn't hurt anyone."

"Have you seen Jamal recently?" asked Roberto.

"*Cierto*. He was here Monday."

Salinas and Claire exchanged glances. "Jamal was here Monday?" Salinas asked.

"Yes, just before lunch. He brought *gifts!*"

Pedro pointed to a large cardboard box in the corner of the room. Claire stood to examine its contents, a collection of new Spanish language children's books.

Don Pedro said, "He's giving them to the library."

Claire squatted to look through the books, admiring the generous gift. "You have a library?"

Pedro laughed. "We built a room behind the school, but we hope to build a real library soon."

When Claire had settled back into her chair, Roberto asked, "What was it like to have an anthropologist in your village?"

"Sometimes it was fine, and other times…" he smiled, "you have to teach them everything. They think they know everything but know nothing." Pedro laughed at his joke and Claire smiled because she knew the truth in what he said.

Roberto asked, "Did everyone like Jamal?"

"Yes," Pedro said, remembering. "Children were afraid of him at first, rubbing his skin and touching his hair. He took it very well, he braided the girls' hair like his, and played *futball* with the boys. The young girls all liked him. They had—how do Americans say—crush?"

Claire laughed at his pronunciation—cruush. Jamal had the same effect on young American coeds.

Pedro added, "Children followed him around all the time. He taught them English."

Roberto waited a moment, considering his words. "We understand that he was studying with the *h-men*, and that he was interested in medicinal and ritual drugs?"

Pedro tensed again. "I don't want to make trouble for him."

Roberto shook his head. "Nor do we."

Pedro's eyes moved from Roberto to Claire as he considered his answer. "I don't really know about drugs. The *h-men* would know, but he died, and we don't have one now."

"When Jamal lived here, did you hear about him using drugs?"

Pedro thought about this. "Jamal...that is...people thought that Jamal used drugs. Some thought that he was interested in healing and ritual because he thought they involved drugs. But *h-menob* don't use hallucinogens or drugs."

"What kind of drugs was Jamal interested in?"

He shrugged. "Perhaps marijuana."

"Any other drugs?"

"People said he asked about mushrooms, but I don't know."

"Do you know where he might have bought marijuana?" Roberto asked.

"*No sé*," Pedro said. I don't know.

"*Don* Benito, perhaps?" Salinas asked.

Don Pedro shrugged but looked away from the detective. "Perhaps."

Roberto folded his hands on his lap and leaned forward. "I'm not interested in what *Don* Benito or Jamal did. I only want to know who killed *Don* Benito."

Pedro took his time. "He sold artifacts...but I heard he also sold drugs."

"Do you know that for sure?"

"No, but people say that is why there were always young Americans hanging around. Not all of them were buying Mayan pots."

CHAPTER FORTY-EIGHT

Thursday Morning/Afternoon

Claire held her hair back from her face as it blew in the wind, the open car windows bringing both hot breezes and dirt particles into her face. Like her rental car, Roberto's state-issued sedan had no air-conditioning, and her dress stuck to the back of the car seat. They sped down a major road back toward Tixbe, Brad's research village. They drove past Motul and turned onto a secondary road that took them past another hacienda and abandoned henequen fields.

Salinas said, "So Jamal was there Monday. He could have stopped in Motul first."

"Do you actually think Jamal would kill Paul or *Don* Benito to hide marijuana use?" Claire protested. "Who cares?"

"You know Jamal. What do you think?"

"I don't think so, but, of the KC faculty, he seems the most insecure about his position."

"How so?" Roberto slowed as they passed through a tiny *pueblo*. The car plodded slowly over speed bumps as they both watched for children and dogs that might cross in front of them.

"Jamal has a joint position in anthropology and biology. To earn tenure, he has to be approved by two departments."

"Wasn't that Tanya's situation also?"

"Yes, linguistics and anthropology. They're both academically vulnerable, but their strategies are different. Jamal is deferential, especially to Brad, but also to George. He rarely makes a stand on an issue. Tanya was demanding, irreverent. She didn't pander to the senior faculty."

While Roberto concentrated on the road, Claire's mind wandered. A week ago, her life had seemed so empty that she had considered leaving her profession and becoming what…a photographer, a writer? But suddenly, she felt energized and alive. This worried her. How could she feel invigorated by a murder investigation that might involve her friends and colleagues? Or was it something else, or *someone* else, who brought back that sense of adventure she had lost in the pursuit of her career?

She jerked back to reality as Roberto approached Tixbe, and once again they crept over speed bumps toward the plaza. Tixbe resembled Yaxpec, with a large plaza and impressive church along one side. Unlike Dzab, the government office doors were open. Roberto stepped into the large room, once part of the colonial government building. Claire remained just outside the door.

Claire heard a booming voice from within: "*Pasen ustedes.*" Come in.

Claire gazed up at the high cement walls and corrugated tin roof. Industrial-sized electrical lights hung from exposed ceiling wires, and huge fans blew the hot air down from makeshift shelves along the high walls. Several smaller floor fans redirected the stale air toward the desk where a middle-aged man with graying hair and a mustache sat, a newspaper opened on his desk.

"I am looking for the president," Roberto said.

"You have found him," the man said, smiling. He stood to shake Roberto's hand. "I am Juan Chavez."

Salinas introduced himself and Claire, providing the reason for their visit.

Juan's face sobered. "You are here about Benito?"

"Yes. Did you know him?"

Don Juan squinted slightly. "Yes, I knew him." He called to a young man wearing a Texas Rangers baseball cap and a brown shirt adorned with a tin deputy's badge.

"This is Raul," Juan said, "our one and only deputy."

"*A su servicio,*" Raul said as he offered them chairs.

"I understand that an anthropologist lived here some years ago," Roberto said. "Bradley Kingsford?"

Juan's face became more solemn with each question. He smoothed his mustache with his hand and looked at the deputy. "Bradley?" He pronounced it "Bladley."

Salinas said, "I can show you a photograph."

Roberto had asked Claire to bring certain photographs with her. She pulled the one he requested from her purse. Juan studied the photograph of the Keane College faculty and pointed to Brad. "That's Jaime."

Roberto said, "We know him as Bradley Kingsford. Why do you call him Jaime?"

The president laughed. "Because no one could pronounce it, so he said to call him Jaime…and we did. I forgot his real name."

"Do you know why he chose Jaime?"

Juan shrugged. "*No, Señor.*"

"Have you seen him lately?"

"We thought he would come. Raul's brother saw him in Motul Monday, but he never came." Juan sat forward and looked at Salinas with concern. "That was the day my cousin was killed."

"Benito Suarez was your cousin?" Roberto asked, startled.

"*Sí, Señor,*" he admitted. "My distant cousin."

"Ah," Roberto said. "Did Jaime know *Señor* Suarez?"

"I think so. In fact, I told him about Benito's souvenir shop. Jaime was interested in religious items."

"Have you heard that Benito might have sold real artifacts, legally or illegally?"

"No, *Señor Detectivo.* Nothing like that."

"What about drugs?"

"*Drogas?* No, *nada.*"

Roberto repeated his mantra. "I only want to find out who killed your cousin."

Juan studied his hands before returning his gaze to the detective. "I didn't know him too well. His family left Tixbe many years ago. And I don't think Jaime would be involved in anything illegal. He was a good person."

Roberto asked, "Were you president when Brad—Jaime—lived here?"

"No. I worked in Motul—in a factory—I wasn't around during the week. But Jaime played *futbal* with us on the weekends. We are close to the same age, but I was married and had two children. He was married but had none. I joked about that…that maybe he didn't know how to do it." He laughed at his joke. "But then his wife wasn't here with him—that's not a good thing."

"Did he buy souvenirs from *Don* Benito?"

"*Sí*, but all Americans buy that stuff to take home. They love it."

"Do you know for sure he only bought souvenirs?"

Don Juan tipped his head slightly and looked down at his desk. "*Cierto*. I don't think Benito sold real artifacts…or drugs." He looked at his hands again. "But it's possible."

CHAPTER FORTY-NINE

Back on the highway, Roberto and Claire were silent, both digesting the information they had obtained.

Finally, Roberto said, "Did you notice how *Don* Juan reacted when I asked if Brad bought items from Benito?"

"Yes, he seemed surprised at the question," Claire said. "What are you thinking?"

"I'm thinking he expected a different question." He glanced at her briefly. "I think he expected me to ask if Brad *sold* artifacts to Benito."

Roberto's cellphone rang. He listened and ended the call. "Do you mind a detour?"

Claire looked at her watch and calculated the time she would need to get to Merida. She had hoped for a shower before Jamal's presentation. "I need to be in Merida by three-thirty."

"I can drop you off at your car," Roberto said, "but you might want to see the scene of the crime?" He glanced at her again, his eyes teasing. "I promise a quick stop. Rosa—Sergeant Garza—is at *Don* Benito's store."

This news piqued Claire's curiosity, and she agreed. They turned back onto the highway toward Motul, but instead of stopping in town, they continued to a small plaza and cluster of buildings that resembled a rural truck stop in the United States. At the corner of the plaza Claire saw a small grocery store and café. *Don* Benito's artisan shop sat between the store and a gas station. Several cement block houses filled the gaps.

They parked alongside a Merida Police car, a beat-up Ford Fairlane with the seal of the City of Motul, and a black Volkswagon Beetle that Claire guessed must belong to the young detective sergeant. Inside, Sergeant Garza perched on a stool behind the counter, examining a composition book identical to the one Paul had used. Garza looked up and raised her eyebrows when she saw Claire enter with the detective.

"*Profesora* Aguila gave me a tour of the countryside today," he said lightly, as they joined her at the counter. "We visited the villages where Doctor Kingsford and Doctor Kennedy worked."

Garza's frown indicated a suspicion that a tour wasn't the only thing Claire had offered. While Claire felt an affinity to the young sergeant, she feared that the feeling wasn't mutual.

Roberto leaned on the counter. "Sergeant, what have you learned?"

"We have new information about the cars and visitors." Garza looked at Claire and then at Salinas, indicating her hesitancy to talk in front of the intruder.

Roberto reassured her. "Doctor Aguila has been very helpful and understands the situation."

Garza nodded gravely. "The rental agency confirmed that Doctor Ramirez rented a black sedan; Doctor Kingsford rented a tan-colored Ford Focus, and Doctor Kennedy rented the white Fiesta. So, it's possible that all three were here, but we can't confirm it."

"Who identified the drivers?" Roberto asked.

Garza pulled her copy of the Keane College group photograph from her satchel and placed it on the counter. "*Señor* Masa at the gas station saw a man in a straw hat knock on the door of the store and then go around to the back. He couldn't see the man's face or hair because of the hat, but he drove a tan-colored car. It could have been Doctor Kingsford.

"*Señora* Mendez, the café owner, identified Doctor Kennedy as the black man in the white Fiesta. Several men saw the black car early in the morning, but no one got a good enough look to describe him, and I didn't have a photograph."

"Good job," Salinas said. "We have a witness who saw Doctor Kingsford in Motul sometime Monday morning, and Jamal may have passed through on his way to Dzab. What about Paul? Did he rent a car?"

Garza brightened. "No, but he was here, before the conference started. He's in the book." She smiled as she turned the notebook around so Salinas could see the page she had been studying. "Paul and Cody came by bus and walked from town."

Salinas raised his eyebrows. "Really? How did you learn this?" he asked.

"I interviewed Benito's nephew, Justo, who works in the store. He remembered two men who fit the description of Cody and Paul. They came into the store on May third and bought a corn-god statue. Justo said the men showed Benito a drawing of the statue and wanted one like it. After they bought it, the dark-haired man asked to take a photograph of *Don* Benito with the statue."

"Photograph?" Salinas said. "Did he have a camera?"

"He took it with his phone," Garza said.

Claire and Roberto looked at each other. "Phone?" Salinas said. "We haven't found a phone."

"Or a statue," Claire added.

"Is Justo still here?" Roberto asked.

"He's with Juarez." She pointed toward the back of the store.

Roberto and Claire passed by a small office and through a door that connected to the house where Benito had lived. It was a small cement-block house, cluttered but otherwise amenable to comfort. A small stove and refrigerator sat along one wall and a large wooden table served as both work and eating space. A young man in his late teens, wearing a Black Sabbath T-shirt and jeans, sat at the table with Sergeant Juarez.

Juarez stood, eyes widening when he saw Claire with Salinas.

"Who do we have here?" asked Salinas.

"This is Justo Suarez, *Don* Benito's nephew. He worked with his uncle in the store." Juarez introduced Salinas and Claire to the young man, whose eyes were red from crying.

The young man looked up from his chair. "*Buenas tardes.*"

A local deputy led Salinas to a small file cabinet that had been hidden in a locked closet. Claire heard the deputy say, "*Documentos y papeles de certificación.*"

Claire recognized Deputy Chan, Sergeant Juarez's partner, in the doorway of a small room off the main living quarters and joined him there.

"*Buenas tardes,*" Claire said. He too looked out into the main room at Salinas, then back at her. Claire did not explain her presence.

"Look," Chan said.

He motioned her into the room where another deputy squatted at a small refrigerator. The sweet smell left no doubt as to what had been stored there.

"So, he did have a side business," Claire said.

"More than one, we think," said Chan.

Roberto and the deputy joined Claire and Chan at the marijuana refrigerator. Claire moved away, allowing them to speak. She studied a photograph of a middle-aged couple that hung on a faded green wall. It resembled many old photographs she had seen in Mexico, the subjects staring at the photographer, their faces somber.

"Is this *Don* Benito?" she asked Justo.

"*Sí,*" he said. "It was taken before my aunt died."

Roberto joined Claire at the photograph. Their eyes met, and she nodded. It was the man she had seen in the slide presentation, and she was quite sure it was the same man who had tried to sell her artifacts years before.

Salinas asked Claire to show Justo the Keane College faculty photograph. Justo took his time studying the faces. "I know Sergeant Garza showed this to you, but please look again, carefully."

"I don't recognize any of these people," Justo said.

Claire flipped through the other photographs, locating a group photo Claire had taken at the reception. "Do you recognize this man?" she asked, indicating Paul.

"Yes, he's the one who was here that day—with the other man. They bought a statue and took a photograph of my uncle."

"Thank you," she said.

"But," he squinted to look at the photograph again and pointed to Laura, "I've seen her too."

"Where?" Claire asked.

Roberto stood over Justo's shoulder, his brow furrowed.

"In Motul."

"Has she been in the store?" Roberto asked.

"I haven't seen her here, just in town."

Roberto and Claire exchanged glances. Claire flipped through her stack and extracted another photo. She showed it to Justo. "Have you seen this man here?"

"No."

"Does the name Eduardo Ramirez sound familiar?" Roberto asked.

"Is that who this is?"

"Yes," said Roberto.

"I've heard the name, but I don't know him."

They thanked Justo, and Claire looked at her watch.

"I have to go. I can walk to my car. It's not far."

"I'll drive you."

They returned to the store where Garza was still examining the accounting book.

"Sergeant," Roberto said, "see if you can learn anything else from Justo about Laura Lorenzo or Eduardo Ramirez. It appears she has been to Motul."

She raised her eyebrows. "Are you leaving?"

"I'm taking Professor Aguila to her car. I'll be back *ahorita*."

At a stop sign just inside the town, Claire said, "We have obsessed about Paul and now *Don* Benito, and who could have killed them. Have you forgotten about Tanya?"

"Not at all," he said as he drove through the intersection.

"And what about Cody?" Claire persisted. "He was here. Could he have killed Benito, Paul, and Tanya?"

Roberto frowned. "I don't see how he could come here alone, without Paul. He doesn't know Spanish or the local geography, and it would be impossible to make a round trip on a bus before breakfast. But, you are right about one thing. I haven't talked much about Tanya..." Claire studied his face, thoughtful and unexpressive, as he parked next to Claire's car.

He turned to face her, his expression solemn. "I think I know who killed Tanya." He reached over and touched her hand lightly. "And the dagger?" he said, raising his eyebrows, "Tanya stole it. Didn't I tell you?"

Claire stared, her mouth open. "How do you know that?"

"You're in a hurry," he said, smiling. "I'll tell you later. Now I know you'll meet with me again."

Claire barely remembered the drive back to Merida. Her head spun with Roberto's words.

Tanya stole the dagger? Who killed her? How could he know, and she not have a clue? Worse, how could he spend all day with her and not tell her these important facts?

She arrived at the hotel a mere twenty minutes before Jamal's presentation. She grabbed her travel bag, her gifts having been distributed to her friends and happily received. She hurried to her room to freshen up. A shower was not to be, but she took time to check her email. There it was—the email from Emily at Lake Odawa, with photographs attached. She glanced at them briefly before forwarding them to Roberto. She grabbed her purse and hurried downstairs.

CHAPTER FIFTY

Thursday afternoon

Sergeant Rosa Garza sat at her desk typing notes from her own investigation, murmuring as she typed. She speculated on a profession where one studies other people, teaches, and attends conferences when she worked fifty hours a week while her mother watched her kids. She wondered if it was worth it, struggling for ten years to prove herself to the men who controlled the police force—she was smarter than most, and more dependable. Then, after her promotion to sergeant, her husband, *el conejo,* left her for another woman, one who, Rosa assumed, would stay home and cook for him. *Good. They deserved each other.* Thank God Detective Salinas had taken her under his wing.

In fact, Rosa currently held all men in low esteem, except Detective Salinas. Those who might be murderers particularly irritated her, especially in cases like this one where she didn't understand the motives. Lust, love, greed, revenge…these emotions she understood. None of the motives in this case seemed worth the effort—threat of blackmail? Smoking marijuana? Not getting a job you want? *¡Carajo!* Why bother?

Personally, she preferred the artifact angle. *Don* Benito was into something, and he probably didn't really understand the seriousness of what he did. He was the middleman between the source of the artifact and the purchaser. Yet her boss, Detective Salinas, had not pursued the person most likely involved in smuggling and even murder, Eduardo Ramirez. Her money was on him.

From her perspective, Salinas was wasting his time following Jamal, the handsome druggie, and the gay guy. Then of course, there was the pretty professor, Claire. Salinas was showing all the symptoms of love sickness: preoccupation, daydreaming at his desk, moodiness. She wondered what would happen when *la professora* returned to the United

States. Life could get interesting around here. She pressed the print button and sent her report to the printer.

Roberto Salinas sat at his desk, typing up his own notes from the two days he had worked without his sergeant. He could hear Rosa mumbling as she worked in the next room. He admired his sergeant for all the challenges she had faced. She would be a good detective someday, but an attitude adjustment would benefit her progress.

A notification beeped on his computer and he opened his email screen to find the photographs Claire had forwarded. He opened the attachment and perused the Stuarts' photographs, enlarging, rotating, and deciphering the location and people in each shot.

As he stared at the screen, Rosa knocked and entered with her report. Rosa always looked neat, the picture of professionalism. If only he could get her to smile periodically. He took her report and asked her to sit down.

"*Que?*" she asked as she sat stiffly in the chair opposite him.

"I am wondering, Rosa, what you think of this case?"

Rosa squirmed in her seat. "Do you think that Jamal or Cody are involved in the murders?"

Salinas shrugged. "We need to follow every lead," he replied. "Jamal keeps lying to me, and I need to find out why. Cody keeps throwing evidence at me, which makes me suspect him."

Rosa cleared her throat and said, "But the murder of *Don* Benito is something else. Cody had no reason to kill him, and we know of no reason for Cody to kill Tanya."

"What is your theory?" Salinas asked.

"Jamal is harmless."

"So why does he lie to me?"

Rosa shrugged. "Perhaps he is worried about his past..." She bit her lip. "Or, he is covering for someone else."

"Who?"

She shrugged again. "Brad Kingsford?" Rosa bit her lip again. "If I can say so...?" She looked at her boss.

"Yes?" Salinas prompted.

"I prefer the smuggling angle."

"And who do you think I should be looking at?"

"Eduardo Ramirez."

"For smuggling or murder?"

"Smuggling for sure, but I think he could commit murder."

"I don't disagree with you," he answered. "Smuggling is a serious crime, perhaps worth killing for." He folded his hands on the table. "That's why the Homeland Security Investigation Team, HSI, is here, working with our Federal Police. They are watching Doctor Ramirez."

Rosa had been excused from part of Doctor Banks' interview, and that of the retired professors at the Casa Montejo. She had resented it at the time. "Those old archaeologists are Homeland Security Investigators?" she said, amused. "Why wasn't I told about this?"

"It was confidential then, but you are included now."

She leaned forward. This case suddenly became much more interesting. "Ramirez may have gone to Motul early in the morning."

"If that's true, it means the agents lost track of him." He furrowed his brow. "But we have no evidence that he has a history with *Don* Benito, other than the initials ER, which are very common in Mexico."

Rosa said, "But Paul Sturgess has a history with *Don* Benito."

"As do Jamal and Brad Kingsford," he agreed, "but let's put Jamal aside for now, as I agree with your assessment." He tented his fingers. "According to the president of Tixbe, Brad, aka Jaime, knew *Don* Benito and had been to his store, despite what he told his colleagues."

Salinas watched Rosa closely. He knew she was weighing the evidence. He gave her time to put the pieces together for herself.

"If Brad was involved in something illegal involving *Don* Benito," Rosa reasoned, "and if someone knew about it—Paul Sturgess perhaps—he might be desperate, but we have no evidence of illegal involvement. But, if Doctor Kingsford was the man in the straw hat, Benito was already dead by the time he arrived in Motul that morning." She paused, thinking. "Perhaps he made two trips—one to kill and a second to set an alibi."

Salinas nodded. "But you are wrong in thinking I have not considered him, or Eduardo Ramirez, or even Doctor Kennedy," Salinas said. "We know Doctor Kennedy went to Dzab on Monday, so he is likely the black man who stopped in Motul."

"But he was there much later. *Don* Benito was already dead," Rosa insisted.

Salinas smiled at his sergeant. "You and I will be interviewing Doctor Kennedy later today, and Doctors Kingsford and Ramirez tomorrow, after Doctor Kingsford's keynote address."

Rosa clenched her fists on her knees. "Aren't you afraid the murderer might leave?"

"I have their passports. I am playing the professors and Doctor Ramirez differently than the other faculty members, primarily because of the American and Mexican interest in Ramirez. I would rather the anthropologists think we are incompetent Mexican policemen, chasing our tails, than to push one or all of them too soon."

"Do they think that?" Rosa asked, frowning.

"They watch movies and the American news."

He watched her deflate, sigh, and sit back in her chair. "What's your theory?" she asked.

Salinas told her. When he finished, he folded his hands on the table, looking at his sergeant. "You don't think much of this group, do you?"

"I think these people are *muy estrañjos*, very strange. They aren't like real people."

"Of course they are," responded Roberto. "They are just like you and me."

"We don't go traveling around to sit in meetings."

"Actually, I do that, and you will too, when you get rank. It's part of being a professional."

"The one professor, Claire, she wants me to like her," Rosa said. "But I wonder if she should be involved. Can we trust her?"

"I thought we agreed that Professors Aguila, Carmichael, and Banks were reliable."

"Yes, but…"

"You object to Doctor Aguila, because…?"

Rosa squirmed in her chair and looked at the photograph of Salinas's family on the shelf behind his desk.

Roberto followed her gaze. "You think I am compromising the investigation for personal reasons?"

"No, but…"

"Rosa," he said, "I met Claire Aguila many years ago. There has never been anything between us that would hinder my judgment. I promise you that I have investigated her connections with the deaths as carefully as the others, as have you. More carefully, in fact, as she always seemed to be in the center of the drama."

Rosa shrugged and rose from the chair. "Is that all?" she asked.

"Yes…no." He remembered the photographs. "I have forwarded an email to you from Doctor Aguila with photos. Can you print them off on regular paper for me now, and have photographs ready for our interview with Jamal this afternoon?"

"Yes, sir." She moved toward the door.

"Sergeant," Salinas said. Rosa stopped and turned back toward Salinas. "Mr. Detwyler should be here momentarily. Don't scare him away, okay?"

She scowled, but Salinas thought he saw a corner of her mouth rise just a little.

CHAPTER FIFTY-ONE

Cody sat in the chair that Rosa had vacated, his hand shaking as he placed his backpack on the floor and crossed his legs. Rosa followed him in and sat next to Salinas, notebook in hand.

"Mr. Detwyler," Salinas said, "I have learned more about the death of your friend, but I still have questions. The sooner I have answers, the sooner you can go home, and the sooner Paul's family can have their son's funeral."

Cody looked from Salinas to Garza, and back to Salinas. "Do I need a lawyer? In the United States we can have a lawyer." He shifted his ankle/knee posture, still trying for casualness.

Salinas leaned forward. "Remember, we have an agreement." Salinas paused as Cody nodded. "Are you comfortable?" Cody nodded again.

"Good," Salinas said. "You have been very cooperative. You completed a written statement with the group on Tuesday and you have spoken with my team twice. And you reported the missing computer. I believe you are telling the truth about your actions. Today, I hope you can help me visualize the events surrounding the deaths this week."

"I told you the truth. I didn't kill Paul or Tanya." Cody blinked back tears.

Salinas studied the young man, Cody's hands shaking uncontrollably. "Before we start, did you bring the items I asked for?"

Cody reached into his bag and pulled out a pair of tennis shoes and three statues of Mayan gods. He handed the shoes to Salinas and placed the statues on the detective's desk.

"Did you find the cellphone?"

Cody gulped and shook his head.

"Would he have carried his phone with him that day?"

"He always carried it."

Salinas opened his notebook and flipped through a few pages. "I'd like to start at Uxmal. I will summarize what I know. Please don't interrupt unless you disagree with my understanding." Salinas waited for Cody to nod agreement, then continued. "I understand you and Paul argued sometime after the reception, and you were also seen talking, perhaps arguing, near the pyramid before the Sound and Light Show." Salinas paused, but Cody did not contradict him. "After the argument at the pyramid, you returned to the Cultural Center. When you heard that there had been an accident, you rushed back to the site."

"Paul said he wanted to be alone, and that he would come back for me," Cody said. "I wrote in my journal until Jamal rushed in after the program."

"What did you and Paul argue about?"

Beads of sweat popped up on Cody's hairline and dripped down his forehead. He raised a hand to wipe the perspiration off his face. Salinas nodded to Garza, who rose and turned the room fan so that it vacillated between Cody and Salinas. "I can order you to give me your journal," Salinas warned.

Cody shifted his feet again. "I thought he wanted this job as an excuse to break up with me." Cody's face, burnt from his day at the archaeological site, blanched as he reconsidered his words. "But I would never hurt him!" he blurted. "I…loved him."

"Did you see anyone near the pyramid while you and Paul argued?"

Cody considered this. "I think I saw Brad and Laura near the far side of the pyramid…and Jamal ran by me when I returned to the Cultural Center. I think he might have been late for the show."

Salinas pulled a sheet of paper from a stack on his desk and placed it in front of Cody. "This picture is blurred because the photographer was taking a photo of the sun setting over the site. It is also a copy, but it will serve our purpose."

The photo depicted a male, in deep shadow, about half-way up the steep stairs of the back side of the pyramid. He wore a hat and a large backpack that hid his shirt. Cody picked up the photo and looked closely.

"It's not Paul," he said.

"You're right. The photographer saw Paul on the ledge of the pyramid. He seemed to be waiting for someone."

Cody's eyes got wide. "It's not me!" he protested. "I'm afraid of heights!"

Salinas nodded. "Do you recognize the backpack or the person?"

Cody shook his head. "Nearly everyone had a backpack and a hat."

"The next morning the police picked you up and brought you here. You told the same story you told just now, except on Monday, you left out the fact that you had argued at the pyramid before the program."

Cody's eyes widened and he slouched back in his chair. "I'm sorry. I—I was scared."

"I understand," Salinas said. "On Monday, you realized that the computer was missing, and you told Doctor Aguila. Why did you choose her?"

"She was the first person I saw when I got off the elevator, but I was glad it was her. She seemed the friendliest of all those people. Some of them seemed a little hostile."

Salinas tented his fingers. "There's evidence that leads us to believe Paul's death was not accidental, and, in fact, you were the obvious suspect. But when you reported the computer, I thought differently. If you had been guilty, and if the computer held damaging information, you could easily have disposed of it. We didn't even ask about a computer. But then you did something else that puzzled me."

Salinas pulled the composition notebook out from his desk drawer, and Cody stiffened, perspiration once again forming at his hairline. "You recognize this, I see," Salinas said as he ruffled through the pages. "You found this notebook on Tuesday?" He paused, and Cody nodded. "And once again you seek out Doctor Aguila, entering a reception uninvited. Why not bring it to me? It's important evidence."

"I wanted her to see it first. I thought it might provide motives for Paul's death."

"What made you think that?"

Cody sat back in his chair, wiping his face once again with his sleeve. "When I read through the notebook, I realized Paul had been collecting information on the Keane College faculty. I wanted her to read it and then pass it on to you."

Salinas located a gap in the notebook. "It seems that several pages are missing. There's a page for all Keane College faculty except Doctor Aguila."

Cody swallowed. "I tore out two pages."

"Why?"

Tears welled in Cody's eyes. "Because the back side of her page and the front side of the other had some notes he made about me, like a pro/con list for deciding to leave me. I don't know why he wrote that in his field notebook, but I was afraid you would see it as a motive."

"As we could have," Salinas said. "Do you remember what he wrote about Doctor Aguila?"

"Something about religion and artifacts."

"Was there anything else in the notebook?"

"On the back side of that second page, he had written a few notes on Laura Lorenzo, something like she wasn't who she said she was."

Salinas leaned forward. "Did you realize that by giving the journal to Doctor Aguila, you compromised her? It appeared to me that she might have torn those pages out."

Cody's mouth dropped. "No! I didn't mean that. I…"

Salinas interrupted him. "Let me tell you what I think." He leaned toward Cody. "You wanted Doctor Aguila to know that one of her group might be involved, and you trusted that she would pass the notebook on to me. You entered the reception uninvited to play detective and question those named in the notebook who might have motives, before I got the notes."

"I just wanted to talk to them, but only Tanya would talk to me, and she acted drunk."

"I understand that you two argued about something, and Jamal rescued her."

"Nonsense!" Cody protested. "She was acting crazy. She had it in her head that I had pushed him or caused him to fall. She said she saw us by the pyramid—I don't know how she got that idea. I told her I didn't climb the pyramid, but she yelled that she didn't believe me."

"You talked to no one else?"

"Just Claire and Professor Madge. Jamal yelled at me. I tried to talk to Brad but he blew me off, so I left."

"You didn't go into the bedchamber to talk to Tanya?"

"No."

"You didn't know that Tanya had died?"

"No, I didn't see her again."

Salinas turned to the drawings at the back of the notebook, indicating the drawing of the jade corn god statue. He sat it next to the crude replica Cody had brought him. "Where did you get these replicas?"

"In Motul." Cody paused, thinking. "We visited several shopkeepers, and Paul questioned them all about pots and statues, and if they knew Doctor Kingsford or Jamal Kennedy. The man he bought the corn god statue from acted miffed when Paul asked to take his picture."

"Did you see the slide presentation Paul prepared for the faculty?"

"Yes."

"Was that photograph part of the presentation?"

"Yes, that was the man."

"That man, *Señor* Benito Suarez, is also dead—murdered." He paused and looked at Cody. "It's possible that Paul caused his death."

Cody lurched forward in his chair. "No! He wouldn't kill anyone!" He paused, as if fearing a trap. "When was he killed?"

"Sit down, Mr. Detwyler," Salinas warned. "He died sometime between late Sunday night and early Monday morning."

Cody sat down, confused. "Paul was already dead."

"True, but after Paul talked to *Señor* Suarez, the vendor called someone, and that person might have killed him."

Cody sat back. His hands went to his face. "That's not possible!"

Salinas spoke softly, "But let's continue." Cody had turned pale and clenched his hands in his lap. "Did Paul make the drawings while you were here in Merida, or had he done them earlier?"

"Earlier, I think. He wanted to purchase some statues, and he had drawings of those he was looking for. He seemed happy when he found them."

"Did *Señor* Suarez see the drawings in the notebook?"

"He might have. He had other customers and moved around the store. He certainly took the correct statue off the shelf for Paul to view."

"Did he seem happy to have his photo taken?"

Cody frowned. "Not really. He acted like he didn't want to be bothered."

Salinas gazed at the young man and furrowed his brow. "You didn't by chance return to Motul early Monday morning, before you met the anthropologists at the hotel restaurant?"

"No! I had no reason to return there, and I wouldn't know how to get there if I wanted to."

Salinas squinted as he stared at the young man. "Deputy Chan will take you back now."

CHAPTER FIFTY-TWO

Jamal stood at the podium, outlined by the large screen displaying the final slide of his presentation. In the back of the room, someone turned on the lights, illuminating the room. Jamal was accustomed to large audiences. The topic of shamanism and ethno-botany appealed to those interested in ethno-pharmacology, as well as new-age spiritualism. However, he feared the crowd here today was more interested in Tanya's murder.

As his eyes adjusted to the light, he scanned the audience. "Thank you for attending today. Are there any questions or comments?"

After several questions, the one he feared came from a young woman. "Do the police have any leads on Doctor Petersen's death?"

Jamal sighed, resigned. "Tanya was a close friend to all of us at Keane College, and we are saddened by her death. However, I cannot discuss the investigation."

Jamal thanked the audience, and people rose to leave. Several students approached the podium to talk to Jamal as he sorted his notes. He tried to concentrate on their questions, but his eyes followed Claire as she moved along her row to the aisle. As if reading his thoughts, Claire looked at him from the aisle, and he motioned her to wait. They walked to the lobby and sat together on a sofa.

"I have a meeting with Detective Salinas," Jamal said, stuffing his papers in his satchel.

"When?" Claire asked.

"In a few minutes. What does he want?"

"I'm sure it's just follow-up questions."

"You can't tell me more?" His eyes narrowed. "I heard that you've spent time with him."

Claire understood his concern. She would feel the same if the situation were reversed. "There is nothing between us," she said, "but we do

263

know each other from many years ago. Detective Salinas was in Motul on business, and I met up with him there. That's all." Claire avoided his accusatory stare.

"Motul?" Jamal said.

Claire watched the changes in Jamal's face as his emotions shifted from surprise to fear to resignation.

"Claire," he pleaded. "What's going on?"

"I can't say any more. I don't know what he will ask you."

Claire, facing the front entrance, saw Salinas and Sergeant Garza enter the hotel. Jamal caught the look of caution in her eyes and turned to watch them approach.

Jamal asked, "Will you sit in with me?"

"If Detective Salinas approves, I will."

Salinas and Garza led Jamal and Claire to a small conference room assigned to them by the hotel management. Jamal tried to look inconspicuous as they made their way back through the lobby. All he needed was a coat over his head to finish the image, he thought. *It's always the black man*, he also thought unpleasantly.

After settling into leather chairs, Garza opened her notebook and Detective Salinas looked from Jamal to Claire. His tone was cool and controlled. "Has Doctor Aguila discussed the reason for this talk?"

Jamal looked at Claire, and his hand moved to finger his earring. "No."

"I asked Claire to accompany me to Dzab and Tixbe today, not to accuse you or Brad of any crime, but to learn if Paul had a connection with your villages. We wanted to know if there was any reason for Paul to blackmail either of you."

Jamal glared at Claire, then turned to Salinas. "You went to our villages looking for evidence of blackmail...and Claire is helping you?" Jamal stood and moved toward the door.

"I'm sorry, Jamal," Claire whispered.

"Sit, Doctor Kennedy." Jamal returned to the chair, his eyes dark.

"Our investigation seems to be moving toward blackmail," Salinas said. "I asked Claire to go with me, as I trust her judgment and her knowledge of Mayan culture. She will correct any of my statements today if they are unfair."

He turned to Claire and she nodded.

"*Don* Pedro, the village president, told us that you had been to Dzab and delivered books for their library. That's very generous."

Jamal relaxed and put his hands in his lap. "It is my way of paying the village back for their hospitality."

"That is commendable," the detective said. "Why did you go to Dzab on Monday instead of the Wednesday free day?"

Jamal licked his lips. "I wanted to use Wednesday to work on my presentation."

"Did you visit Motul on Monday?"

Jamal stiffened, and he pulled his hair back from his face. "I… no… yes, I did. I went to see a man I know."

"*Señor* Benito Suarez?"

Jamal looked confused. "Yes. How do you know?"

"A black man was seen at *Señor* Suarez's home Monday morning."

"Why is this important?"

"Because he's dead," Salinas said.

Jamal pulled at his hair. "*Señor* Suarez is dead? It's not possible!"

Salinas asked the sergeant to get some water, and she left the room. Salinas turned to Jamal. "He was murdered sometime very early Monday morning."

Jamal visibly relaxed. He sat back in his chair and his shoulders released their tension. "I stopped there much later, almost noon."

"After you entered Paul's hotel room to look for the computer?"

Jamal looked at Claire, who did not react. *She already knows about the computer.* "Yes," he said softly. "But *Don* Benito wasn't home, so I went on to Dzab to deliver the books."

"But you could have gone to Motul very early and returned before breakfast."

"But I didn't," he pleaded. Jamal squirmed in his chair.

"Why did you visit Benito?"

Jamal sighed and looked at Claire again. "I wanted to know if he had told anyone about my visits to his store during my fieldwork year."

"And why was that? Did you buy souvenirs or gifts?"

This question startled him. "Well, yes, I did."

"Anything else?"

Jamal sat quietly, except for his hand continuously clenching and re-clenching. Rosa entered the room with four water bottles. Salinas summarized the interview in Spanish for her notes. The pause to open water bottles and resettle gave Jamal a few minutes to collect his thoughts.

Salinas continued, "Personally, I don't care what you purchased, Doctor Kennedy. I'm trying to solve a murder."

"I'm an ethnobotanist and anthropologist," he started by way of explanation. "I'm interested in the use of medicinal plants and hallucinogens in ritual contexts."

"But Mayan shamans don't use hallucinogens. Why research here?"

"Yucatán is one of my research sites. I have also worked in northern Mexico and in South America. Here, I am mainly interested in medicinal herbs and the use of *copal*, incense, in ancient and modern healing."

"So, how does this relate to *Don* Benito?"

Jamal looked to Claire. "*Don* Benito sold marijuana," he finally confessed, "and I had studied its use elsewhere as a medicinal plant, and…"

"And liked to smoke it—how do you say—recreationally?" Salinas finished for him.

Jamal sighed. "Yes."

"Now that wasn't so hard, was it?" Salinas smiled. "You bought pots and pot."

Salinas smiled at his own joke, then turned serious. "Why did you think that *Don* Benito might have passed this information to Paul, and what made you think Paul would use it against you?"

Jamal slouched in his chair. "During his presentation to our faculty, Paul included a photograph of *Don* Benito as one of his informants.

Paul asked Brad if he knew *Don* Benito. Brad said he knew of his store, or something like that. But I knew *Don* Benito."

"And Paul knew this."

Jamal nodded. "That day, at Uxmal, Paul asked me if I had purchased anything special from *Don* Benito. It seemed odd that he would make innuendos like this when he was applying for a job. We all laughed, thinking it was a strange way to interview, but I worried about it. The information wouldn't destroy my career, but it could be embarrassing. Later, we learned he had done similar things to others."

Jamal drank from his water bottle. "I told the truth about seeing Cody running away from the pyramid before the program. But Tanya's accusation that she saw me with Paul at the Governor's Palace wasn't true. When I objected, she admitted that it had probably been someone else."

Salinas pulled a packet of photographs from his briefcase. "These photographs were taken by a tourist Sunday at Uxmal. Some of them are quite informative." Claire watched as Salinas ruffled through the stack, and Jamal leaned forward to look at them. Salinas drew them back toward himself.

"We know that Doctor Sturgess was not on the pyramid alone," Salinas said as he pulled a photograph from the stack. "We have a blurry photograph of someone climbing, or descending, the pyramid from the back side. We can't see a face or head, but we can see a backpack."

Jamal glanced briefly at the photograph. "It could be Paul."

"Alas, we have no photograph of Paul on the pyramid," Salinas said, "but we have two eye-witness accounts of him walking along the base of the second level at about the same time."

Jamal glanced at the photo again. "Lots of people bought those stupid hats, and nearly everyone uses backpacks. It wasn't me, anyway," he protested. "I didn't climb the pyramid to meet with him."

"Do you recognize the person in the photograph?"

"No."

"You're sure?"

Jamal hesitated. "I think so."

Claire looked at the photograph again and thought she recognized him. She said nothing.

Salinas tapped the photograph. "We know Paul wore a backpack that day, and that his computer was inside. However, no backpack was found on him or near him where he fell."

Jamal slumped back. "What does that mean?"

"We think that whomever Paul met on the pyramid took his backpack, stuffed it inside his or her own backpack, or hid it somewhere."

Jamal sighed in relief. "So, that lets me off. If I had been there and taken the computer, I wouldn't be searching his room for it the next day. I would already have it."

"But you might have been looking for something else?" Salinas put the photograph away. "You're free to go, Doctor Kennedy."

CHAPTER FIFTY-THREE

Thursday Evening

Jamal sat at the bar, nursing a beer, struggling to find meaning in the events of the past week—the death of Paul, Tanya, and *Don* Benito—they couldn't possibly think he would kill any of these people, could they? What motives had they come up with? He had asked Claire to drink with him, but she had declined his offer, pleading exhaustion from her two days on the road. She was obviously involved with the investigation, if not with the investigator, and Jamal knew that she had information she wasn't sharing with him. *Does she suspect me too?*

He felt a slap on his shoulder and looked up to see George at his side. "Come join us," he said, pointing to a table in the corner of the lounge where Madge sat, looking at a menu. Jamal took his beer and joined the elder anthropologist at her table.

"Congratulations on a great paper, Jamal," Madge said. "You always have the perfect balance between theory and ethnographic detail."

Jamal snorted. "Thank you, but I hardly remember what I said. It could have been gibberish, for all I know."

"Well, it wasn't," Madge said.

Jamal shrugged. "But really, I can't get my mind off Tanya. I keep expecting her to appear and hiss at me for something." He blinked away tears. "Who could have killed her?"

George returned to the table with a beer for himself and a margarita for Madge. "They're bringing another beer for you, Jamal. I know you can use it."

Jamal nodded his thanks.

"I heard Detective Salinas interviewed you again today," George said. "How did it go?"

"He grilled me pretty hard. They still don't seem to have a handle on either death." Jamal finished his beer as the waitress brought him another. He considered telling his colleagues about *Don* Benito but was interrupted.

"Can I join you?"

Jamal looked up from his beer to see Brad at his side. George pushed the extra chair out to him.

Brad collapsed into the chair. "Have you heard? Cody's gone."

"How do you know?" George asked.

"I went to his room to apologize for brushing him off at the reception. I was hard on him. Did he go home?"

"How could he?" Jamal asked. "We don't have our passports."

Brad shrugged. "I have no idea. Does anyone know when we'll get our passports? I planned to leave tomorrow after my talk."

"We should get them back by then," Madge said, "but if Salinas doesn't have a suspect in hand, we might have to change our travel plans."

"Damn," Brad exclaimed. "Salinas hasn't been hanging out at my door, so I guess I'm in the clear." He laughed, but it was forced and didn't reach his eyes.

"Jamal had the pleasure of an interview today," Madge said.

"Oh?" Brad said. "Do tell. What is '*el detectivo*' thinking?"

Jamal shrugged. "Who knows?" Still stung from Claire's deception, he clenched his bottle with both hands. "Claire visited our villages with him."

Brad's head came up in surprise. "Our villages?"

George gave Jamal a sharp look, his eyes narrowed. "Don't forget, he interviewed all of us after Tanya's death, and he has our written statements. We can't blame Claire for what he knows."

Madge sipped her drink and said, "There is also the notebo..." She stopped mid-word, but it was too late. George gave her a warning look, and Madge took a quick gulp from her margarita. Both Jamal and Brad looked at Madge, their eyes a study in confusion.

Brad spoke first. "Notebook? What notebook?"

"I...I heard that Cody found a notebook...Paul's journal," Madge stammered. "The police have it."

"Why is that important?" Brad asked.

"I don't know," Madge lied.

"Have you seen it, Madge?" Jamal asked.

Madge looked at George, who looked at her menacingly out of the corner of his eye. "I haven't read it," she lied again.

"Has Claire seen it?" Brad demanded.

George answered before Madge could say more. "I'm sure it's just a field notebook...we all have one."

Brad studied his colleagues. "You're probably right."

Jamal stared at Madge. "But it might have more," he said. "Remember all the strange questions Paul asked us?"

"What kind of information could there be?" Brad asked.

"What worries you?" George said, addressing Brad. "Or any of us?"

"Nothing," Brad said. He looked around the room. "Where is Claire? I wonder if she knows where Cody is."

Jamal said, "She's in her room, I think."

CHAPTER FIFTY-FOUR

Claire showered and dressed in a pair of shorts and a T-shirt. She uncorked a bottle of wine she had purchased in the market, climbed onto her bed, and opened her latest Elizabeth George novel at the bookmark. Although her eyes faced the printed page, her mind focused, not on DI Thomas Lynley, but rather Detective Roberto Salinas and more immediate murders. If she were writing this script, she would plot Cody as the murderer, but the evidence, as she knew it, did not allow for that more convenient solution. Rather, it looked more like the murderer might be someone she knew.

Frustrated, she reached for her computer and reopened the email from the Odawa County supervisor. She clicked on the photographs one by one, seeking the photo of the man on the pyramid.

A knock on the door startled her. She closed her computer and opened the door to see Brad smiling on the other side.

"Jamal said you were avoiding us tonight. Can I come in?"

Claire hesitated, silently cursing Jamal. Brad breezed into the room carrying two airline-sized bottles of gin and a small tonic water.

"I'm really tired. I told Jamal I needed to be alone tonight."

"I promise I won't stay long." He saw the wine bottle on the dresser. "Ah, drinking alone, I see."

Claire ignored him. She took her wine glass off the bedside table and sat in the wingback chair. She motioned to him to take the other chair.

"Can I talk you into a G&T?"

"No, thanks, but help yourself. Glasses are in the bathroom."

Brad frowned and did not follow her instructions. He placed the bottles on the table and sat, fumbling with his ponytail.

Claire waited for him to start the conversation. When he didn't, she asked, "Are you ready for your keynote address tomorrow?"

"I guess so. Are we ever really ready for public speaking?"

"I'm not, but I have always felt that you had no fear."

"I'm just a good actor, I guess," he said, looking around the room. "I'd feel a lot better if our passports had been returned so we know we can go home." He looked at Claire expectantly.

"I changed my ticket to visit my daughter," Claire said. "I would hate to cancel my trip."

"I heard you spent the last few days with Salinas. I thought you might have some information."

Claire cleared her throat. "That's not true."

"I didn't mean…"

Claire crossed her arms, irritated at the insinuation, "He was investigating a murder in Motul and knew I was in Yaxpec. He asked me to go with him on a few interviews."

Brad frowned and pulled on his ponytail. "Who was murdered?"

"Benito Suarez. The vendor in Paul's presentation."

Claire watched Brad closely as he responded to the news. He blanched, and Claire thought, *He didn't know about this.*

"I remember Paul asking you if you knew him," she mused.

Brad stood and began to pace. "I recognized his face and his store. I had forgotten about him until I saw the photo. I didn't know his name."

"Have you seen him recently?" Claire asked, and immediately regretted it.

Brad's demeanor changed. His face hardened, and his eyes pierced into Claire's. "Listen," he said, standing over her. "I don't know what you have going with that detective, but you need to decide where your loyalties lie."

"It's just a question."

"Be careful. I imagine he's pumping you for information on your colleagues and you're spewing all kinds of gossip."

Stunned, Claire stood, her five-foot-six frame dwarfed by his six-foot height, but she did not back down. "Three people have died—all of them have links to us. Detective Salinas is smart. He doesn't need an anthropologist to make connections between these deaths."

Claire stepped to the dresser and refilled her glass of wine. She knew this wasn't wise, but she needed alcohol-induced courage. She said, "Has Detective Salinas talked to you since Tanya's death?"

"Not since *Casa Montejo*." Brad's expression changed again, and his face softened. He sat down at the table and busied his hands by lining up the small liquor and tonic bottles on the table. "He wants to talk to Eduardo and me after my speech tomorrow. I didn't know about a murder in Motul. I suppose I'll find out more tomorrow."

"Yes, I suppose you will."

He tensed again. "I heard the police have a notebook, and that you might know something about it. The fact that you kept this information from me means your loyalties have shifted."

"There is nothing to tell."

His face hardened again. "You'll be sorry, Claire. If our program is slashed because of scandal, we will all suffer, and it will be your fault for betraying your friends."

"Betraying, Brad? Are you serious? This isn't who hit a baseball through a living room window. This is murder!" She lowered her voice as she felt it go up in register to a near-shrill.

Brad moved away from her. "It had to be Cody. He had a motive, I'm sure." He sat back down, the reasonable Brad returning. "And he was at the reception. He could have killed Tanya." He paused and said, "Cody's missing, by the way. Do you know where he is?"

"I have no idea," Claire said, "but if Cody killed Paul and Tanya, we should get our passports soon. But remember, there have been three deaths. These defy coincidence, don't you think?"

Brad picked up the bottles and walked to the door. "Be careful, Claire. Don't sell us out. You'll be sorry you trusted a Mexican cop."

He closed the door behind himself; Claire locked it and put the chain in place. Then she called Roberto Salinas.

Ten minutes later, Claire heard another knock on her door. Roberto had told her to expect this visit, and she opened the door to George.

Her hands still shook as she invited him in and offered him the last glass of wine from her bottle. He looked at her curiously as she emptied the wine bottle into a water glass and asked him to sit where Brad had sat minutes before.

"Are you okay?" George asked.

"Wine helps," Claire quipped, too casually. She couldn't fool George.

George took a sip of the wine. "Roberto asked me to come. He told me Brad threatened you."

Claire sipped her wine. "I'm not sure he meant to threaten me, but it felt like a threat."

"You need to know that it is almost over."

"Salinas knows who did the killings?"

"I think so, but he needs to talk to Brad and Eduardo tomorrow. In the meantime, Salinas asked that I give you some background on the other investigation." He paused and sipped again. "He didn't want to compromise your safety by telling you himself, in person."

"Other investigation?"

"There have been two parallel investigations going on this week. They have crossed paths in a very complex way, and Salinas has given me permission to put you in the loop, so that you can watch out for yourself."

Claire leaned forward in her chair. "Tell me."

"Over the past few months, I have been indirectly involved with HSI."

"Homeland Security? Like immigration and terrorism?" Her eyes widened as she tried to fit her colleagues into the same category as Osama bin Laden.

George cleared his throat impatiently. "No, Claire. The Cultural Property, Art and Antiquities Program, part of Homeland Security Investigations."

"Smuggling?" Claire asked. "Artifacts? *Don* Benito?"

"Yes."

"How does this relate to us?" As Claire waited for George to speak, pieces of the puzzle began to coalesce in her own mind. "Your friends... Carlos Gonzalez and Pablo Perez?"

"They are retired archaeologists who work for HSI."

"And you too?" asked Claire. "How could I not know this?"

George laughed. "I'm a lowly anthropology department chair at a small university, but I have known Carlos and Pablo for many years, and they asked me to help with their investigation since I was here for the conference. That's why this notebook is so important, and why I am upset with my colleagues who didn't share it with me."

"How could I know?" Claire asked, then thought a moment while she sipped her wine. "Does Madge know?"

"I just told her recently," he raised his eyebrows. "I'm amazed it's not on Facebook. That woman can't keep a secret."

Claire smiled in agreement. "Who are they investigating?"

"Eduardo is their major focus. So, you see the problem. Eduardo is loaning us part of his collection, and now we find that a dead anthropologist has a notebook that contains drawings of artifacts, some of which had suspicious provenance. And," George reminded her, "a replica of one of these was presented to Brad publicly."

"Does this mean Brad is involved with smuggling?" This relieved Claire somewhat. However serious smuggling might be, murder was far worse.

George answered, "We have no evidence that Brad is involved. Being a long-time friend with a suspected smuggler does not mean that he's involved. But when HSI hears that they had a falling out, then they are interested. And when people around Eduardo start dying, Salinas is interested."

Program for the 10th Annual Meeting of the Society for Mayanist Studies

Events for Friday, May 8
Resistance, Resilience, and the Future of the Maya

Morning Sessions:
- Janet Jensen, *Pan-Mayanism and the Resurgence of Mayan Oral and Written Language*
- Evelyn Nielander, *The Zapatista Movement as Post-Modern Resistance Movement*
- Orien Osterman, *The Role of Computers in Incorporating Mayan Language and Culture into Mexican Curriculum*

No Afternoon Sessions

Farewell Luncheon: 12:00 noon in the Intercultural Hotel Ballroom

Keynote Address
Doctor Bradley J. Kingsford, *"After the 2012 Mayan Apocalypse: Mayans in the 21st Century"*

CHAPTER FIFTY-FIVE

Friday Morning

"You can't just leave me here, hanging!" Desperation flooded through Brad as he stood behind Eduardo, who was carefully wrapping a small piece of hieroglyph in bubble wrap. Brad recognized the collection of items on the bed as those that had been on display in the Exhibit Room.

"You knew I had to leave early."

"But we're meeting with Salinas," Brad groaned.

"I'm not waiting for that thrill," Eduardo snorted. "If it hadn't been for you, I'd have left two days ago."

"Why is that my fault?"

"Because I had to clean up your mess. Now my contacts are skittish, and my delivery has been delayed." He placed the hieroglyph in a hard-covered case with several items already wrapped. Brad noticed that Eduardo's suitcase was already packed and sitting open on the second bed. "As soon as I get confirmation on my destination and word that my shipment has been delivered, I'll be gone."

"My mess? I just learned that Benito's dead! If you had left things alone, nothing would have happened. Paul fell, pure and simple: everyone said so, even the cops."

"And then what? Wait for the old man to tell someone else? You don't even understand how much trouble you were in. There's nothing to link me to the old man. He was a smuggler and a dope pusher. He had lots of potential enemies."

"But the cops have already linked him to me, Paul, and even Jamal." Brad's voice fell as the seriousness of his situation settled in. "And what about Tanya?"

"I took care of that too, you're welcome." Eduardo lifted the last statue from the bed, the jade corn god. "Take it." He handed it to Brad who took it and stared at its beauty. "It's yours now."

Eduardo's smile was cruel, and Brad flinched, "I don't want it." He dropped it on the bed.

His friend picked it up and handed it to him again, "You earned it. No one will know."

Brad gazed at the statue, then stuffed it into his suit pocket. "What about the future artifacts you send us? Are we legal?"

"Legal?" Eduardo sneered. "You're worried about legal now, after you begged me for the collection?" He closed the small case and went into his bathroom to collect his toiletries. "Don't worry about it."

Brad sat on the bed, his hands shaking. "Where's the shipment you're waiting for?"

"If I tell you, then you're an accessory," Eduardo said, his voice coming from the bathroom. "Leave it be and leave me alone."

"What am I going to do?" Brad fingered the statue in his pocket as Eduardo returned and placed his toiletry bag into his suitcase.

"You could leave, if you have something to hide," Eduardo chided.

"Where would I go? I don't have a passport." Brad looked at Eduardo. "Don't they have your passport too?"

"Poor you, with only one passport. Being bi-national has its advantages, especially when the cops are too stupid to check if I might also have American documents." Eduardo picked up his American passport and flashed it at Brad before tucking it into his pocket.

"How do you know they haven't checked? How do you know they're not sitting at the airport waiting for you?"

"To do what? Arrest me? For what? My hands aren't on any of those deaths. Besides, I'm not going to the Merida airport."

"Where are you going?"

"Again, you don't want to know."

"They'll catch up with you some day."

Eduardo's face became stern. "Not unless someone tells the authorities. Remember, we have a relationship, and you have a museum."

Brad stammered, "If I am arrested, they'll find out about you."

"Are you threatening me?"

Brad leaned forward on the bed, elbows on knees, and covered his face with his hands. "No, but I don't know what to do."

Eduardo looked at his friend in disbelief. "How can you be so naïve? You brought all this on yourself."

"How can you say that?" Brad's face reddened in anger. "You started it when you took advantage of my financial problems."

"You have selective memory, my friend. You brought those artifacts to me, remember?"

"To show you."

"But you were eager to sell them. I saved you from personal embarrassment, allowed you to finance your research, helped you extricate yourself from that bitch you called a wife, and now, I have saved you again. Don't bother to thank me."

"Jeannie warned me about you. She wanted me to end it and turn you in."

"And that would have ruined you too." Eduardo smiled.

"But she left me."

Eduardo snorted. "Good riddance."

Brad stood and walked over to the dresser. He looked at himself in the mirror. He was wearing his suit, dressed for his keynote address, but his eyes, framed by his shoulder-length hair, were embedded in dark circles. He took his hair in his hands and pulled it back. Ponytail, no ponytail…God, what was he thinking? He looked at Eduardo via the mirror. "Where's Cody?"

Eduardo surveyed the room for anything he'd missed. "I have no idea. Is he missing?"

"What did you do?" Brad said, turning away from the mirror.

"Nothing." Eduardo put on his jacket and opened the door.

"Are you calling a porter?" Brad asked.

"Are you stupid? While you're delivering your speech, I'll load my car and wait for my signal." He motioned to Brad. "You should go. Good luck on your speech, my friend." He held the door open, and

Brad left, the statue weighed him down as if his pocket held every artifact he ever sold to his friend.

CHAPTER FIFTY-SIX

Claire picked up her pace. Earlier, she had attended, but couldn't concentrate on, Evelyn Nielander's talk on the Zapatista movement. Her mind had been on Brad's threats, George's revelations about smuggling, and her immediate need to get a print of one of the Stuart's photographs before the luncheon.

George had told her not to leave the hotel today, but she didn't consider herself in danger. She couldn't imagine Brad a serious threat, despite his words. What could he do to her? But Eduardo? Why had he offered her a job? Was he buying her silence? About what? Had Brad been involved in smuggling? Murder? Impossible…Eduardo maybe, Brad… no, Jamal…never! Her head spun as she turned into the Kodak store.

Later, the photograph in her purse, Claire rushed into the second-floor hotel dining room, her heart beating wildly. She had missed the introductory remarks, and the participants were already eating their meals. Despite (or perhaps because of) the tragedy that marked the event, the room was abuzz with conversations.

A large easel had been set up next to the speaker's podium. It held a large sheet of poster board with photographs of both Tanya and Paul and the words 'In Memoriam.' At the head table, Brad sat with George and several others who had been part of the planning committee for the conference. Brad glared at her as they made eye contact. Claire tried to smile as if nothing were wrong, and George gave her a questioning look when their eyes met.

Claire scanned the tables to find her group. She looked for Eduardo but remembered that he had planned to leave the conference early. Wasn't he supposed to meet with Roberto today? The Feds were responsible for Eduardo, she told herself. He was their prey. She breathed in deeply to quiet her heart.

She spotted Madge and Jamal seated near a side entrance to the dining room, and she weaved her way toward them. Madge had saved her a seat, and a waitress approached immediately with her lunch.

"Where have you been?" asked Madge.

"Photo store," she replied, poking at her pasta salad.

"We were worried about you," Jamal whispered. "George told us about Brad."

"I'm so sorry I slipped about the notebook," Madge whispered. "George is furious."

"At least I understand what Salinas knew about my past," Jamal said. "I'm sorry I blamed you, Claire."

Claire could feel Brad's presence in the room. "I think everyone is nervous and just wants to go home."

The room quieted as Brad approached the podium to deliver his speech on the modern Mayan experience. Brad had always been the consummate speaker, but today he stammered, and his eyes skittered around the room. He scanned the assembly, looking for someone— Eduardo? Claire tried to concentrate on the speech, but her thoughts dwelled on his words the night before. He *had* threatened her.

Finally, unable to sit calmly, she opened her purse under the table, extracted the photograph that Salinas had shown to Jamal, and handed it to Madge. Brad's lecture lurked at the back of her consciousness. Madge stared at the photograph of the man climbing the back side of the Magician's Pyramid. She froze. She recognized the hat and the backpack, just as Claire had. Jamal took the photograph from Madge and looked at it for a second time. He glanced at Brad.

Claire sensed a hesitation in Brad's narrative and looked up to see his eyes locked on her. Her blood turned cold, and her mind flew in multiple directions. Finally, too nervous to sit still, she took the photo from Jamal and stuffed it into her purse. She touched Madge lightly on the arm.

"I'm going," she said. Claire could feel Brad's eyes on her as she moved along the wall to the side entrance of the room. In the hallway, she took a deep breath and noticed several police officers near the door she had just exited. Around the corner, Roberto and Sergeant Garza stood at the main entrance to the dining room. Roberto approached her. Fingers shaking, she handed him the photograph.

"I thought I recognized him when you showed the photograph to Jamal yesterday, but I wasn't sure. I made my own copy and showed it to Madge just now. We think it's him, but I can't believe it," Claire said as Roberto led her away from the door. "I hoped…" she grimaced at her choice of words, "…wanted it to be Eduardo. I could see him hurting someone, or even Cody in desperation. I didn't want it to be Brad."

"It's not over yet," Roberto said. They heard applause and chairs shuffling through the closed doors. Roberto said, "Be careful." He looked around. "Was Eduardo in there?" Claire shook her head.

"His car is still here," Salinas said and pointed to a windowed alcove away from the dining room exit. "Can you watch for him and call me if you see him leave?" He looked at Claire. "Stay away from him, promise?"

Claire nodded. She followed his instructions and sat in a wing chair overlooking a hedge separating the pool from the parking lot. She located his car in the lot and calmed herself by watching children splash in the sparkling water. Minutes later, the doors to the dining room opened and diners emerged, a flood of colorful clothing and chatter moving either toward the wide stairway leading to the lobby or the elevators across the hall.

Madge, Jamal, and George emerged from the crowd and joined her at her look-out. In pain and disbelief, they witnessed Salinas and Garza meet Brad at the door. Salinas attempted to make their meeting casual. He smiled at Brad and made light conversation with him as they walked away from the crowd, presumably toward a back stairway. Brad turned back toward his colleagues, and glared at them as Salinas led him away.

The foursome sat in silence for a long time, watching the parking lot and reluctant to speak. Claire's attention had diverted to a Mexican family playing together in the pool below when Madge tugged at her sleeve.

"There he is." They watched as Eduardo hurried toward his car. George reached into his pocket and retrieved his phone and a business card. He punched in numbers and waited.

Looking over George's shoulder, Claire noticed the Homeland Security seal on the business card. Jamal jumped and ran after one of the officers who had lingered behind the departing detective.

Claire had already forgotten Salinas's warning. "We have to follow him," she said, grabbing her purse. "George, do you still have your rental car?"

George was on hold, impatiently fumbling with his glasses and watching Jamal gesticulating to the officer. He scowled at the phone. "I returned it, but this isn't our business."

Claire reached for the card, but George held it tightly in his fist. "It *is* our business," Claire insisted. "Brad didn't kill Benito. Eduardo did. Please, give me that number. I'll keep in touch."

George held up his finger as his call went through. He reluctantly handed the business card to Claire but pointed a finger at her. "Be careful!" he demanded between clenched teeth.

Claire whispered a 'thank you' as she grabbed the card. She turned to Madge. "Come with me. I need a navigator."

George struggled with the phone, nearly dropping it as he tried to catch Madge's arm. "Madge!" he growled. "Stop!" But she ignored him. George had never seen Madge move so fast, holding tight to the railing as she followed Claire down the hotel staircase.

"Gonzalez, *Bueno?*"

"Carlos? This is George. I'm at the hotel. Ramirez just left. Where are your people?"

Gonzalez replied, speaking slowly to calm George. "We have Perez at the Merida airport and others stationed at the air and seaports at Chetumal on the Caribbean coast, and in Campeche on the Gulf of Mexico. We have just received word that his shipment has been delivered in New Orleans, an unusual destination for his material. He must have hustled to find a new drop-off. We're holding the person who picked it up."

"Claire and Madge are following Ramirez," George said, his voice shaking. "Claire has your card. She should be calling you."

"Tell Salinas what Claire's doing," Gonzalez warned, "and I'll wait for her call."

Stupid woman. She will get herself and Madge killed, George thought as he disconnected and rummaged in his wallet for Salinas's card. His call went directly to voicemail. He left an urgent message and ended the call.

As he did so, Jamal appeared at his side. "I told the cop, but I think he was trying to find a reason to arrest me. Where are Madge and Claire?"

"On a fool's chase, damn them." He looked out at the parking lot. Claire's car was already gone. "Stay here," he demanded. "Call me if you hear from Claire or Madge."

"Where are you going?

"To find that damn police station."

CHAPTER FIFTY-SEVEN

Claire ran to her Volkswagen, stuffing the business card into her skirt pocket and rummaging in her purse for her car keys. Madge straggled behind her. The car was hot to the touch, and the interior seats burned Claire's legs when she sat, but she barely felt it in her haste. She opened her window and had the engine started by the time Madge caught up with her. Madge squeezed into the small car, pulling the seat belt around her ample middle, and opened her window.

Because the central city consisted of one-way streets to alleviate traffic, left was the only direction she, or Eduardo, could turn. She merged into the traffic, looking for his black sedan as she maneuvered around both moving and parked vehicles.

As they proceeded through an intersection, Madge pointed forward. "He's turning right."

Claire squeezed into the right lane, caught the light and turned the corner. At the next block he turned right again, following the one-way traffic.

"The car rental," Claire said as she crept up to the corner and turned.

Eduardo turned left into the rental parking lot, and Claire had no option but to pass by.

"Why is he turning his car in?" Madge said. "He'll have to get a taxi."

Claire drove to the next corner and made two right-hand turns, taking her back to the hotel, and then repeated their route back to the rental agency.

"Do you have a map?" Madge asked as Claire squeezed into a parking space reserved for taxis.

"In the glove compartment." Madge reached into the minuscule compartment and pulled out a folded Yucatán map. She unfolded it as an angry cab driver approached their car. His face softened somewhat when he saw the two women.

"You cannot park here," he said in stilted English.

Madge performed her best befuddled elderly woman routine. "*Lo siento, Señor*. I'm looking for the Intercultural Hotel." She fumbled to find the enlarged map of Merida. As the driver began to use arm motions to direct her to the hotel they had just left, Claire saw Eduardo pull out of the rental car lot and turn into traffic, now driving a white car. She pulled out from the parking spot, leaving the taxi driver mid-sentence. Madge waved to him as they pulled away.

"*Muchas gracias!*" she called from her window. Madge turned the map over, still trying to find the Merida insert, blocking Claire's view.

"Madge!" she said. "I can't see."

"Where is he?" Madge said, pulling the map down on her lap.

"Up ahead. He changed cars…it's the white Ford Escape."

Claire moved over into the left lane as Eduardo turned left at the corner. A driver in a 1950 vintage pickup truck of indeterminate color honked at her as she nearly missed clipping what was left of his front fender.

Madge folded the map into a large square, giving Claire a sideways glance. "Shouldn't you call that number George gave you?" she asked. "Or are we doing this alone?"

"You're right," Claire conceded. "Get my phone." Claire struggled to extract the business card from her pocket as she turned left at the yellow light, earning her a whistle from the traffic officer.

Madge pulled Claire's purse onto her lap and extracted the phone. Claire handed her the business card, and Madge punched in the numbers. She held the phone out to Claire.

"I can't talk, Madge."

Claire listened as Madge identified herself and uttered a series of 'u-huhs' and 'yeses.' She turned to Claire. "Where are we?"

"Calle 55 going west." She gave the make of the car. "The license number is YUC 2398."

Madge relayed the information, said a few more 'a-huhs' and ended the call. "It was Carlos Gonzalez," she reported. "He wants us to follow Eduardo as far as we can. They're setting up roadblocks outside of town, and he'll let us know when to fall back. If Eduardo changes direction or realizes we are behind him, we are to pull away immediately and call him."

Madge looked around for a cup holder, found none and tucked the phone under her skirt. She opened the map again, carefully this time, finding their location. "He talked to George, and George is calling Salinas," she added. Claire pointed at Eduardo's car a block in front of them, and asked Madge to watch him carefully.

The afternoon traffic was increasing, and Madge struggled to keep the car in sight, a difficult chore as most cars were light-colored. Claire had difficulty keeping close enough to get through the lights while avoiding being identified.

She braked quickly to miss a young tourist couple with two children who stepped into the street in front of them to hail a taxi. The taxi driver, appearing out of nowhere, swerved in front of her to collect his fare. At the next light, a city bus turned in front of them, spewing smoke from the exhaust as it stopped and started. Claire thought she had lost Eduardo for sure. *What was I thinking?*

The bus turned several blocks later as they emerged from the downtown area. They approached a major thoroughfare that led toward the airport. Just as Claire was about to give up, Madge stuck her arm in front of Claire's face.

"There he is!"

Claire followed him at a comfortable distance. There were fewer pedestrians, but traffic moved faster. "Phone, please," said Claire, her nerves on edge as she maneuvered through traffic, keeping Eduardo's car in view.

Madge pulled the phone out from under her skirt. "Who are we calling?"

"Agent Gonzalez," Claire said as she stopped at a light and watched Eduardo slip through ahead of her.

Madge punched the recall button and handed the phone to Claire. "Gonzalez."

"This is Claire Aguila. I'm on Avenida Itzaes heading toward the airport." She moved forward as the light turned green.

"We have it covered," Gonzalez said. "Don't follow him into the airport access, but call us when he turns in, if you can."

Claire handed the phone back to Madge. She reported the conversation, and Madge pointed ahead to where Eduardo had been stalled at the light ahead of them. Nearing the airport, Claire slowed so they could watch Eduardo turn into the access road, but he drove past it, without slowing.

"Shit," Claire said. "Now what?" She glanced over at Madge. "Phone, please."

Madge pulled out the phone, but it caught on her skirt and flipped onto the floor. "Damn!" Madge said. She tried to kick at the phone with her foot, but her bag was in the way. She reached as far as her seat belt and arms would allow but couldn't touch it.

"Madge!" said Claire.

"Damn car...no cup holders, no air-conditioning." She unhooked her seat belt and felt around the floor. "Got it." She punched re-call and handed the phone to Claire.

"He drove past the airport," Claire told Gonzalez when he answered.

"Where are you?"

"Avenida Itzaes turned into Highway 180 toward Uman."

"What? You're breaking up."

"Toward Uman," Claire yelled into the static, her phone out of Merida's range.

"Okay," came the muddled response, "....on course....helicopter..... Campeche."

"What?" Claire said. She handed the phone to Madge. "Get the message."

After a few more disjointed sentences and requests for clarification, Madge ended the call but held onto the phone. "Someone is coming up behind us, and a helicopter is being activated. They think Eduardo is heading toward Campeche."

CHAPTER FIFTY-EIGHT

Brad sat in a closed room furnished with a wooden table and two additional chairs. He avoided looking into the two-way mirror as he contemplated his worst nightmare—being held in a Mexican police station with the possibility of spending the rest of his life in a Mexican prison. His life up to this point flashed before him: the regrets, the years wasted in fear of discovery, and the lack of fortitude to shed himself of his toxic friend.

The windowless room was stifling hot. Brad felt the sweat soaking through his suit, and his hair clung to the back of his neck. An idle floor fan sat in the corner. He considered turning it on, but before he could act, Detective Salinas entered the room with the female sergeant, whose name he couldn't remember, and another man, tall, middle-aged, with steel-gray hair and gray eyes. The man wore a light gray suit, resulting in an eerie, ghost-like appearance. A policeman Brad recognized from the Casa Montejo followed the trio into the room, delivered a third chair, and then retreated. The two men carried briefcases, the sergeant a notepad.

Salinas reintroduced Sergeant Garza and introduced the man as Michael Morgan. "Mr. Morgan is from the American Consulate, Doctor Kingsford. He is an attorney, though his role at this point is not to represent you in any criminal sense but to protect your rights as an American citizen during this interview."

Brad stared at the man, but no words came. Instead, he folded his hands and placed them on the table as the officials settled themselves in the chairs. Salinas sat across from Brad, his back to the two-way mirror. Sergeant Garza moved her chair off to his side and Mr. Morgan moved his chair next to Brad, a symbolic gesture Brad did not miss.

The door opened again, and the officer entered with a small pushcart. He unloaded a digital recorder and four bottles of water. Salinas took his time testing the recorder as the others opened water bottles. Sergeant Garza stood and turned on the fan, activating the oscillate function.

Brad could feel the smallest of breezes waft in his direction. His heart pounded in his chest, and he could barely breathe, but he forced himself to ask, "Am I under arrest?"

"As I told you at the hotel, this is an interview," Salinas said.

"Then why did you make a spectacle of me, and why is the Consulate here?" He looked at the attorney, who instilled almost as much fear in him as did the detective.

"I'm sorry, Doctor Kingsford. I needed to make sure you didn't leave before we spoke. Mr. Morgan is here on my request, so that there are no questions as to your treatment."

"I can't leave. I don't have a passport."

The Consulate representative spoke for the first time. "Doctor Kingsford…Brad…let me explain why I'm here."

Salinas held up his hand and Mr. Morgan paused until Salinas clicked on the recorder.

Morgan continued, "Normally, the Consulate does not get involved in Mexican police matters unless an arrest is made. In this case, Detective Salinas has asked me to come because he suspects that you have been involved in several serious crimes, but he is not yet ready to arrest you."

"If you aren't here to represent me, shouldn't I have an attorney?" Brad struggled to control his speech. He could not afford to be weak now.

"I'm here to protect your rights as a U.S. citizen. If, at any time during the interview you would like to request a criminal attorney, the interview will stop, and I will help you find one. If, at the end of the interview, Detective Salinas feels he has enough evidence to arrest you, he will do so, and an attorney will be found for you. At that point, your case will be turned over to the *ministerio publico*, their version of a district attorney. The district attorney will then present his case to a judge and a judgment will be made."

"Is that at a trial?" Panic rose in Brad's voice again.

"Yes. If you are charged here, the district attorney and defense attorneys will make arguments and may call witnesses before a judge, but there is no jury. The judge will decide guilt or innocence." He paused. "But it's too early to think about that. For now, you need to cooperate with Detective Salinas."

"I didn't kill anyone!"

"Our purpose today is to ask you a few questions about the events of this week," Salinas said. "Sergeant Garza and I have interviewed all your colleagues twice, except you. We don't want you to feel left out." He smiled.

Brad watched Salinas reach into his briefcase and pull out a notebook and two bulky manila envelopes. "I would like to start with Paul Sturgess's death." He reached into one envelope and pulled out a stack of papers Brad recognized as the witness statements completed after Paul's death. Brad's statement sat on top of the pile.

"In your written statement, you stated that you didn't see Mr. Sturgess before the Sound and Light Show that evening." Salinas looked up from the statement. "Do you stand by that statement?"

"I...I don't remember seeing him. If I did, it was from a distance." Brad placed his hands on his legs. "I don't remember speaking to him."

Salinas thumbed through the stack of statements slowly. "It seems that several people saw you at the pyramid, near Paul and Cody, just before the show started."

"That doesn't mean I saw him. It's a big pyramid."

"Did you climb the pyramid that evening to meet with Paul, or to follow him?"

"No, of course not."

Salinas reached into the second envelope and pulled out a stack of photographs. He made a show of looking through them, but Brad figured Salinas knew exactly where the damaging photograph was located. He first suspected its existence when he watched Claire hand a photograph to Madge at the luncheon. Salinas was dragging out the process to unnerve him, and it worked.

The detective pulled two photographs from the middle of the stack, laid them upside down on the table and said, "An elderly tourist couple took a photo of your group." He paused and turned the top photograph over to show the group photo.

Brad glanced at it but didn't see the significance of the photo. "Yes, I remember."

"Well, it turns out they took many photos that day, including this one of a man climbing the pyramid at sunset." Salinas tapped the upside-down photo with his index finger. "The photograph is not very clear, but the time stamp indicates six-fifty, just prior to the program."

He turned the photograph over and slid it across the table for Brad to see. "Is this you, Doctor Kingsford?"

"I didn't have a hat."

Salinas laid the two photos side by side and pointed to a small space between Brad and Tanya. Brad looked carefully at the space and saw the straw hat he had removed from his head for the photo. He blinked back drops of perspiration that had run from his hairline into his eyes. His knees began to pump uncontrollably.

"I…I forgot that I climbed it. I wanted to see the lighting of the show. But I didn't see Paul up there. Really!" he pleaded.

Salinas made a sympathetic noise. "But unfortunately, the elderly couple has better observational skills than you, because they did see Paul on the pyramid at the same time. They reported it to the local police at the scene."

"Do they have a photo of Paul?" Brad pressed his hands on his knees to still them.

"No. Unfortunately for you, they took this photograph…" he tapped the photo of the man climbing the pyramid, "…without even noticing you. Their attention was on the sunset over the pyramid, not on someone climbing it."

Salinas pointed at the backpack worn by the climber. "Is this you?"

Brad's knees pumped again. "Lots of people had backpacks," he persisted. "This could be Paul."

"So I have been told. But your backpack is distinctive...and Paul had dark curly hair and was not wearing a hat."

Brad sat back in his chair and grabbed his water bottle.

Salinas continued, "What did you do with the computer, Doctor Kingsford?"

"Computer?"

"Yes. Paul had it that day, but it has not been seen since his death. I think you killed him for whatever he had on his computer."

"I didn't push him!" Brad shouted and jumped up.

Mr. Morgan took his arm and said, "Sit down, Doctor Kingsford. Think carefully. What happened?"

Brad sat, leaned forward and put his head in his hands. Lifting his head, he blinked to keep the tears from beading up in his eyes. "He tried to blackmail me. He thought he had some information that would hurt me professionally. He wanted me to assure him that he would get the job, then we would be best friends and colleagues. I don't know what he was thinking."

"Tell me how he fell," Salinas said.

Brad pulled his hair away from his face. "I wanted to see what he had, and he kept pointing to his backpack. He leaned back and...he fell. I tried to catch him, but he tumbled down." Tears began to flow freely. "I ran down the pyramid stairs. I hoped that, even though he fell a long way, he wasn't dead, but he was...dead. I didn't know what to do. He was on his back, so I turned him over and took the backpack. I stuffed his pack into mine. It barely fit, but what could I do?" Brad paused as if waiting for a response. "Then I realized that he would be seen easily when the show ended, so I dragged him up to the balustrade so he would be hidden in the darkness. It was awful, but I couldn't let him ruin my life."

"That was extremely cold and calculating," Salinas said. "He was dead. How could he hurt you?"

"By what was on his computer."

"What did you find on the computer?"

Brad's legs bounced up and down, and he held his hands on his thighs to calm himself. "A journal, but I didn't take time to read it. I just deleted the files."

Salinas glanced at Garza, who was frantically writing. She looked up at him and held her hand up to let him know she was lost. He waited a moment for her to catch up. Brad tipped the water bottle back to sip, but his hand shook too much to drink. He put it down.

"Did Eduardo see this happen?"

Brad collapsed back into the chair. "He was nearby and saw everything. When I reached the bottom of the pyramid, he came close…but not close enough to leave his footprints, I know now. He told me what to do, and then he walked with me to the Nunnery Quadrangle. I think Tanya saw us approach. I told him I didn't want to go to the program. I couldn't do it…sit there with everyone after what happened." He set his elbows on the table and put his head in his hands. "Eduardo told me I had to go, and he would handle it…and he did. We sat behind them, so I could calm myself down during the show."

"We found the computer, Doctor. Our people are working on it now. Did you take Paul's phone, too?"

Brad slumped into the chair. "It was in his backpack. I smashed it and threw it away with the computer."

Salinas paused again. "What can you tell me about *Señor* Suarez? You might know him as *Don* Benito?"

"Not much," Brad said. "He sold artifacts in Motul. Lots of tourists bought souvenirs from him. I didn't really know him."

"You never purchased anything from him?"

"Some souvenirs. Nothing more."

"What do you mean, nothing more? What else did he sell?"

Brad could feel the sweat pouring down his shirt and pooling around his hairline. "I…I heard he sold marijuana."

"Anything else?"

"No."

Salinas shook his head. "Doctor Kingsford, I understand that *Don* Benito had another, more lucrative business than selling grass to gringos. He had a business arrangement with your friend, Eduardo; you two have been involved in smuggling artifacts into the United States. Am I wrong in this assumption?"

Brad swallowed, his eyes darting between Salinas and Morgan. "No...I mean yes, you are wrong."

Salinas continued, "It would be best for you to tell me about this. If it happened a long time ago...so much the better, but if it relates to these unfortunate deaths, you will need that lawyer after all."

"I didn't smuggle artifacts into the United States," Brad pleaded. "You have to believe me!"

Salinas looked at his notes. "Did you go to the beach Monday, Doctor Kingsford?"

"Yes."

"Did you stop along the way to throw away the computer and phone?"

"Yes."

"And did you stop off in Motul on your way?"

"What?"

"Well, it seems that a car fitting the description of your rental was seen in Motul Monday morning. The driver wore a straw hat."

"It could have been anybody."

"Perhaps," Salinas agreed. "But this car pulled away from *Don* Benito's store around eleven o'clock. There's only one major road to Progresso. We can estimate from the mileage records on your rental car that you took a detour to Motul, or another destination of equal distance, on your way to Progresso." Salinas turned his hand upward. "Were you there, Doctor Kingsford?"

Salinas stopped to take a drink of water, allowing Garza to catch up. Brad could feel the sweat on the back of his neck, despite the fan. All attempts to control his leg movements proved unsuccessful. "Yes... yes, I was there." He ran his hands through his hair, pulling it up to allow the fan to cool his neck. "Seeing Benito's photograph in Paul's presentation reminded me that I hadn't seen him for a while. I wanted to stop in and say hello. He wasn't there, and the store was closed, so I left."

Salinas frowned and started to speak, when a knock at the door interrupted him. The officer entered, his face flushed. "*Por favor, Señor,* can we speak?"

Salinas stood. "We will take a short break so Doctor Kingsford can use the restroom. Perhaps we can have more water brought in?" He looked toward the officer, who nodded. Salinas followed him out and closed the door.

CHAPTER FIFTY-NINE

Salinas stopped short when he saw George Banks pacing at the station desk, his face red in frustration. Salinas feared that a heart attack might be imminent. He had a bad feeling about this.

"What happened?" he asked, looking from the anthropologist to the desk sergeant.

"*Señor*," said the officer, "Mr. Ramirez is gone."

"Gone? Where?"

"We don't know, sir."

"*¡Mierda!*" exclaimed Salinas.

"That's not the worst of it," George said. "Claire and Madge are following him."

"Following him? How?"

"In Claire's car."

"*¡Dios mio!* Salinas groaned. "What happened to his tail?" He looked sharply at the officer, who just shrugged. "I had men in that hotel, and the Federal Police at the airport."

George said, "Claire and Madge are in contact with HSI, but Eduardo is on the move, probably toward Campeche."

"Do we have a team there?"

"The Mexican Feds are at the airport and seaport."

Salinas ran his fingers through his hair. "Claire is still following him?"

"Yes, and Madge!"

"*¡Chinga!*"

Salinas pulled his phone out of his jacket pocket and scanned his recent calls. He punched in a number. "Claire?" Pause. "Doctor Carmichael? Let me talk to Claire."

Back in the interrogation room, Salinas took a few deep breaths to calm himself. Luckily the others had not returned from their break. He leaned back in his chair. *That woman! She'll get herself killed for sure.* But he could do nothing. He had to trust the team.

Brad and Mr. Morgan returned from the restroom, taking their seats. Garza had not yet returned. Salinas tried to calm himself as he rechecked the recorder. He concentrated on keeping his hands from shaking as he tested the sound. Garza returned several minutes later with more bottled water and handed them around the table. She took her chair and pulled her notebook out again.

"Doctor Kingsford, where is your friend?" Salinas asked, struggling to maintain a level monotone.

Garza looked up sharply as did Brad, whose eyes darted between Garza and Salinas.

"I…I thought he was being interviewed," Brad said. "I assumed he was here someplace."

"Doctor Kingsford." Salinas stretched out every syllable. "Come now. This is the point where you help us so you can avoid any further charges of aiding and abetting multiple felonies."

Brad slunk in his chair. "He wouldn't tell me. He said he didn't want to implicate me."

"How considerate of him," Salinas said. "How about a guess?"

Sweat seeped through Brad's suit coat, and his leg recommenced its bounce. "His family has a residence in Mexico City, and I know he has family and business partners in Monterrey, Chetumal, and Campeche also. He has lots of contacts in the port cities."

"I'm sure he does." Salinas paused. "Does he have a second passport?"

Brad nodded. "He gave his Mexican passport to the police. He also has an American passport."

"Under what name?"

"I don't know."

"So, if he were driving southwest from Merida, would you suggest he might be heading toward Campeche?"

"Yes," he squeaked. Salinas nodded at Garza, who rose from her seat and left the room. Brad opened the water bottle, lifting it to his mouth, but the liquid splashed over his suit pants. Rosa returned and took her seat.

"Now let's get back to your relationship with Eduardo Ramirez."

"We have been friends for many years…"

Salinas interrupted him. "Yes, I have heard the official story. I want to know how you got involved with smuggling artifacts for him."

"I didn't smuggle!"

"What did you do for him?"

Brad put his elbows on the table and covered his face with his hands. The vision returned to him. The two old Mayan men and the dirty white handkerchief.

"Doctor Kingsford?" Salinas paused patiently, giving him time. "We need to know."

Brad looked at Mr. Morgan, whose face reflected deep concentration, as if he were already trying to prepare a defense for this defenseless creature. "I didn't smuggle artifacts," Brad said finally, pulling his hair behind his ears. "I bought and sold them."

"Tell me about it."

"I needed money. My wife and I were both pursuing graduate research; hers was at the same university as mine, but she didn't need to travel. I came to Mexico alone, but my grant ran out, and my wife was sending me money to help me finish." He pressed his hands on his legs to control their bouncing. "I had hired a local woman, Mercedes, who did my laundry and sometimes cleaned for me. I lost my grant, so I let her go. Even though I didn't pay her much, I needed to economize."

Brad wiped his eyes and continued, "One night her husband and father came to my house with a small artifact. Her husband told me that he and Mercedes had a sick child, and they asked me to purchase this artifact from them—it was a small chunk of hieroglyph. They said they knew a man in Motul who would purchase it, but gave them only pennies. I felt obligated, since I had let her go…even though I didn't want to spend the money, I couldn't refuse their request."

"How many times did this happen?" Salinas asked.

"About three or four times over the next six months. The artifacts were small, and I didn't pay much for them. I didn't know what do to with them, so I stored them in my suitcase."

"How did you become involved with *Don* Benito and Doctor Ramirez?"

Brad took another sip of water, trying to hold the bottle without spilling its contents. "Late one night, the old man came to my house with a small statue of a corn god with jade eyes. It was so beautiful that I couldn't resist it." Brad looked at Morgan, then Salinas. "Several months later, Eduardo came to Merida and I visited him here. I showed him my collection and he was very quiet. Then he introduced me to his friend, *Don* Benito."

Salinas said, "You became a supplier of artifacts to Eduardo's middleman, Benito Suarez."

"Yes."

"You knew these artifacts were discovered after the 1972 law had gone into effect, and thus illegal."

"Yes." Brad pressed his hands on his knees. "But, at first, I was helping a poor family. I didn't mean to profit."

"At first," Salinas repeated. "How many years did you buy and sell for Doctor Ramirez?"

"During my field work...and several times a few years later when I returned to Tixbe for more research. But it destroyed my marriage."

"How so?"

"My wife learned what I had done and demanded that I tell the authorities what Eduardo was doing. She thought that I could keep out of trouble...after all, technically, I didn't know what he was doing with the artifacts."

"But you chose your friend, a thief and smuggler, over your wife?"

"My career would have been ruined."

"What happened next?"

"My wife left me, but she didn't tell anyone about what I had done. I finished my doctorate, wrote an ethnography about the rituals and

culture of Tixbe, taught in Texas, and eventually was hired as the director of the Mayanist Program at Keane College." He paused to sip water
again. "I tried to put it all behind me."

"But you couldn't?"

"I thought I had, until last year. And I brought it on myself. I really
wanted the job at KC, and I thought that, with all I had done for
Eduardo, I could ask a favor of him."

"The museum?"

"I was only asking for a commitment for a future loan of artifacts,
so I could bring that to the table during my interviews. It wasn't a big
deal. Museums loan items out all the time."

"What did he say?"

"He said 'sure, anything for my friend,' so when I got the job, I
called him. A week later, I received a formal letter from his business,
Galerías Indíginas, proposing a generous loan of artifacts. It was an
offer I couldn't refuse."

"Were you suspicious about the origins of these artifacts?"

"Eduardo assured me that they were legal."

"But you were suspicious?" Salinas paused for Rosa to catch up,
then said, "You could have refused the offer."

"I needed that loan to establish my position in the program. I
wanted to show that I could build a successful museum."

"So, you brought the offer to the faculty members in the program
for approval?"

"Yes."

"Did the question of legitimacy come up in the discussion?"

"It was Madge who brought it up. She doesn't trust galleries...nor
does George."

"But they agreed to accept the loan."

"Yes, primarily because it was a loan, not a gift." He paused again.
"But Madge started researching Eduardo's business behind my back."

"Is this why you wanted to hire someone else as curator? Someone
less...enthusiastic?"

"No...not that."

"But it seems that perhaps Doctor Carmichael was correct in her suspicions? When Eduardo presented you with the statue, you knew it was the original statue you bought from the village men, all those years ago." Salinas reached into his briefcase and pulled out the replica that Cody and Paul had purchased from *Don* Benito. "For days, the original statue sat in the case, archaeologists and other experts walked by admiring the replica...and you knew what it was."

Brad moaned. "Yes. And then I knew it was a bribe...the whole collection would be tarnished."

"And you could be linked to him criminally."

"Yes."

CHAPTER SIXTY

"Well, let's talk about Tanya," Salinas said.

An involuntary groan escaped Brad's lips.

"You didn't think I forgot her, did you? Let's see if my narrative is accurate. Please tell me if I am wrong in any way."

Brad sat back against the chair. His leg bounced uncontrollably, defying any amount of pressure he placed on it.

"Over the years," Salinas said, "I have learned that to understand a murder it is important to understand the victims. In the last few days I have learned much about both Paul and Tanya. I never met Mr. Sturgess, but I understand he was an ardent believer in the adage, 'Knowledge is Power.' I believe that knowledge resulted in his death. I met Tanya only once, but I have learned that she and Paul had something in common. They both used soft blackmail." Salinas tented his fingers. "First, she mentioned at breakfast that she saw someone talking to Paul during the day at Uxmal…"

"That was Jamal," Brad interrupted.

"Jamal denied it, and photographs show you and Paul speaking on the platform of the Governor's Palace. I think Tanya was sending you a message."

"I just forgot. Who remembers those things?"

"Fair enough," Salinas said. "But Tanya also saw something odd that evening that didn't register with her until after Paul's death. She saw you twice before the program, first at the base of the pyramid as she passed by. Then, with binoculars, she saw you and Eduardo walking away from the pyramid toward the bleachers. When you joined her in the bleachers, Eduardo said something about rescuing you from Laura Lorenzo, but she had seen Laura already in line ahead of her."

"How do you know this?"

"It seems that, like Paul, she also kept a journal on her computer, and you didn't get to that one before we did."

"What does that prove?"

"It proves that you lied." Salinas checked his notes and the tape recorder. "And Tanya knew you lied, but she didn't know why. She was intuitive, like Paul. She wrote in her journal that you had pressed the theory that Cody might have killed Paul, and that you seemed most intent he not be hired. She recognized Paul as someone like herself, and she sensed that he had something against you that might help her." Salinas paused, waiting for a response, but Brad did not speak.

Salinas continued, "I doubt she knew about your illegal activities, but you didn't know that. She may have suspected that you had something to do with Paul's death, without knowing your motive. Her brilliant but fateful use of the dagger symbolized what she thought you had done...sacrificed Paul for whatever he might have known about you."

"That's crazy!" Brad protested.

Salinas shrugged. "It's in the computer... in our evidence room... safe.

"I think you felt desperate," Salinas continued. "She passed the dagger to you as a threat and asked for a meeting. So, you went to her room. Doctor Banks saw two small airport-sized vodka bottles on the dresser. I am not sure what you had planned but, whatever it was, George Banks interrupted you. You noticed she had been taking pills, and you got the idea you might be able to—keep her quiet? Harm her? When you all left for the reception, you pocketed the pill bottle, scooped up the vodka, and contrived some sort of plan. The open bar gave you opportunity to use the pills. I don't know when you crushed them. Perhaps they had already been crushed, but you somehow got the drink to her. This was very risky."

Brad protested. "I—did—not—kill—her!"

"Then perhaps you can give me your version. This is your chance, Doctor Kingsford."

Mr. Morgan, who had not spoken since the meeting began, interrupted, "Do you want that lawyer, Doctor Kinsgford?"

"I'm innocent," Brad repeated, then held his hands firmly on his thighs. "She did pass me the dagger, and we met in her room."

Brad paused for a breath. "She told me she saw me kill Paul, but of course she didn't. If she had seen what happened, she would have known he fell on his own. But the truth wasn't important to her. She wanted the curatorship. It seemed like such a small favor to her. She didn't want money, just a job."

"Like Paul," Salinas said.

"Yes," Brad admitted.

"I told her that I couldn't do it alone, like I told Paul. We have a committee, and besides, George had already crowned Madge queen of the museum before I even arrived on the scene. I didn't like it, but I had to accept it. Tanya thought I could use my influence on George because of the museum gift. She demanded that I announce at the reception that she would be the curator. It would be a coup for her, and would prick Madge's bubble besides. She didn't like Madge, or any of us really. She wanted to be somewhere else, a more prestigious university, and she saw the curatorship as a step up the academic ladder."

Salinas nodded. "Did you bring the alcohol to her room?"

"Yes. I thought I would offer her a drink and find out what she wanted, but she said she didn't want it. I saw the bottle of wine and poured two glasses while she went into the bathroom, but she wouldn't drink that either, so I poured it into the bathroom sink and rinsed out the glasses. I was desperate. I didn't want to make a fool of myself announcing an appointment I had no intention, or even ability, to make. She took a pill from a prescription bottle just before George arrived, and she perked up when she saw him, and said, 'This will do me good,' or something like that. I saw her put the bottle next to her purse on the dresser."

Brad ran his hand over his face. "George and I both tried to convince her to stay in her room, but she refused. She took her purse and demanded we leave. I took the pill bottle from the dresser. When I put it in my pocket, I realized I had the dagger in there too, but I couldn't do anything about it with George present."

Rosa waved her hand and Salinas paused. After a few moments, he said, "So you left together."

"Yes, but when we got there, I found a quiet spot and opened the plastic bottle. There was just one pill left. I didn't take it out—I just crushed it in the bottle with my ink pen. Jamal sat at the bar watching Tanya with the other man, and I poured the contents into a drink. I told Jamal that Tanya might want a margarita and pushed the glass toward him. When Tanya came toward the bar, he took the glass to her. I didn't think it would hurt her. It was just one pill. I just wanted her to leave. I thought if she felt sick enough she would, and I could save myself, and her, from embarrassment."

"What happened then?" Salinas asked. He looked at his watch.

"I didn't want to be anywhere near her, so I wandered into the sitting room. A while later, Laura Lorenzo come into the sitting room, and the docent followed her back into the bedchamber. The docent returned and told me that Tanya was resting there. I remembered the pill bottle and the dagger in my pocket and thought I could return the dagger to her, and perhaps get rid of the pill bottle. She was still awake, but before I could give her the dagger Jamal came in and I left."

"You still had the pill bottle?"

"Yes."

"What did you do with the dagger?"

"I saw Eduardo sometime later. I passed the dagger to him and asked him to get rid of it for me. He was angry that I had it."

"When did you put the pill bottle in her purse?"

"I checked on her later, and she looked very bad. I wiped off the pill bottle and put it in her purse. I found it under the blanket."

"You assumed she was alive?"

"Yes! That is, until the ambulance came. Then I learned she had died, and that someone had stabbed her. I knew that Eduardo was responsible." He pushed clenched fists into his lap. "She was alive when I saw her last!"

"But you can't be sure of that. You could have killed her with the drink."

Brad sobbed. "It was just one pill." He pressed his quivering lips together. "Eduardo stabbed her with the dagger. He told me."

Salinas put his notes down. "The coroner agrees, but she was just barely alive when she was stabbed. She might have died anyway."

Brad's eyes widened in horror. "That can't be true!"

Salinas said, "I am afraid that you will be arrested for attempted murder of Tanya, and an open murder charge for the death of Paul Sturgess. You will need that lawyer after all, and you will have to convince a very skeptical judge you did not push Mr. Sturgess off the pyramid. You have a very difficult time ahead, my friend."

Brad couldn't control the shaking in his hands or his legs. "I didn't kill the old man either," he said pathetically.

"I know," Salinas said. "Eduardo did. But we don't know where he is."

CHAPTER SIXTY-ONE

"Campeche?" Claire exclaimed.

As she spoke, the phone rang again and Madge answered it, peering up at Claire as she saw the name and number pop up on the screen. "Hello? *Bueno?*" She covered the receiver with her hand and tried to hand it to Claire. "It's your boyfriend," she whispered.

"I can't take it, Madge." The thoroughfare had widened, and Claire struggled to keep up with Eduardo as he sped along the highway.

"She's driving," Madge said. She listened for a few moments. "Repeat please. We have poor service here." She nodded as she understood his side of the conversation. "He passed the airport. We're still following him." She listened again and whispered to Claire, "He's yelling at me."

Claire grimaced and passed a pickup truck piled high with cement blocks. Madge's eyes grew wide as Claire blew past the truck. Madge was listening to what Claire assumed was a tirade from the detective. Finally, she said, "We're in Claire's rental Volkswagen...hmm...yes, the red one." She listened more, then hung up.

"What did he say?"

"He said next time rent a white Ford."

Claire rolled her eyes. "And what else?"

"Keep following him, but not too close. Someone will call back when the police have him in their sights."

They followed Eduardo through Uman, a colonial city that reminded Claire of Motul. They skirted the central plaza, past the market and through a residential area. Eduardo's clean white SUV contrasted sharply with the old, rusted cars driven by most of the locals.

Just beyond Uman, Eduardo stopped at a Pemex gas station. Claire parked in front of a small roadside *refresquería* across the street and watched as the gas station attendant filled his tank. He opened his window and yelled at the young boy attempting to clean his windshield, handed the attendant a bill and pulled away. Claire waited until he had merged into traffic and pulled into the gas station. She understood Eduardo's impatience as she waited for the attendant to fill the small tank. She waved away the young boy with the squeegee, paid the attendant and rushed back into traffic.

They caught up with Eduardo just north of the town of Chochula, where he was tailgating a pickup truck with ten adults and children bouncing around the truck bed. Claire slowed down to put distance between them. The phone rang and Madge answered.

"Yes, Agent Gonzalez." Madge listened with only a minimal number of interruptions, then disconnected.

"What?" asked Claire.

"He told us to stop in Chochula. There's a helicopter in the area and a road-block down the road." She aimed the phone at Claire. "He said to turn around when we can. We're done…got that?" Madge said, shaking the phone at her friend. "We are done."

Claire nodded, her shoulders relaxing. She took a deep breath. Just before the town, Eduardo turned onto a bypass road, so Claire took the smaller road leading into town. She didn't want to pass through Chochula in fear of catching up with Eduardo where the bypass rejoined the road, so she slowed, looking for a place to turn around.

"I seriously need a bathroom," Madge said, "and perhaps a beer."

They stopped at a small house-front *refresquería*. Inside, they asked a young, very pregnant, woman if they could use her bathroom, hoping that the house attached to the store had such a luxury. They were in luck, and afterwards they bought soft drinks and pastries before returning to their car. Turning back north, they passed a small two-track path that led to a set of thatch traditional homes. They paused at the speed bump, and Eduardo's car pulled out in front of them. Claire gunned the engine to go around him, but the Volkswagen bumped into Eduardo's vehicle. Her front fender crumpled against the sturdier model.

"Damn," Madge said.

Claire tried to imagine the wording of her insurance policy and the disclaimers on her rental agreement. "Shit."

Eduardo glowered at them through the windshield and said something they could not hear, but they understood. He got out of the car and came to Claire's window. She locked her door and told Madge to do the same. Claire rolled her window up, leaving a small opening so she could hear him.

"Come, let's take a ride." Out of the corner of her eye, Claire saw Madge pull the phone under the map. Claire attempted to draw his attention away from her friend.

"Eduardo, just go. You're free."

"I'm sure there's a small army behind you," he growled, "and in front of me, too. They don't care about the niceties of a trial here. They'll kill me, but they hate to kill tourists." His mouth turned up into a sneer. "Get out." He pulled a small handgun out of his pocket and put it against the window. "Get out of the car now!"

A small group of villagers formed around them, women carrying fiber shopping bags, their children huddled behind them, and men carrying machetes on their way to or from their fields. They all moved toward the tall Mexican man who was obviously not Mayan.

The women began screaming at Eduardo, admonishing his lack of shame, "¿No tiene vergüenza?" The men hoisted their machetes, demanding that he put the gun away. Claire watched the scene play out in front of her, in awe of her unlikely rescuers. She thought if foreigners and non-indigenous Mexicans learned anything, it should be: don't mess with the Maya.

Eduardo raised his gun and aimed it at the growing crowd. The women grabbed their children and moved them behind their own bodies. The men moved forward, their machetes aimed at Eduardo.

"Move back!" Eduardo shouted, and the gun shook in his hand.

An elderly man limped toward Eduardo, leaning on a cane made from a tree limb. He looked up at the tall man and stared at him with piercing eyes. "You don't belong here. *Vaya*."

Eduardo stared back, but he couldn't hold the ancient man's gaze. He glanced from person to person, at the older children carrying their younger siblings, and at the growing crowd flowing out of houses and stores from all directions. He stepped back, aimed the gun at Claire, then lowered his aim, shooting into one of the Volkswagen tires, causing gasps among the onlookers. He stuffed the gun back in his pocket and ran to his car, squealing the tires as he pulled away from the crowd, nearly hitting an emaciated dog that had chosen that moment to take a nap in the middle of the road.

As his car stormed through the village, careening over speed bumps, Claire sat back against the car seat, putting her hands up to her face. Recovering her nerve, she left the car to examine the flat tire and crumpled fender. Her audience crowded around to make sure Claire and Madge were unharmed. The Mayan women immediately began to admonish them for traveling alone. "Where are your husbands?"

Inside the car, Madge pulled the phone out from under the map. Through the open door, Claire could hear a stream of expletives erupting through cyber-space. After a few moments, Madge said, "We're okay."

"Who was that?" Claire asked, holding back the children who tried to climb into the car.

"George," Madge said. "I don't know if he is mad as hell or worried sick."

Claire watched as a black official-looking SUV approached, bouncing over the speed bumps. It slowed as it turned into the small road, easing its way through the growing crowd of townspeople. Claire squinted at the driver and her mouth opened in disbelief. Laura Lorenzo exited the SUV, strode over to her and gave her a hug. "Are you two okay?"

CHAPTER SIXTY-TWO

Saturday

An exhausted group of Mayanists and one detective sat at a large table at the Caracol Bar, where Claire and Salinas had met for drinks four days earlier. The co-owner, Todd, had set up a long table in an alcove away from the television screens. He placed buckets of beer and platters of appetizers along the center. Madge and Claire were the focus of attention as the group bombarded them with questions about their car-chase adventure. Claire, aware that Salinas held very mixed emotions about her behavior, sat quietly and let her colleague tell the story.

With a chicken wing in one hand and a beer in another, Madge related the tale of the chase, Claire's driving ability, and how Eduardo had accosted them with a gun. "You wouldn't believe it!" Madge exclaimed. "It was like the movies, and Claire acted so cool. She didn't even blink when she saw the gun."

"Not true, Madge. I just react slowly," Claire smiled. "Besides, he was surrounded by the entire village of Chochula, brandishing shopping bags and machetes. What could he do?"

"And then..." Madge said, "...after Eduardo shoots our tire and takes off, the HSI team arrives and guess who it is!" Everyone knew the answer because they had already heard this part of the story. Madge tipped her bottle of beer to Laura Lorenzo, who just at that moment entered the bar and walked toward their table, followed by Cody, pulling a rolling suitcase and his backpack.

Madge opened her mouth to make a loud announcement, but Claire nudged her friend and gave her a warning glance. Madge whispered and said, "Agent Lorenzo."

Laura and Cody sat, and Jamal handed them beers.

Laura said, "You should have seen the looks on your faces." She laughed and, finally, Salinas smiled too. "But thanks to Claire and

315

Madge, we captured Eduardo, and he has exchanged his Armani for Mexican prison garb. He'll have to learn to live in his own country with a much less extravagant lifestyle."

"And I can finally take Paul home," Cody said, smiling sadly, "though not in the way I thought."

"We are so sorry this happened, Cody," Claire said.

Cody shrugged. "I am too, but he brought his fate on himself. He chose the wrong people to blackmail."

Madge reached over and patted his hand but addressed Laura. "Where did you hide our friend?" she asked.

"The undercover professors grabbed him from the Casa Montejo and moved him to their hotel. They knew he was in danger."

"From whom?" Jamal asked.

"At that time, we weren't sure if it was Brad or Eduardo," Laura admitted. "In Cody's statement, he wrote that he saw Brad and me at the pyramid, and Tanya close by. Neither Brad nor Tanya mentioned this in their statements. Then Cody did a silly thing…"

Cody clutched his beer. "I went upstairs at the Casa Montejo to talk to Brad. I asked him if he would vouch for me by telling Detective Salinas that he had seen me leave Paul at the pyramid, but Brad got agitated and accused me of blackmailing him."

"I was watching," Laura added. "I called Carlos Gonzalez, and he and Pablo went outside to watch for Cody. In the meantime, Jamal found me and sent me in to see Tanya. Things were happening too quickly."

Cody took the narrative back, "Brad scared me, and I decided I better leave the party. I was relieved, though a little frightened, when the professors intercepted me and one of them took me to their hotel. They moved my things and Paul's belongings that night."

George pursed his lips, thinking. "After Jamal's presentation Brad met us in the lounge. He said he had gone to Cody's room, and that someone else had moved in. I wondered at the time why Brad would do this. Now it looks like you all might have saved his life."

Cody took in a breath. "Oh, God!"

Jamal asked Laura, "How did this work? Did you apply for the job to get close to Eduardo? Did you know you would get an invitation for an interview? Are you even an anthropologist?"

Laura took a long gulp of beer before answering, "Yes, yes, and yes. I'm an anthropologist who has studied in the Mayan region, as my vita shows. It is a legitimate vita, except that my relationship with the university is a cover. I have a Ph.D. under my real name, but became a doctoral candidate for the purposes of this job, to investigate Eduardo's role in smuggling and purchasing undocumented artifacts. The Mexican Federal Police and HSI worked together."

Laura took another sip of her beer. "George, as a silent partner with Carlos and Pedro, wooed you all into thinking that I would be a good candidate to interview since I would be here at the meeting. If you had not invited me to interview, I would have come anyway, but it would have been more difficult to get near Eduardo. In a morbid way, if Paul hadn't fallen, Eduardo might well have gotten away."

"Were you also investigating Brad?" Claire asked.

"We knew of his past association with Eduardo but didn't know if he was involved in Eduardo's current activities. We suspected Brad might have smuggled artifacts out of Mexico for Eduardo, but we didn't have any proof. Brad denies smuggling but has confessed to selling artifacts to Eduardo through Benito Suarez."

Roberto picked up the narration. "Their friendship story is generally true, but they have created a myth of that relationship. Instead of one in which Brad is the idealistic graduate student who takes a foreign student under his wing, it was really a relationship in which Eduardo groomed a naïve American for future collaboration. When Brad approached him about the museum donation, Eduardo saw his opening."

"Is Brad still involved?" Madge looked at George, her eyes wide with fear. "Is Keane College liable for his actions?"

"You haven't received any artifacts yet, so, no," Roberto assured them. "But you were close. The jade statue is real. If Brad had managed to get it through customs and you had displayed it, it would have been a different story. Don't worry, we have it now."

"I knew we shouldn't have trusted the proposal," Madge said.

"You didn't," George reminded her. "You started researching Eduardo's collections. Brad complained to me about it."

"I'm sure he regrets this decision now," Roberto said. "We suspect Eduardo planned to use the museum as a kind of front for artifact laundering. That may be why Brad hoped to hire someone more pliable into the position of curator."

"So how did Paul come into the picture?" Madge asked. "He came here to apply for the job, but it seems that he had other motives."

Salinas nodded. "Paul interviewed vendors as part of his research on tourism. He knew many of the store owners and what they sold. He also researched Eduardo's business, *Galerías Indígenas*, and he recognized the replicas that Benito sold were similar to those on the business website. Finally, he learned that Benito's cousin made souvenir replicas, and that Brad had connections with Benito. Paul seemed to be very efficient at researching people for his own purposes."

"I still don't know if Brad killed Paul, or if it was an accident," Jamal said.

"We may never know. He insists it was an accident," Salinas said. "But Brad clearly fled the scene, and, remember, he also stole the computer."

Jamal pulled his braids back from his face and turned to Salinas. "Did you suspect me of killing Paul?"

"I did, but your friends—" his hand swept the table, "—convinced me that you weren't a likely suspect. Despite your suspicious behavior, there would be no reason for you to enter his room if you already had the computer, so I agreed with them."

"When did you start to suspect Brad of being involved with Paul's death?" Madge asked.

"I didn't suspect anything at first," Salinas admitted. "The Uxmal Police, as well as my captain, wanted the death to be an accident. I was forced to reconsider that assessment when two things happened: Paul's notebook, and meeting Laura."

All heads turned to Laura as she reached for a second bottle from the bucket. "When I was introduced to Paul at the Uxmal reception, we recognized each other," she explained. "We had both attended the same anthropology program, but I was a few years ahead of him. I knew him mainly by his reputation of soliciting confidences and using them to his advantage. I left Chicago to finish my doctoral program and forgot about him. When I saw him at Uxmal, I began to worry, knowing he was interviewing for a teaching position with Keane College."

Laura looked at Salinas, who nodded, and she continued, "When I saw him talking to each of you individually, I observed—as both an anthropologist and federal agent—the body language these conversations elicited."

Claire said, "He wrote something in his notebook about you. I think he called the university for information. Tanya complained that someone had called to check your credentials."

"He probably suspected that I already had a Ph.D."

"Laura, what were you really looking for when you climbed the pyramid?" Claire asked.

"I noticed the drag marks on the ground, as you did, and I climbed up a few steps for a different perspective. I took a few photos with my phone, and those confirmed the shots you had taken from the ground." She paused. "I was very impressed that you had the foresight to document the scene."

"Your photographs helped us put the pieces together in Paul's death," Salinas added. "The drag marks, blood, and footprints all helped us piece together what happened."

"What did you find out from the footprints?" Claire asked.

"We collected shoes from some of you," the detective said. "Jamal's prints were found only at the periphery, but so were Eduardo's, confirming Brad's statement that Eduardo helped him cover for the crime. Cody's were there, but only found on top of other prints, indicating he walked there later. Sadly, the footprints of the medics obscured many prints, but Brad's prints dominated the scene. By working around the body, he thought he could confuse the prints, but it was clear he had been at the scene earlier."

Claire recalled how Brad had turned Paul's body over, straightening it out, as if looking for something. She asked, "Did you ever find Paul's phone?"

Salinas nodded. "It was in the backpack. Brad destroyed it and threw it away with the computer. The kids found it, but it was beyond repair."

"Tell us about *Don* Benito," Madge said. "How did Eduardo know about Paul's visit to Motul and his interest in the statue?"

Salinas folded his hands on the table. "Phone records show that Benito called Eduardo after Paul had visited. Deciding that Benito could be a threat, Eduardo went to Motul and killed him. Brad arrived later. He had already dumped the backpack and wanted to make sure that Benito would not betray him. When Benito didn't answer the door, he left, not knowing that Eduardo had gotten there first. Then Jamal wandered through, for the same reason." Salinas smiled again. "It was a busy morning in Motul."

"But I had nothing to do with the smuggling or selling of artifacts," Jamal protested.

"But your initials were in Benito's contacts —JK," Salinas said.

"But that wasn't me."

Salinas smiled at Claire. "It was Brad…Bradley James Kingsford… aka Jaime because villagers could not pronounce his name."

Cody, who had been sitting quietly, teared up. "That means Paul caused not only his own death, but that of Benito Suarez also."

"Your friend was devious," Laura said.

George frowned. "Just like Tanya."

CHAPTER SIXTY-THREE

There was a pause as everyone took food and drink and shifted their thoughts to Tanya.

"Who will be charged for Tanya's death," Madge asked, "Brad or Eduardo, or both?"

"Probably both," Salinas said. "Eduardo for murder and Brad for attempted murder. Toxicology determined that the dagger hastened Tanya's death, but she already had enough oxycodone and alcohol in her system to kill her. No one knew Tanya had a drug problem except Jamal. She hid it well. Brad suspected she had taken a pain pill, and he sealed her fate when he added a fatal dose of the crushed oxycodone to her margarita."

"I can't believe I considered him my friend," Jamal said.

Madge, seeing the pain in Jamal's face, said, "But Tanya contributed to her own death by drinking and taking prescription drugs. It was only a matter of time before she would have a fatal overdose."

"But I gave her the margarita," Jamal said, his eyes tearing.

"Brad made sure you took it to her," George said.

"And worse," Laura said to Jamal, "you put the empty glass on the waiter's tray, but I don't think you remember doing it."

"Oh, my God," Jamal said. "I don't remember it at all, but what about the wine? She didn't drink it with me."

"Brad poured the wine, but she refused to drink, so he poured it into the sink," Salinas said. "He had brought a few sleeping pills with him and small airplane-sized liquor and tonic bottles, but she refused all alcohol, claiming she wanted to wait until the reception to drink."

Jamal said, "What information did she have on Brad?"

Salinas said, "I don't think she knew about the smuggling at that time. She was fishing...is that what you say? Her interrogation at breakfast sent Jamal to Paul's room looking for a computer and

Brad to Motul. But Eduardo, having been alerted by *Don* Benito, got there first."

Madge said, "So what *did* Tanya know?"

Salinas described Tanya's computer journal. "She *was* devious, your Tanya. But unwise, with no sense of her danger."

"I remember that she took my binoculars when she joined us in the bleachers," Madge said.

Salinas nodded. "She saw Brad at the foot of the pyramid with Eduardo, and Jamal talking to Laura in the bleachers above them."

Claire thought back to that night. "Then Brad and Eduardo rushed to the seats behind us, laughing about how Eduardo had to rescue Brad from Laura. Tanya knew they were lying."

"And she noticed that when Brad put his backpack on the step next to his feet, it looked bulky," Salinas added. "He laid it down carefully instead of dropping it at his feet. She wrote about it in her notes."

"She suspected that Eduardo saw what happened and provided Brad with an alibi?" Madge asked. "When did she steal the dagger?"

"Tanya heard Brad and Eduardo argue about the statue after the presentation," Salinas said. "From her vantage point just outside the door, she not only heard enough to guess there was tension between them that might involve the museum, she also saw where the key to the display was kept. Later, she simply found a time when the exhibit room was empty and used the key to steal the dagger, probably sometime between the Tuesday morning meeting and George's presentation."

Salinas continued, "Once stolen, she put the dagger in an envelope, wrapped it in a note, and gave it to Brad surreptitiously after George's talk. Evidently, Tanya couldn't resist the symbolism."

"Did you find the note?" Jamal asked.

"We found the envelope at the reception, ripped up in a waste basket. We never found the note. We don't know what it said, but we suspect it merely set the time and place for the meeting."

"So, she had two accusations against Brad: the suggestion that he had caused Paul's death and a suggestion of some sort of professional impropriety," George summarized.

"Yes," Salinas said. "She told Brad that for her silence, he needed to give her the position of curator." Salinas gave an apologetic nod to Madge. "And she demanded that he make the announcement at the reception. Brad panicked. He had no intention of naming her curator at a public event. So, when she refused to stay behind, he took the pill bottle with him."

"He was probably relieved when he learned that Laura had taken her to the bedchamber," George added.

Salinas agreed. "Yes, but then he had to do something about the pill bottle and the dagger. He entered the bedchamber several times. The first time, Jamal interrupted him. The second time she was unconscious, and he placed the pill bottle in her purse."

"And the water glass?" asked Claire.

"Ah, Brad saw the water glass and thought himself lucky. It would show that she took the pills herself. Unfortunately for him, the docent took the glass away."

"How did Eduardo get the dagger?" Claire asked.

"Brad gave the dagger to Eduardo to get rid of it," Salinas said. "Eduardo denies the stabbing, but I'm quite certain that he did it. Even though Eduardo denied knowing Tanya was in the bedchamber, the docent saw Eduardo entering just before he asked Claire outside for a chat."

"I was his alibi?" Claire said miserably.

"You still want that job?" Madge smiled.

Tears came to Jamal's eyes. "I've been foolish. She acted so strangely in the market. She told me there was something wrong with the backpacks at the pyramid. I accused her of using drugs again, because she was rambling, almost incoherent. I shouldn't have dismissed her accusations. She was so fragile," he insisted.

Salinas said, "She was fragile, but manipulative. She usually got what she wanted, but when thwarted, she kept everyone on edge—Jamal, Brad, and Cody." He looked at Cody, who was on his third beer and staring into space until he heard his name. "You weren't her first victim, Jamal. She also used Thomas Freeman to further her career."

Laura interjected, "We thought at first Tanya might be involved with Eduardo, and that she might have had a hand in the Palenque case, but it seems that Freeman's other graduate student had a connection with Eduardo."

"But Tanya took advantage of Freeman's situation to request that he serve on her dissertation committee and support her candidacy," Salinas said.

"Perhaps she started as a victim," Claire argued. "She was beautiful, and perhaps the relationships with professors and others started as flirtations, before she realized that she held power over these men as well."

Madge said, "There she goes again. Claire the naïve."

George turned to the detective who sat pensively, twirling his beer bottle between two hands. "What will happen to Brad in the Mexican legal system? We hear horrible stories, sorry to say," he added to lessen the accusatory tone.

"He is being charged with a felony misdemeanor in Paul's death, and attempted murder of Tanya," Salinas said. "He is lucky because of new laws that give defendants the opportunity to provide witnesses, but it is still the judge who decides guilt or innocence. There are no juries. Since Eduardo's crimes are under federal statute, he will be treated according to federal laws."

Claire asked, "Might we be called back as witnesses?"

"Perhaps."

"What are Brad's chances?" asked Madge.

Salinas said, "In his case, he will need to convince a judge that he did not push Paul from the pyramid or administer a lethal dose of a powerful drug to Tanya with the intent to kill her. Since both defenses depend on his word against a dead victim, he may have difficulty doing that."

Salinas looked at his watch and turned to Cody. "*Dios*, we're late. Tanya's parents are arriving from Detroit in less than an hour, and Cody has a plane to catch."

Cody stood and grabbed his suitcase. Claire rose to give him a hug. "Good luck with your writing career," she said.

Cody smiled, "Maybe someday I'll write about what happened here...but not yet."

"If it becomes a movie, I get to play Claire," Madge said laughing.

Jamal turned toward the detective. "Can I come? I want to speak to Tanya's parents."

"Will they want to see you?" Salinas asked.

"I need to see them. Please?"

Salinas nodded, and Jamal jumped up to follow them.

Madge stared after them. "Do you think Jamal and Salinas should meet the parents with beer on their breath?"

George said, "I think that might be the only way to do it."

Laura, who sat quietly during the conversation, stood to leave. Madge said, "Are you sure you don't want this job? You are still qualified."

Laura smiled as she pulled a wad of pesos from her purse. "Are you kidding? At an assistant professor's salary?" She smiled. "Besides, your jobs are too dangerous." She giggled and waved as she walked away.

Todd came to clear the table. Everyone reached into wallets and purses, but Todd waved them away. "Bill's paid, my friends."

They emerged into the hot Merida afternoon.

CHAPTER SIXTY-FOUR

Saturday Afternoon/Evening

Madge, George, and Claire walked together back to the hotel to collect their bags and leave for the airport, clutching their precious blue passports. Madge and George arranged to take Jamal's luggage to the airport and meet him there later. Claire's flight to Madison, Wisconsin, wouldn't depart until early evening. She hoped that Cristina could forgive her "mother hen" behavior. Her daughter was determined to go to Africa, and to Africa she would go, regardless of Claire's fears and concerns.

Madge interrupted Claire's thoughts. "Did Salinas ever suspect Cody?"

Claire said, "He did at first, because of his strange behavior. Cody tried to hide the fact that he and Paul were having difficulties, and he realized that if Paul was murdered, he would be the primary suspect. No one else knew Paul well enough to kill him, at least that was his fear, and his actions with the notebook drew Roberto's attention."

Madge shook her head. "He wanted to conduct his own investigation. But, once inside, no one wanted to talk to him, except Tanya, and her outburst drew attention to him."

"But Cody also talked to Brad," George said. "Remember, he wanted Brad to give him an alibi for Paul's death. That could have killed him."

They reached the hotel and stood together in the lobby, reluctant to say goodbye after all that had happened that week. All signs of the conference had already disappeared: the daily schedule board, the multicultural crowd, and the familiar faces at the bar.

"What's going to happen to us?" moaned Madge.

George cleared his throat. "I talked to the dean. She knows the entire saga and has apprised the provost of our situation. I'll meet with them when we return, but for the time being, they have advised that we continue with our program development."

"Who will be interim director?" asked Claire.

"Well," admitted George, "the dean suggested that I be the director, since I started in that role before we hired Brad and," he paused, looking at Claire, "she wants Claire to replace me as anthropology chair."

Claire protested. "Me? I don't want to be chair. Don't I have a say?"

"Tell that to the dean. She thinks you are the best suited to take over in a crisis. I just happened to recommend you on those grounds. You did a great job here, mediating between the police and the anthropologists."

"Is that what they call it?" Madge chided, and cast a knowing glance at Claire, who blushed and turned to look at George.

Claire asked, "And Madge? Will she continue as curator? Or is the museum defunct?"

"Madge will be curator and will compile an inventory of our holdings. It will be an awesome chore."

"And she gets to seek legitimate gifts to our museum."

Madge turned to Claire. "By the way, Claire, what was your sin?"

"Sin?"

"What did Paul find out about you?"

Claire told them about how a younger Benito Suarez had approached her and Aaron during their field work year, trying to sell them artifacts. "Paul wrote my initials on a page set aside for Benito. Laura even investigated me, but they decided I was harmless."

"Did you buy artifacts?" asked Madge.

"Of course not. That was rule number two for anthropologists in the field, right behind 'never loan money to villagers.' We failed on *numero uno* but obeyed *el secundo*." She paused. "I never heard about you two." She pointed to George and Madge. "Tell me your secrets."

Madge smiled and said, "I had no secrets."

Claire guffawed. "Come on, Madge. No one believes that...look at you. You look like you got caught in a time warp at Woodstock. A little too much sex, drugs, and rock and roll—the Weather Underground?"

"You give me too much credit," Madge said, blushing.

George smiled, a once-in-a-month smile. "Madge and I were married."

"What!?" Claire exclaimed. "That's incredible!" She looked from Madge to George. "But it's not a crime. It's kind of cute. And it explains why you seem so comfortable together." She looked at them again, to see if they were joking. "Why didn't you want anyone to know?"

Madge said, "Back then a husband and wife wouldn't be hired together, so we lied about our status to get our first jobs. I was a true feminist—I kept my maiden name—and we pretended that we met at the university. It was no big deal—nothing that would give us a reason to kill Paul. He had nothing on us—that's why Salinas brought us into his investigation so readily."

"But you divorced?" Claire asked, incredulous.

"Oh, yes," Madge laughed. "Long ago."

"I was Husband Number One," George said, smiling.

"No man can handle me, not even George. The marriage ended, but the friendship continued." Madge and George smiled at each other as Claire looked on in amazement.

In the lobby, Claire hugged her colleagues farewell. Even George allowed for a brief hug before he hailed a taxi for himself and Madge.

CHAPTER SIXTY-FIVE

Claire's flight didn't leave until evening. She had several hours before her dinner date. She had stored her luggage at the hotel guest storage room, and her Volkswagen had been hauled back to the car rental to be repaired at U.S. Government expense. The damp heat accosted her as she left the air-conditioning at the hotel. It was the hottest part of the day, but at least the crowds and traffic would be lighter. She walked slowly toward the central plaza, perspiration seeping down the back of her sleeveless blouse. She would have to retrieve her suitcase and change her clothes before she met Roberto for dinner.

She had calculated the space available in her suitcase for gifts. Instead of a long walk to the market, she decided to shop in the small stores near the central plaza. She found colorful silver and gold earrings for her daughter, mother, and sister, and, in a corner liquor store, she purchased bottles of Kahlua for her brother and father.

Next, she crossed the plaza and sought out the hammock salesman she had talked with on her first day in Merida. She found him in his usual location, on the edge of the plaza. She purchased the largest, most colorful hammock he had. Now, she had to find a way to get it to Lake Odawa, Michigan.

Her arms heavy with gifts, she made her way back to the hotel. She retrieved her suitcase from the hotel storage room, packed up the gifts, changed her clothes in the lobby restroom, and returned the suitcase to storage. Thus refreshed, she left the hotel, took deep breaths and absorbed as much of her surroundings as she could, for she had no idea when she would return. She entered her favorite restaurant, La Chaya, and requested a table for three near the window.

She ordered a Corona with lime and settled herself in, reflecting on this past week—and what might be in her future. She was unprepared to take on the role of department chair, and she hoped she might talk the dean out of her decision. But, in a sense, she felt new, fresh. Her life had been stagnant, her emotions flat. Her daughter sensed it—thus her insistence that she spend Mother's Day in Wisconsin. It was more than an attempt to appease her mother's fears.

A knock on the window pulled her out of her thoughts. Roberto stood outside the restaurant with a young woman whom Claire recognized from the conference—his daughter.

Roberto introduced Claire to Marta Salinas, and they joined her at the table. Marta, tall like her father with dark skin and thick dark hair held in place with two barrettes, dominated the conversation for the first fifteen minutes, from their drink orders, through the toast of beer bottles, and into the ordering of dinner. Marta was ebullient, passionate about anthropology and her dream to study Mexican women and economics.

As they spoke, Claire noticed that Roberto sat quietly at the table, listening. During dinner, the conversation shifted to the events of the past week and the conference. Marta hoped to finish her degree at the University of Yucatán but pursue graduate school in the United States. To Marta's glee, Claire invited her to Michigan to look at universities there. "I would love to show you around," Claire said. Marta looked at her father. Her face flushed.

Claire didn't mention the murders. She didn't know how much Roberto wanted Marta to know about his job, especially this past week, but eventually, after the dinner plates had been cleared, the conversation turned in that direction. Marta had been watching closely as she attended the sessions and the reception. She had talked to her father about the Keane College group, a fact that disconcerted Claire somewhat; she was observant, like her father.

Marta had watched Tanya as she rambled about backpacks and pyramids at the reception. She had watched Jamal talk to Tanya and saw the look of concern on his face when Laura took Tanya into the parlor. She had seen Jamal pacing while the reception guests waited to talk to her father and had told Roberto that the black man could not have killed her.

"There was too much love and concern in his eyes," Marta said.

"But he was breaking up with her," Claire protested mildly.

Roberto finally spoke. "I think he was...how do you say...in conflict?"

"Conflicted," his daughter corrected him, and smiled.

"But I think Marta is right," he conceded. "Jamal loved Tanya, probably much more than she loved him."

Claire thought about this. The truth of it made her very sad. She looked at her watch. "I have to go," she said. "It may take a few minutes to find a taxi."

Roberto said, "I'll take you."

Claire looked at Marta. "How will you get home?" she asked.

Marta stood to leave. "I'm going to the library. I have a ride home. And thank you for signing your book," she said.

"Thank you for buying it." Claire stood and hugged her.

Roberto kissed his daughter on the cheek and led Claire to his car.

They collected Claire's luggage at the hotel and rode in uncomfortable silence to the airport. Claire, for her part, was exhausted. She did not want to talk about Brad or Eduardo or their questionable futures. She was done with them.

Her thoughts involved her own future, in the short term, as chair of a department from which she had felt disengaged for the past two years. In the long term, she wondered about her personal life. Would she ever find happiness again like she had felt with Aaron? How did she feel about the man sitting next to her now, driving her to the airplane that would transport her to another world? She couldn't really conceive of an intimate relationship with anyone new...not yet...not ever? How did he feel about her? What did his silence mean?

At the airport, Roberto parked the car and took her large suitcase while she pulled her carry-on behind her. Inside, she checked her luggage through and got her boarding pass. They stood awkwardly near the security area.

"Will I see you again, or will you disappear like you did before?" Roberto asked. His smile was tinged with uncertainty.

"I promise to email. And besides, I'll always come back to Merida. It's my second home."

"And what if I wanted to take a vacation, or accompany Marta on her university search?"

"I would love it, but don't come in winter," she said, smiling. "You won't like it." They stood close together, uncertain.

"I have to go," Claire said. She tugged at the handle of her rolling carry-on.

Roberto reached down to give her a hug and she moved in toward him. He kissed her briefly on the cheek, very lightly.

Claire said, "*Hasta que te vea de nuevo.*"

"*Que le vaya bien*, Clarita."

Acknowledgments

Throughout my life, I have loved mystery novels, from Nancy Drew to my current favorites. My fascination doesn't lie with bloodthirsty serial killers and horrific crime scenes, but within the dynamics of family and social ties; where murders are solved, not by car chases or gunfights, but by careful investigation and intuition. I am hooked on stories where murderers may live among us and perhaps live perfectly normal lives, except…something happens. To me, these murders may be the most terrifying.

When I retired from academia, I resolved to write a mystery novel. I had read thousands, what could be so difficult? I learned very quickly the discipline and organization necessary to plot a murder mystery and develop characters that resemble real people. I have benefited from workshops offered by local mystery authors Aaron Stander and Elizabeth Buzzelli, whose enthusiasm inspired me to keep writing: thank you! I also would like to thank authors Mardi Link and John Pahl, who read early versions of the manuscript and offered valuable comments and suggestions.

I am forever grateful to my husband LaVail, who has read multiple versions of the book and has been a compassionate editor. Many thanks also to my son, Nathan, who has been a patient reader and consultant on crime scene and police procedures—for both *Human Sacrifice* and my current project, *Culture Shock*. I am lucky to have friends who share my love for mysteries and who were willing to read early drafts of the manuscript: thank you, Sandy Seppala Gyr, Valerie Hover, and Susan Grant. Thanks also to new friends and "old" colleagues who read the pre-publication versions: Mary Kay Eastman, Marina Call, Dr. Janet Brashler, and Dr. Heather Van Wormer.

Two wonderful writing groups nurtured and encouraged me during this journey. In Big Rapids, Michigan, the ArtWorks Group guided me through the beginning stages of my first draft; in Traverse City, the Old Town Writer's Group both challenged and encouraged me through the late drafts of Human Sacrifice and the early drafts of Culture Shock. Two more eclectic and awesome groups of people I have not had the pleasure to know! Thank you!

Thank you to the staff of Mission Point Press for their guidance throughout the process: Heather Shaw, Doug Weaver, and especially Scott Couturier, whose hard work and excellent editing strengthened this book. I am forever indebted to Sandy Seppala Gyr, an expert in all things murderous, for her careful copy-editing and proofreading. A very special thank you to Jim DeWildt for his great artwork, his friendship, and for his patience in working with a fretful author.

Author's note on the locations described in the novel

Merida, Yucatán is a beautiful colonial city. The plazas I described exist, as do some of the restaurants, though some are fictionalized. The Casa Montejo also exists but has been renovated several times since my first visit. The general floor plan remains, but I have made some artistic adjustments to facilitate the movements of people and plot. The Intercontinental Hotel is a composite of the many tourist and conference hotels that exist in the city, but where I never stay. The police station is a figment of my imagination.

Uxmal is an extraordinary archaeological site, and the Sound and Light Show is a real event. Until recently, visitors to Uxmal have been allowed to climb the Magician's Pyramid. That changed prior to my last visit in 2018. Now, the stairways ascending the Magician's Pyramid have been blocked off, though the other buildings are still accessible to tourists. These sites are national treasures that require protection from the elements—and humankind.

The three villages that Claire and Roberto visit—Dzab, Tixbe, and Yaxpec—are composites of the types of villages and towns visitors will find beyond the colonial cities. Motul and the towns that Claire and Madge race through are real towns, but their descriptions are fictionalized.

All the names and characters in the book are fictional, and any resemblance to real characters is coincidental. There is no Keane College, nor is there a Keane College Mayanist Program. Any resemblance to an existing program is also coincidental.

A note on *Compadrazgo*: *Compadrazgo* (co-parenthood) resembles our concept of godparents. In Mexico, it represents a social relationship between the godparents and the parents of the child. Families seek compadres for all special events: baptism, confirmation, weddings; and these sets of compadres share responsibility for the child throughout his or her life. It is a special bond that links families and friends in a complex social web.

You can read more about stolen artifacts and the ownership of national treasures in the following academic sources, among many:

Loot: The Battle over the Stolen Treasures of the Ancient World, Sharon Waxman, Times Books, Henry Holt and Co., NY (2008)
Art and Crime: Exploring the Dark Side of the Art World, N. Charney, ed., Westport: Greenwood Publishing (2009)

About the Author

Dr. Cindy Hull is an anthropologist and retired Professor Emeritus from Grand Valley State University. She has published two ethnographies: *Katun: A Twenty-Year Journey with the Maya;* and *Chippewa Lake: A Community in Search of an Identity. Human Sacrifice* is her first novel. It takes place in the Yucatán Peninsula, where she lived and studied among the Maya. Cindy currently lives with her husband and night-stalker cat in Traverse City, Michigan.

(Photo: Keith Vandenbergh)

Made in the USA
Lexington, KY
15 November 2019